"Wonderful ... great dialogue ... Sophia the seasoned courtesan [is] so feisty and fun ... Don't miss this fresh and extremely fun romp through romantic London. It is, as Sophia would say, 'simply too delicious to miss!'"
—*Night Owl Romance*

"Riveting! This wonderful story is filled with so many secrets, intrigue, and even revenge that you are captured and held to the very end ... Steamy romantic scenes and delightful dialogue ... This is one historical romance you do not want to miss."
—*Coffee Time Romance*

"This cleverly orchestrated, unconventional romp through the glittering world of the Regency elite—both admirable and reprehensible—is filled with secrets, graced with intriguing characters, laced with humor, and plotted with Machiavellian flair. A joy to read, it ends with a hook for a sequel involving the remarkable countess herself. Readers will be waiting."
—*Library Journal*

"Dain shows a fine flair for subtle touches of humor and clever dialogue and tops everything off with a most engaging mother who is a master at manipulation."
—*Romantic Times*

"*The Courtesan's Daughter* is a ribald romp through English society and the rules of the ton that prevailed at the time. Ms. Dain has captured the sensuality of the period perfectly and treats readers to a rather steamy romance while creating a thoroughly enjoyable laugh at society."
—*Affaire de Coeur*

continued ...

Praise for *The Courtesan's Daughter*

"[Dain's] new book tells a tale of impropriety and independence, and a mother and daughter determined to bend the rules of society in their favor. The author never fails to write challenging and complex romances that challenge the reader to enjoy and beg for more; this novel will steal your breath away! Claudia Dain has proven yet again that her books are completely and utterly sensual and from the heart. *The Courtesan's Daughter* is HOT!"   —*Book Cove Reviews*

And more praise for Claudia Dain's novels

"Claudia Dain's emotionally charged writing and riveting characters will take your breath away."

—*New York Times* bestselling author Sabrina Jeffries

"Claudia Dain writes with intelligence, sensuality, and heart and the results are extraordinary!"

—*New York Times* bestselling author Connie Brockway

"Claudia Dain never fails to write a challenging and complex romance."   —*A Romance Review*

"Dain is a talented writer who knows her craft."   —*Romantic Times*

The Courtesan's Secret

Claudia Dain

BERKLEY SENSATION, NEW YORK

THE BERKLEY PUBLISHING GROUP
Published by the Penguin Group
Penguin Group (USA) Inc.
375 Hudson Street, New York, New York 10014, USA
Penguin Group (Canada), 90 Eglinton Avenue East, Suite 700, Toronto, Ontario M4P 2Y3, Canada
(a division of Pearson Penguin Canada Inc.)
Penguin Books Ltd., 80 Strand, London WC2R 0RL, England
Penguin Group Ireland, 25 St. Stephen's Green, Dublin 2, Ireland (a division of Penguin Books Ltd.)
Penguin Group (Australia), 250 Camberwell Road, Camberwell, Victoria 3124, Australia
(a division of Pearson Australia Group Pty. Ltd.)
Penguin Books India Pvt. Ltd., 11 Community Centre, Panchsheel Park, New Delhi—110 017, India
Penguin Group (NZ), 67 Apollo Drive, Rosedale, North Shore 0632, New Zealand
(a division of Pearson New Zealand Ltd.)
Penguin Books (South Africa) (Pty.) Ltd., 24 Sturdee Avenue, Rosebank, Johannesburg 2196,
South Africa

Penguin Books Ltd., Registered Offices: 80 Strand, London WC2R 0RL, England

This book is an original publication of The Berkley Publishing Group.

This is a work of fiction. Names, characters, places, and incidents either are the product of the author's imagination or are used fictitiously, and any resemblance to actual persons, living or dead, business establishments, events, or locales is entirely coincidental. The publisher does not have any control over and does not assume any responsibility for author or third-party websites or their content.

First edition: May 2008

Library of Congress Cataloging-in-Publication Data

Dain, Claudia.
    The courtesan's secret / Claudia Dain.— 1st ed.
        p. cm.
    ISBN 978-0-425-22136-5
    I. Title.
    PS3604.A348C685 2007
    813'.6—dc22   2007049677

PRINTED IN THE UNITED STATES OF AMERICA

10 9 8 7 6 5 4 3 2 1

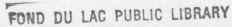

For Kate, who makes everything better

One

London 1802

"THERE are certain circumstances upon which it is absolutely essential to seek out a courtesan," Louisa Kirkland snapped.

"If you're expecting an argument from me . . ." the Marquis of Hawksworth drawled, and gave a halfhearted shrug.

"Oh, shut it, Hawksworth," Louisa said. "Why should I expect something as energetic as an argument from *you*, of all people?"

It was entirely within her rights to talk to a marquis in such an abrupt manner, or at least this particular marquis. Hawksworth was not only her cousin, but he was an unrepentantly lazy boy of twenty who ought to have better things to do than lie around all day dozing on a sofa.

Which is exactly where she had found him when she had insisted he accompany her to Sophia Dalby's town house. Not that she would permit him to enter with her. No, that would not do at all. No, Hawksworth had to remain outside, engaging in whatever activity best suited him, likely a nap, while she went inside to face Lady Dalby in what was certain to be a most uncomfortable conversation.

But then, most conversations with Sophia Dalby were uncomfortable. She was entirely certain that it came from Sophia having been a noted courtesan in her day, though it was equally possible that Sophia had always been a woman other women found uncomfortable.

"And what am I to do whilst you're with the delightful Lady Dalby?" Hawksworth asked, neatly proving her point. Louisa had yet to meet a man who did not find Sophia Dalby delightful. It was most annoying.

"Isn't there someone you might call upon? Someone in the vicinity who would admit you?" Louisa said, straightening a seam on her glove as she prepared to approach Sophia's door on Upper Brook Street. It was a very nice address, the houses quite respectable, and Dalby House was a literal stone's throw from Hyde Park. Of course, Sophia had married into her fine address, but didn't most women? It had been a neat bit of work, and if Sophia could manage that, she could certainly manage the little thing that Louisa needed of her. "Doesn't Mr. Prestwick live on this street? Go and call upon him."

"And his lovely sister," Hawksworth said with all the laziness he could muster, which was considerable as he had such practice at it. "I could do with another look at her."

If there was one woman Louisa disliked, a ridiculous notion as she found it necessary to dislike quite a few women, most particularly Anne Warren, it was Miss Penelope Prestwick. Miss Prestwick was that impossible combination of sweetness and seduction that Louisa found intolerable and men found compelling. That the Prestwick viscountcy had more money than was entirely in good taste only made her more irritating, obviously.

"Of course you could," Louisa said. "I'm quite certain you are not the first man to get a good look at Miss Prestwick. I should be careful around her, Hawksworth. She wouldn't mind being a duchess one day and you would so nicely fill the bill."

"Thank you," Hawksworth drawled politely, missing the point entirely. "Shall we say half past? Or shall you require more time with Lady Dalby?"

"I shall be brief. I would advise you to be the same."

"Half past, then," he said agreeably. Hawksworth, for all that could be said against him, had a most even and agreeable disposition. It was his finest trait. It may also have been his only trait.

Louisa wasted no time in watching Hawksworth amble down Upper Brook Street toward the Viscount Prestwick's town house. She had other matters entirely occupying her thoughts.

Louisa was admitted, looked over not at all discreetly by Fredericks, the Dalby House butler, and a most inappropriate butler he was, and ushered into Sophia's famous white salon. Everything connected to Sophia was famous in one fashion or another, and Louisa did not waste time in ferreting out the particulars as to the source of fame for the white salon. It was a salon, like any other, except that it had the obvious distinction of being swathed in various shades of impossible to maintain white.

It looked immaculate, of course.

Sophia rose to her feet, greetings were exchanged, and Louisa, without shame and certainly no hesitation, proceeded to the point of her visit.

"Lady Dalby, thank you for seeing me."

"Not at all. Can I offer you a cup of chocolate?"

"Yes, thank you," Louisa answered.

She didn't particularly care for a cup of chocolate, but it served its purpose in getting Fredericks out of the room to send someone for another cup. In the silence and quiet of their momentary solitude, Louisa studied Sophia briefly.

She knew her, of course. They were not strangers to each other, though they were hardly friends. Louisa had studied Sophia as much as anyone else in London had done, which is to say, minutely. Yes, she was beautiful, darkly aristocratic, flawlessly seductive, relentlessly charming. But what woman could not claim the same list, with some little bit of effort?

Which was the entire point, really. Sophia, as far as Louisa could discern, accomplished her list of credits entirely without effort.

"I find myself in a bit of a dilemma, Lady Dalby. I don't quite know how to go about . . . fixing it," Louisa said.

Sophia merely raised her eyebrows in pleasant curiosity and kept stirring her chocolate.

"I," Louisa said, a faint blush heating her cheeks. Blast having red hair and the complexion that went with it. Every emotion showed on her skin. It was beyond embarrassing. "I . . . am certain that I don't have to tell *you* about . . . well, about my pearls. About the entire pearl evening that took place at Hyde House two nights ago."

"No," Sophia said in obvious amusement, "you don't have to tell *me*."

Obviously not, as Sophia, somehow, had orchestrated the entire shameless event. Shameless, yes, but so very to the point. Caroline, Sophia's daughter, had in a single evening, acquired three very likely men: the Lords Dutton, Blakesley, and Ashdon. Each man had presented her with a pearl necklace, and each man had sought her favors, shamelessly and ruinously. The obvious problem being that Caroline had not been ruined in any meaningful sense of the word. No, Caroline had made her choice, the handsome though somber Lord Ashdon, and she had been married to him the very next morning. It was perfectly obvious to Louisa that Caroline had married the man she'd wanted and that she'd arranged things perfectly to get him.

It was even more obvious that Caroline Trevelyan, at the innocent age of seventeen, could have arranged no such thing. Her mother, the ex-courtesan, had been behind it all.

If it could be done for Caroline, Louisa saw no reason why it could not be done for her. Unless, of course, Sophia did not care to help her get what she wanted. Sophia, rather too intelligent for comfort, likely suspected that Louisa did not hold her in the highest regard. Or she hadn't. Until now.

"I don't know how it happened exactly," Louisa said, plunging forward and ignoring the clever glint in Sophia's dark eyes, "that is, I don't know all the details. But I was given a rather lovely strand of pearls by my grandmother, and somehow Lord Dutton got them from my father, Lord Melverley, and attempted to give them to your daughter."

"Well, my dear," Sophia said, taking a small sip of her drink, "Caro doesn't have your pearls. Why come to me?"

It was perfectly obvious to Louisa that Sophia knew *exactly* why she had come to her, but that, being Sophia, she wanted Louisa to crawl over broken glass and beg for her aid.

Fine. She could do that.

"I would like, that is, I noticed, we *all* noticed, how well things have gone for Lady Caroline and I was wondering . . . I was thinking that you might . . . be . . . able . . ."

It was far easier to contemplate crawling over broken glass than to actually do it. This begging for help business was decidedly difficult. She was completely certain she did not like it one bit. Even Lord Dutton's dashingly beautiful face grew a bit dim in the light of the amusement in Sophia's eyes.

"You would like your pearls back, wouldn't you?" Sophia said, setting down her cup on a very elegant Directoire table.

"Yes," Louisa said, holding Sophia's dark gaze. "I want my pearls back."

"Then, darling, we shall simply have to get them for you."

IT was as Lord Henry Blakesley was leaving the Prestwick town house that he bumped into the Marquis of Hawksworth about to go in. Where Hawksworth was, Louisa was not far distant. Where Louisa was, Dutton was almost certainly to be.

Louisa made rather a point of that.

"All alone today, Hawksworth?" Blakesley asked. "Dutton left Town, has he?"

Hawksworth smiled slightly. "Certainly you'd know that as soon as I."

A point, and well taken. Louisa not only made use of her cousin to escort her around Town, she made equal if less comfortable use of him. He did not particularly like being used as a sort of tame hound to sniff out the elusive Marquis of Dutton, but that was how Louisa chose to use him.

Blakesley knew precisely how that sounded and he didn't care for it in the least. Unfortunately, he did nothing about it. He didn't care to think too deeply about why.

"You're calling upon Mr. Prestwick?" Blakesley asked, changing the subject.

"Or Miss Prestwick," Hawksworth said casually. Hawksworth did most things casually; he was becoming almost famous for it. "They are a pleasant family, are they not?"

"Most pleasant," Blakesley said. "Mr. Prestwick is just within. I believe you were at school together?"

"Yes, and he spoke so often and so well of his sister."

Blakesley smiled. "She is eager to wed, so I'm told."

"Aren't they all?" Hawksworth said with a pleasant smile. "She is in season, I should think, her age and circumstances being at that precise point."

"You are not afraid of getting caught in the matrimonial net?"

"There is a season for everything, Lord Henry," Hawksworth said languidly. "It is a waste of energy to fight against the seasons. They change most regularly, no matter our preferences."

"And you will ride the change, enjoying all of spring's abundant pleasures?" Blakesley offered.

"Precisely."

"You are of a mind to marry Miss Prestwick?"

"I do not know Miss Prestwick," Hawksworth said pleasantly. "It is not the season for me to wed, and so I may dally where the mood takes me. Miss Prestwick might be pleasant enough to dally with in this off season for me, in all propriety, of course. I find myself here; there is no reason why I should not avail myself of blessed proximity."

"Of course not," Blakesley said, more amused by Louisa's cousin than he had ever been before. For such a young man, he was either more naïve than his peers or more sophisticated. It was so very difficult to decide which. "You have left your cousin somewhere safe, I trust? Or did you come to Upper Brook Street on your own?"

Blakesley knew Louisa's habits well enough to know that she had dragged her cousin here and then shucked him off like so much mud on her shoe. Hawksworth was of a disposition to allow it. Blakesley was not.

Hawksworth smiled in lazy good humor. "She is calling upon Lady Dalby. She made it very clear that she did not want my company when she did so. Perhaps she will welcome your company more than mine. It is hardly possible that she would welcome you less."

Or was it? Gone to see Sophia Dalby? Blakesley did not like the sound of that. Sophia Dalby had a way of managing things, a way of manipulating events and people until things were all muddled into a pattern that no one could have foreseen and few would welcome.

Except, he suspected, Sophia herself.

What was Louisa doing tangling herself up in Sophia's skirts?

"I think I shall call upon Lady Dalby. Care to join me, Lord Hawksworth?" Blakesley asked. "I can promise you that Sophia is more entertaining than Penelope Prestwick could dream of being."

Hawksworth smiled languidly and shrugged slightly. "I am at your disposal, Lord Henry. It is to Dalby House for the both of us. I do not care to think what Louisa will do when she sees us."

"It will be entertaining, at the very least," Blakesley said with a slanted smile. "What more can be asked of an afternoon call upon a countess?"

Two

LOUISA had no idea why Sophia would help her; there seemed no logical reason for it, but she was not going to spoil what she hoped would be a profitable alliance by looking for reasons. That Sophia was willing to help her was more than enough and, frankly, more than she had dared hope to achieve on a single visit.

"Now, darling," Sophia said, leaning forward in her chair, "you simply must promise me that you will do everything exactly as I tell you. Delicacy and a certain precision are absolutely essential in affairs of this sort."

It did not escape Louisa's notice that obeying Sophia, a woman who truly had no reason to help her, might possibly be the worst course of action she would ever undertake. She had, to be brutally honest, never been particularly nice to Sophia. In fact, it could be argued that she had occasionally behaved in a rather nasty fashion to her. It was not beyond the realm of possibility that Sophia, rumored to be rather ruthless when she chose, might choose this exact moment to be ruthless with Louisa.

Dutton was worth the risk. Oh, and the pearls as well. She couldn't let herself forget that this was all about getting back her pearls. That Dutton was in possession of them was glorious serendipity.

"I shall do whatever you think best," Louisa said, leaning forward in her own chair.

Sophia nodded and smiled in approval.

Whatever alarm Louisa felt upon receipt of that rather calculating smile, she suppressed. Ruthlessly. Dutton, and her pearls, were worth it.

"Perfect," Sophia said softly. "We shall get on splendidly. I do so enjoy it when my dictates are followed to the letter."

"Dictates?" Louisa said, her previously repressed alarm baying vigorously.

Sophia shrugged delicately. *"Mandates? Counsel? Instruction?* Choose the word that best pleases you. As long as we are in agreement as to what shall happen. I shall instruct and you shall obey."

Louisa was almost entirely certain that she had never obeyed anyone in her life. If not for the compelling nature of Lord Dutton and her compelling need to get possession of her pearls, she would have refused Sophia baldly. But she could not. She needed her pearls. She wanted Dutton. Or perhaps it was that she wanted her pearls and she needed Dutton. She didn't suppose it mattered as long as she gained possession of both.

"In the pursuit of my pearls," Louisa qualified.

"Naturally," Sophia said, her dark eyes gleaming. "A woman simply must have her pearls. And the man who took them from her must be punished."

"Punished? Oh, no. Not at all necessary," Louisa said abruptly. "I'm quite certain that my father is entirely to blame for selling my pearls. Lord Dutton can hardly be held at fault for buying them."

"Really?" Sophia said softly. "I'm equally certain that he could have purchased someone else's pearls with little effort. It seems entirely too convenient to me that he would practically steal your pearls from off your very elegant neck and proceed to make a public spectacle of presenting them to another woman. Though the other woman happens to have been my daughter, it wasn't very chivalrous of him, was it? I can state without hesitation that Caroline in no way expressed an interest in either Lord Dutton or any pearls he might happen to have found himself in possession of. The entire pearl spectacle as it involved Caroline and Lord Dutton was entirely Lord Dutton's idea."

Louisa hadn't considered that. *Had* Dutton made it a particular point to acquire *her* pearls? Had he done it to entice her? Or had he done it to insult her? And why had he done it with Lady Caroline at the most interesting assemblie of the Season?

With Dutton, either course was as likely. He was flagrantly adept at both enticement and insult. It made for a most exhausting romance, particularly as she was becoming more and more certain that she was the only person *present* in the romance. Dutton, inexplicably, did not seem to have succumbed to her obvious appeal and she had, to be brutally honest, given him ample opportunity to succumb.

She was, she was becoming increasingly certain, hopelessly in love with the Marquis of Dutton, and he was not, despite her best efforts, falling hopelessly in love with her.

It was inexplicable. Yet, it appeared to be true.

It was on the heels of that rather unpleasant thought that the door to the white salon opened and Fredericks entered with her cup.

"The gentlemen have returned, Lady Dalby," Fredericks said in an undertone. "With guests. Will you admit them?"

Sophia turned her dark gaze to Fredericks and said serenely, "With guests? Male, I presume." To which Fredericks nodded with entirely more amusement than was proper in a proper butler. He was an American; Louisa supposed that must answer for his coarse familiarity. "By all means. Admit them," Sophia said, her eyes on Louisa. Louisa resisted the urge to shift her weight on the fine white silk damask of her chair. "I think this will be most instructive, Lady Louisa. Do try and enjoy yourself fully."

It was a most odd remark to make. Louisa did not like it in the least.

And it was on the heels of *that* rather unpleasant thought that the door to the white salon opened and a parade of men of the most singular attractiveness walked into the room. It was quite impossible to form a coherent thought of any sort for quite some time after that. It was only at Sophia's amused cough that she managed to stand and curtsey her greeting at the gentlemen presented. They were introduced to her in the proper fashion and she supposed she made the proper replies; she had been the recipient of a more than passable education, after all, and one expected certain rules of etiquette and deportment to rise to the fore in uncomfortable circumstances, and meeting the men of Sophia's family certainly qualified as an uncomfortable circumstance.

Louisa sat back down upon Sophia's white silk damask, arranged her skirts, and tried not to stare.

No exercises in deportment could have been sufficient to the task.

First, of course, should have been Sophia's son, the rather remarkable Earl of Dalby. Wavy dark brown hair, liquid dark brown eyes, an expression of smoldering amusement tracing every line of his chiseled features; for all that, he was a boy compared to the man that was Dutton, she forcefully reminded herself. It was unexpected in the extreme that the Earl of Dalby was almost completely eclipsed by the man introduced as Sophia's brother.

He was a complete shock as he was clearly one of those American Indians one heard so much about. He certainly looked the part. Tall, bronzed, his dark hair falling straight into roughly cut chunks about his harshly chiseled face. His dark eyes were mere slits of speculation and he looked at her rather more closely than she was accustomed to.

She was dismayed to realize that she was not revolted by it.

He was introduced as Mr. John Grey, though it became immediately clear that everyone in the room addressed him as John.

Simply John. Impossible, really, as she couldn't go about addressing him by his given name; though she didn't suppose she would have any need to address him at all. She rather hoped not. Mr. John Grey looked entirely capable of cutting her heart out of her ribs without so much as a hitch in his breathing.

John Grey was the father of three sons, hardly more than boys in age, really, but again, like Lord Dalby, very forbidding despite their physical youth. George was likely her own age of twenty, and possessed of dark good looks and good height. In all, she was forced to admit, despite his primitive origins, he did rather look the part of a Greek statue. A dark, tousled Greek statue with the most startling dimple in his left cheek, which she knew existed because of his absolute cheek in smiling at her. Really. Hardly appropriate behavior but one entirely to be expected of an Indian, if one could believe the romantic and highly suspect rumors of them.

She was beginning to believe that the rumors might have more merit than she had at first supposed.

John the Younger was the middle son, and a more aristocratic face would be difficult to imagine. Of course, like the others, he was unfashionably dark of complexion, but it did not at all diminish his elegant athleticism. He looked to be about eighteen. Another mere boy when compared to her Dutton.

The youngest of Sophia's surprising nephews was introduced as Matthew, and he was surprisingly stunning in appearance. Young, yes, too young, but with the cleanest features and the bluest eyes set beneath the most classic brows; he looked what he was, that is, an Indian and savage. But therein lay the problem; savagery had never before looked quite so compelling.

It was completely inappropriate for her to take any note at all of these savages when there were two very likely titled gentlemen in the room as well, besides Lord Dalby. They were the guests, apparently, and Sophia seemed quite as surprised and perhaps slightly delighted that they'd joined her son's party.

"One would think you'd ridden to the hunt, Markham. Just look at what treasures you've brought home for me to enjoy," Sophia said, smiling at the Lords Penrith and Ruan, the *treasures.*

"Now, Mother," Dalby, who clearly also answered to Markham, said, "don't frighten them with your particularly odd strain of humor. I told them they'd be quite welcome."

"And so they are, darling," Sophia said. "As to being frightened . . . have I frightened you, Lord Ruan?"

"I'm forced to admit you have not, Lady Dalby," Lord Ruan said in a low voice.

"Then I shall just have to try harder, Lord Ruan, shan't I?" Sophia answered softly. "Now that you've found your way to my door, I daresay I shall have ample opportunity."

"Let us be precise, Lady Dalby," Ruan said silkily. "I have found my way *past* your door, past all your defenses, which, I find I am also forced to say, were rather more meager than I had expected."

"You had expectations," Sophia said, raising her black Wedgwood cup to her lips. "And they were not met." The contrast to her pale skin was particularly flattering. "Have I just been insulted, Lord Ruan? Shall it be pistols at dawn?"

"If we must duel," Ruan answered softly, his voice a deep rumble of amusement, "I have a sword of which I am particularly fond."

Upon which Sophia let her dark-eyed gaze travel the long length of Ruan's form before saying, "I don't doubt it, Lord Ruan."

Louisa could feel herself blush. This is what came from taking chocolate with a former courtesan; the conversation could not help but be coarse and rife with innuendo. Louisa looked at the Marquis of Ruan: a startlingly tall man with black hair and piercing green eyes in a face that had seen a good share of life. He looked only slightly older than Sophia, and what was more, he looked entirely and inappropriately at ease with the conversation.

" 'Tis obvious you've met," Dalby said in an undertone that could be heard by the entire room.

"Only recently, at the Duke of Hyde's assemblie where Caroline became so delightfully engaged," Sophia said, turning her gaze from Ruan to Penrith. "But you, Lord Penrith, you are an old friend. Tell me, how is your darling mother? Are she and your sister still traveling through Greece?"

"Yes, Lady Dalby," Lord Penrith answered, "and enjoying it immensely according to mother's last letter. They were hoping to visit Lord and Lady Elgin."

"How lovely that will be," Sophia said. "By all accounts Mary, Lady Elgin, is the most pleasant of women. I do envy them their ability to travel so widely upon the world."

"And what keeps you from traveling, Mother?" Dalby said from his elegant slouch upon the milk blue damask sofa.

"Why, my children, darling," she answered with a soft smile. "A mother simply should not leave her children at such a sensitive time in their lives as this."

"Sensitive? Sensitive in what regard?" Dalby asked.

"She means to see you married," Penrith said, his golden green eyes sparkling. Lord Penrith, whom Louisa had never had occasion to meet, was a remarkable looking man. Everyone, absolutely everyone, commented upon it.

He was tall, as fashion preferred, and golden, which fashion perhaps did not prefer but which compelled everyone who saw him to immediately discount fashion. His hair was longish and dark blond. His skin was dark gold. His brows were straight and cleanly drawn over almond-shaped eyes. His nose was shaped with poetic beauty and his brow was noble and intelligent.

But, of course, he could not truly compare to Dutton.

"Married?" Sophia said to Penrith's remark. "Without question, Markham. You must marry, but not yet. You are far too young to marry."

"Thank God we agree on that," Dalby muttered.

"I am quite certain I shall embarrass you by saying that I should be much surprised if we did not agree on absolutely everything," Sophia said. "Take, for example, Lady Louisa."

All eyes, male eyes, turned to look at Louisa. Louisa did not find it in the least agreeable. She lowered her eyes to her cup of chocolate and gazed into its brown depths as if it were the most fascinating object on three continents. Poise at its best, actually, as there was nothing even remotely interesting about a half-drunk cup of chocolate.

"I'll take her," a male voice said. Louisa's head jerked up to connect the voice to the man. It was one of the Indians, the one called George. Impertinence at its most extreme.

"Now, George," Sophia said on a trill of laughter, "you know quite well that things are done differently here in England."

"Too bad," George practically grunted.

Well, *really.*

"I'm afraid that I must be off," Louisa said, laying aside her cup on an elegant little table and rising to her feet. All the men in the room rose with her. She was beginning to feel like a player in a particularly bad farce.

"Now look what you've done, George," Sophia said from her poised perch on the damask sofa. "You've frightened Lady Louisa off. And we were having such a productive conversation."

Louisa sank back down to her seat. The men sank with her.

Frightened off? Hardly. And not by a mere primitive who didn't appear to have access to a good tailor. His coat was a positive lump of fabric that hung from his shoulders to his hips. Distasteful. Sophia really should see her relatives better turned out before she let them loose upon London.

He needed a good shave as well. She could actually see the dark shadow of his beard growing out of his jaw. Savage. Her stomach was quite turned by the sight. She could feel it flipping around even now.

And someone really should tell Mr. George Grey that staring was completely reprehensible. She might just tell him herself.

Someday.

His looking so completely savage was just the tiniest bit off-putting.

"Oh, good," Sophia said softly. "You've decided to stay. How tolerant of you, Lady Louisa. Having no brothers, you cannot image how unruly a house with men in it can become."

"Yes," Louisa said awkwardly, trying desperately to keep her gaze from George and his rather too snug leather breeches buttoned above a pair of soft leather boots. She was only marginally successful. He had spectacular legs and they were compellingly long.

"She's not married," George said, staring at her with his dark, savage eyes, his gaze entirely too direct and his manner disturbingly bold.

"No," Sophia said with a smile. "Not at present."

Not at present? Sophia made it sound as though she could be picked up and purchased as a matrimonial parcel with just a nod to the clerk. Indeed.

"I have no immediate plans to marry," Louisa said.

"I applaud you, Lady Louisa," Lord Penrith said, his voice a husky murmur.

People talked about that as well, about his voice and what it could do to a woman if she happened to find herself talking to him behind a hedge or a screen. Of course, the women who did talk about it were soon shuffled out of the best houses in London. A respectable woman did *not* go about talking to attractive gentlemen behind the furniture.

"I should say so," Lord Dalby echoed. "It's a rare woman, one of exceptional virtue, who does not make marriage a priority."

"Markham," Sophia said liltingly to her son, "please do try not to appear an idiot. Virtue has very little to do with anything, particularly where women are involved, and most decidedly where women are involved with men."

Lord Ruan laughed under his breath. John, Sophia's startling brother, made some noise, but she couldn't be certain if he wasn't simply coughing.

"I beg your pardon," Dalby, or rather Markham, said to his mother.

"As well you should," Sophia said. "Of course Lady Louisa plans to marry; she is simply wise enough not to rush precipitously into anything as permanent and as costly as a marriage."

"Costly?" Ruan asked.

He was a most compelling man and spoke in that distinctive drawl which showed the world that he had absolutely nothing to do with his time but enjoy it. While Penrith's green eyes were hazy and golden, much like a cat's, Ruan's eyes were like emerald blades, piercing and hard and entirely too knowing. It was a strange relief to find that he could spare his gaze for little beyond Sophia.

Louisa was not in the habit of pleasantly sharing the attention of any man with any woman, but in this case she was more than a little relieved. Lord Ruan looked entirely too experienced and was entirely too unrepentant of that fact.

That Sophia Dalby could manage him wasn't even a question worth asking.

"But of course," Sophia answered Ruan, looking at him rather more intently than was commonly considered proper. Not that Louisa was surprised by that; Sophia made it something of a routine to do things that weren't considered proper. Which was the entire reason for coming to her for aid in obtaining both Dutton and her pearls, now that she thought about it. "You of all people, Lord Ruan, must know that when a man and a woman join there are inevitable costs."

"Inevitable?" Ruan asked in a manner that was just this side of seductive. Louisa felt a slight tingle of feminine awareness in her toes. She jammed her toes into the tips of her shoes and silently insisted that her toes behave.

"Definitely," Sophia said with a small smile.

"The marriage contracts, of course," Dalby said.

"Of course," Sophia said sweetly, looking at her son. "What else?"

"What else, indeed," John said, giving his sister a most peculiar look.

John Grey was even more intimidating a man when giving out peculiar looks. Sophia's wild brother looked quite capable of killing a man for his snuff box. Of course, when a man had a sister who had been a courtesan, he might find that more than the usual number of occasions arose for killing a man. Odd, but she hadn't heard any rumors of men being killed in unusual number while Sophia had been, what must honestly be termed, *in trade*. It was entirely likely that Mr. Grey had remained in America and, since she had never heard of him, continued to do so.

Now, why was that? And what had brought him to England now?

Interesting questions, to be sure, but as they had absolutely nothing to do with Lord Dutton she could hardly be expected to actually *care* about Sophia and her family situation.

"But, as I was saying," Sophia said silkily, "I'm quite certain we can all agree, even you, Markham, that Lady Louisa is possessed of the most luscious shade of red hair that I have seen in twenty years."

Louisa fought the urge to clamp her hands down over her head. Naturally, Sophia had hit upon the one point most likely to prick: her hair. Her hair was the reason her father hated her. And because her father hated her, she returned the feeling in good measure. She was not going to be outdone, and certainly not by her father.

Louisa lifted her chin and her resolve and did *not* put her hands over her head.

"Twenty years?" Ruan said, looking casually in Sophia's direction and yet not looking the least bit casual.

"At the very least," Sophia said. "Such intensity, such brilliance, quite above the mark. Very much indicative of the girl herself, I daresay."

It was fair to say that all the men in the room, and that would be seven if one did not count Fredericks and she most certainly did not count Fredericks, were staring at her. Seven men, staring at her hair. She didn't like it in the least. *This* is what became of girls who called upon disreputable people without a proper chaperone, or even an improper one. What her cousin Amelia would think when she found out about this she didn't care to deliberate.

It was entirely uncertain whether she would tell Amelia anything at all.

"I hope so," George said in a husky undertone that practically echoed off the walls, rebounding the comment into every ear in the room. Lovely.

"I do believe, George, that you're halfway to being besotted by the girl," Sophia said. "Have a care. English women of a certain coloring are rumored to have a certain temperament."

"Good," George said, obviously ignoring his father's stern glance and grunt of disapproval.

"No, darling," Sophia said, "I believe you're missing the point entirely. Lady Louisa, with her fiery hair, coiled like twisting flames, will burn you dreadfully, if given half a chance."

George nodded and, smiling that rather too cheeky smile, revealing that startling dimple, said softly, "Good."

Blast. She was never leaving the house again without a chaperone, and she was *never* going to pay another call upon Lady Dalby. Some experiences were too vulgar to be endured. Why, she felt as if the floor itself were heaving around her legs. It was an entirely unfamiliar and unwelcome sensation.

"Oh dear," Sophia said softly. "I do believe, Lady Louisa, that you have an admirer."

Yes, well, it was the wrong one, wasn't it?

Three

LOUISA put the best face on it as possible, she was quite certain of that, but she had not come, without proper chaperone, into Lady Dalby's rather infamous salon to meet men. Hardly. She had come to discuss methods and means of reacquiring her pearls. She did not see how being subject to inappropriate conversation and, it might be argued, lewd stares, was helping her efforts to obtain Lord Dutton and her pearls. She sniffed in delicate disapproval, shifted the hem of her skirts in cold disdain, and waited for Sophia to do the right thing. The right thing being, in this particular instance, the removal of the men in her salon.

Although why Louisa expected a former courtesan to remove men from her presence was perhaps reaching a bit too high. Unless Lord Dutton was expected? Louisa lifted her bosom just slightly and arranged her hands most prettily and, without being entirely aware of it, looked expectantly and with rather too obvious hope at Lady Dalby.

Sophia Dalby seemed to read her expectant look rather more effortlessly than was entirely complimentary.

But as it was developing into the most unusual sort of day,

Fredericks did, at that precise moment, announce yet more callers. Dutton, certainly.

Actually, not Dutton at all, but her cousin Hawksworth, fully before his time, and Lord Henry Blakesley, Blakesley wearing a very sarcastic sort of look, one which he wore upon almost all occasions. If it was meant to chasten her, which it almost certainly was, he was failing wretchedly, as he always did.

She was not the sort of woman to be subdued by a look. She had not been the sort of *child* to be subdued by a look, which was certainly an advantage when dealing with Melverley, her father. Melverley, almost completely by accident, had taught her quite a bit more than was customary about how to manage a man, particularly if that man was proud and given to making sarcastic pronouncements.

Louisa could manage Lord Henry Blakesley quite well.

She had spent the better part of two years in her quest for Lord Dutton, and Blakesley had been a sly partner in her quest, not that he had done her any good. She wasn't Dutton's wife, was she? But Blakesley, blond and bored and rather more sharp of wit than was entirely comfortable, did entertain her whenever she found herself wandering from room to room during an evening out, searching for the elusive Dutton.

Blakesley, attractive in a rather sharp sort of way, was never boring. In fact, in an odd and completely unexpected fashion, he amused her as few others could.

"Isn't this charming?" Sophia said, smiling seductively. Louisa could almost ignore her as Sophia seemed to make a point of doing everything seductively. She found it tiresome. The gentlemen, it was quite clear, did not. "A room full of interesting and worldly men. What a delicious day it has become. Don't you agree, Lady Louisa?"

As Dutton was not among them, she was hardly disposed to agree.

"Completely, Lady Dalby," Louisa said in the sweetest tone imaginable.

Blakesley chuckled softly and eyed her in almost open derision.

After two years, he knew her too well. It was clearly not to her advantage.

"Lord Hawksworth," Sophia continued, holding court among the men crowding her salon in complete ease and one would even say delight, "how is it that we have never met? You are, by all appearances, a delightful man of rare deportment."

Hawksworth, that ill-trained boy, blushed.

Blakesley allowed half a grin to slide across his features before regaining his composure.

Ruan, his green eyes glittering, did not smile.

Neither did Sophia's son.

"He does not get out much, Lady Dalby," Louisa said with only the smallest snip of sarcasm. "My cousin is most devoted to his health and the hours of sleep he requires are quite precisely measured out."

"How very wise of you, Lord Hawksworth," Sophia said smoothly, in complete contrast to Louisa's sharp observation. "I, too, spend as much time as I possibly can in bed."

Upon which, Lord Penrith choked ever so politely on nothing whatsoever.

Of course, it was completely obvious what he had choked on. Certain innuendos simply would not go down without a fight.

It was at that awkward moment that Mrs. Anne Warren entered the white salon. As Louisa did not care for her in the slightest, she was not at all pleased. Things were not going at all as she had hoped. But when did they ever?

Anne Warren was, unaccountably, a special favorite of Sophia Dalby's. She had been something of a companion, being that she was the very young widow of a minor naval officer, to Sophia's daughter, Caroline. Now that Caroline was married and out of the Dalby household, one would have thought that Anne Warren would have been out as well.

She was not.

She had, for reasons unexplainable, become engaged to Lord Staverton. Viscount Staverton was old, cross-eyed, and very rich. He was also a very well-established friend of Sophia Dalby's and had been for as long as Sophia had been in London. Of course, everyone knew what that meant. Staverton had been one of Sophia's many protectors while she had been on the Town. It was perfectly obvious to everyone, particularly Louisa, that Sophia had arranged for Anne Warren to marry Staverton. It was not at all obvious how she had done so.

Sophia was, by anyone's reckoning, extremely good at getting what she wanted.

Of all the skills to possess, certainly that was the one to have. That Sophia had, for reasons unexplainable, decided to help Louisa get her pearls back from Lord Dutton was to her very good fortune. She was not going to antagonize Anne Warren and thereby risk offending Sophia.

Or at least, she was going to try not to. Where Anne Warren was concerned, Louisa had very little self-control. Anne Warren, apart from Sophia's protection, also had the attention of Lord Dutton. That, clearly, was more than Louisa could be expected to endure.

It was also clear that she was going to have to endure it.

"Oh, Anne, how timely you are," Sophia said as Anne entered the room.

The men rose, introductions were made, the Marquis of Penrith looked at Mrs. Warren entirely longer than was necessary, as did her cousin Hawksworth, as did Lord Ruan. The Indians smiled rather too broadly at Anne, and Lord Dalby even went so far as to kiss her on the cheek. The only man in the room, in fact, who did not positively swoon over the completely ordinary Anne Warren was Blakesley. Blakesley was looking at her, a twisted smile upon his face, his blue eyes almost maliciously amused.

"I am so delighted that you made it back in time. It would not have done at all for you to miss this impromptu gathering of London's most interesting people," Sophia said.

It was completely obvious to Louisa that Sophia had intended to say London's most interesting *men*, but she had remembered Louisa at the very last moment and amended her statement so as not to obviously insult her. Not *obviously* insult her. Still, the unspoken word hovered in the air of the white salon like rotting herring.

Blakesley, as usual, was silently laughing at her.

Louisa, as usual, did her very best to ignore him. She was very good at it as she had had so very much practice.

Anne, looking typically and irritatingly beautiful, said, "I'm so sorry. I do hope I'm not interrupting, Lady Dalby. I'll just tell the boy to put the fabric in my room until—"

"No, no, not at all, Anne," Sophia said. "Have it brought in. I'm quite certain it will amuse the gentlemen to help us decide upon which fabric to use in this room. I'm redoing it, you see," Sophia said to the men scattered about the room, "and I do so enjoy a man's opinion on something as essential as the proper color for my favorite room."

Oh, bother. It was perfectly obvious to Louisa, indeed, to any girl over the age of six, that men of any age disliked looking at anything that did not involve either breasts or triggers.

But, as it was Sophia Dalby making the request, the men in this particular room looked positively delighted at the opportunity to consider swatches. All except Blakesley, that is. He looked undelighted, yet undisturbed. But then, Blakesley had that way about him of looking undisturbed by most everything. She found it a particularly restful quality, truth be told.

"What of the white?" the Earl of Dalby asked. "This salon has been white for years."

"And, while it amused for a while, all pleasures must eventually pall," Sophia said, gazing at the Marquis of Ruan. "I do so enjoy a change of scene."

The Marquis of Ruan returned Sophia's gaze with the barest smile touching his lips. It was a look which quite suited him, and Louisa, for all her devotion to Lord Dutton, could feel her heart flutter in something very close to titillation just watching him watch Sophia.

What must it be like, to have a man of Ruan's obvious appeal look on with such obvious interest and in a room full of witnesses? Certainly, Dutton had never looked in any way approaching interest at her. She would have known it if he had for she was always watching to see exactly what he did or did not do.

What he did not do always far exceeded what he did do.

"What color would interest you, Lady Dalby?" Ruan asked, moving closer to Sophia as the footmen came in holding bolts of costly fabric in a variety of hues. The whole room shifted and parted, forming smaller groups within the whole. Blakesley took the opportunity to move next to her, while Hawksworth, that coward, took the opportunity to move away from her, closer to Anne Warren, she could not but note.

"Which of these colors intrigues *you*, Lord Ruan?" Sophia asked in reply.

"I've always been fond of blue."

"How very unfortunate," Sophia said. "Blue would not compliment the light in this room at all. We see things very differently, I am afraid."

"I am not so untutored that I cannot find my pleasure with other hues," Ruan said.

"How very accommodating you sound," Sophia answered softly, running her hand over a lovely length of crimson velvet.

"How very practiced at accommodation. One can't but wonder where you learned the skill."

"At my mother's knee?" Ruan said, lifting a dark brow.

"At someone's knees," Sophia said softly, smiling in a brief flash of humor.

Louisa was aware that she was witnessing something that she should pay careful attention to, but she was not at all certain what to do with it.

"What are you doing here?" Blakesley said in a harsh whisper, dragging her attention completely away from the exchange absolutely rife with undercurrents between Sophia and Ruan.

"Choosing fabric?" Louisa said. "What are *you* doing here? And what are you doing with Hawksworth? I thought he was for the Prestwick town house?"

"Which is where he found me."

"What were *you* doing there? Not to see Penelope?" she said with more snap than was entirely appropriate, but Penelope was practically desperate to marry and everyone knew it. Blakesley could and should do far better than Penelope Prestwick.

"And why not? She's pleasant enough," Blakesley said.

"At the moment, I'm quite certain that's true," Louisa said. "She is, after all, determined to marry the first man who asks her. I should be very wary, were I you."

"Why? I don't plan to ask her and she can hardly ask me."

An answer which calmed her considerably. She liked Blakesley too much to see him saddled with Penelope, who might be both beautiful and wealthy but was hardly the sort of girl one wished upon a friend. And Blakesley was her friend, albeit a rather odd one in that he never complimented her or cajoled her or loyally took her side in every debate. A very odd sort of friend, indeed. One had to wonder why she tolerated him as well as she did. A mark of her good character, no doubt.

"I'm delighted to hear it, Lord Henry," she said. "I value you too much to see you in a misalliance of even the most casual sort."

Blakesley made a face, just this side of pleasant, and then indicated with a motion of his head that she should stand and accompany him to a more private part of the room. As the occupants of the white salon were shifting quite drastically, the Indians leaving and Anne Warren more fully surrounded than ever by Penrith and Hawksworth and Dalby, Louisa was more than happy to follow Blakesley to whichever corner he wished.

"Why are you here, Louisa?" Blakesley said in a hoarse undertone, his blue eyes a trifle more sharp than was usual. "You don't have any special fondness for Lady Dalby."

"I'm paying a call, Lord Henry," she said primly, though it was difficult to maintain a prim exterior when Blakesley adopted that particular look and that particular tone. Nevertheless, she did it. "I have been known to do so."

"Not at Dalby House," he said. "You want something, and I think we both know what it is. Or who."

That was a little too close to the mark for her enjoyment and, naturally, she was left with no other recourse than to do something about it. Namely, to redirect his attention to other, less humiliating, conclusions.

"If you must know," she hissed, turning so that she faced the room from beyond the mound of Blakesley's shoulder, "I want my pearls back. Melverley had no right to sell them."

Blakesley looked rather more closely at her than was entirely comfortable, but she bore up admirably and returned his speculative look with one of pure annoyance.

"He had the right," Blakesley argued, "but perhaps not the need."

"Trust you to cut it so finely," she snapped. "I want my pearls."

"Sophia doesn't have them."

Louisa snorted delicately. At least, she was fairly certain it was delicately. "Can you think of a better person to advise me on how to get them back? If any woman knows how to wring a strand of pearls from out of a man," she said, and then added, "and speaking of that, why did you give Caroline pearls that night? I had no idea she was such a favorite of yours."

"And you had no idea about Penelope Prestwick either, Louisa," he said stiffly. It was absolutely impossible to talk to Blakesley when he got his back up. Bother it. "There is much you are not aware of, apparently."

"Apparently," she said, moving away from him. He followed her, which she had anticipated. At least she knew how to manage Blakesley. Usually. When he was in the proper mood. "But I do know that I want my pearls, that Lord Dutton has them, and that Sophia Dalby is more than willing to help me get them back. I think I know enough, don't you, Lord Henry?"

Blakesley didn't answer directly. No, he was too contrary for that. He looked at her in what could only be called bald speculation, his eyes positively gleaming as he studied her. She stood up to it rather well, in her experienced opinion. Blakesley could often be found studying her; she'd developed quite a talent for enduring it placidly.

"But why would Sophia help you?" he murmured.

It was hardly flattering. It was so very difficult to remain placid when one was continually being insulted in one manner or another.

"Because, darling," Sophia said, coming up behind Blakesley as silently as a swan on a lake, "I do so ardently believe that a woman should never be separated from her jewelry. You can believe that, can't you?"

"I suppose I can," Blakesley said, turning his gaze to Sophia and studying her with the same intensity that he had been showering upon Louisa. It was most annoying. "But how do you think to manage it, Lady Dalby?"

"Between Lady Louisa and I, we shall work something out, don't you think?" Sophia said, smiling politely. "I'm quite certain that Lord Dutton can be persuaded to part with a strand of pearls he can have no use for."

"Persuaded how?" Blakesley said, ignoring Louisa completely to discuss her pearls, *her* pearls, with Sophia. It was beyond tolerable.

"Darling," Sophia said, laying a slim white hand upon his arm, "if you don't think that, between the two of us, we can manage a single pearl necklace, you don't know women as well as I thought you did." And then she laughed.

Feeling like the most common of whores, Louisa felt her cheeks burn bright red in shame.

"I was under the impression, which I see now was mistaken," Sophia said gaily, continuing on as if Louisa's face were not the approximate color of a strawberry, "that you and Lady Louisa were rather special friends. You clearly do not understand her at all, Lord Henry. She is a woman most determined. She *will* have her pearls again. One only wonders what paltry defense Lord Dutton will manage to summon. I do so love a mystery, don't you?"

Blakesley was kept from answering by the arrival of Lord Penrith to their number. Lord Penrith, after the most cursory of greetings and with a passing remark as to the particular attractiveness of the bolt of gold and red brocade, drew Blakesley off for a conversation about hunting dogs, of all things. Not actual hunting dogs, mind you, but the artistic merit of the hunting dogs on a very pretty length of green and red pictorial fabric. Lord Penrith seemed quite outraged at the angle of one of the dogs' rear legs.

What was even more remarkable was that Blakesley did not hesitate to argue that he had once owned a dog with precisely that angle of leg.

Perhaps men did care about more than breasts and triggers.

"Such an interesting man," Sophia said when they were alone in a relatively quiet corner of the white salon. Ruan and Dalby appeared to be getting into quite a heated discussion about the merits of ivory damask as compared to brown on cream pictorial. Dalby, it seemed, favored the damask. Anne Warren looked almost amused by the argument. "I do think Miss Prestwick will be most satisfied with him."

"I beg your pardon?" Louisa said. If it wasn't Anne Warren, it was Penelope Prestwick. She was clearly destined not to have a moment's peace between the two of them, though they could not have been more different.

Sophia looked at her, her black eyes dancing in amusement. "Why, I assumed you knew. You and Lord Henry have a special bond, do you not?"

There was no answer to that which was proper, so Louisa said nothing. She merely looked expectantly and pleasantly into Sophia's clearly sadistic face.

"I was talking with the Duchess of Hyde recently," Sophia continued, "and she was quite of the opinion that one of her sons must do his duty and marry. And, of course, I quite agree with her. It is a man's duty to marry and protect the line. Well, you may or may not be aware," Sophia intimated, as if they were the closest of friends, which they were not, "that the Marquis of Iveston, Hyde's heir, is extraordinarily . . ."

And here Sophia clearly searched for the appropriate word. It took all of Louisa's self-control not to offer *backward.* Because, of course, she had heard about Iveston. Everyone had.

"Private," Sophia eventually said, "and, even with five sons to choose from, Lord Henry is the likeliest to marry first and so," Sophia said with a shrug, "there you are."

"I beg your pardon?" Louisa said again.

"Oh, haven't I made myself clear, darling? I'm so sorry," Sophia said, not looking sorry in the least. "I suggested that Miss Prestwick might do quite well for Lord Henry and the duchess quite agreed and so . . ." And here Sophia shrugged expressively, again.

No.

Louisa was quite well aware of what she was feeling and thinking and it was a profound and permanent *no*.

She was not at all certain why she was so intensely opposed to Penelope Prestwick marrying Blakesley, but she was. That was all there was to it. She didn't suppose she need bother thinking anything more about it.

No.

"I happen to know," Louisa said haltingly, "that my cousin, Lord Hawksworth, has expressed an interest in Miss Prestwick, though I have no idea how serious his interest is." It was truly amazing how quickly she threw Hawksworth into the gaping jaws of Penelope Prestwick. Truly amazing. "Certainly, as Hawksworth will be a duke one day, Miss Prestwick should not rush into anything with Lord Henry."

Upon which, Sophia laughed most delicately. "But, darling, Hawksworth is a boy. He is far too young to marry, and Miss Prestwick is most eager, I'm told. As is the Duchess of Hyde, to be perfectly honest. No, it must be one of hers to satisfy her. It is not for Miss Prestwick that the deed shall be done, you understand; it is purely to satisfy the needs of the Hyde line. As it ever is."

Yes, that was certainly true, but Blakesley? Why did it have to be Blakesley who was to be sacrificed to Penelope Prestwick?

"I'm not at all certain that Lord Henry is ready for marriage," Louisa said.

"And what man is?" Sophia said. "It is a woman's pleasant duty to bring a man to a point of readiness, is it not? And what fun it can be to do so."

It sounded quite wicked, but then most of what Sophia Dalby said sounded quite wicked. She clearly did it intentionally.

"I think, Lady Louisa, that you must learn the pleasant art of a proper pursuit. I shall instruct you, shall I?"

Positively wicked.

"Now," Sophia said, "first let us talk plainly about your pearls and Lord Dutton's possession of them."

Finally.

"It is perfectly obvious," Sophia continued, "that he had some devious purpose in acquiring them."

"I believe it was because your daughter requested a strand of pearls," Louisa said stiffly. *She* knew the facts of the situation, and she was *not* going to allow Sophia Dalby to lay any blame on Dutton. Caroline had been the instigator, with a very healthy prompt from Sophia, of that there was no doubt whatsoever.

Sophia smiled and said, "Isn't it rather odd that Lord Dutton presented Caroline with a strand of pearls when she had no interest in him at all and had certainly never made her preference for pearls known to him?" And when Louisa opened her mouth to defend Dutton and only mildly castigate Caroline, Sophia continued, "If further proof is required, you have only to consider that Dutton presented *your* pearls to Mrs. Warren only minutes after Caroline refused him."

Mrs. Warren?

It could not be true. And yet, it sounded so exactly like Dutton.

"I beg your pardon?" Louisa said, her voice sounding quite unattractively tight. One might well have said she *squeaked* the question. "I mean to say, did she . . . are you saying that Mrs. Warren is now in possession of my pearls?"

To which Sophia laughed in delighted cruelty. Oh yes, laughter could be quite cruel. A fact which Sophia Dalby proved most regularly. Louisa did not know what she had been thinking to come here, to this house, to this woman. She felt positively ill.

"Darling," Sophia said softly, leaning forward in deceptive sympathy, "you know quite well, from Mrs. Warren's own lips, that she has no interest in Lord Dutton." An obvious lie. There wasn't a woman alive who didn't have an interest in Lord Dutton. It was a well-known fact that he was irresistible. "You must have no worry from that quarter. I promised you that I would help you get your pearls back around your lovely throat and that is exactly what I shall do. Unfortunately, it is not as simple as asking for them from Mrs. Warren. No, Lord Dutton has them still. And it is from Lord Dutton that we shall get them."

Well. That sounded better. She could almost breathe again. Having to beg Mrs. Warren, possessed of red hair much like her own but with the inexplicable addition of having somehow gained Dutton's attention, for the return of her necklace would have been too, too much to bear. But she would have done so, for her pearls. And for Dutton. Unfortunately and inconceivably, Mrs. Warren, for all that she claimed she did not want Lord Dutton, could not return his affections to her. Although *return* may have been a most inaccurate word since, as far as she could tell, she had never had Dutton's affection to begin with.

Love, she had well learned, could be almost as cruel as laughter.

"How shall we accomplish it?" Louisa asked, leaning forward so that she and Lady Dalby could whisper comfortably. "Shall I chance upon him in the park?" She had heard a rumor that Caroline had done just such a thing with Lord Ashdon in Hyde Park and that the results had been remarkable and swift.

"No, no," Sophia said, shaking her head and, yes, laughing at her. Really. Lady Dalby was possessed of the most awkward sense of humor. She appeared to enjoy laughing at anything. Most unrefined. "Nothing so forward with the skittish Lord Dutton," Sophia continued, after she had stopped chuckling. One could almost believe that Louisa was the butt of some very tawdry jest. "We must proceed circuitously. He must never see it coming."

Odd phrasing, to be sure. One would think they were planning an assault upon Lord Dutton's very compelling form.

Louisa felt a thrill of excitement down deep in her heart just thinking of it. She'd been right, after all; coming to a former courtesan had been *exactly* the right idea.

"Now, I will assume," Sophia said, "that you wish to begin immediately."

"Of course," Louisa said, nodding her head in what she was certain was a most unbecoming and eager fashion.

"What are your plans for this evening? I assume you have plans?"

"Naturally." Really. Did Lady Dalby think she sat at home waiting for the elusive Lord Dutton to call? No, she did what any intelligent and attractive young woman did: she went out and hunted him down. "Lady Amelia and I, attended by Hawksworth, are to enjoy dinner at the Duke of Hyde's."

"Most convenient," Sophia said, her dark eyes sparkling with an altogether dangerous gleam. "How very astute of you and your cousin to manage an invitation to a ducal residence. I do think," she said, rubbing her ring finger against her lower lip, "that a ducal residence is *just* the place to launch our initial attack in what I am certain will be a very brief, but perhaps amusingly bloody war."

"War?" What sort of courtesan spoke of war? This was all of love, of deep and lasting love. "I have no intention of making war against Lord Dutton."

Sophia eyed her with a frozen gaze.

"You want your pearls, am I correct?" Lady Dalby said, her voice soft and chill.

"Of course."

"Then a small war may be necessary, Lady Louisa. You must trust me. I do know more than a little about the various ways of acquiring jewels."

There was hardly any doubt about *that*.

"It is only that I," Louisa said in a hesitant manner that was positively mortifying to her and which she was incapable of stopping, "I should not enjoy causing Lord Dutton any . . . unpleasantness."

Sophia's left eyebrow rose fractionally. "Surely Lord Dutton can tolerate some unpleasantness in his life. He is a man, after all, and men are rather good at tolerating unpleasant things. The same should never be said of women. We may occasionally be required to endure unpleasantness, but we should, at all costs, avoid become adept at it."

Louisa could only gape. She had never in her life been exposed to such a philosophy.

As philosophies went, this was by a wide margin the most sensible and appealing one she had ever heard. She planned to adopt it immediately.

"I daresay I agree with you completely, Lady Dalby," Louisa said in that same earnest tone that she feared was becoming a rather permanent feature in her conversations with Sophia Dalby.

"I daresay one would hardly know it from your past behavior with and toward Lord Dutton," Sophia said coolly. "Now, about tonight. I think your aunt would be better suited to our plans than your charming cousin. The proper chaperone is so important, isn't it?"

Louisa blanched and then flushed. She could feel the ebb and flow of emotion all over her face and throat.

"Darling," Sophia said, leaning forward with all the grace of a swan and laying a white hand upon Louisa's arm, "all will be avenged. Trust me to see it done. You shall have your pearls and, upon my word, Dutton shall feel the sting of it."

"And my past behavior?" Louisa managed to ask. If her devotion to Dutton was obvious to Sophia, then she was of half a mind to speak openly of it. Pearls or not, she meant to have Dutton, and perhaps Sophia could help her more if she better knew her desires.

"Will remain in the past," Sophia said. " 'Tis a new day, darling, and we will accomplish *all* your desires. All," she finished with a knowing gleam.

Then again, it was entirely likely that one did not need to flagrantly discuss such things with a former courtesan. Louisa was more than certain that Sophia knew exactly what she was about.

Which was entirely the point.

Four

WITH Hawksworth having fulfilled his purpose and been dispatched, Louisa walked in to her father's house with all the casual innocence of a woman who'd been out shopping and returned home more bored than when she left. It was a fine bit of acting. Not that anyone was around to notice.

According to Anderson, the butler, her aunt Mary, Lady Jordan was napping. Her father, the Marquis of Melverley, was out, likely at either White's or his current mistress's house on George Street. Of course, as the innocent and unmarried daughter of a marquis, she wasn't supposed to know about such things, but as her father made rather an open habit of having a mistress or two, she didn't suppose she could be blamed for knowing what was obvious to all.

The only person who was home was the same person who was always home, Louisa's younger sister, Eleanor. There was absolutely no point at all in acting a part with Eleanor as an audience. She was the most jaded cynic Louisa had ever met, and that included the cynical Henry Blakesley. Having Melverley for a father gave one rather a hand up on being cynical.

Eleanor was in the library, just to the left of the vestibule. It was a massive room, fully the largest in the house, and had the happy situation of being flooded with western light for the better part of the day. But it was not the light that drew Eleanor; it was the books. Row upon row of the most beautifully bound and inexpressibly boring books. Louisa didn't know how Eleanor stood it, being surrounded by so much reading material of the most tedious variety. Why, there was a whole shelf devoted to classical architecture. She knew for a fact that Melverley had bought the books by the crate and for the prettiness of their spines. He had as much care for classical architecture as she did, which was to say, none at all.

"How's Lord Dutton today?" Eleanor said from her slouch. She was buried in her usual spot, a pile of faded silk cushions cocooning her upon the sofa, a book in her lap.

"I haven't seen Lord Dutton," Louisa said, plopping down upon the opposite end of the sofa and reaching up to take off her hat.

"He wasn't in the park?"

"I would hardly know as *I* wasn't in the park."

"Nor on Bond Street?"

"I did not travel to Bond Street."

Eleanor put her book completely down and stared at her.

"What does Lord Henry Blakesley say to this? Isn't it his duty to track Lord Dutton down for you? You shall need to find a new hound, Louisa, if this is the best he can do."

"Don't be ridiculous, Eleanor," Louisa snapped. "Lord Henry is no such thing."

"Isn't he?"

"Naturally not."

"What *have* you been doing, Louisa?"

"I've been calling on . . . a friend."

"A . . . friend?" Eleanor said, tucking her feet up underneath her and dislodging one pale blue pillow from its nest. "Is this friend a man? Don't tell me you went *alone*. Where's Amelia?"

"Of course I did not go calling on a man," Louisa said sharply.

"With or without Amelia, I would never do such a scandalous thing."

"But you did go without Amelia."

"She was engaged."

Eleanor only raised a dark red eyebrow at that rather blatant evasion.

"You didn't go calling on Lord Dutton, did you?" Eleanor said.

"Of course not! And I've already told you," Louisa said, "I haven't seen Lord Dutton today."

"That doesn't mean you couldn't have called on him," Eleanor said matter-of-factly, dipping her head back into her book. "You could have called on him and found him not at home. You then, if you were very silly, might have walked past St. James Street in hopes of seeing him."

"I would do no such ill-bred thing!" Louisa said. "What nonsense are you reading that gives you such forward and ill-mannered ideas?"

"Shakespeare," Eleanor said lightly, "but that is not where I get my ideas. You could then have wandered along the edge of Hyde Park, hoping to see Lord Dutton riding by, and having failed at even that, you might then have walked across Park Lane onto Upper Brook Street and knocked upon the door of Dalby House."

Louisa was standing by this time, her hands clenched into white knots of fury and mortification. Eleanor did not seem at all intimidated, which was precisely what was wrong with Eleanor; she could not be intimidated. A most irregular and even more irritating trait for a younger sister to possess. From what Louisa could gather, younger sisters were supposed to live in absolute terror of their older siblings. Not so Eleanor. It was most, most inconvenient.

"You followed us," Louisa whispered hoarsely, stating the obvious.

"And a merry chase it was," Eleanor answered brightly.

"Alone?" If Eleanor had wandered London without an escort at the tender age of sixteen, her aunt Mary would never forgive her. What her father thought she could hardly have cared less.

Though she didn't suppose he had to know about it, did he? Let him worry about his mistress. His daughters would, could, and did take care of themselves.

"Of course not," Eleanor said. "I'm not so foolish as all that. I went with Amelia and two footmen. She didn't want to accompany me, of course, but as I told her rather directly that I would proceed with or without her, I suppose she felt compelled to attend me."

"I suppose she did," Louisa said crisply, sitting back down on the sofa next to Eleanor. It might have been better said that she *collapsed* upon the sofa, not that it mattered. It was patently obvious that she could keep no secret from Eleanor. "I don't know where you get these schemes, Eleanor, to go running about London, spying on your only sister."

"That bit I suppose I do borrow from Shakespeare," Eleanor said. "So much running about in his comedies. It did sound like fun."

"I trust you found it wasn't."

"Not really, no," Eleanor said with a grin. "Following you about was very entertaining, not that Amelia shares my opinion. She was shocked beyond words when you walked past St. James Street. According to her, there is no more efficient way to ruin a woman's reputation. Of course, that was before you went to visit Lady Dalby. What *did* you do there, Louisa? Is your reputation ruined now?"

"Hardly," Louisa said, tucking a foot underneath her and sprawling against the arm of the sofa. "In fact, if all goes as it should, it might be the making of me."

"Really?" Eleanor said, leaning forward and putting her book down once again. "What happened? Was Lord Dutton there?"

"No, he was not. You do know, Eleanor, that not everything revolves around Lord Dutton."

To which Eleanor, the imp, only laughed.

Yes, well, perhaps that was the only response possible to what could only have been termed wishful thinking.

"What are we laughing about?" Amelia said, entering the library.

Lady Amelia Caversham, only daughter of the Duke of Aldreth and only sister to the Marquis of Hawksworth, was cousin to Louisa and Eleanor through their Aunt Mary. Mary had been the oldest of a trio of girls who had, according to gossip, taken London by storm twenty-five years previous.

Martha, Amelia's mother, had acquired herself a duke in the form of Amelia's father. Margaret had done just slightly worse in acquiring for herself the Marquis of Melverley. But of course, that was the tale as the public told it. Louisa knew without a doubt that her mother had done very much worse in finding herself saddled with Melverley.

Both Margaret and Martha were dead now, leaving their children in the care of less than diligent fathers and leaving Mary, their sister, the field. Mary, to hear her tell it, had married for love. Mary had married badly, a mere baron who had died ten years ago leaving his wife without children and without funds. Marrying for love had not been the wisest course for Aunt Mary. Louisa was going to do much better at it when she married Lord Dutton. Marrying for love was not a bad idea if one married the right sort of man. Lord Dutton was precisely the right sort of man. To start, he was a marquis, a very much better sort of man than a mere baron.

Eleanor did not agree with such sound and logical reasoning, however. She loved to read Shakespeare, and who knew where he had gotten his rather odd ideas about love and marriage. Amelia, on the other hand, agreed with her completely. Amelia was possessed of an entirely practical frame of mind about things romantic. Louisa rather liked that about her.

She also rather liked the fact that Amelia cared absolutely nothing for Lord Dutton. For that reason alone, Amelia could not possibly have been a more delightful companion.

"*We* are laughing because Louisa just announced that not *everything* revolves around Lord Dutton," Eleanor said with a chuckle.

"After the day you've had?" Amelia said, sitting down on a well-padded chair and stretching out her legs. "That takes cheek, Louisa. Now, tell me everything. What did you discuss with Lady Dalby? Was Lord Dutton there?"

"No, he was *not* there, nor did I expect him to be," Louisa said, coloring it just slightly. It would not have been at all amiss if he *had* been there, though since she had not expected him to be there she did not think it at all amusing that everyone assumed she'd gone to Dalby House looking for him. It was a fine point, but in a courtship such as the one she was almost having with Lord Dutton, fine points became excruciatingly important.

"I must say, I think it's for the best that he wasn't there," Amelia said, brushing a hand over the back of her golden hair. "It's scandalous enough that you paid a call upon Lady Dalby without an escort. It would be altogether worse if you'd been closeted within with Lord Dutton."

"It was hardly scandalous," Louisa said. "After all, I've paid more than one visit to Lady Dalby in the past."

"Yes, but always with a chaperone or escort and always when she was hosting a party. To plop yourself upon her doorstep in the middle of the afternoon . . . well, I must tell you that I tried to stop you, or to at least accompany you, but Eleanor prevented me."

Louisa raised her ginger brows and looked at her sister in surprised curiosity.

"I thought you should have a go at her," Eleanor said, shrugging. "At Lady Dalby, I mean. They say she's very clever about things, and very wicked as well. But then, I don't suppose it is very unusual to be both clever and wicked. Based upon my reading, I should say it was rather unlikely to be one and not the other."

"Don't be absurd, Eleanor," Louisa snapped. "Of course a person may be both clever and good."

"Name three," Eleanor countered with a straight face. "And don't bother naming Lord Dutton as I am completely certain he is as wicked as the worst rake in Town should be, though I'm not at all certain he is clever in the least."

Into a silence that stretched rather uncomfortably as they each tried to think of someone, anyone, who was both clever and good, Amelia said, "One thing can be said for Dutton; he is remarkably clever at avoiding—"

"Louisa?" Eleanor chirped.

"Marriage," Amelia said instead, her blue eyes betraying not even a hint of amusement, which was another reason why Louisa so appreciated Amelia. She was incapable of malice, which, as everyone knew, was nearly impossible for the daughter of a duke. "Now, what happened at Lady Dalby's? Did she receive you?"

"Of course," Louisa said, although, truth be told, she had experienced a flutter of nerves the second before she knocked at the door. One never knew how Sophia would respond, most especially since Sophia Dalby was entirely capable of malice. "We had a lovely conversation which was cut just a bit short by the arrival of the male members of her family and the Lords Penrith and Ruan."

Upon which, Eleanor dropped her book; it landed awkwardly on her foot and flopped onto the floor. Amelia's mouth was just slightly agape and her eyes unblinking. All in all, it was a rather satisfactory response.

"Lord Penrith?" Amelia finally sputtered.

"What do you mean *male members of her family*?" Eleanor said as Amelia spoke. "Is there more than the Earl of Dalby?"

"Much more," Louisa said smugly to her sister.

"Are Lord Penrith's eyes truly green? Did he speak? Is his voice all that they say?" Amelia asked.

"Why should you care, Amelia? He isn't in line for a dukedom," Eleanor said. "I want to hear about Sophia's family."

"His eyes are very green," Louisa said to Amelia, "and his voice is very . . . very . . ."

"Very what?" Amelia breathed.

"Very," Louisa said on a sigh of breath.

"Oh, my," Amelia said, standing up to walk behind her chair. She looked a bit flushed. Lord Penrith was entirely worthy of a healthy flush. It was just possible that Louisa herself had flushed upon seeing him for the first time; she was quite certain that she would not flush upon meeting him again. Quite certain.

"Did you blush like that when you met him?" Eleanor asked, her elegant brows raised quizzically.

"I'm not blushing," Louisa said, banishing all memory of Penrith's rather startling green eyes and languid voice to their proper place in her thoughts, namely, the thinnest sphere of consciousness. Only Dutton deserved a maidenly blush from her. How Penrith had got hold of one was beyond speculation. "Do you want to hear about Sophia's family or not?"

"Definitely," Eleanor said. "There are her children, Caroline and Dalby, though don't they call him something besides Dalby?"

"Markham, I believe," Amelia said, sitting back down upon her chair, her color restored to its normal flawless ivory. "A childhood name, according to Aunt Mary."

Louisa refrained from stating that Sophia's son looked anything but a child. Given that she was devotedly in love with Dutton, it was not at all appropriate for her to notice the particulars about any other man. Even if she did notice them, the particulars, in other men. Highly and completely inappropriate. She did not quite know what was wrong with her.

It must be something to do with having spent time with Sophia Dalby. It just proved how wicked influences were so completely *wicked.* She had never looked at another man since first seeing Dutton. Now it seemed that she couldn't stop herself from looking.

Wicked.

"But do tell us about Sophia's family," Eleanor said, sitting up completely, her thin arms crossed, her pointed chin resting in her hand, eyes alight with mischief and avid curiosity. "Are they as wicked and clever as she?"

"They are," Louisa said dramatically, "*Indians.*"

"From America?" Amelia said in awe, to which Louisa nodded, smiling.

"*Truly?*" Eleanor said dreamily, her eyes going to the ceiling, and then she jerked her gaze back to Louisa, jumped up off the sofa, and said, "I want to meet them. How many of them are there? Are they all men? Are they all *grown* men? Where's my shawl? Louisa, help me find my shawl. Amelia, didn't I have my shawl while we were out walking?"

"You are *not* serious," Louisa said, knowing full well that Eleanor was completely serious. This was just the sort of thing to titillate her, which was absurd as sixteen-year-old, well-brought-up young ladies should not be titillated by anything, and certainly not the thought of meeting savage Indians from America. George Grey, in particular, had been particularly savage, dimple and all.

"Were they . . . savage?" Amelia asked, her own gaze going dreamy.

Eleanor was lifting cushions and pillows and books, looking with frantic eagerness for her shawl, but she stopped at the question and stared at Louisa.

"They were, weren't they?" Eleanor said on a hush of breath. "Savage and wicked and—"

"And they were," Louisa interrupted, slyly kicking Eleanor's rather nice cashmere shawl underneath the nearest bookcase with her foot, "the blood relations of Lady Dalby."

She had meant it as a rebuke. It was not received as such.

"Blood relations," Amelia mused softly, "that explains quite a lot about Lady Dalby, doesn't it?"

"They must certainly be *very* savage and very, very wicked if they are related to Lady Dalby," Eleanor said with a very wicked gleam. Things were not going at *all* the way Louisa had hoped. When did they ever? "But why are you certain that these men are her blood relations?" Eleanor continued. "Perhaps they are only related through marriage."

"And perhaps not even by that," Amelia said somewhat wickedly.

Louisa shrugged over Eleanor's shocked gasp. "As different as they are, they bore a resemblance to each other, particularly between Markham and John the Younger."

"John the Younger?" Eleanor said. "That sounds rather dynastic. But stop all this empty chittering and *tell* us about them and about your visit and about Lady Dalby. *Everything*, Louisa. Try to push Dutton out of your thoughts for just a moment or two, if you would."

Actually, now that she looked at it, she hadn't thought about Dutton for a full five minutes. Remembering all those unimportant men littering Lady Dalby's white salon had quite distracted her.

And so she told them, but while she was rendering a rather rushed version of the events and men that had occasioned Sophia's salon, she avoided mentioning that, by express instruction from Lady Dalby, her attendance at the supper at Hyde House that evening was nearly compulsory. Amelia, for all her pleasant manner and easy temper, was altogether ruthless when it came to invitations to a ducal residence. Amelia would not at all enjoy knowing that anyone else at Hyde House that evening had important plans of her own to put into play. At least, Sophia had implied there were important plans in play.

At this beginning stage of events, Louisa supposed she could allow Sophia some measure of trust. Some small, unimportant measure, certainly. After all, she had planned to attend the dinner before even discussing her pearls with Lady Dalby. There was nothing Sophia could do to disrupt her evening at Hyde House.

She was almost certain of that.

"And of course, she didn't explain to me how she happened to have a brother who is an American Indian," Louisa said, hopefully in conclusion.

"How utterly fascinating," Eleanor said. "Do you suppose I could meet one or two, perhaps if I loitered about in front of Dalby House? I suppose it's not entirely unlikely that I should stumble over one or more of them."

"You shall do no such vile thing!" Louisa said.

It was quite more than enough that *she* was called upon to loiter about Dalby House in her quest to attain Lord Dutton and her pearls. She did not suppose she should be called upon to sacrifice her sister to any such low endeavor. Though, to judge by Eleanor's face, it would not be much of a sacrifice.

"Will they be attending the Hyde House affair tonight?" Amelia asked. "I should so like to study them up close."

Louisa squirmed just the slightest bit and said, "I do not think they care to be studied." Though it was just possible that George might not mind in the least. "Anyway, I am not at all privy to the so-cial schedule of Lady Dalby's rather unusual relatives."

"Pity," Eleanor said with an altogether unattractive snap. "I do think that had I been dallying about all afternoon in Lady Dalby's salon I should have come away with rather more information than you have done, Louisa."

"I rather doubt it," Louisa said stiffly, running a finger delicately over her right eyebrow.

"In fact, had I any money at all," Eleanor continued as if Louisa had not spoken, a habit of hers that Louisa found inexpressibly irri-tating, "I should wager that you spent your entire afternoon with all those compelling and interesting men talking only of Lord Dutton."

At which point Amelia giggled in an entirely unattractive and uncalled-for manner.

"If you had any money to wager you would lose it all," Louisa said, rubbing her eyebrow with slightly more than delicate vigor. "I did not speak of Lord Dutton at all. I spoke exclusively about my pearls and how to reacquire them."

"I suppose it is a coincidence that Lord Dutton is in possession of your pearls, which would mean that they are his pearls now," Eleanor said.

"Only until I get them back," Louisa said.

"And did Lady Dalby suggest a means to get them back?" Amelia said.

"Not . . . precisely," Louisa said, rising to her feet. Really, this conversation was becoming entirely too uncomfortable and she did not see any reason why she should endure another moment of it.

"Then you truly have wasted your time, Louisa," Eleanor said. "When I think of how you must have squandered all those wonderful men—"

"There was nothing at all wonderful about them," Louisa snapped.

"That," Eleanor said, "is something I should like to determine for myself."

"So would I," Amelia said as Louisa crossed the library.

Which, it must be noted, was the entire trouble with women in general: they were prone to lose sight of the proper man whenever an improper man made an appearance. Louisa prided herself, not unjustly, with having risen above that tendency entirely.

"But, admit it, Louisa, Lady Dalby is advising you," Amelia said softly, her eyes betraying a most avid and unattractive gleam.

"On how to attain Lord Dutton," Eleanor finished, gleaming in perfect partnership with Amelia. It was most unattractive.

"Don't be absurd," Louisa stated. "She is merely advising me on how to reacquire my pearls."

"She should be quite good at that," Eleanor said with a sage nod of her red head.

"Lord Dutton has your pearls, Louisa," Amelia said with a very smug smile.

"That is hardly the point," Louisa said grimly. Really, it was bad enough that she rather suspected the ton found her pursuit of Lord Dutton profoundly amusing; she didn't have to tolerate ridicule in her own library, did she? "Melverley might have the right to sell my pearls for a horse, but he hardly has the need. I want my pearls. They are mine and I'm going to get them back."

"Even if you have to tackle Dutton in a dark alley to get them, is that it?" Amelia said, grinning.

"I rather think she would prefer it that way," Eleanor said.

Eleanor was, without qualification, the most annoying person Louisa had ever had occasion to know, and that included her acquaintance with Sophia Dalby, which, it must be admitted, was saying quite a lot.

Five

THE Marquis of Dutton sat in a quiet corner of White's and considered his options. Caroline, a bit of a tempest, though a beautiful one, was cheerfully saddled with Ashdon. Why she would choose such a dour fellow, one so given to the sulks, was beyond what little comprehension he reserved for other men. He much preferred giving his thoughts, and his attention, to women.

Which put him in mind of the devious and desirable Anne Warren. She had turned into one surprise after another. Though surprises could be delightful, too many at once and they became tedious. He decided that Anne Warren had become tedious.

Why he kept thinking of her, he couldn't quite say.

He certainly didn't need a wife, at least not yet, and Anne was hardly wife material, being the daughter of a less than successful courtesan as she was. Though she had been taken in and was currently under the protection of the Countess of Dalby, an ex-courtesan of rather legendary status, Anne had none of the flair of a practiced ladybird. At least that he could see. But could a girl fall that far from the proverbial tree? Didn't blood, after all, tell?

It was just such speculation, hovering dangerously near obession, that had driven him to kiss Anne in the privacy of Sophia's famous white salon. It had not gone as planned, not that he had worked up much of a plan. But, with most women, a heated look, a torrid kiss, and they were muddled nicely, primed for whatever he decided to do next either to them or with them. It hadn't turned out that way with Anne. He'd spoken seductively, kissed her decidedly, and waited for her to melt in his arms.

She hadn't melted. In fact, she became engaged to Lord Staverton, an old, wrinkled, cross-eyed gentleman of, by all accounts, a rather nice estate, the very next day.

It was difficult to remain pleasantly neutral about things of that sort, and in that particular order.

He had kissed her. He had expressed a most earnest interest in her. She had chosen another man.

Yes, very difficult to remain neutral.

Of course, he hadn't offered marriage, nothing of the sort, but she couldn't have expected that. Who was she? The by-blow of an indiscreet whore and the widow of a minor naval hero of a minor battle. No, marriage was not on the menu. And neither, obviously, was Anne.

Pity.

"Lady Louisa's pearls must be burning a hole in your pocket."

Dutton sighed and looked up from his slouch. Lord Henry Blakesley stood looking down at him, his blond good looks lit by a sardonic light that emanated entirely from the man himself. Most unwelcome.

"Hardly," Dutton answered in an only slightly drunken drawl.

One half of Blakesley's mouth tilted in a thin smile. "No? The word is that after Caro rejected your pearls in favor of Ashdon, you presented them to Mrs. Warren. And that she rejected you as well. Hard night, when a man can't give away a fortune in jewelry."

"In both cases, the women were previously engaged. Literally."

"That's what they're saying," Blakesley agreed, pulling up a chair and signaling for a drink.

Most, most unwelcome.

"You had your pearls rejected as well," Dutton pointed out.

Blakesley shrugged. "Entirely expected. Caro was all for Ashdon from the moment she set eyes on him. My pearls were merely a prod."

Dutton sat up straighter and pushed his hair back with both hands. "You let yourself be played as a mere pawn in a mating ritual?"

"I hardly care as long as I am not the one being mated. Besides, it was amusing, and I am hardly a pawn if I am fully aware of the game and my place in it."

The next sentence remained unspoken, but only because there was no need to say it out loud. Dutton had been played, masterfully, by Caroline. Which meant, obviously, that he had been played by Sophia. He was not the first man in London to have come to that conclusion, but that didn't make it any more palatable.

Sophia had used him to snare a husband for her daughter. How she had done so he could not imagine. It had been his idea to help Ashdon acquire a strand of pearls, just as it had been his idea to keep them for his own purposes, the first of which was to present them to Caroline at the Hyde House assemblie. How Sophia had arranged for him to do what he himself had decided to do on his own volition he could not fathom. But the results spoke for themselves. He had the pearls. He had given them to Caro, or had tried to. He had also tried to give them to Anne Warren. She had also refused his pearls.

Women were an odd lot, taken as a whole. The best that could be said for them was that they were fairly tolerable and occasionally amusing when taken one by one.

"The pearls were my idea," Dutton said stiffly.

"Of course they were," Blakesley said sarcastically. Blakesley had the rather annoying habit of speaking sarcastically whenever possible. "You decided to sell a horse to buy a pearl necklace off of Melverley and then you decided that you simply had to give them to Caroline Trevelyan. You came up with this plan when? Last month? Last week? Or on the very day that Caroline was in need of a pearl necklace?"

Blakesley then had the cheek to laugh.

Dutton was not so foxed that he couldn't find his own reason to laugh. Blakesley was not without his own Achilles' heel.

"And you presented your own strand of pearls to Caro in full view of Louisa Kirkland. A happy coincidence, I suppose?"

Blakesley lost both his laugh and his smile. Perfect. It was flagrantly obvious to anyone who cared to look that Blakesley followed Louisa Kirkland around like a very well-trained dog.

"As I remember, the yellow drawing room was filled with people," Blakesley said, "which was entirely the point."

"Oh? You arranged with Sophia to ruin her daughter in front of as many people as possible? How very odd."

"I don't claim to understand how the woman's mind works, but I can hardly argue with her success. Caro is married to Ashdon. That was the point of the whole event, wasn't it?"

"Was it?" Dutton said.

"Obviously," Blakesley said crisply, taking a full swallow of his drink. Dutton took a full swallow of *his* drink, matching him. Blakesley, watching Dutton over the rim of his glass, kept swallowing his whisky until the glass was empty, as did Dutton. A ridiculous competition, but satisfying nonetheless.

For some inexplicable reason, his thoughts turned to Anne Warren again. They'd played at something and he'd lost. It was a state of affairs that was completely unacceptable.

"What is it you want, Blakesley?" Dutton asked in irritation, Anne Warren's rather pretty face floating through his thoughts in a sea of whisky.

"Nothing in particular," Blakesley said, pouring them both another glass. "I was just curious as to what you were going to do now. Now that you have sold a rather stellar horse and have a pretty string of pearls instead."

"I could sell the pearls, though they are rather fine and I suppose someday, when I simply must marry, I could give them to my wife. They make a pretty gift," Dutton said. "Or, as I said, I could sell them," he added, studying Blakesley's sardonic face over his glass.

Dutton took a swallow. Blakesley took a swallow. They stopped and stared at each other over their respective rims.

"You could," Blakesley said.

"It would enrage Louisa, I expect, as I imagine she considered them hers and would likely do anything to get them back, don't you think?"

"I have no idea."

A ridiculous assertion, and they both knew it. Henry Blakesley had made it something of a point to know every thought in Louisa Kirkland's pretty red head, not that it had done him any good so far as all her thoughts were aimed precisely at Dutton's head. Of all the positive attributes that could be laid at Louisa Kirkland's well-shod feet, an aptitude for subtlety was not one of them.

"You could buy them from me," Dutton suggested, leaning back in his deeply upholstered chair.

"Dutton," Blakesley drawled, "how can you have forgotten? I am currently in possession of a very respectable pearl necklace, a gift for my future wife at some future date. I hardly need two pearl necklaces and I most assuredly don't need a wife who *requires* two pearl necklaces."

"Don't you?" Dutton said before he took a very long swallow of his drink. Blakesley merely watched him, his own drink untouched. He'd won the drinking competition, though he wasn't certain at the moment what the prize was supposed to have been. He supposed it didn't matter; winning was quite enough of a victory, the only victory, in fact, that he cared about.

Which brought to mind Anne Warren again. He'd lost in his game of seduction with her and that was flatly intolerable.

Blakesley stretching out his long legs in the chair opposite him and crossing them at the ankle in the most relaxed pose imaginable swung Dutton's only slightly drunken thoughts back to Louisa, the pearls, and women in general. Here he'd tussled with Anne Warren, a woman who, no matter who she was currently engaged to, was obviously enamored of *him*, no matter that she'd not reacted to his kiss and no matter that she'd shown him nothing but cold civility since that kiss, not to mention that she'd hurriedly gotten herself engaged to a peer of the realm.

Ridiculous. The whole thing was flatly ridiculous. He *knew* she wanted him and, what's more, she knew he knew.

Women really were, as a whole, incapable of subtlety and most assuredly not of secrecy. Why, they wore their desires and intentions all over their rather lovely faces. Not only was it endearing, it was supremely useful.

Take Louisa Kirkland . . . well, actually, he could take Louisa Kirkland any time he wanted. Poor Blakesley could hardly say the same. Dutton snickered and closed his eyes with a smile.

"Something amusing?" Blakesley asked blandly.

Though slightly more foxed than was usual for him at this time of day, Dutton was not so completely in his cups that he would descend to the vulgarity of plain speaking about the very obvious Lady Louisa.

"I was just wondering to what lengths Louisa Kirkland would travel to regain the Melverley pearls. She's not a woman given to half measures, is she?"

Blakesley, his face rather too carefully composed, said nothing.

"It should make for a very interesting Season for me, not that I don't always find something to amuse me while I'm in Town," Dutton said.

"Don't you mean to say 'someone'?" Blakesley said.

"Actually, yes," Dutton said with a soft smile, studying Blakesley over the rim of his now empty glass. "Someone."

Blakesley leaned forward and filled it with whisky. An obvious attempt to get him completely foxed, but, really, it was fine whisky. Dutton took a healthy swallow. Blakesley took a sip of his drink and watched him like a hawk watches a snake. Though he was hardly a snake and didn't enjoy being compared to one, even if he had made the comparison himself.

Dutton put his drink down on a side table. He might have been more deeply into his cups than he had at first thought.

He decided in the next instant that he didn't care.

"Now, if you were to find yourself in possession of the Melverley pearls, then *you* might have an interesting Season in Town," Dutton said. .

"I don't need help in finding amusement," Blakesley said softly, his icy blue eyes glittering in the candlelight.

Dutton didn't care what Blakesley's eyes did in the candlelight. He picked up his glass and took another swallow of whisky, his plan forming in somewhat liquid fashion as he swallowed. Liquid plans were the best, the brightest, the most dependable. Odd how he'd never made that connection before.

"But perhaps a bit of help with Lady Louisa wouldn't be amiss," Dutton said. His voice sounded sloppy to his own ears. He didn't care about that, either.

Blakesley smiled. Or it looked remarkably like a smile if he closed one eye.

He closed one eye.

"You're foxed," Blakesley said.

"Not enough to matter."

"Open both eyes and say that," Blakesley said pleasantly.

Dutton opened both eyes and leaned his head back against the chair cushion.

"I propose a bargain," Dutton said.

"Didn't you propose a similar bargain with Ashdon?"

"Which is the reason I now find myself in possession of the Melverley pearls."

"And not in possession of a woman to wear them," Blakesley said.

"Ridiculous. I can have any woman I want, with or without pearls."

"Can you?"

"I can have Louisa Kirkland, certainly."

Blakesley leaned forward, his eyes increasingly icy. "You bandy her name about with unpleasant regularity and familiarity, Dutton. I should stop that, were I you."

"Which is the entire point, Blakesley," Dutton said, ignoring icy eyes and the outraged tone. He had a plan and he was going to make it work, no matter Blakesley's stubbornness over tedious and inconsequential details. "Take the pearls. Give her a reason to chase you about town. Do with . . . them what you will, when you will."

It was perfectly clear to both of them that he had been about to say "do with *her* what you will." He was not as foxed as all that.

"You sound as though you were selling her to me."

"Ridiculous," Dutton said. "I am merely selling her interest in me, for a time, to you."

"The pearls being the price of her interest."

"It should do for a start. I'm certain you have the means and the ability to build on that foundation."

Actually, he possessed no such certainty. Louisa Kirkland had been following him about for the better part of two years, calf-eyed, and Henry Blakesley had been trailing after Louisa for almost as long, letting her lead them both where she willed. Ridiculous. One took matters in hand with a woman, and whatever other juicy bit he could put his hands to as well, as the situation and the woman dictated. How Blakesley had come to his majority without knowing this most basic of truths about women was a complete mystery.

Though Blakesley's lack of the most basic knowledge of women might have something to do with his mother, Molly, Duchess of Hyde, being originally from Boston, Massachusetts. The colonials of the previous generation were universally known for being more than passing peculiar. It was not entirely impossible that Lord Henry Blakesley had picked up his odd habits from her.

Blakesley considered him in icy silence, his eyes narrowed. Dutton took the man's need to ponder his offer as an occasion to get a few more swallows down his throat. It was *damn* fine whisky.

"And what would you get out of this bargain?" Blakesley asked softly.

"A bit of peace, for one," Dutton drawled. "And a bit of amusement."

"With the elusive Mrs. Warren, perhaps?" Blakesley asked.

"Perhaps," Dutton said stiffly, or as stiffly as five glasses of whisky would allow.

Blakesley smiled sarcastically. "If a pearl necklace could not rope her, I daresay nothing can."

"The price is not always pearls."

"True," Blakesley said, tipping his chair back on its rear legs. "Perhaps you ought to try diamonds."

"Not every woman has a jewel price, Blakesley," Dutton grumbled.

"Don't they? I would never have guessed you for a romantic, Dutton."

"Though I would have guessed you for a—"

Dutton stopped abruptly. Foxed, yes, but not blind. If he continued on with his thought, that Blakesley was a fool for the rather too obvious Louisa Kirkland, he would likely end up on some dueling field at some ungodly hour. He hated ungodly hours as a general rule.

"A cynic," he finished.

Blakesley merely smiled in response, cynically.

"I can live without your pearls, Dutton."

"I believe the question is whether or not Louisa can live without the pearls. Or whether she will have a rousing good time in trying to win them back."

At that remark, rather coarse, he must admit, but also exceedingly true, Blakesley's frigid blue eyes burned.

Dutton didn't care what happened with Blakesley's eyes. At that particular moment, he only cared about causing a bit of mischief. He could not have said why. It was a particular pleasure of his that he lived his life without looking for reasons behind every action, which anyone would be forced to admit was bound to be a very tedious way to live.

Dutton, as a rule, avoided tedium. Which, oddly, made him think once again of Anne Warren.

Six

IT was quite obvious to the most casual observer, which Lord Henry Blakesley was most decidedly not, that the Marquis of Dutton was completely foxed. It was also equally obvious that Dutton had struck upon a plan that might, in the most generous interpretation, have merit.

Louisa had seen the Melverley pearls, *her* pearls, presented to another woman in the most flagrant manner imaginable by the man she had an unhealthy and illogical fascination for, namely, Lord Dutton. Louisa would want her pearls back. That Dutton was in possession of them would be an irresistible combination for her; and it should be noted that Louisa, for all her charms, was not possessed of a nature that practiced resistance regarding much of anything.

In all, he could not quite name what it was that he found so fascinating about her. But he was. Fascinated. Aroused. Enamored. All the stupid and ridiculous nonsense inked by poets and fools, and yet he could find no escape from the nonsense.

He was in love with her. Stupidly. Ridiculously. Illogically.

Stupidly, because she did not love him. She was pointlessly

enamored of Dutton, and there was simply no putting her off the scent. He had tried. That was the ridiculous bit. He had seen her at his parents' assemblie two years previous and the look she had given him from across the capacious yellow drawing room had snared him. Bold and daring, amused and superior, her ginger hair a torch of fire in that crowded room, her skin so flawlessly white it glowed . . . well, that was the long of it. The short of it was that he had made it a point to be in her company whenever possible ever since.

And she had illogically chosen to be in the company of Dutton whenever possible ever since.

He supposed his memory must recite that Louisa met Lord Dutton on the very same evening and that, henceforth, all her daring and amused looks had been saved for Dutton from that day to this.

And the poets wrote of love. They deserved to starve.

It had been no coincidence that he had given Caroline a pearl necklace worth an earl's estate in the same yellow drawing room just days ago, and that he had done it when he was certain Louisa would have a stellar view of the event. Some ironies were just too perfect to avoid and it did have the added tang of bearing the most delicate flavor of revenge.

It should have been Louisa. She should have been the woman wearing his pearls. She should also have been wearing his name.

But she wanted Dutton and Dutton did not want her.

But she did want her pearls.

Yes, Dutton's idea had definite merit. The only sticking point was what Dutton would want in return. Dutton, for all that he was a gentleman of the first mark, was a bit of a scoundrel. It was, in fact, what made him such interesting company. It was also most likely what Louisa found so fascinating. Girls of good family inevitably found men of questionable character fascinating. Call it a law of nature. He had, especially since meeting Louisa.

"If I take the Melverley pearls off your hands," Blakesley said, "what will you require as recompense?"

Dutton opened one eye to peer at him from his slouch. "What can you offer?"

He was being made to bargain for the attentions of Lady Louisa Kirkland; he was well aware of that. It was distasteful in the extreme. It was also, unfortunately, apparently necessary.

"I'm not aware of having anything you would find interesting," Blakesley said.

Dutton's eye closed again and he sighed. "I'm afraid that's likely true. I believe the crux of the entire situation is that *I* have the one thing *you* find interesting."

"*Have* is rather too strong a word," Blakesley said softly.

"Is it?" Dutton drawled, his eyes still closed. "If you had the pearls we could put the matter to the test." Dutton opened his eyes and pierced him with his famous blue gaze. "Take the pearls. Find out where her interest lies. If she continues to seek my company, then the question is settled."

"And if she pursues me? Then she is simply interested in her pearls? Hardly flattering to me."

"My dear Blakesley," Dutton said, "if this is about finding ways to flatter you, then we must come up with another game entirely. I thought this was about Louisa."

Which was, of course, true. Most everything in his life for the past two years had been about Louisa. It was tiring and monotonous and, unfortunately, that was not enough to put him off. Not even close.

"She must know that I have them," Blakeley said, "or else the point is missed."

"I'll take care of that," Dutton said, straightening in his seat.

"It must be handled delicately," Blakesley said, by which he meant that Louisa must be handled delicately. He would not have her know of this bargaining as it would hardly flatter her. "And I must know what you expect from me in return. I am not going into this blindly, Dutton."

Unless love made one blind, which it quite possibly did to judge by his behavior for the past two years and, most especially, in the past two minutes.

He must be mad. The proof being he did not care if he were mad.

"Let us wager on it," Dutton said. "A simple wager for simple stakes."

It was well known to every man in London that there was no such animal as a simple wager for simple stakes. And, being mad, he still didn't care. He would get this thing settled with Louisa Kirkland one way or the other before he truly did go mad.

"Which are?" Blakesley asked.

Dutton shrugged and looked idly across the dark interior of White's. "I will let it be known sometime before dawn that you have the Melverley pearls. If, shall we say, in three days time, she does not, oh, what is a polite way of expressing what I'm trying to say?"

"There is no polite way of saying it," Blakesley said with a cold smirk.

"Then I am saved," Dutton said. "I shall just have to say it, shan't I?" Dutton returned Blakesley's smile with equal chill. "If she does not leave off my scent and chase after yours, then we shall know that pearls are not what interest the lady. Fair?"

"Not quite," Blakesley said. "How will this interest be measured? Neither one of us is hardly objective."

Dutton looked at him squarely, his nostrils flaring in indignation. Dutton's nostrils could rot in hell for all he cared. He was not going to lose this bet, and Louisa, on some fragile claim made by a man who was foxed more often than not.

"You think I would cheat?" Dutton said. "Dissemble?"

"I think you would flatter yourself," Blakesley said, crossing his legs casually and leaning back in his chair. "You are not a stranger to self-flattery, after all. I'm merely protecting my interests. You can hardly find fault with that."

"Then let's name an objective third party to arbitrate," Dutton said with a half smile.

Bloody hell, the last thing Blakesley wanted was someone else knowing what was afoot. Louisa would rage if she ever found out.

The obvious point being that she must never find out.

"Fine," Blakesley said coolly, looking around the room and finding the perfect choice almost instantly. "Shall we ask the Duke of Calbourne?"

"Let's," Dutton said, rising to his feet, rather sloppily, he might add.

The Duke of Calbourne was easily the tallest and most rugged duke in England. That he was a widower with a young son, that his estate was formidable, that he was a good-tempered though private man, meant that he was, for all the aforementioned reasons, privy to the most delightful gossip in the ton. Or that was the speculation. Calbourne was not a man given to gossip, which naturally made him a magnet for all the most scandalous *on dits* imaginable.

Calbourne, sitting alone in a heavily tufted leather chair and sipping a brandy, did not rise upon their approach. Blakesley was just as glad; no need to call attention upon this impromptu meeting. The sooner, and the quieter, the whole mess was done with, the better. Calbourne sat listening to Dutton's drunken explanation of the situation with Louisa and the Melverley pearls with an expression of amusement he did not bother to hide.

Blast. This is where love led a man. He might as well put a gun in his mouth and be done with it.

"It certainly is turning into a season for pearls," Calbourne said with a grin. "If this continues for even another week, the price of pearls, never reasonable, will triple."

"No one is buying pearls," Blakesley said. "We're simply making use of the existing supply."

"Aren't you, though," Calbourne said, leaning back in his chair. "What's my part in this?"

"A simple case of observation," Dutton said. "Simply observe where Lady Louisa's interest falls."

"I'm almost afraid to mention this," Calbourne said with a lazy smile, "but suppose her attention wanders to another quarter entirely. Where does that leave you?"

"Small chance of that," Dutton said.

"Confident, isn't he?" Calbourne said to Blakesley.

"Hence, the wager," Blakesley said tightly.

"So, no chance of her interest wandering," Calbourne said, his eyes lit with suppressed laughter. "That makes it so much simpler. For me. Very well. I'll arbitrate your little wager. Is there a time limit to this or must I make Louisa Kirkland a particular point of interest for the entire Season?"

There was something in the way Calbourne said that, some hint of good-natured malice that set Blakesley's teeth on edge. It was not beyond possible that Calbourne, in looking so diligently in Louisa's direction, might not develop a *tendre* for her himself.

"Three days," Blakesley said.

"Only three?" Calbourne sighed. "That hardly seems enough time to judge the true direction of a woman's heart. Besides, the lady is quite lovely. I shouldn't mind spending more time in her presence. Or do you think that the truth will be so evident that a mere day will reveal it? Perhaps we should keep this wager to an hour. An hour, in the right circumstances, should reveal all."

At that precise moment, Blakesley couldn't decide how Calbourne had ever been deemed good-natured. The man was positively malicious.

"Two weeks," Dutton said, blinking heavily.

"Three days," Blakesley softly snarled.

He was not going to have Calbourne, a most eligible duke, nosing about Louisa for a full fortnight, yet he knew Louisa well enough to know what would happen after just an hour. No, the thing had to be managed precisely.

And by that he meant Louisa.

Dutton raised one dark brow. "Confident, aren't you?"

"Just impatient," Blakesley answered.

"One would hardly know it," Dutton drawled in insult.

What happened next was quite beyond the norm for White's. Although, as it had happened just two days previous, to the same gentleman, it might be said that the norms of gentlemanly behavior at White's were in flux. How else to explain the fact that Lord Henry Blakesley slammed his fist into Lord Dutton's belly much as Lord Ashdon had so recently done? That the Duke of Calbourne was on hand to disrupt the melee in both instances put the entire event rather above coincidence, though no one would ever imply that the Duke of Calbourne had been an instigator in the dual attacks.

At least, not to his face.

Seven

IT had been a very simple matter to invite the Marquis of Penrith to Dalby House early that evening. Invitations issued by Sophia, Dowager Countess of Dalby, to eligible men who had achieved their majority were rarely declined and certainly never ignored.

"Darling Penrith, it was so good of you to come and see me on such short notice, especially as I am quite certain that you have made lovely plans for yourself this evening," Sophia said as she lounged against the back of the white salon's milk blue damask sofa.

Penrith lounged equally comfortably on an identical sofa. The sofas were paired and positioned to face each other in front of the marble fireplace. It was a most convivial and attractive situation, as well as being most productive. She had arranged not a few alliances on these sofas.

"One always makes plans, Lady Dalby," he replied in that particularly languid way he had of speaking, "but whether or not they bear fruit is a matter of destiny."

"Destiny?" she said on a soft laugh. "Are we to be as serious as all that? And at this early hour? I would think that destiny must wait until the early hours after midnight, at the very earliest."

"Must it?" Penrith smiled, a singularly seductive action on his rather leonine features. "And what destiny awaits me then?"

"You assume I have a passing acquaintance with destiny."

"Lady Dalby, it is well known that you and destiny are on extremely intimate terms."

"Lord Penrith, that is quite the nicest compliment I have had all day," she said, smiling. "May I compliment you in return?" At his nod, she continued. "You are quite the most talked of man in London, my lord, and in entirely complimentary terms. 'Tis a rare thing, to be talked of and complimented in the same breath."

"And yet," he said with the smallest of frowns, "perhaps not entirely complimentary to a man of my station and my years?"

"My Lord Penrith, I am not at all certain what you mean."

"My Lady Dalby, I am quite as equally certain that you do. No man likes to be thought entirely well of. It puts one in mind of a long in the tooth gelding. Particularly galling as I have not been gelded."

Sophia laughed in delight. What a lovely son Julia Aubourn had managed for herself. Penrith was truly a jewel in her crown.

"Don't be ridiculous, Lord Penrith. You and I both know that a young woman of innocent aspect is quite nervous about standing behind even a small table with you at her side. Your reputation for scandalous behavior is quite up to the mark."

"If you say so, though I am not at all certain that there can be a mark of excellence regarding scandalous behavior."

"Oh, I assure you, there can be," Sophia said with a smile that was quite intentionally wicked.

"I do believe you, Lady Dalby, I most assuredly do," he said, grinning back at her.

He was devilishly handsome, was Lord Penrith, and so charmingly decadent. It was a complete pleasure to spend time with such an engaging and agreeable young man.

"Of course, I suppose that even the lily looks better for a little gilding," she said, eyeing Penrith.

"First a gelding and now a lily," Penrith said dryly. "My reputation *is* in a state. What do you advise, Lady Dalby? I am yours to instruct."

Such a delightful man, truly, to put himself into her care so swiftly and so completely. There really was nothing more a man could offer, other than a nice cash settlement, and she certainly was not in the market for that, not from *this* man and not at this stage of her well-ordered life.

"Darling, I promise you," she said, grinning at him fully, "you shall enjoy every minute of this."

DUTTON had drunk just enough so that he didn't feel a thing; not his toes and not his fingertips and not the outer edge of his tongue. Granted, walking and talking were a bit of a challenge, but he enjoyed a challenge from time to time. Now was clearly one of those times.

He and Blakesley had spent the best part of the day drinking excellent whisky at White's with the very amused Duke of Calbourne. What Calbourne had to be so amused about he couldn't imagine, not without serious effort, and he was not in any frame of mind to attempt any sort of serious effort. And that included acquiring the delectable Mrs. Warren.

Mrs. Warren, though he had yet to quite puzzle it out, was going to fall into his very deserving hands. When he was finished with her, and he had no doubt at all that he would finish with her if he could figure out how to start with her, he might even take a second look at Louisa Kirkland. Redheads were looking altogether on the up for him and he suspected rather strongly that Mrs. Anne Warren, with her bright ginger hair, was entirely responsible.

"Was there a reason why we had to *walk* to your house?" Blakesley snarled at his side.

Really, was the fact that he was being made to walk any reason to snarl? Blakesley was about to get a fortune in pearls *and* Lady Louisa, if he could manage to keep his wits about him.

Yes, well, no wonder he snarled so often. Blakesley had the most abominable knack with women, or at least with women as defined by Louisa Kirkland.

"I wanted to clear my head," Dutton replied cordially. If he wasn't the most cordial, affable fellow of his acquaintance, then he didn't know a thing about affability.

"Optimist," Blakesley said softly, snarling only slightly. Small wonder Louisa wouldn't look twice at Blakesley when perpetual snarling was the reward.

Dutton would have made some remarkably witty rejoinder but his tongue wouldn't cooperate at that precise moment. They turned onto Jermyn Street and were at his front door not a minute later. High time, too. He had to dress for the Hyde House dinner, where he happened to know that Louisa was expected and where he would tell her that her pearls now resided in Blakesley's rather pedestrian pocket. One would have thought that the son of a duke, albeit the fourth son, would have made it a point to have a more presentable coat. The only thing Blakesley seemed to make a point of was Louisa Kirkland, and just look where that had got him.

Women were far better behaved when one didn't focus too much pointed attention upon them, which was exactly what he had done with Louisa Kirkland and just look where that had got *him*.

Really, even with the Melverley pearls, he didn't hold out a speck of hope for Blakesley's chances with Louisa. Which was precisely why he'd proposed the arrangement in the first place. It was going to be amusing in the extreme to watch Louisa darting after him even with the inducement of the Melverley pearls in Blakesley's inept grasp. And it was not beyond possible that Mrs. Warren would find the continued sight of Lady Louisa stalking him through London's salons a proper prod to give in to his considerable charms.

All in all, it was a plan that, even if it failed, could not fail to amuse.

Eight

WILLIAM Blakesley, Marquis of Iveston, heir to the Duke of Hyde, was twenty-nine this very day, very eligible, and avoided absolutely everyone who knew he was very eligible and Hyde's heir, family excluded, naturally. That the family was only very rarely gathered together at any one time, in any one location, had prompted his mother, Molly, many years ago now, to arrange for this annual celebratory dinner for Iveston.

Henry Blakesley had never missed it. None of his four brothers had. His father, who positively loathed evenings of this sort, wouldn't have thought of missing it.

The fact that Louisa was certain to be at the annual Hyde House celebration of Iveston's birth had no bearing at all upon Henry Blakesley's intense anticipation for a dinner that was scheduled to begin in a mere hour. He was not yet dressed for dinner. Molly was not pleased.

"Blakes," she said sharply. *Blakes* was her pet name for him; it was with some relief that no one outside of the family had taken up the habit of it. "You are not dressed. I daresay that Louisa Kirkland is responsible."

"I beg your pardon?" he said stiffly. Never once had his mother so much as mentioned Louisa's name to him, a fact he had taken particular pleasure in.

"As well you should," she said, setting aside her embroidery. "I have been made to understand only recently the depth and scope of your involvement with Lady Louisa. Certainly she is a questionable person at best. Her behavior regarding Lord Dutton has become the stuff of legend. Your own involvement with her has become nothing short of ridiculous."

"I am not in the habit of being thought ridiculous," he said through tight lips.

"I'm afraid that's quite untrue, Blakes. You are particularly in the habit of being ridiculous where she is concerned."

"She is a friend, nothing more."

Molly rose to her full, petite height and fixed him with a hard gaze. "You are still being ridiculous, Blakes. Men and women are never *friends and nothing more.* It is a blatant fact that a man's sole purpose in befriending a woman is to seduce her, which, by your continued friendship, I will assume you have not yet done."

Blakesley could only stare, openmouthed, at his mother. Being from Boston, she had the habit of being plainspoken, but never *this* plainspoken.

"And of course, you should not," Molly continued, walking out of the room and motioning for him to follow her, which he did. "No matter her father's slipshod upbringing of her, no matter her loose behavior with Lord Dutton, you should make it a point never to seduce girls of good family. And her family name is quite good, even if Lord Melverley leaves much to be desired."

"Lady Louisa should not be judged based on her father's handling of her," Blakesley said.

"Perhaps not, but she *will* be judged on her handling of herself. And she is handling herself very ill. The Town does nothing but talk of her, and by extension, of you. This cannot and will not be tolerated, Blakes. You do understand," she said, not asking for his understanding at all. "Think of Iveston's reputation if you cannot be compelled to think of your own."

"Set yourself at ease, madam," he said, the words barely escaping his compressed teeth.

Molly appraised him silently and with obvious skepticism. "Then you'll amend your appalling behavior in regards to Lady Louisa?"

"Completely," he said with a frosty bow of his head. "You are content?"

"Most tolerably," Molly replied sharply, snapping her fan closed in concert with her words. "It is most disagreeable to have one's son disparaged so publicly. Having him disparaged privately is quite disagreeable enough, which is what I must put up with regarding Iveston and his peculiar ideas about socializing with his peers. Ridiculous, to avoid people the way he does. One would think he was damaged in some horrid fashion when, of course, he is the most handsome and pleasing sort of man. But that is beside the immediate point," Molly said. Blakesley sighed and lowered his gaze to the floor in exasperation. "You simply must hold yourself in check, Blakes. This fool-for-love drivel is perfectly fine when played out upon the stage, but it has no value at all in life. One must keep to the priorities."

"Which are?" he said blandly. Really, this was becoming more than intolerable. He was being dressed down like a runny-nosed child of three.

"To make a proper marriage, obviously," his mother said on what was perilously close to a snort. "It is equally obvious that Louisa Kirkland is clearly the wrong sort. Any woman who runs around Town after a man the way she has done will hardly be a fit mother to any man's heirs, for how could he fail to wonder if the heirs are, in fact, his?"

Blakesley held himself very erect and said, "These are matters which, perhaps, a man may judge better than a woman."

"I doubt that very much," Molly said, "but I would prefer to leave the subject of Louisa Kirkland altogether."

"As would I," he said, a gross understatement.

And with that, he left the music room, the heels of his shoes clicking like gunshot against the marble floors.

"ALL you had to do was find one," Iveston said from deep within the tufts of his red leather chair, facing the fireplace as it cast its golden glow. "One woman willing to take you on. And you find Louisa Kirkland."

"If you say anything about love making its mark on my wayward soul, I'll blacken your eye nicely. Explain that to your guests," Blakesley said, tucked within his own chair, brown leather and only slightly smaller, facing the same golden glow.

"Please do," Iveston said. "It would provide the most delightful excuse not to attend tonight's torture. And it would have the added benefit of setting Mother on your tail and getting her off of mine."

Blakesley grunted and hunched his shoulders up around his ears. "I've reached my limit of endurance on that, thank you very much. You shall remain unmarked, at least by me. I happen to know that there are at least ten young and very eligible women coming tonight for the particular purpose of presenting themselves for your approval. Which is to say, they are here to look you over."

Iveston huddled deeper, the red leather squeaking. "As always. I came to the conclusion, and a rather dismal conclusion it is, that Mother has not arranged for these dinners to celebrate my birth in a show of familial devotion and affection, but merely as a sort of marriage fair for the unmarried ladies of the ton. It goes without saying that I am perceived to be the prize."

"How long did it take you figure all that out, Ives?" Blakesley asked sarcastically.

Iveston leaned back in his chair, his long legs stretched out in amiable misery, his blond eyelashes gleaming in the firelight as they shaded his blue eyes. "I believe it was as I was chewing a particularly tough piece of mutton and looked up to find no fewer than eight of the finest women of Mother's acquaintance staring at me in undue fascination and obvious speculation. I was seventeen at the time, so, twelve years ago now? Twelve years of being the fox to a field of matronly hounds, and my own mother the master of the hunt. If I didn't feel that your situation with Louisa Kirkland was so damnably ridiculous and endlessly amusing, I would say I was the most ill-favored man in town. But, of course, you have that distinction."

Blakesley didn't have any trouble at all in knocking his older brother out of his chair and sitting on his chest. He did, however, have trouble keeping him there. In an entirely friendly tussle of not less than three glancing blows, the two men were able to make their point, which was that neither one of them was willing to tolerate being thought of as either ridiculous or amusing. At least not for much longer than they had already done.

When they had straightened their cuffs and smoothed their cravats, they once again resumed their lazy posture by the fire, the creak of leather as they shifted their weight a comfortable accompaniment to their grunts of affable irritation and general surliness.

William Blakesley, better known as Iveston, and Henry Blakesley, lovingly called Blakes by his intimate family, were, in all manner and in every detail, brothers. They were both blond, both jaded to an appropriate and entirely useful degree, and both possessed of a more than sarcastic wit. In that Iveston was heir to a rather substantial dukedom, it was more than enough to convince the most particular observer that Iveston's wit was a shining example of a stellar mind. In Blakesley's case, the determination was more often that he was a scoundrel of the first water.

Such was the price one paid in Society for being the fourth son of a duke.

"I'll say this for Louisa," Iveston mumbled, rubbing his left ear, "she may not hound after you, but she's also never hounded me. She follows her heart and not her purse."

Blakesley grunted and slunk lower in his seat. "Which makes the whole pearl situation more questionable."

Iveston cocked his head at Blakesley and said softly, "Have you considered casting your net in another pond?"

"Have *you* thought of just being done with the entire chase and marrying the biggest dowry in the neatest package?"

"Actually, yes," Iveston said, sighing. "What else is there to it, anyway? A dowry, an heir, one's duty to one's family done in the most ridiculously easy fashion; one can hardly call it hard duty."

Blakesley snorted his amusement. Iveston kicked him on the foot.

"But you want love," Blakesley said, still chuckling. "You want to *suffer*, as I suffer."

"Don't be absurd," Iveston said stiffly. "I will manage it much more efficiently than you have done. Love does not demand suffering. It is a noble emotion, properly managed."

"Yes," Blakesley said dryly, "you've made your point. I should like to see you manage a woman as easily as you speak of managing love. The two do, unfortunately, travel in tandem and women are not so easily managed as all that."

"I should say that depends upon the man," Iveston said loftily.

Which naturally required that Blakesley launch himself in a physical attack upon his eldest brother.

LADY Dalby looked like a woman who expected to be physically assaulted at any moment, and as if she would have enjoyed the experience immensely. It was a look that was peculiar to her and was, by any man's reasoning, the cause for her spectacular success both in Society and out. She looked a woman simply begging to be seduced, though it was a well-known fact that Sophia Dalby never begged for anything.

The Duke of Calbourne was as fascinated by her as any man, which is to say, he would have seduced her if she gave any indication at all that she was interested in his particular brand of seduction. Unfortunately, she had not.

Yet.

Calbourne, having conspired only slightly with Sophia this very week to get his closest friend married to Sophia's daughter, was under the rather slippery impression that he and Sophia Dalby were friends of a particular sort. Namely, friends who would one day become lovers.

Naturally, things being what they were and events proceeding as he hoped they would, Calbourne had lost no time in telling Sophia about the wager regarding the Melverley pearls as they pertained to Louisa Kirkland, Dutton, and Blakesley.

He rather suspected that someone was going to find himself married very soon. As long as he was not the lucky man, Calbourne was very much intrigued to watch Sophia manage things from a safe position. And he was in a very safe position regarding all things matrimonial. Calbourne did not seek a wife as he already had produced one perfectly satisfactory heir in the person of his seven-year-old son, Alston.

If there was one particular skill at which Sophia Dalby particularly excelled it was in arranging wives for men who were not in the market for wives. Just look at what she had done in a matter of days to his friend Lord Ashdon, who had been minding his own business on a Monday and found himself married by Thursday.

Chilling bit of management, that.

"You are intrigued by this news, are you not?" Calbourne asked, crossing his legs as he sat on one of the yellow salon's more sturdy chairs.

"Very," Sophia said softly. "It is endlessly fascinating to watch what a man will do to possess the particular woman of his choosing. Do you not find it so?"

Given that he had told her of the pearl wager in the hopes of finding his way into her bed, Calbourne felt the sting of indictment in her remark rather more than he would have liked.

Being a duke, he was not at all accustomed to feeling stings of any sort whatsoever, and he fully intended for it to stay that way. Even if he and Sophia did find themselves tangled in the sheets at some future date, he was not going to allow himself to be manipulated or insulted or any of the other things Sophia Dalby was wont to do to a man. There was no time like the present for making that singular point very clear to her.

"But, of course, it is always the woman who does the choosing in these matters," Sophia said pleasantly, her dark eyes shining with mirth, cutting him off before he had even begun to lay down the ground rules of their association. "Not that most men realize that, naturally. But *you* realize that, don't you, your grace? It is your most enchanting trait, as you must surely know."

He knew nothing of the sort. He was somewhat dimly aware that Sophia had redrawn the lines of their relationship, insulted him, and complimented him all in the same breath. He found himself in the odd position of wanting to agree with her. And that is exactly what he did.

She was a most confounding woman. Perhaps he did not want to be tangled in her sheets after all.

"I daresay I understand completely what Lord Dutton hopes to achieve by such a tawdry wager," Sophia continued languidly. "He is a most forward man, is he not? As for what Lord Henry Blakesley was thinking, well," she said with a slow smile, "his actions must speak for themselves. I don't know what his mother will do when she finds out. Surely Dutton will bear the brunt of responsibility for instigating this shameful wager, putting a gently reared girl's reputation in peril. Of course, one could argue that Blakesley went along with it quickly enough," Sophia said silkily, "but from your description, it sounds as if he did it to protect the girl from harm, as you have in alerting me to the sordid details of this ill-conceived wager. Lady Louisa must be protected from callous and opportunistic men, must she not? And who better to see to her protection than a duke of the realm? And, of course, a woman well-versed in protecting herself from opportunistic men." Sophia laid a white hand against her equally white bosom; Calbourne followed the movement of her hand to her breast and found his gaze ensnared. Sophia smiled over a sigh. "Would that be a correct interpretation, your grace?"

He was being managed. He could feel it.

He didn't like it one bit.

"Completely accurate, Lady Dalby," Calbourne said softly. One did not get to be a duke by being manhandled by anyone, even a very seductive and entirely too clever woman of extremely uncertain, but entirely intriguing, reputation. "I thought you would be able to . . ." He paused.

In point of fact, he wasn't entirely certain what he had thought. He hadn't thought much beyond the desire to tell Sophia the current state of affairs regarding the Melverley pearls. She *did* have something of a sliding interest in them as they had been almost directly responsible for Caroline's quick marriage. Yes, pearls had been the weapon in that particular courtship. It was not too far afield to think they might again play a part in the London Season of 1802.

"You flatter me," Sophia said, rescuing him from any attempt he would have been forced to make to finish a thought that was unspeakable. He appreciated her effort. Dukes did not go about mismanaging simple things like pearl necklaces and private wagers. "An activity I find especially appealing." Sophia smiled slowly and touched the dangling pearl earring in her left ear with the tip of her finger. It was the most devilishly erotic gesture he had seen in a week and he could not possibly have explained why.

Calbourne recrossed his legs. Firmly.

Sophia smiled more fully, lowered her gaze, and relinquished the pearl.

"Certainly, your chivalry is to be admired," she said. "One hardly expects less of a duke, yet expectations so rarely bear the desired fruit. How thrilling it is to find that the fourth Duke of Calbourne exceeds both desire and expectation."

For a man with a most comfortable chair, he was becoming damned uncomfortable.

He was entirely certain that Sophia was responsible; as a duke, he was not in the habit of being uncomfortable.

"But I must confess to you," Sophia said, tilting her head in thought, "I simply cannot allow things to stand as they are."

"I beg your pardon?"

" 'Tis simple enough, your grace. I simply cannot allow this wager to continue for, what was it? Three days?"

"That it is what they eventually agreed upon, and not without some disturbance, I assure you. I suggested a fortnight, Dutton proposed a week, and Blakesley insisted upon three days."

"Yes, he would," Sophia said with a half smile, her gaze lowered momentarily to her lap. "And I do agree with him in theory. In practice, I must do all I can to deliver Lady Louisa from such coils as you rash men have set upon her."

"I have done no such thing," Calbourne said.

"Of course you have not, not *actually*, yet you are deeply involved as a sort of referee, are you not?"

"It is a simple wager, Lady Dalby. You have made more than a few of your own, have you not?"

"Caught out, I see," she said, grinning fully at him. "I have been guilty of such, and I daresay will be again, but dear Louisa must be saved, must she not? Only think of my reputation if I do nothing to save her."

"Save her, Lady Dalby? There is no force at work here. The

lady will do what she will do. She either will pursue her pearls or she will not. What's to be done?"

"What indeed?" Sophia said on a soft and feminine sigh of docile acquiescence. "You put it most clearly and most brilliantly. Of course, everything you say is true. The lady will, most reliably, do what she will do. Indeed, I have no doubt at all that Louisa Kirkland will do what any woman would do in similar circumstances."

Strangely, it sounded slightly sinister when coming from her mouth, but then that was true of much of what Sophia Dalby said. She had an odd way of phrasing things at times.

"She will be at Hyde House tonight?" he asked.

"I believe she was invited."

"Dutton and Lord Henry will be there as well. It should prove an entertaining evening."

"I'm quite certain it will be," Sophia said softly. "I wonder, your grace, if you would be interested in a private wager?"

"Of what sort?"

"Of the friendliest sort," she said, shifting her weight so that suddenly her legs were outlined beneath the fragile silk of her gown. Calbourne shifted his own weight in direct response. "I will wager that Louisa Kirkland will make her choice and make it obviously by tomorrow night. Three days . . . nothing of this sort requires as much as three days to decide."

"So quickly?" Calbourne said slowly, studying Sophia and learning nothing. "You think she will make her choice known by tomorrow night?"

"I think, your grace, that she will make her choice known by tonight, if one measures the length of a night by the dawn," Sophia said with a polite smile. "I'd rather err on the side of prudence, hence, until tomorrow night. Is it a wager?"

"Done," he said.

"And shall we not include the naming of the gentleman?"

Sophia said. "I think you men do, at times, put too much upon what is your fluxuating allure and not nearly enough upon the unchanging beauty of a pearl necklace. But I am likely biased in my views, you will allow."

He certainly did allow. A woman who had made a tidy sum on collecting pearls and other items from men would see things differently, but Louisa Kirkland was no courtesan.

"You think she will prefer Blakesley over Dutton?" he asked.

"Blakesley has the pearls, does he not?" she answered with a smile.

There was plainly no possibility of Louisa choosing any other but Dutton; she had been doing so for two years and there was no reason for her to change her mind now. It was equally obvious that her pearls had been sold out from under her by her father, and none knew that fact better than Louisa. There was simply no getting them back now, no matter who had them.

"Done again. I will back Dutton. The terms?"

"Not money," Sophia said, rising to her feet, "for that would be too crass by any measure. Shall we say an intimate dinner at Calbourne House?"

"I would be delighted," he said, bowing crisply. "If Lord Dutton attracts the lady's interest in the next twenty-four hours, I shall host an intimate dinner at Calbourne House." Where Sophia would be the only guest. A very tidy win, if Louisa behaved as she had reliably done for the past two years.

"And if she chooses elsewhere by tomorrow night, then I shall host an intimate dinner, you being the guest of honor. This gives every appearance of being a wager I cannot lose," Sophia said, smiling up into his eyes. He returned her smile fully. There were many things said of Sophia Dalby, but the one on which all men agreed was that she was charming company.

"Nor can I, Lady Dalby. I shall see you at Hyde House tonight?"

"Your grace, you will most assuredly see me at Hyde House to-night. It promises to be a most entertaining evening, does it not?"

Again, Calbourne could not help but note that there was a slightly sinister, one might even say provocatively malevolent edge to Sophia's question. Most odd.

Nine

LOUISA, looking as enticing as she possibly could in a gown of fine white muslin with a daringly low décolleté, because Lord Dutton required daring décolletés, entered Hyde House for the second time in a single week. It was something of a coup. While hundreds were invited to a Hyde House assemblie, only a few were ever invited to celebrate the Marquis of Iveston's birth. This was her first time doing so. Amelia, dressed in ivory silk with a cunning design of indigo beading at the hem, was at her side, looking equally triumphant.

Tonight, they would achieve their purposes. Louisa would finally ensnare Lord Dutton, and Amelia would entice whatever eligible duke happened to be about.

It promised to be a spectacular evening.

"I suppose I shall have to comment on the wallpaper again," Mary said, none too quietly.

Louisa turned to stare over Aunt Mary's head and shared a subtle grimace with Amelia. Mary, Lady Jordan, was very short.

"You wouldn't think a room needed to be redone every year," Mary continued, fussing with her jade necklace, green being a color that did not suit her at all, "but when one has money, I suppose one must find ways to flaunt it."

"I'm sure I shall," Amelia said pleasantly, arranging her simple necklace of sapphires and diamonds, a combination that suited her to perfection. Naturally. One did not go about attracting the attention of a duke by wearing the wrong color.

"I'm sure I don't know what money is for if not to enjoy spending it," Louisa said. "I expect to have a spectacular time in spending Dutton's money."

"Darling," Sophia Dalby said, entering their company and their conversation without a moment's hesitation. Louisa had not even seen her coming. "While a woman must be aware of a man's financial strength, she must always refrain from discussing such things in public. While a man likes to have a fat purse, he does not want his value to be based upon it."

"I would never . . . I meant no such thing!" Louisa said in a hushed voice, looking behind her to see if Dutton or anyone who knew Dutton had heard her. Which was ridiculous, really, for who didn't know Dutton?

"But, naturally, it must be considered," Sophia said, continuing on as if Louisa had not spoken. "Isn't that so, Lady Jordan?"

Aunt Mary, who had married for love and married badly, simply scowled at Lady Dalby in response.

Mary and Sophia, from what Louisa could gather, had entered London at almost the same instant. That Sophia had clearly worked things to her very prominent advantage was not something Mary enjoyed contemplating. It should not have been so. Logically, it should not have been so.

After two years in pursuing Lord Dutton, Louisa was increasingly aware that logic had very little to do with anything, particularly men and marriage.

"But, of course," Sophia continued, moving their small group by slow degrees through the crowd at the door of the blue reception room, "it is quite clear to me that Lady Amelia understands this very well. How wise of you, darling, to have grasped the situation so fully while so young."

Amelia smiled blandly in response and arranged her necklace more precisely than was necessary. To be hunting for a duke was one thing; to be *known* to be hunting for a duke was quite another thing altogether. It did not put a girl in the most advantageous light, even if it were a very practical goal. Most men did not require practicality in a wife when extravagant prettiness would suffice.

Men were rather stupid.

Louisa and Amelia had both found it annoying on more than one occasion that men were so necessary to a girl's future. That is, Louisa had found it annoying until she had set her eyes and, in rapid succession, her heart upon Lord Dutton. Even if she did think Dutton rather stupid for not falling to her charms after two years, she did not find him annoying. Dutton was too splendid to be annoying.

Sophia had gracefully led them to the Duke and Duchess of Hyde and their eldest son, Iveston, who stood near the far wall of the blue reception room to receive their guests. It really was a wonder how she had done it. The room, though as fully large as a duke's London residence ought to have been, was still quite full of people in the finest of gowns and the whitest of linen cravats.

Sophia smiled and dipped her greeting to the duke and duchess, leaning forward to whisper something in the duchess's ear. Molly, the duchess, turned a bright eye upon first Louisa and then Amelia. It was not friendly in the least. One might even have said her look was one of blatant suspicion and imminent dislike.

This is what came of trusting a courtesan.

Mary, Louisa, and Amelia made their dips in their turn, Amelia's curtsey was especially pretty as she faced the Marquis. Iveston was truly a man to remark upon, even if he had not been in line for a dukedom. He was flagrantly tall and fashionably lean and quite blatantly blond. Not the blond of his younger brother, Lord Henry Blakesley, whose hair was more golden, more the shade of his mother's, now that Louisa thought about it.

In fact, there was quite of bit of Henry in Molly's cynical and rather too observant eyes. A point that was made even more forcefully as Henry appeared next to his brother Iveston and smiled at her in a manner that could only be described as sarcastic.

Smiling in sarcasm ought to have been impossible, yet Blakesley managed it quite handily.

He looked splendid in evening dress with his sardonic smile and his calculating gaze directed exclusively at her.

She liked that about Lord Henry Blakesley. She liked that when she was in his company, no matter the expression he wore upon his face, he gave her his full attention. He could wear whatever expression he liked, for she was quite certain she had seen them all: indifference, annoyance, impatience, amusement, boredom, pleasure, interest. Whatever his expression, whatever his mood, he always was fully attentive. It was so unlike Dutton, so completely the reverse of Dutton, that she had become increasingly aware and increasingly appreciative of the difference. It was, after all and for whatever reason, nice to be *noticed.*

"Lord Iveston, how remarkably splendid you look this evening," Sophia said with a snap of her ivory fan. "In the flush of full manhood and health. How the ladies must swoon."

She was flirting with him. But then, Sophia had the nasty habit of flirting with every man. Louisa had even observed her flirting with Dutton on more than one occasion, and, worse, Dutton had appeared to enjoy it very much.

"If they swoon, Lady Dalby," Iveston answered softly, "I fear it is in response to my father's title, not my flushed manhood."

To which Sophia laughed in a manner not entirely modest and to which the Marquis of Iveston blushed. Louisa was entirely sympathetic. Obvious blushing was the curse of those with skin like snow and blushing was the curse of those who parleyed with Sophia Dalby.

"And modest besides," Sophia said with a grin. "You will never convince me that ladies do not swoon when faced with your . . . flushed manhood? What a charming turn of phrase you possess, Lord Iveston. You remind me of your brother Lord Henry. He, too, has a way with words."

"I did not intend that the way—" Iveston began in a voice barely above a whisper.

"Don't apologize, Iveston," Henry Blakesley interrupted. "You'd have to know Lady Dalby better to know that you have charmed her completely. Is that not so, Lady Dalby?"

"Completely so, Lord Henry," Sophia said, tilting her head charmingly. It was beyond irritating that every movement of Sophia Dalby's was done charmingly. Louisa could only conclude that Sophia had spent hours and hours in front of a mirror, practicing charm.

That she had spent hours in front of her mirror practicing looks with Lord Dutton in mind, and with such scant results, made the whole thing intolerable.

"I do so enjoy Molly's sons, each and every one," Sophia said. "I trust that all the Blakesleys will be in attendance this evening?"

"We have yet to find the excuse that our Mother will accept," Lord Henry Blakesley said. "And we have tried."

"I can't think why you should want to avoid a dinner given in your brother's honor," Louisa said. "At worst, it seems quite unfamilial."

"And at best?" Blakesley said, giving her that hard look that was so common to him and which she found not at all intimidating.

"At best, it seems quite wise," Sophia answered in her place.

Louisa did not appreciate it in the least. She could converse quite well with Blakesley, no matter how surly he became, and she did not appreciate any doubts that she could. Of all men, she could at least claim to manage Lord Henry Blakesley.

"Wise?" Amelia said, angling her body so that her bosom was shown to her best advantage. Iveston was not looking at Amelia's bosom, at least not obviously so. Pity. "I cannot think why it should be thought wise."

"Can you not?" Sophia said, looking at Amelia and her well-displayed bosom, her dark eyes twinkling. "Five sons in the house and not a one of them married. They must long to run like rabbits through the tall grass and there is so little cover to be had over a dining table."

"There are always the candlesticks," Lord Henry said, smiling crookedly, one side of his mouth lifting almost reluctantly.

He *liked* sparring with Sophia Dalby, that much was patently obvious. Just let him try and deny it. When she next got him alone, she would give him the opportunity to do just that.

"Are we to pretend that men do not enjoy being wanted?" Aunt Mary said, her words not slurring in the least and her manner most abrupt. Louisa and Amelia exchanged a look over her head again. Mary was a much more pleasant chaperone, that is to say, much more manageable, when she was in her cups.

"Let us not pretend anything," Sophia said, "for, at best, it is a waste of time."

"And at worst?" Blakesley said.

"A waste of opportunity," Sophia promptly rejoined, smiling seductively at him.

It was too much. Louisa was not about to stand about all evening and watch Sophia Dalby seduce every man who spoke to her.

"Then men do enjoy being wanted?" Louisa said, forcing Blakesley's attention back to her. He swung his gaze far too casually to her, letting it linger for far too long on Sophia Dalby. A full two seconds at the very least.

"Wanted, yes, naturally," Sophia said, "but not . . ." She let her voice trail off softly and looked expectantly at Lord Iveston, blatantly attempting to draw him out. Louisa let her gaze slide to Amelia. Amelia did not look at all pleased.

"Pursued," Iveston said in a soft undertone, smiling at Sophia, his rather cunningly shaped blond head dipped in her direction.

It was appalling and revolting and beyond tolerating. Sophia clearly did not know how to talk to a man without attempting to seduce him. Worse yet, she apparently always succeeded.

Louisa would have given her right eye, or a pearl necklace, to be able to accomplish half as much in twice the amount of time.

"Ridiculous," Aunt Mary said. "Men love pursuit above all else."

"As the hunter, not the hunted," Louisa said. "Is that the truth of it, Lord Henry?"

"I would have no way of knowing, Lady Louisa," he said on a soft snarl of sarcasm.

He was angry about something, though she could not imagine what it could possibly be. She was the one who had the right to be annoyed. And she was. Very annoyed. The whole world seemed, in that instant, to be arrayed against her happiness. Actually, the whole world had seemed arrayed against her happiness from the moment she left the nursery, but she was not going to whine about it. She had more fortitude than that.

"Now that's ridiculous," Sophia said, looking with open amusement at Blakesley. In point of fact, Sophia was looking him up and down like some carnal treat she couldn't wait to pounce upon. Disgraceful, decadent woman. Louisa resisted the impulse to shake her head in disapproval. "You cannot claim that women don't find you irresistible."

"I am not entirely certain that this conversation is in good taste," Iveston said, glancing at Amelia. Amelia's throat turned a delicate shade of pink, which served to highlight her exceptionally creamy bosom.

"Have we offended you, my lord?" Sophia said.

"In point of fact, I cannot remember ever having been so entertained at my own party," he said. "Lady Dalby, you are splendid. I must seek out your company more often than I have done in the past. I can see why Blakes finds you so fascinating."

Upon which Amelia's throat, breast, and cheek turned chalky white and Louisa's breath caught in her throat. This was not *at all* what she had hoped to achieve by seeking out Sophia Dalby.

"Blakes?" Sophia said with a charming lilt.

"A family name," Blakesley gritted out, "and not one that should have left the family."

"It's charming beyond description," Sophia said. "I'm surprised not to have heard it mentioned before now. Certainly, Lady Louisa has kept your secret, Lord Henry, for as close as you are, she has not breathed a word of it."

Blakesley looked at her with the most odd expression. She didn't like it in the least.

"I'm as surprised as you are, Lady Dalby," Louisa said. "I am certainly not privy to the intimacies of Hyde House."

The look in Blakesley's normally cynical blue eyes was chilling and, uncomfortably, far from cynical. Why, he looked almost wounded.

"How very odd," Sophia said, watching Blakesley. "I had gathered that you two were rather more intimate than that. Oh, well," she said, shrugging, "I was clearly mistaken. I hope you will not be offended if I call you Blakes on occasion, Lord Henry."

"As long as the occasion is intimate, Lady Dalby, then I shall not mind in the least."

"I see we are of a mind, Lord Henry. How enjoyable," Sophia said, looking at Blakesley from beneath her dark lashes. As Louisa's lashes were golden red, she could not duplicate the affect. Not that she wanted to, not with *Blakes.*

She most certainly did not.

"While it may be common for you to speak of intimacy with a gentleman," Mary said stiffly, "it is not common for the ladies in my charge. I must ask you to excuse us."

Mary was entirely too sober to be made proper use of. The situation must be rectified before the first course or this dinner would be a useless exercise. That was made perfectly clear in the next instant, when Mary was trying to herd Amelia and Louisa away from the heir apparent to the Duke of Hyde, of all the idiocy, and upon the imminent arrival of the Duke of Calbourne to their small gathering.

Amelia looked ready to faint from delight. Louisa would have looked equally overcome if only Dutton could be found in the ever-growing crowd in the blue reception room of Hyde House. She could not find him. If he were present, he was not making any attempt to join their party.

Dutton truly did, most regularly, behave in the most annoying fashion.

The Duke of Calbourne made his bow and joined their small and entirely too intimate party. Amelia was not to be moved from that moment onward. *Here* was a duke who was in the full force of his title; albeit that he already had an heir, which meant that any children of Amelia's would *not* have that distinction; still, as matters went, it was a small one. Amelia had been very clear on one point since the approximate age of four and that point was that she was going to be a duchess.

Louisa had no doubt about it whatsoever. Amelia was just the sort of woman who *should* become a duchess; she would appreciate it so very much and, consequently, would appreciate the man who had made it possible. A happier marriage could not be conceived. Or so Amelia had maintained since the approximate age of six.

Amelia was a very forward-thinking girl. Louisa had always admired that about her. Truly, they each had such good plans in place for their individual futures, it was an amazing bit of rotten luck that they both still found themselves unmarried. Unthinkable, really, when they had come out two years previous. Things had not gone at all to plan from that day to this.

Of course, things had not started out at all as they should have done, before Aunt Mary had been, with only the barest nudge, encouraged into becoming a two-bottle-a-day drinker. Things had gotten immeasurably more convenient since then.

One simply could not manage a man at all with a sober and vigilant chaperone at one's side. It was difficult enough when the chaperone was deeply in her cups. Of course, dukes being what they were and Dutton being what he was, this whole marriage business had become more complicated than either one of them had imagined at the start. Even a drunken chaperone hadn't helped much.

Oh, very well. Hadn't helped a bit.

Neither she nor Amelia were any closer to their marriage goals than they had been, which explained her rather desperate bid for help from Sophia Dalby. Not that it was doing her any good whatsoever and may, in fact, have been the worst step she could have taken, which was exactly what Amelia had been telling her all afternoon. Eleanor had simply laughed and kept laughing, barely bothering to hide her face in a book.

With the way things were going now, Sophia flirting rather too obviously with both Iveston and Blakesley, Louisa was more than a little inclined to regret the whole thing. The whole thing as it pertained to Sophia. Certainly she was not at all inclined to regret her devotion to Lord Dutton. Never that.

Louisa's attention was drawn by the sight of Amelia's graceful curtsey to the Duke of Calbourne, her bosom and creamy cleavage very nicely displayed for a gentleman to consider for the second time that evening. The Duke of Calbourne hardly graced any of them with a glance, never mind noticing Amelia's bosom; his attention was all for Sophia.

It was beyond annoying.

"Lady Dalby," Calbourne began, his eyes nearly devouring the woman. Naturally. "What a pleasure to see you here tonight. Lord Iveston, may I wish you well on your natal day? You're looking well."

"Yes, we were just commenting on that," Sophia said with a gently tipped smile. "You don't think Lord Iveston looks flushed, your grace?"

Upon which, Lord Iveston flushed pink and ducked his blond head.

"The pink of health," Calbourne responded, looking not at Iveston but at Blakesley. Most odd. Blakesley looked as he always did; bored and superior and more muscular than pure elegance would allow.

But Blakesley's sharp blue eyes never left her face. Most gratifying. Blakesley could be counted upon for that singular brand of attention; she was not at all surprised to find that she had grown quite comfortable with it. Perhaps even dependent upon it?

It did not bear scrutiny as it did not pertain even remotely to her goal of ensnaring Lord Dutton. All thought and, indeed, all action had been sublimated to that goal these two years past. Blakesley understood that perhaps better than anyone.

He was a most understanding, most accommodating man.

"Exactly so, your grace," Sophia said smoothly.

"Lord Iveston looks exactly as a man should," Amelia ventured.

Which effectively stopped the conversation. All female eyes looked at Amelia and all male eyes looked to the floor.

"Charming," Sophia said softly, eyeing Amelia, whose bosom was flushing in quite the same shade as Lord Iveston's cheek.

"Quite charming," Blakesley said. "Quite the nicest compliment a man could receive upon his natal day, Lady Amelia. You are to be congratulated."

"I'm not at all certain I can allow any congratulations that are not directed at me to be tolerated," Lord Iveston said, his very attractive mouth turning up in a wry smile. "My stellar good looks were being remarked upon. I must insist that all future conversation remain exactly there."

Lord Iveston, from a first impression of being rather awkward socially, was proving himself quite the sarcastic equal of his brother Blakes. How entirely pleasant for Amelia. Iveston would make such an agreeable husband for her.

Louisa looked at Blakesley and found him almost smiling at Iveston, who was definitely smiling at Amelia. How completely lovely.

"Very sensible," Calbourne said. "I must agree, of course. All conversation should and must remain solely on Lord Iveston. Don't you agree, Lady Dalby?"

An odd turn, it must be admitted. Why should Calbourne care and why should he care that Lady Dalby agree?

"I promise you, your grace," Sophia said, "nothing has or will be said which will offend your dictates. All conversation will remain precisely where you and Lord Iveston have placed it. I trust you are satisfied?"

"As I am ever satisfied in your presence, Lady Dalby," Calbourne said, bowing briefly, a smile hovering at the corners of his mouth.

Most definitely odd, even for a duke.

"I sense a wager has been agreed upon," Blakesley said. It was so like Blakesley to say precisely whatever was on his mind. It was one of the qualities which made him such a dangerous companion. Louisa, against all caution, had always liked that about him. "Shall I guess what it concerns or would that be in poor taste?"

"I am quite certain that you could not behave in poor taste if you tried, Lord Henry," Sophia said.

"Shall we put it to the test?" Blakesley rejoined. "And, better still, shall we wager upon it?"

Whatever had got into Blakesley? This was not the sort of conversation that helped anyone achieve anything. The entire tone of the evening was going most determinedly sour. What the devil was the man thinking to speak out so, without any consideration for how it would affect her? It was quite his worst quality.

"I am always interested in an interesting wager," Sophia said blandly, her glance touching lightly upon Louisa's face. As was to be expected, Louisa blushed.

She was quite disgusted with herself. At that moment, in fact in most of the moments of her life, she would have given anything to be dark-haired, with the quiet complexion that came with it. Her own complexion, as lovely as it was, fairly shouted to every passerby whatever her current emotional state happened to be. It was mortifying in the extreme.

"I can't think why I should allow these innocent girls to be privy to such debauched talk."

Aunt Mary couldn't seem to understand that her role was to stand quietly and allow Amelia and Louisa to be about the business of finding husbands. Where *was* the liquor in this room?

"Don't say you never wager, Aunt Mary," Louisa said, trying to keep the cutting edge of irritation out of her voice, somewhat unsuccessfully, "for I have heard you wager with Lady Edgeware over the size of Lord Ferndon's—"

"Louisa!" Aunt Mary snapped loudly.

"Next foal," Louisa finished innocently.

At which point, Blakesley laughed, an abrupt bark of laughter that he quickly swallowed. Louisa smiled in spite of her irritation with Aunt Mary; she did so enjoy making Blakesley laugh.

"A wager among ladies can never be coarse," Aunt Mary said primly. Being prim was not a natural fit for Mary, Lady Jordan, even when she was sober. It hardly became her. "This, however, this intersex wagering is common in the extreme."

"*Intersex.* Is that a word?" Lord Iveston mused.

"Oh, I am quite certain it must be," Sophia said pleasantly.

"Perhaps that should be our wager? On whether *intersex* is a proper word or not?" Blakesley said in exaggerated innocence. Innocence, rather like Aunt Mary's primness, was not a natural fit for Lord Henry Blakesley.

"But who would judge the propriety of *intersex*?" the Duke of Calbourne asked, a wicked twinkle in his eyes.

"Common," Mary muttered under her breath. She was not so bold as to openly rebuke a duke.

"I should think that would be obvious," Sophia said.

"It is," Mary said sharply. "*Extremely* obvious."

Sophia merely laughed at Aunt Mary's sharp tone and sharp look. In that instant of pure, inexpressible annoyance, even Mary's nose looked sharp. It was an unfortunate truth that Louisa had seen that particular sharp look many times before. It was not an accident that her father had expressly picked Aunt Mary to be her chaperone. Her father knew *exactly* how sharp Mary could become. What her father didn't know was that Mary became beautifully fuzzy when filled with liquor of any variety and that it was ridiculously simple to encourage Mary to become fuzzy. If only she would start on that process immediately. Louisa couldn't help looking around the room for a bottle.

"It's in the next room," Blakesley said under his breath.

He'd moved within their circle of conversation so that he was just to her right, which had moved Lord Iveston to almost touching distance to Amelia. Blakesley was always doing nice things like that, no matter what came out of his mouth. She rather suspected that he was less cynical than he led one to believe.

"Then let's move to the next room," Louisa murmured back. "I shan't have a hope of making any meaningful . . . conversations . . . if she continues on this way."

She had been on the verge of stating that she hoped to make progress with Dutton, but she had never been so forward in her marriage goals with Blakesley before tonight and she saw no reason to begin now. She was well aware that Henry Blakesley was no

one's fool, but being blatant about her own objectives seemed unnecessarily blunt, not to mention counterproductive. It would be
just like Blakesley to throw a hammer into her plans just for the
sport of it. He did find the most odd things amusing.

"About that," Blakesley said softly, his breath moving the hair
next to her ear. She did so hope he wasn't disarranging her hair.
She had been quite particular with her maid about arranging that
particular curl to fall just so. It wouldn't do at all if she appeared too
rumpled, and of course it would be even worse if she appeared
too prim. Dutton positively loathed *prim*, though Mrs. Anne Warren was rather more prim than rumpled and Dutton seemed to not
loathe her in the least.

Louisa was becoming more certain by the hour that she loathed
Anne Warren.

"Yes?" she said, but the conversation of the group swept them
back in, cutting off his chance to answer her.

"Darling," Sophia said to Mary, at which point Mary's nose
looked something like a dagger in its sharpness, "you misunder-
stand me. Obviously, none of us can arbitrate the officiousness of
the word. We shall have to depend upon a completely neutral party.
One who has nothing to gain from the outcome."

"Which is to be?" Calbourne asked.

"Oh, something simple and very pleasant, I should think,"
Sophia said. "Shall you not decide it, Lord Iveston? It is your day
and your celebration. You should have the honor of setting the
terms."

"I don't wish to offend Lady Jordan," Iveston said.

Upon which Amelia looked at Aunt Mary with only barely concealed panic in her blue eyes. If Mary was foolish enough to insult
their host and heir apparent to one of the finest dukedoms in England, then Louisa was not in any doubt at all that Amelia
would . . . Amelia would . . . well, she was positive Amelia would
get some delicious revenge upon their aunt, maintaining her own

reputation in the bargain. Amelia was quite clever that way, almost devious, but in the most appealing way imaginable.

Mary seemed, thankfully, to understand the situation suffi-ciently to respond in the appropriate way.

"You could not possibly offend me, my lord. Please, have your fun and enjoy your day."

"You are certain?" Lord Iveston asked.

He clearly had a devious streak of his own for he was obviously rubbing it in. Louisa could not possibly have been more delighted. Aunt Mary *should* be punished for trying to throw a hammer into the works.

"Determinedly," Mary answered. It was not the most pleasant answer, but it served. That was all she cared about.

That, and Dutton. Where *was* he?

"Then I propose that once we have an answer to our *intersex* question," Iveston said. He clearly enjoyed saying *intersex* whenever possible. He might be, even though a future duke, a bit crass for Amelia. Not that Amelia would ever let something as minor as that get in the way of her plans. Louisa was not at all certain that Amelia thought it was possible for a duke to even be crass. "I propose," he said again, "that the wager be whomever is *for intersex* should have to drink a glass of port wine without taking a breath and whomever is *against intersex* should abstain for the entire evening."

"Perfectly logical," Calbourne said, almost completely drown-ing out Aunt Mary's grumbling that dukes and almost dukes of to-day's age were completely common and most decidedly immoral. No one bothered about anything Aunt Mary said, drunk or sober, which was such a relief, truly. No wonder she had got herself noth-ing but a beggarly baron for a husband.

"Now, who shall be our arbiter?" Iveston said, looking to Sophia, though why Sophia should decide Louisa had no idea. Men simply deferred to her at every opportunity. It was almost ludi-crous.

Louisa would love to know how she did it.

"I think my escort for this evening should do nicely," Sophia said, tracing a finger over the edge of her bodice. Louisa had the unpleasant experience of watching the gaze of every man within a range of six feet go straight to Sophia's completely obvious bid for attention. "I do not see him at the moment," she said, turning this way and that, giving glimpses of what had to be admitted was a flawless cleavage. Poor Amelia let her breath out in defeat. "Oh, there he is."

It was to be expected that everyone in their small group would turn at her prompting to see to whom she was referring. Louisa naturally assumed that Sophia would have attended this event with her son, the Earl of Dalby, but Louisa did not see Dalby, no matter how she looked.

Instead, across the crowded room, she saw Anne Warren, her red hair gleaming in the candlelight and her skin looking entirely too perfect. But what was worse was that Mrs. Warren, that upstart, was talking pleasantly and entirely too comfortably with Mr. George Grey, that *Indian*.

Mr. Grey turned as if summoned, which was impossible as he was at least forty feet away and there were at least thirty people between them, not a one of them Lord Dutton, it should be mentioned. Yet turn he did at Sophia's remark and his gaze, dark and dangerous, went directly to Louisa.

Louisa felt her stomach tumble in almost the same instant that she heard Blakesley mouth an oath under his breath.

Blast. It always was the wrong man, wasn't it?

Ten

MR. George Grey, his evening attire completely appropriate, if one discounted his disheveled hair and glittering earring, which Louisa was not at all disposed to discount, placed the tips of his fingers against Mrs. Warren's white-gloved elbow and led her across the room to their party.

Of course he did. George Grey, even in evening dress and still looking far too savage for any sensible woman's peace of mind, seemed determined to irritate her by his rather too close attention to her; the fact that he was cordial and in the company of Anne Warren only proved the point that he was a troublesome man and Louisa should and would avoid him at all costs.

That she would also be avoiding Anne Warren was an added bonus.

The wager be damned, she was not going to stay and pretend to make polite conversation with a woman who had the temerity to draw Lord Dutton's attention. She might be able to tolerate an Indian of slovenly manners—he was, after all, related to the Dalby earldom—but that was quite as far as Louisa was willing to bend. She did not and would not make the same allowances for Anne

Warren. It was a particularly popular *on dit*, and therefore as close as possible to being a well-known fact, that Mrs. Warren's mother had been firmly in the demimonde, and on the dreary and unprofitable side of it, at that.

Louisa was not supposed to know such things, but again, having Lord Melverley for a father made all sorts of knowledge almost impossible to avoid. It was equally true that Louisa Kirkland had no intention or inclination to avoid any knowledge of any kind. A point which may, upon reflection, have indicated a very strong resemblance to her father.

It was with the greatest relief and profound satisfaction that Louisa prided herself on rarely wasting time in reflection of any sort. Action was the order of this day and any day.

She was just turning to Lord Iveston to make her excuses when Lord Dutton entered the room. She knew he entered the room, the exact instant in which he entered, by the complete and immediate absence of blood in her veins and breath in her lungs. Dutton did that to a girl.

She absolutely adored that about him.

Truth be told, and why not be truthful about it? She *was* going to marry him, after all. She adored everything about him. His smoldering gaze, sardonic grin, lean form, leonine walk; the sum total of his being called to her, and while she was completely certain that his charms called to every woman of his acquaintance, she was the woman who was going to capture him.

Of that she had no doubt whatsoever.

Mr. Grey and Mrs. Warren reached their group and were introduced properly, which Louisa barely noticed as she was too busy studying the beautiful line of Dutton's leg and the perfection of his tailoring. As she was trying to think of a dignified way to exit her current clique and make her way to Dutton, he spied her and almost immediately made his way to her.

Her heart skipped a beat.

"Try not to faint, will you?" Blakesley said.

"Don't be absurd," she whispered, throwing out her bust and hoping that the candlelight would cast the most flattering shadows upon her rather ordinary bosom. "I never faint."

"You'll do something if you keep straining your bosom like that," he said, and none too quietly either.

"Be still!" she hissed, though she did relax a bit and allow her bosom to fall a little closer to its natural position. At least Mrs. Warren's bosoms were no larger than hers.

"Why is it that women think men are only interested in the heft of a woman's bodice?" Blakesley murmured almost directly into her ear. She did hope he wasn't spoiling her perfect curl.

"You *are* being contrary tonight," she whispered back, hiding her mouth behind her fan. It would not do at all if Dutton thought she felt anything beyond the most tepid friendship with Henry Blakesley; the field was clear and she was determined that Dutton know it. "Of course men are positively *consumed* by the exact dimensions of a woman's bodice. What else does a man want, if not that?"

"Oh," he drawled just before he made his bow to Mrs. Warren, "a sweet disposition?"

She had never heard anything more absurd in her life. Louisa just barely managed to paste a pleasant look upon her face by the time Dutton reached them. She certainly hadn't bothered to produce any sort of pleasing look for George Grey or Anne Warren.

It was patently obvious, at least to *her*, that men, as defined by George Grey, Indian, did not require any sort of pleasing countenance whatsoever. He had been staring boldly at her and did not look at all displeased by what he saw.

Which was entirely appropriate. She looked, at the risk of sounding immodest, spectacular. Her dress was perfection and her hair, well, her curls tonight were arranged to give just the sort of demure innocence that was the apex of fashion and tasteful seduction.

If Blakesley didn't breathe the whole, careful arrangement into disaster, that is.

He was just the sort of man to ruin a girl's hair for the sport of it. The look in his blue eyes as she glanced at him over her fan confirmed it. Blakesley looked ready for fun, and that was dangerous to everyone around him.

Normally, she enjoyed that sort of evening with Blakesley, but not tonight, not when Dutton was so close and she had Sophia's counsel ringing in her ears. Tonight . . . tonight anything was possible.

"You have need of me, Sophia?" George asked of Lady Dalby, but his eyes never left Louisa's face.

She was becoming so accustomed to his blatant fascination with her that she failed to blush, which was such a relief. Louisa took a deep breath in satisfaction and held it, lifting her bust to a lovely advantage.

Blakesley snorted softly in amusement.

"Yes, George," Sophia said, "we are engaged in a wager and have need of an arbiter."

"A wager?" Anne Warren said, her pretty mouth smiling softly. Louisa didn't happen to like Anne Warren, but even she could see that the woman had a pretty mouth. It unfortunately was not her only good feature. Mrs. Warren was possessed of a flawless complexion of the creamiest white, lustrous hazel green eyes, and glossy red hair.

A thoroughly dislikeable woman.

"What are the terms?" Mrs. Warren said, intruding herself into a *private* wager without any invitation whatsoever. That said everything which would ever need to be said about her general character and the blatant lack of delicacy in her deportment.

It was particularly satisfying as Mrs. Warren had made such a mess of it in front of Dutton. Of course, he didn't seem to grasp the situation at all. Dutton, oddly enough, was looking at Anne Warren with a blatant lack of delicacy, as much as she hated to admit it. But admit it she did. One did not go about seducing Lord Dutton into a proper courtship without the necessity of admitting certain things. Namely, that Dutton was a bit of a rogue.

Which was completely charming on him, certainly.

"Ah, another participant," Calbourne said. "There is nothing so interesting as having lovely women involved in wagers. It leads to such interesting results."

"Do not listen to him, Mrs. Warren," Lord Iveston said. "It is a completely innocent wager with completely reasonable terms. The loser must drink a glass of liquor without taking a breath. Simplicity itself."

"Simplicity itself," Mrs. Warren said, "unless the glass be the size of a demijohn and the liquor be rude gin."

"The lady has wagered before," Calbourne said with a smile. Amelia wilted even further, her bust sinking almost with every breath. "She is wary."

"Mrs. Warren lives with Lady Dalby," Louisa said. "Perhaps she has been tutored to be wary."

She had spoken impulsively, more to steal Dutton's attention away from Mrs. Warren, and his attention had most definitely been on Mrs. Warren. Why, he scarce had been able to look at anyone else since joining their small party within the greater confines of the blue reception room at Hyde House. Impulsive, yes, and perhaps a tad cruel.

Oh, very well, cruel indeed, but what was a young woman to do when the man she adored was standing before her and did not so much as glance her way? What attention Anne Warren had not gar-nered, Sophia Dalby had. She and Amelia might have been made of bronze for all the attention they were receiving. Hard times called for hard measures.

Yes, and a bit of cruelty as well.

Sophia Dalby saved her, and knew she did, too, which made it all the more horrible.

Into the slightly shocked silence her observation had merited, Sophia turned her dark and liquid gaze upon Louisa and said, "How clever you are, Lady Louisa, and how very true your words. Mrs. Warren has indeed been under the careful guidance of my tutelage. And an apt pupil she is. I daresay the proof of it, aside from her spectacular marriage to Lord Staverton in a fortnight, is that she is most careful to get all the terms of a particular understanding well defined before plunging."

Which, of course, was a direct and cutting remark aimed precisely at Louisa. Any fool could see that.

"Have you entered into some arrangement with Lady Dalby?" Blakesley said in an undertone, trying to edge her away from the group. As the group contained Lord Dutton, Louisa held her ground and would not allow herself to be moved.

"Hardly," she muttered behind her fan. She was going to have to insist that Blakesley stop speaking to her as she could not possibly conduct an adequate seduction of Lord Dutton from behind her fan. She happened to know that her mouth was one of her better features and her teeth were practically a miracle of nature. Small help it would be to her if Dutton were sheltered from their impact.

"But something," Blakesley insisted, his hand going to her elbow.

She shifted her elbow, lifting her hand to touch the back of her neck. She had a lovely neck, too; though perhaps not as slender as Anne Warren's, it was certainly as white.

"Nothing to speak of," she hissed.

"Speak of it anyway," Blakesley snarled softly.

He seemed to care nothing for propriety, or the position of her hand on her neck; Lord Henry Blakesley stepped on the back of her skirt so that she could not move. By some strange concert of movement, Lord Iveston turned his body and shifted his weight from one foot to the other so that in a matter of seconds, she and Blakesley were separated from the wagering clique. The clique that contained *Lord Dutton.*

"What are you about?" she said, turning to face him as far as his big foot on her hem would allow.

"I'm asking that of you, Lady Louisa," he said. "Kindly answer."

The group shifted yet again and now there were three people between them, a barrier comprised of Lord Hartley, his unattractive and unsurprisingly unmarried daughter, and his third wife, Millicent or Margaret or some such thing.

Blast.

"Isn't there a wager we should be a part of?" she said, turning so that she could almost face him. He still stood on her hem. If she twisted much more she would rip a seam.

"There is a wager we *are* a part of," he said, stepping back, releasing her hem. She almost lost her balance, but he still had hold of her elbow so she didn't tip even the slightest degree. Small thanks for that. "I must speak with you, Louisa."

"You *are* speaking with me, Lord Henry," she said, trying to move through the crowd to the tallest man in the room, the tallest man in any room: the Duke of Calbourne. They were all still gathered. She could just make out Anne Warren's red hair and the welcome gleam of Amelia's blond hair. That Indian, George Grey, who should have been effortless to spot, didn't seem to be a part of their number any longer. He was likely stealing the silver.

"Kindly listen to me," Blakesley said. "I am trying to get your pearls back for you."

That got her attention.

"How?" she said, turning to face him.

She didn't often look at Henry Blakesley directly as his gaze was rather too clear-sighted and incisive for comfort. She also rarely, if ever, stood as close to him as she did now because of the very particular discomfort such proximity always engendered in her.

No, one did not go to Blakesley for comfort. One went to him for amusement of a most jaded and cynical variety. He was not looking very cynical at the moment and amusement was the farthest thing from her mind. She wanted her pearls back, that was certain, and if she could reacquire them through Blakesley rather than through a questionable alliance with Sophia Dalby, well, things couldn't have looked more encouraging.

"Did you say we were part of a wager?" she said a moment later. "A wager involving you and I? What possible wager could have us as its heart? Did *you* make this wager, Blakesley? Because if you did, it was not at all in good taste. I should not at all like being part of any man's ill-conceived wager. Is it on the book at White's? I should certainly hope you have enough decency to not bandy my name about in a gentleman's club."

Though it was true that Sophia's daughter had got her name on the betting book at White's and it hadn't appeared to hurt her in the least. She had even heard a rumor to the effect that Sophia had insisted that that particular bet had been the making of Caroline. Preposterous, obviously, yet Caroline *had* made a stellar match . . .

"Shut it, can you?" Blakesley snapped, escorting her none too gently toward the rear of the reception room and a small door very tastefully concealed in the paneling.

Well.

"If you could force yourself to be quiet and ignore the fact that Dutton is in the vicinity, I believe you'd be interested in what I have to tell you."

No, one did not go to Blakesley for comfort.

They were at the complete rear of the room, and a quiet spot it was, when he finally stopped hauling her about like a load of wool.

"I'm listening," she said, not able to resist the urge to cross her arms over her chest in exasperation.

"I can see that," he said wryly. "You are very fond of striking that pose when listening to something that you anticipate will annoy you completely."

She uncrossed her arms as casually as possible and checked her curl. It felt distinctly droopy. Of course it did.

"Is that better, Lord Henry? I would so hate to strike a pose which offends you."

"Yes, pleasing me has always been your highest priority."

"Is that the wager? That I arrange myself in a manner which pleases you? Pray, who would ever be found to arbitrate that?"

Blakesley's lips turned up in the most cynical of smiles; really, it could hardly be called smiling, what he did with his mouth. Snarling was the truth of it. Civilized snarling. Blakesley was many things, but he was always and eternally civilized.

"We require no arbiter, do we, Louisa? Things stand as they have ever done."

What the devil did that mean? Of course things stood between them as they ever had done. What else? Of all the tumult of her life, of all the trouble with her father and with snaring Dutton, she found her time with Blakesley to be the most welcome respite of every day.

"I have no idea what you're talking about, Lord Henry. Is this to do with the wager you mentioned? Is that what you've been doing all day? Making wagers with my name upon them?"

He smiled again, a soft smile that nevertheless had a sharkish look to it. Blakesley was not himself at all tonight, which was most inconvenient as she had hoped for at least some assistance with Dutton.

"The wager is this, Louisa," he said, leaning forward, his shark smile very bright, "and do try not to faint or blush or snap your bodice ties when I tell it. I don't know how I should explain such things to my mother."

Well, *really.* Blakesley could be so insulting when he was of a mind to be so. Louisa couldn't help but look across the room to where the Duke and Duchess of Hyde stood to greet their arriving guests. It was purely coincidence, she was almost completely certain, but Molly Hyde was staring at her with undisguised suspicion at that very moment.

"My bodice is none of your concern, Lord Henry," she managed, not blushing in the least. She was too angry to waste time in blushes.

"How well I know it," he murmured.

Of course, *then* she blushed.

"Could we get on with this, please? I should like to talk to Amelia before we enter for dinner," she said.

"About the hunting season, no doubt," he said, looking over the top of her head to where Amelia still stood, with Dutton, it should be mentioned yet again.

Blakesley was standing very close to her, too close. If he were not something of a brother to her, and if he had not behaved very publicly in that capacity for nearly two years, it would have looked entirely too intimate. Even with all those qualifiers, she was not entirely comfortable with his proximity. She could smell the faintly blended scents of his linen shirt and wool coat and under those familiar and highly pleasant scents, the scent of his skin.

It was most distracting.

His hair looked rather fine tonight, gleaming like old gold coins in the candlelight, and his eyes, gazing out at the crowd behind her, searching the room like a wolf on the edge of the shadows, looked particularly piercing.

And then he dropped his gaze to hers and she was forcibly reminded that his eyes were a very pleasing shade of blue and that they could see things in her which she much preferred to remain hidden.

Blakesley was too discerning by half.

"This is not the hunting season," she said sternly.

"There's not a man in London who doesn't know that it is," he said lightly. "Which brings me to my point. Kindly stop distracting me, will you?"

"I haven't done a *thing* to distract you! I'm trying to drive you to the point, Lord Henry, which you clearly haven't noticed."

"True," he said, nodding amiably, when she knew that he hadn't an amiable bone in his body. "It must be that I was distracted by your hair. It looks especially pretty tonight. That one curl, just there," he said, and he touched the curl she had arranged for Dutton, the curl that he had been breathing on from almost the moment she walked into Hyde House. He touched it with his finger, almost carelessly, almost caressingly, and the curl became *his*.

She didn't like it in the least.

"One perfect curl," he breathed softly, "fondling your neck, tumbling against your skin, sliding delicately by your very pretty ear . . ."

Her ear, pretty or not, grew hot and pink in mortification. Blakesley's breath brushed against her skin, tickled her ear, and heated her face with embarrassment and confusion. He never spoke like this. They might have teased, but they never flirted. He was flirting with her. She'd been Out for two full seasons; she knew full well what flirting looked like.

Heaven knew, she'd seen Dutton flirt often enough.

Just because no one had ever flirted with her before did not mean that she did not know it when she saw it. She was an observant girl, after all.

And, when no one was about, she practiced flirting in the mirror.

It was easier in the mirror.

This being coquettish did not seem to be in her nature. She felt something turn over in her belly and squirm about under her ribs.

She did not like that in the least, either.

"My hair is naturally curly, as you know," she said stiffly, arching her neck and her curl away from him. "One perfect curl, indeed.

One would think you are a romantic of the worst sort, Lord Henry, to hear you talk so."

He released his breath in a sigh that was not romantic in the least. "And you know I'm no such thing, don't you, Louisa?"

"I think too highly of you to call you any such thing, Lord Henry. You are far too clever to be ruled by emotion."

"Thank you," he said softly, his clever blue eyes studying her rather more closely than she liked. "And what rules you, Louisa?"

"I don't like to think of myself as being ruled by anything."

"I know that well enough," he said, smiling slightly. "Yet each one of us is ruled by something, some ideal or desire, something which drives us onward, even to destruction. Care to name your destruction, Louisa? Or shall I name it for you?"

He breathed the last, a breath of pain, she would have said, had she a romantic bone in her body, which she joyfully did not. Life did not reward the romantic and she fully intended to get her reward, all those things that had been denied her thus far. It was a perfectly logical goal and she had a perfectly logical plan to achieve it, if only Blakesley would step out of the way and allow her access to Dutton.

There was that. This delay, this careful seclusion, seemed all too calculated of a sudden. Was Blakesley trying to keep her from Dutton? To what purpose?

No, it was too ridiculous. Blakesley had nothing to gain by such an act.

"My destruction?" she said, trying to step away from him, but unable to do so by the wall at her back. Blakesley seemed almost to be looming over her. It was a most uncomfortable sensation and she didn't intend to tolerate it for one instant more. "I don't know what is wrong with you tonight, Lord Henry. Your behavior is highly irregular and most odd. One might conclude that you don't wish your brother well, to behave to his guests in such odd fashion."

"Odd fashion? You find it odd that I take you off to enjoy you in whatever privacy is allowed by the standards of the day?"

Whatever did *that* mean? Blakesley was becoming more disturbing to her sense of order and expediency by the minute. After all, she had cultivated his acquaintance precisely because he *was* so perfectly placed within Society and allowed himself to be used in such noble fashion—namely, her respectable pursuit of Lord Dutton.

There was no understanding him now. He jumped from one thing to another and not a one of his topics made sense. There was only one explanation for it.

"Lord Henry, I think you are deeply in your cups."

To which, Lord Henry Blakesley laughed. It was not a pleasant laugh. What with Lady Dalby's practically incessant and unpleasant laughter and now Blakeley's odd humor, one would think that there was no one left in London who knew how to appropriately laugh. It was certainly clear that far too many instances were found in which to laugh at *her*, which didn't make one bit of sense.

It looked to be a most trying evening and not at all as she had expected when her curls were being so artfully arranged.

"I find everything about this encounter odd, Lord Henry," she said, not at all pleased to find her back literally pressed against the wall. "I am not at all accustomed to being cornered and—"

"And," he interrupted, leaning over her in a most uncivilized posture, "you are not at all accustomed to being pursued by a man into the quiet corners of a room for a most appropriate, most respectable, seduction."

Seduction?

"I think the time has come, Louisa, when that must change. I would not be at all adverse to being the man who is responsible for the change, and I would not need to be in my cups to do so. I am not drunk," he said softly but so very sternly.

When had Blakesley learned how to be stern? And yet it could certainly never be said that he had ever been soft.

"A man does not need to be foxed to find your company compelling. Whyever would you think so?"

A thousand responses rose in her mind, but strangely, none could find their way to her lips. She was, for perhaps the first time in memory, too stunned for speech.

His face was very close, too close. She could feel his nearness like a fire in a winter room, his hair gleaming gold and hot, his eyes blue and piercing. This was not Blakesley as she knew him. This was not Blakesley as she wanted to know him. This man was too much the man and, though it galled her to admit it even to herself, she was not adept at managing men. She was no Sophia Dalby and that was the sad truth of it.

"Speechless, Louisa?" he taunted. "I would not have thought it possible."

Which, naturally, was exactly the prod she needed to find her tongue.

"I wish you *were* drunk, Lord Henry, for that would be some excuse, however feeble, for presuming there ever could be such a thing as a respectable seduction. I thought you knew me well enough to know that I am not particularly interested in behaving respectably, and I am not at all interested in being seduced. You misspoke completely. If you are not drunk, you should get drunk at the earliest opportunity. I know I shall, if only to wash this memory from me as thoroughly as possible."

It was a good speech, a fine speech. It was both clever and cutting, a pairing she particularly liked.

It was so unfortunate that Blakesley did not respond appropriately. It was completely like him.

Blakesley grinned, showing fully half his teeth, the imbecile.

"How fortunate that you don't care particularly for respectability or for seduction, Lady Louisa. It makes my proposal ideal for you. You shouldn't have any trouble at all in arranging yourself and your schedule to the terms of the wager," he said.

She didn't have the faintest idea what he was talking about, naturally, but she did know that her evening was not going at all as planned. When did it ever?

"Are we back to the wager? I was beginning to think you made it up to get me alone," she said sarcastically.

They were hardly alone, the room being almost full now, but she wasn't anywhere near Dutton and that was all that mattered.

"Alone? We have never been alone, Louisa, not truly," he said, echoing her own thoughts, which was highly annoying as she wished her thoughts to be her own and no one else's. "If we ever are alone, you shall surely note the difference."

"Yes, I'm sure," she said dismissively. "A great difference, as you say, but as we shall never put it to the test, it is hardly the subject for a wager. We were talking of a wager that concerned me, were we not?"

She did not particularly care for the look in his eyes as it was rather more speculative than was entirely complimentary. Not that Blakesley was ever complimentary in the slightest, but this look was almost rapacious. The small hairs on her arms stood up in rigid alarm.

She most definitely needed a strong drink. This evening was becoming more uncomfortable by the instant and Blakesley, her comfortable ally on every other evening for the past two years, was the cause.

Men were such a nuisance.

"Yes, Lady Louisa, the wager," he said softly. The room was not at all crowded, it was simply too large for that, but it was noisy and full and they were hardly alone. Yet the look in his eyes, the tenor of his voice, captured her as nothing had done for years. Nothing with the exception of Lord Dutton, of course. "As we are not alone," he said, his gaze leaving hers to scan the room. He echoed her thoughts again and it was as equally annoying as it had been the last time.

"I believe that point has been made and made again," she interrupted. "Can we not move from it?"

The fact that they weren't alone and would never be alone was becoming a point of increasing irritation. Blast it all, but now she wondered what it *would* be like to be alone with him.

A minor point. She was quite certain it would pass.

"Certainly," he said, sounding not at all amiable. "I'll state it plainly, shall I?" He did not pause for her consent. It was completely like him. "A wager has been made, a wager concerning you and your pearls—"

"They are no longer my pearls, are they?" she interrupted. "They are in Lord Dutton's possession, are they not? A condition made most obvious in this very house not a week ago."

"And the wager springs from just this foundation," he said. "You would like to reclaim the Melverley pearls, wouldn't you?"

"Of course, but—"

"Then you must do as I tell you, Louisa, and you must do it quickly and without argument."

If that wasn't the most likely of male orders to a female, well, then she didn't know men at all. And she did know men, she understood them very well, she just couldn't seem to manage them efficiently. Certainly it was a skill which could be learned?

"On the points of a wager?" she said with no little sarcasm. "Not at all probable, Lord Henry."

She felt a stirring behind her and turned her head slightly to look, which put her precious and not so perfect curl dangerously near Blakesley's shoulder; he could muss it beyond repair with a shrug. He probably would, too. He was in the most peculiar mood tonight.

"Why is the Marquis of Penrith coming this way?" Blakesley grumbled.

It was with great delight that she answered, "I met him for the first time just this afternoon at Dalby House. He's a most *agreeable* man, don't you think?"

She had turned slightly more and saw Penrith sliding through the crowd. Penelope Prestwick, that cow, turned a simpering smile upon him, but Penrith slipped past her efforts. Good man.

"How lovely Miss Prestwick looks tonight," Blakesley said. "I see she's wearing diamonds."

"Yes, doesn't she always," she said tartly. Penelope Prestwick had the annoying habit of wearing diamonds on every occasion. It was becoming something of a joke about Town.

"And they look so well on her," Blakesley said softly, looking down at Louisa with a very amused expression. "She's such a pleasant girl, so agreeable."

"Is she?" Louisa said stiffly. "I hadn't noticed."

"No, you wouldn't."

"You were going to tell me something, Lord Henry? If not, I would like to rejoin my cousin," she snapped. "Perhaps Lord Penrith will escort me. He looks so very eager to reach my side, does he not? I am almost certain he will do whatever I ask. Such an *agreeable* man."

"Yes, well, whatever he's coming to do, he's going to have to wait," Blakesley snapped, cutting her off *again*. Blakesley really was quite a horrid man; she didn't know why she had tolerated him for as long as she had. "The points of the wager are these," Blakesley said, his mouth quite close to her ear. His breath washed over her neck and against the delicate back of her ear with alarming intimacy. She almost shivered. Almost. "If you want your pearls back, you must pursue *me*, Louisa."

"I beg your pardon?" she said, pulling away from him and his intimate breath. Unfortunately, there was not much room to move and all she succeeded in doing was to plant her shoulder firmly against his chest. He had a very hard chest.

"A wager was made today at White's. Would Lady Louisa Kirkland pursue her pearls, which are now in my possession, or would she continue in her pursuit of the Marquis of Dutton?"

"Continue?" she gasped. "At White's?"

She couldn't quite grasp it. Did all the world know of her *tendre* for Lord Dutton? She couldn't breathe. If Blakesley would only move his very hard chest away from her, she might be able to form a coherent thought.

Blakesley wasn't cooperating at all tonight, on any point.

"Listen to me, Louisa," he said, pulling her arm, the arm that was wedged against his chest, and turning her to face him. His face was very close and his eyes very blue, she did notice that through her haze of confusion. "If you want your pearls back, pursue me. I shall win them for you. The question is, do you want your pearls?"

"Of course," she said. It was the one clear thought she could formulate. "But how is this the subject of a wager? Who would make such a bet?"

"It hardly matters, does it?" Blakesley said softly, looking down at her with what she would have called tenderness on anyone else's face. On Blakesley's face, she didn't know what to call it. "Avoid Dutton for the next few days, enjoy my company as you have in the past, and the pearls are yours. Can you do it?"

"Can I do it? Of course I can do it," she snapped. "I can and would do anything to get my pearls. Melverley should never have sold them."

There were many things Melverley should not have done, as well as all the things he should stop doing immediately, but she had given up on her father long years ago.

"And what were you doing at Dalby House today?" he asked with a snarl. Blakesley was of the most uneven temper tonight. "You can't have imagined Dutton would be there."

"I imagined no such thing!" she snarled right back at him. "I do have female friends, you know."

"Not at Dalby House, you don't," he snipped.

Really, this entire conversation was devolving into the ludicrous.

It was at that moment that their conversation was blessedly interrupted. She turned to face Lord Penrith, for certainly he had made his way to them by now. Louisa wiped every trace of annoyance off her face and, flicking her rumpled curl into place, turned to face him.

She heard Blakesley snort in either amusement or derision, though she couldn't possibly have cared which.

But it wasn't Penrith with his tousled dark blond locks and green eyes who faced her. No, of course not, nothing that simple.

It was the Indian.

Eleven

FROM across the salon the Marquis of Dutton watched with a careless eye the conversation between Lady Louisa and Lord Henry Blakesley. He rather suspected that Blakesley was cheating at their wager. He also, not without some vanity, thought that even cheating would not change the outcome.

Louisa Kirkland was as besotted as any woman could possibly be. He had enough experience of women to know that. Which was precisely why he was standing directly across from Mrs. Anne Warren. She might be pledged to marry the ancient Lord Staverton, but she was his for the taking. They both knew that, even if she was currently ignoring him completely.

A woman never wasted time ignoring a man she didn't want.

Anne Warren stood politely ignoring him, pretending to listen to the Duke of Calbourne go on about something, likely his latest foal, which in normal circumstances would have interested him. But these were hardly normal circumstances.

Louisa Kirkland must find him available when she rushed over to present herself in all her virginal splendor.

Anne Warren must find him irresistible so that she gave him a tumble either before or after her wedding, he hardly cared which.

And Sophia Dalby must somehow be made to stop laughing at him. She was laughing, silently to be sure, but laughing nonetheless.

He looked at her and raised a single eyebrow to lofty heights. He'd quelled more than one rebellious mare with that look.

Damned, if the woman didn't chuckle.

"Your plate is quite full, Lord Dutton," Sophia said, her dark eyes gleaming with humor. "I should not think you have the resources to take on yet another female. Best you save your censure for less experienced prey."

Upon which, Mrs. Warren turned just enough so that she fully faced Lord Iveston and presented him with her back. A lovely back it was, too. The more fully she shut him out, the more fully he knew how hungry for him she was.

He could not help but smile in anticipation.

"I do so like to see confidence in a man," Sophia said, taking a step toward him and turning slightly so that they were separated from the party made up of Lord Iveston, the Duke of Calbourne, Mrs. Warren, Lady Amelia Caversham, and Lady Jordan. Mr. George Grey, to whom he'd been introduced just a few minutes earlier, was making his way across the salon to where Louisa and Blakesley stood in heated conversation. He did not have to imagine what they were discussing.

"You do have your share and then some," she continued, forcing him to give her his full attention.

It was not difficult. Sophia Dalby was a compelling woman. She also neither avoided him nor sought him out. Clearly, she had no interest in him whatsoever. It did happen, now and again. He had learned not to take it to heart.

"I have often wondered how sturdy your confidence is, Lord Dutton," she said, taking yet another step nearer to him and giving him a wonderful view of her décolleté. He enjoyed it immensely.

"I have never had it put to the test, Lady Dalby," he said. "Would that make a good wager? You seem ever to be instigating wagers."

"I turn a profit when I can, my lord," she said cheerfully. "But I would not wager against your confidence. It is such a rare trait in a man. I should so hate to be the cause, however indirectly, of shattering it."

"Perhaps in the men of your usual acquaintance," he said, stung more than he wanted to admit by her statement, ridiculous though it was. Why his gaze turned to Anne Warren in that instant he could not have said. Well, perhaps he could, but he did not want to delve at all into that particular pond.

"I assure you, darling," she said with a soft smile, "that I am acquainted with only the best of men of the highest rank. Is tonight not proof of that?"

"And your nephew?" he asked, turning the dig back upon her. "Is he of the best and highest?"

The fellow was an American Indian, that much was obvious. It had been a surprise, certainly, but he had taken it in good step. Odd, that he had heard no rumor about Sophia's savage family tree. He had, when he had thought about it at all, assumed she was of French descent.

"The very best," she said without hesitation and with complete ease of manner, "and very nearly the highest. Iroquois, specifically Mohawk, if you are at all familiar with the tribes of North America, which of course you must be as they have ever and always played such a large and meaningful part in so many of England's various wars. England is not the only society which has an aristocracy, you realize."

Actually, he had known no such thing about Indian society, and he did not suppose he could have been expected to know. To be honest, he was not at all surprised that Sophia, no matter her background as a courtesan, was from some ancient Iroquois aristocracy.

She had always had a certain manner about her which, according to all reports, she had possessed long before marrying the Earl of Dalby.

"May I ask how you came by such a lineage, Lady Dalby? I must admit to being surprised by the connection," he said, hoping to turn the conversation away from himself and upon her. He was curious, as well. One did not meet an Indian from the forests of America every day of the week.

"Oh, the usual way, Lord Dutton," she answered sweetly. "By marriage."

"Then Mr. Grey is your nephew fully? His father . . . ?"

"My brother," she said, nodding. "Yes, we are fully and completely and most contentedly related. Which means, you understand, that Markham, the ninth Earl of Dalby, is fully related to an Iroquois sachem as well. Did you ever think to hear it? A peer of the realm with Iroquois blood running rampant through his veins? I daresay it will do England some good, wouldn't you agree?"

He didn't particularly agree, no, but as there wasn't a thing he could do about it, he didn't waste effort in turmoil. It was one of the finest aspects of his character that he had determined from an early age what was worth spending one's time and effort on and what was not. Indians in Parliament was not. Mrs. Warren was.

Life was so simple when one had firm priorities and kept to them.

Actually, Parliament wouldn't be harmed a bit if they assumed something of his policy.

"I daresay that England will survive," he said lightly, looking over Sophia's head at the current gathering.

The room was nearly full; they would soon enter into dinner. Mrs. Warren was still with Iveston, Calbourne, and the Caversham girl, who, without any subtlety to speak of, was looking for a duke to wed. Blakesley was still with Louisa, and not making much progress by the angry looks they were exchanging.

Blakesley was one of those odd fellows who apparently couldn't find his way with a woman if he had her naked and tied to a bed. Most peculiar, and endlessly entertaining.

"There's that confidence again," Sophia said softly, waving her fan gently to move the dark curls about her face.

"A family trait," he said, giving her his full attention again.

It was hardly hard duty. Sophia Dalby was both seductive and beautiful and she possessed the added allure of knowing fully the depth of her appeal. It was, to be sure, an elegant and exotic combination of assets.

"Yes," she breathed, smiling playfully at him, "I remember."

As he had no intention of allowing the conversation to drift *there*, he said, "But what of Lady Caroline? Are she and Lord Ashdon thriving in matrimony?"

"They must be," Sophia said. "I haven't heard a word from them since they left for Chaldon Hall."

"You don't expect them to return to Town this Season?"

"Lord Dutton, I have no expectations whatsoever. Should I?"

"It is only that I perceived Mrs. Warren was something of a companion to Lady Caroline. I suppose I had wondered if she would accompany your daughter on her bridal trip."

Sophia smiled serenely, but her dark eyes were gleaming with amusement as she answered what even he could admit was a clumsy sortie into the status of Anne Warren.

"And she did not," Sophia said, looking past him to nod at someone.

Dutton would not have attempted looking behind him to see who it was, but he was tempted to do so. Something in Sophia's eyes had shifted at the nod and he was beyond curious to know who could effect such a change in her. Sophia, it could almost be said, looked suddenly predatory.

"I can see that she did not," he said pleasantly.

Sophia looked at him fully again and gave him a spectacular

smile. "Mrs. Warren is such a charming companion, such a dear friend, but I do her a disservice. I consider Anne Warren a member of my family. Certainly I treat her as such."

"She is in your every confidence," he said, smiling.

Sophia laughed delicately and tapped his shoulder with her folded fan. "Darling, *no one* is in my every confidence. I have far too many confidences which must remain . . . confidential. I'm certain you understand."

"Fully." And he did.

Anne Warren was under Sophia's able protection, but they were not complete confidantes. That boded well for him. He had no direct wish to cross Sophia Dalby, as it was rumored by those in an acute position to know that she was a ruthless adversary, yet it was entirely possible that he could seduce Anne Warren without Sophia being privy to the act.

It was an entirely reasonable supposition and he was entirely committed to acting upon it. While managing a flagrant Louisa Kirkland, he would bed Anne Warren.

Simplicity itself.

∾

OF course it should have been the most simple thing in the world, but it wasn't, and Amelia Caversham was getting so very tired of trying. Here she was, face-to-face, and looking quite marvelous, truth be told, with two, *two*, dukes or nearly dukes and she could barely keep them looking in her direction.

One of *them* being the Duke of Calbourne, a highly eligible duke of rather remarkable good looks and perhaps of slightly more than desirable height; but, he did have a son, which proved he could do the deed. She had heard a rather interesting rumor that the Earl of Summerlund was not up to that sort of performance, the result being that his wife, who was a full year younger than Amelia, had been forced, *forced*, to make good use of the head groom.

The Summerlund heir had been born last summer.

Anyway, the second of them now facing her was the lovely and quite elegant Lord Iveston, heir to the Duke of Hyde, who was terribly old, wasn't he, and could not live forever, could he? Iveston, having not yet married and having never been married and, truth be told, appearing not at all *interested* in being married, was a very handsome prospect. If only he would show some interest. In her. Immediately.

Or the Duke of Calbourne. Either one would do nicely.

The entire problem, as far as she could make out, was that dukes and almost dukes, particularly if they were young, as these two were, but even if they were not, *knew* that they should do very nicely indeed and as a consequence they were not at all cooperative.

It was really most disheartening.

It was particularly disheartening and discouraging and, really, disgusting as she had planned and planned for this evening, when there would be at the very minimum two dukes or almost dukes and she happened, now, at this very instant to see yet *another* duke just entering the salon.

Because he, Edenham, was a duke and behaving perfectly like a duke as she had come to know them, he paid her absolutely no attention whatsoever.

And on top of all that, if that wasn't absolutely enough, Louisa was having the most spectacular time in that not only was Lord Henry Blakesley, brother to Lord Iveston, almost duke, engaged in a blatantly passionate conversation with her, but Lord Penrith, *the* Marquis of Penrith, whom everyone knew was the most exquisite man of the Season, even if he had the misfortune to not be in line for a dukedom, was bowing before Louisa now. Even at this distance and through at least forty people, Penrith looked quite taken with Louisa.

Worse yet, Mr. Grey, Sophia's rather remarkable nephew, was

standing, hovering actually, over Louisa and looking positively and dangerously mesmerized by the very sight of Louisa.

And hadn't Louisa just met Penrith and George Grey in Sophia Dalby's salon this very day?

Amelia loved Louisa as well as any girl ever loved a cousin. Certainly. Without doubt.

But it was not at all a lovely feeling to watch Louisa get so much attention, whether she wanted it or not, and since it was not Lord Dutton who was fawning over Louisa, Amelia was more than certain that Louisa did not realize how fortunate she was because now, more than ever, Amelia was very well aware that no one, *no one*, cared whether she left the room, the house, or the town.

And she wasn't counting her brother in that because brothers were worthless in calculations of that sort.

The evening, just barely begun, was turning into perhaps one of the worst nights of her life, and she had quite a few to choose from. Worst nights, that is.

She had not, despite all her plans, hit London by storm. No, more a light drizzle with not even a promise of lightning.

Her governess, when exclaiming over her shining blond locks and clear blue eyes, had not led her to believe that this, *this*, would have been her future. She was on the shelf, or almost on the shelf, and she was not yet twenty-one. It was failure she was facing and nothing less.

Amelia's gaze, blue and crystalline (a direct quote from Mrs. Weaver, her former governess), lifted again to watch Louisa quarrel, by the look of it, with Blakesley, flirt with Penrith, which would explain the quarrel with Blakesley, and pointedly ignore Mr. Grey, which didn't seem to be working out at all, and let herself drift out of the conversation Calbourne was having with Iveston about the height of his latest foal. They let her drift, the louts, because they didn't care if she stood listening, questioning, sticking her bosom out so far that her back ached, or pulled her hairpins out with both hands. They didn't care. They didn't notice.

They weren't at all interested. In her.

It was a perfectly dreadful evening and they hadn't yet sat down to dinner.

But of course the worst, the complete worst was Anne Warren. It was well-known if one listened to gossip, which of course she did for how else was she to know anything about anyone, that Anne Warren's mother had been only slightly better than a common lightskirt, which clearly meant that Anne Warren herself was only slightly, if at all, better than that. And this woman, this, it must be admitted, widow of a naval hero of the most minor variety, was completely, *completely* riveting to both Calbourne and Iveston.

It was not to be borne.

She felt the distinct and unwelcome urge to cry.

Which she naturally would not do as she had been better brought up than that and besides which, no one would have *noticed* in any regard.

"Do you not care for horses, Lady Amelia?" Mrs. Warren said.

Perhaps someone had noticed after all.

Anne Warren's lovely eyes looked at her sympathetically. Mrs. Warren's eyes were a remarkable shade of light greyish green and matched to perfection the soft pewter-colored trim of her stylish gown, which it must be noted seemed to reliably prove that a friendship with Sophia Dalby had its advantages, for it was flatly impossible for a woman of Anne Warren's background and status to have afforded such a gown otherwise. All of which, naturally, caused Amelia to ponder yet again the wisdom of Louisa's seeking Sophia out for counsel in the matter of her pearls.

In some lights it looked positively wise.

But that had to be absurd as any properly brought up lady knew, *knew*, that listening to anything a former courtesan said would have to rank as one of the most unwise of acts.

Amelia let her gaze stray from the well-groomed Mrs. Warren across the room to Louisa, who was currently engaged in conversation with Mr. Grey, Lord Henry Blakesley, *and* Lord Penrith. *The* Lord Penrith. Why, his voice alone could cause a girl of impeccable breeding to tumble under the nearest shrub. To tumble *him* under the nearest shrub was the actual saying, but girls of impeccable breeding were not supposed to say such things, even to themselves, and as she was fully intent upon becoming a duchess, she had made it a point to do all, *all,* with perfect propriety.

Fat lot of good it had done her.

"Lady Amelia?" Anne Warren said.

"Oh," Amelia said, pulling her gaze away from Louisa and her conversation with two very obviously attentive men, "I find horses and their bloodlines to be very interesting."

What else was she to say when one duke and one almost duke were discussing horses in that very instant? She cared about horses only as a method of transportation, but could she admit that now, in this company? Hardly.

"I'm afraid that I do not. I suppose it is because I was not around horses in my youth," Mrs. Warren said pleasantly. "I suppose I am too old now to acquire the fascination."

Amelia's father had always prided himself on his stables, not that he had let Amelia anywhere near them.

"Calbourne," Iveston said, inserting himself into their conversation, "I do think Mrs. Warren's attention has wandered. We can speak of this later. For now, let us think of the ladies and what would interest them. I do believe," Lord Iveston said with a sweet smile aimed directly and exclusively, *exclusively,* at Anne Warren, "that I saw a very fetching ribbon yesterday that would exactly match your eyes, Mrs. Warren."

Anne laughed in delight, which is exactly what Amelia would have done if anyone had bothered to talk to her, and said, "I cannot believe that you shop for ribbons, my lord, fetching or otherwise.

Talk horses if you please. It is your day and you should and must be indulged."

"I like the sound of that," Iveston said, ignoring Amelia completely and, by all appearances, effortlessly.

"Yes, well, I think you have been indulged quite enough," Calbourne said. "It is time that the ladies be indulged."

"And I like the sound of that," Mrs. Warren said.

Aunt Mary snorted and shook her head loosely. She had found the punch. She had become quite more agreeable since she had done so.

"Young women should never be indulged," Mary said primly, or as primly as three glasses of punch would allow. "Ruins them completely."

"I should say that would depend upon what they were fit for to begin with," Iveston said, fighting a blush.

It was most charming, though if she married Iveston, their children would likely be white of hair and pink of cheek, which could sometimes result in offspring that looked peculiarly like white rabbits. It was something to consider, that was certain.

Not that Lord Iveston behaved as though he were bothering to consider *her*.

"Because in that case," Calbourne continued, "it might be the making of them. Indulgence can be a very satisfying end, wouldn't you say, Iveston?"

"Not in mixed company, no," Iveston said, turning quite pink in the cheek.

Rabbits.

Of course, Lord Calbourne, being older and more experienced, particularly where having wives was concerned, might be more than she was capable of managing.

Ridiculous. If she could manage to marry a duke, she could manage him while married to him. One simply followed the other.

But she did not particularly care for his bold tongue and his unfortunate habit of speaking rather more suggestively than was proper, habits which she would naturally overlook if he expressed even the slightest interest in her.

Amelia, bosom carefully arranged, looked coyly at Calbourne.

He did not look even slightly interested. He was, in point of fact, looking with unbecoming warmth at Mrs. Warren.

It was entirely possible that, like Louisa, she might learn to positively loathe Anne Warren.

ANNE Warren was quite aware that Amelia Caversham was on the road to a very strong distaste for her. She could hardly blame her. The men, Calbourne and Iveston, were behaving dismally. It was obvious to her that they were behaving that way entirely intentionally.

It was equally obvious to her that Amelia had not reasoned that out.

Amelia Caversham, as lovely as she looked and as sweetly as she behaved, was rather too obvious in her pursuits. Namely: a duke for a husband. It was not a bad goal, certainly not, and a woman should have goals, quite firm ones, in fact, but it was best if they were not displayed quite so obviously. And, in fact, it served a woman's best interests if they were not displayed at all.

She had learned that from Sophia, or was learning it, and it was good counsel indeed. She intended to follow it fully and to the letter.

She was going to attain her goals and she was going to do it quietly and with all good taste. She was going to marry Lord Staverton, a lovely man, quite tender in his regard for her and quite charming in his devotion, no matter that he was fully old enough to be her elderly father and that he had the unfortunate aspect of having one uncontrollable eye. He was a lovely man. He was a titled man. She had quite learned to ignore his eye and his age.

The most delightful development of her engagement to the delightful Lord Staverton was that Lord Dutton was completely poleaxed by the news.

It was too wonderful.

Dutton was miserable and confused and surly, which was a condition he entirely deserved. She couldn't have been more delighted to be the cause of such misery on such a deserving man.

Of course, Dutton looked entirely self-satisfied and arrogant and confident to *her*, but Sophia, who surely understood men better than any woman she had yet to meet, had told her in no uncertain terms that Dutton was facing the crisis of his manhood and that it was high time he did so.

Sophia must be believed, and Anne did. Resolutely. Without hesitation, qualm, or doubt. It was the simple truth that ever since she had begun listening to Sophia's counsel concerning men that Caroline had married the man of her choosing a mere three days after choosing him and Anne had become engaged to a perfectly lovely gentleman and had simultaneously cast Lord Dutton into misery.

Things couldn't get much better than that.

If only Amelia could see what was so very plain to her; namely, that Calbourne and Iveston were punishing her after a fashion for her too plain pursuit of a title. It was entirely natural, of course, for a woman to want a title, natural and logical. Why, even a man must admit that he preferred being titled to untitled. That he would become so unreasonable as to expect a woman to ignore such details was beyond logic, but men did so often drift beyond logic into their own strange land of honor and tradition that it could often become difficult to reason with them rationally.

And in those instances, which happened all too often to be entirely complimentary to men, the only course for a woman to follow was to leave them ignorant of events as they stood and for her to proceed with her very logical plans accordingly. Which is exactly what she was doing and which is exactly what Amelia should be doing.

It was unfortunately and flagrantly obvious that Amelia was wanting in sound counsel.

That she should be counseled by Sophia was also obvious.

That Anne could suggest no such thing to her was also, sadly, obvious.

Ah, well, she would do what she could, staying within the bounds of strict propriety as she properly ought. When a woman had a mother such as she had endured, she lived forever within the bounds of propriety or risked immediate censure and expulsion. She had lived after having been expelled. She had crawled her way back in, in large part by Sophia's efforts, and she was not going to risk being tossed back out.

She felt sorry for Amelia, but not so much so that she would risk her own survival.

It was a truth Sophia knew well, as did Anne, because it was a truth they had lived and survived to remain silent about. One did not discuss life on the outer wall of Society because it was simply too dismal to revisit, even in memory. That was another truth they shared, albeit silently.

Anne looked across the small space that separated her from Sophia, who was currently laughing about something with Dutton, who looked as compelling as he ever did, miserable or not, and watched her. Sophia, black haired and ivory skinned, her black eyes shining like polished onyx, was more mother to her than her own mother had been. She owed her a debt of love and gratitude that she paid daily and gladly. Not that Sophia expected anything of her, but the depth of understanding and devotion they shared for each other was precious to her.

If Sophia Dalby had asked Anne to walk through fire, Anne would have certainly tried to do so, which is exactly why Sophia had not told her to marry Staverton. No, she had let Anne make her own mind up about that, and then affirmed her when she had.

It was the right choice. Caroline, Sophia's headstrong, protected daughter and Anne's dear friend, could not see it. Caroline had lived well loved within the bounds of Society all her life. No, she could not see the wisdom, the pure gift, of marrying dear Staverton.

Staverton, charming and sweet, was her salvation.

Anne turned her gaze back to Amelia Caversham. From the slightly haunted look in Amelia's eyes, it looked like she needed some salvation of her own and it was not going to come from either Calbourne or Iveston. Anne was not at all accustomed to behaving in any way that could be deemed heroic, but she was determined all of a sudden to play the hero, in whatever small measure she might, with Amelia. The poor girl looked quite ready to burst into tears.

And the men looked not at all disposed to care.

Men, like the brutes they were on the worst of occasions, had to be managed most carefully, at least according to Sophia. Anne had seen nothing to dissuade her from that observation.

"Then do we agree?" Anne said, compelling the men to look at her. "Is it not the ladies who should henceforth be indulged?"

"I am in complete agreement, Mrs. Warren," Iveston said. "In what fashion would you prefer your indulgence? Wine? Food?"

"A canceling of your debts?" Calbourne said slyly.

The Duke of Calbourne was most captivating when he was acting sly, and she was entirely certain he knew it. Impossible, irrepressible man; it was quite apparent by his behavior that he had been married once before. He was entirely too comfortable around women. Although the same could be said about her, she supposed; having been married, she was quite comfortable with men and their odd little jests and random moods. They often behaved like rather large children and responded best when dealt with firmly and not unkindly. They could not help their limitations, after all, and should not be faulted for them.

"I won the wager over that particular word, your grace, if you remember," Anne said. "Mr. Grey was quite certain that there was no such word."

"As *intersex*," Calbourne said, smiling slyly down at her.

He was rather like one of those imps one read about in children's stories, the smiling monster who laughingly drags one off into a wood. Calbourne was not going to drag her off anywhere.

"Exactly," Anne said primly. "It is not a word, and I won the wager. It is not I who shall have to drink enough to make me lightheaded."

"Pity," Calbourne said, grinning down at her. How did he manage to look so impish when he was roughly the size of an ox?

"But as to how we should like to be indulged," Anne said, forcefully pulling Amelia into the conversation. Amelia looked willing to be pulled, but ignorant as to the procedure.

Virgins.

Well, one worked with what one had.

"Do you have any thoughts, Lady Amelia? I say it is past time for our whims to be indulged, don't you agree?"

"I do," Amelia managed, her voice as soft as white velvet.

Men, as a rule, did not particularly care for white velvet: too difficult to manage.

"In the ways of indulgence," Iveston said, almost completely avoiding looking at poor Amelia, "as I said, there is food, drink—"

"And the other, intensely popular, widely regarded form of indulgence," Calbourne interrupted.

Yes, well, she knew quite well where Calbourne's mind was headed and she thought it entirely horrible of him to try and haul the conversation and their delicate female minds there with him.

Imp.

"Male interests," Anne pronounced, cutting off Calbourne and not one bit apologetic about it. She had to protect Amelia, didn't she? And she was not going to risk anything inflammatory being said about her to worry Staverton. He deserved at least that much from her. "Male interests to the last. Men may indulge in food and drink, but a woman has different, more delicate, interests. Does she not, Lady Amelia?"

Really, on the subject of dragging things, she could hardly do more to drag Amelia into an only slightly scandalous conversation with two eligible men. The girl, virgin or not, could at least *try* to appear interesting.

"I should say so," Amelia said, her voice rising just a bit. White velvet was left behind for pink damask. Well, it was an improvement.

"Did you have a particular indulgence in mind, Lady Amelia?" Iveston asked most cordially. Anne sent him an approving smile. Calbourne chuckled, which was not at all surprising, considering the man.

"Ruined," Lady Jordan muttered into her cup of punch.

The lady, Amelia's aunt and chaperone, after all, had a point. It really was too, too fast a conversation to be . . . indulging in. Anne swallowed a smile at the thought and was rewarded with the sound of Calbourne's snicker.

Wasn't it only imps and small children who snickered?

Absolutely. Calbourne had made her point for her.

"Is it not an indulgence to be the singular point of interest for two very pleasing men?" Anne said, looking entirely at Iveston. She was certain Calbourne would take the point. And he did, to judge by his chuckle. "Shall we not call that our particular whim, Lady Amelia?"

"We could," Amelia said, her blue eyes showing the barest beginnings of a flicker of lively amusement. It was most charming and she looked wonderfully beguiling for the first time that evening. "We probably shall, but shall we not ask for our whim to be perhaps more . . . calculated?"

"A calculated whim?" Calbourne said. "Does that not defy logic?"

"Only a man's logic," Anne said quickly, "which we hold not to have the smallest value in this present circumstance."

"This is turning quite deadly," Iveston said. "Shall I not draw my sword, which would be highly inconvenient as it is stored in a trunk on the third floor in a poorly placed closet? But I must defend myself against such an accusation. Calbourne, naturally, must defend himself. Defending myself will be quite as far as obligation shall take me."

"Gallantry in action," Calbourne muttered good-naturedly.

"That I must defend myself on my birthday must surely be seen as gallantry enough."

"Why must men ever and always resort to force?" Anne said to Amelia.

"Perhaps because they lack the sense to do otherwise?" Amelia responded immediately, her voice a very pleasing shade of hearty plum-colored wool.

At which point, and for one delicious moment, the men were stricken speechless.

Well done, Amelia!

And for the first time that evening, Amelia Caversham had the full attention of two very marriageable men with the exact qualifications she seemed to want in a marriageable man. It was a moment worth behaving the hero for and Anne smiled fully, enjoying every second of her own, lesser, triumph.

It did not escape her notice that Lord Dutton, his conversation with Sophia edging to a close, had heard the last bit of her somewhat saucy exchange with the lords Calbourne and Iveston and was staring at her with what could only be described as shock.

Anne smiled fully and did not so much as lift her fan to hide it.

How remarkable that, in doing a good turn for Amelia Caversham, she had managed to deliver a dagger thrust to Dutton.

Wasn't life lovely that way?

Twelve

NATURALLY, being a normal woman with perfectly normal goals, Louisa had dreamed of having the devoted and exclusive attention of a small gathering of men.

Oh, very well, in her dreams, which were rather more frequent than was charitable, she had captured no less than six gentlemen in her web of beauty and wit and they had fallen like so many autumn leaves in the wake of her charm. She now had three men, for Mr. Grey could hardly be deemed a gentleman, avidly clustered about her, demanding her exclusive attention and becoming quite churlish with each other as they did so.

It was not at all a pleasant situation.

In fact, she was coming dangerously close to losing her temper, something which she absolutely must not do. But really, did Blakesley have to be so sarcastically churlish? Did Penrith have to be so unrepentantly seductive? Did Mr. Grey have to be so dangerously savage?

Having to deal with Dutton's casual dismissal of her would have been a pleasure at the moment. As things stood, she had not a moment's rest to give to thoughts of Dutton.

"And are you finding your stay in London pleasant?" Louisa asked Mr. Grey. She found that keeping him talking was far preferable to having him stand and stare at her in what could only be described as carnal hunger.

Oh, yes, she had read certain sections, the interesting ones, of that author, Fielding. She knew all about carnal hunger, at least as it was described in books. George Grey was, at this very moment, displaying the exact characteristics of one of the main characters in Fielding's most salacious novel. It was more attractive in a novel. In person, it was positively frightening.

"I was finding it interesting. As of this afternoon, it became fascinating," Mr. Grey answered, staring hungrily into her eyes. Most disturbing. She felt almost sick to her stomach.

"Is this your first visit?" she said, raising her chin and quelling her queasiness.

"No, not my first and not my last," he answered.

He had the most disturbing habit of speaking in abrupt phrases. It made conversation so difficult. That, and the look in his dark brown eyes. At least he was sparing her his dimple. His dimple was extremely difficult to ignore.

"And when will be your last visit?" Blakesley said, looking rather rudely at Mr. Grey.

"When I have what I want," Mr. Grey answered, looking not at all offended. In fact, Mr. Grey looked almost amused.

Mr. Grey was a very unusual man, that much was certain. Or perhaps he was normal for an American; she could hardly judge as she didn't know any actual Americans that she was aware of. Unless one counted Sophia Dalby as an American since she had to be half American by any reckoning, American Indian at that. Although, perhaps being an Indian was significantly different than being an American.

Something else she had given no thought to whatsoever in her life to date.

Leave it to Sophia Dalby and her annoying relatives to complicate what should have been a very pleasant evening.

"And what is it you want?" Blakesley said, holding Mr. Grey's gaze like a clenched fist.

"What every man wants. A woman."

Upon which, Mr. Grey turned his gaze away from Blakesley's and stared directly at her.

Oh, dear.

When *would* dinner be served?

"You've come to the right town if you're looking for a wife," Penrith said, his smile plainly showing his amusement.

Yes, well, he could afford to be amused; he was not a *woman.*

"Yes," Blakesley said, looking at her with a half smile, "there's not an unmarried woman in Town for the Season who is not eager to be wed. Even to an American. But aren't there women enough in America?"

"There are women enough everywhere. The right woman is not so easy to find. I thought," Mr. Grey said, staring down at her, practically ignoring both Penrith and Blakesley.

It was, dare she say it, almost flattering. He did seem quite spellbound by her. It was completely beyond her usual experience of men and, now that she seemed to be growing accustomed to it, it was not unpleasant.

In fact, she rather thought she liked it.

Oh, dear.

"I agree with you completely, Mr. Grey," Lord Penrith said, casting his green-eyed gaze down at her. Really, she wasn't a small woman, but what with being surrounded by three unusually tall men, she was beginning to feel positively hemmed in.

She rather thought she was beginning to like that as well.

"Finding the right woman is merely a question of entering the right room at the right time," Penrith continued. "How fortunate I was to happen upon Lord Dalby in the park today, and fortunate that he invited me home with him."

"Seems everyone was at Dalby House this afternoon," Blakesley muttered.

"Yes, I was so surprised to see *you* there today," Louisa said stiffly. "Pity that you left so quickly. Off to White's, were you? We did wonder." Really, Blakesley made it sound as if she had gone to Dalby House for the express purpose of meeting men.

Although, there was nothing wrong in that if it happened to be true, was there? Even though it was nothing close to the truth. She had gone to Dalby House for the sole purpose of seeking Sophia Dalby; was it her fault that the salon had wound up being simply awash in attractive, available men?

She really ought to have gone to Sophia earlier in her life. She couldn't think what nonsense she'd been thinking not to have done so. Sophia truly was a most remarkable woman and she knew absolutely everyone, and that included, naturally, the most remarkable men of the Town.

"Did you?" Blakesley said wryly. "Spared me a thought, did you?"

"If you choose to spend the best part of the day lolling about in White's," she snapped back, "I don't see how I'm to be held responsible for that."

"I was in White's and I was not lolling, though why I should not loll as I see fit is no concern of yours."

Why was it that Blakesley's eyes, which she had always known somewhere in the back of her mind were blue, scalded her in their blueness now? Certainly Penrith's rather remarkable green gaze, which was certainly lovely, did not affect her in quite the same way. Nor did Mr. Grey's, no matter how he leered. No, it was Blakesley, who had always been quite impossible and reliably unpredictable, who made every nerve quiver in both anger and interest.

Blasted man. He was quite the most contrary of her acquaintances. She was not at all certain she would continue to tolerate him.

"Of course, you must spend your hours to please yourself," she said. "I certainly have no need of you."

"They've been friends long?" Mr. Grey asked Lord Penrith.

"From what I've heard," Penrith answered casually, both of them behaving as though they were not being overheard at all. It was extremely aggravating.

But what wasn't lately?

Certainly Blakesley couldn't possibly do more to annoy her than he had done in the last twenty minutes, never mind the fact that he had clearly avoided her for the best part of the day for the purpose of exposing her to public censure by placing her name at the heart of a squalid bet at White's. It was too awful of him. She couldn't imagine what he'd been thinking.

Obviously, he hadn't been thinking at all, which was completely unlike him. Blakesley was the most intelligent man she had yet to meet, though she supposed everyone could stumble into stupidity now and then.

Blakesley had stumbled.

She wasn't sure she would forgive him, at least not until next week.

"It's regular for an unmarried woman to befriend an unmarried man?" Mr. Grey asked Penrith.

"Not entirely regular, no," Penrith answered, his voice so pleasant and so calm that one might have thought he was giving a lecture on the habits of the native population of some backward province. "But, you see, Lady Louisa is not an entirely regular sort of girl."

"True," Mr. Grey responded, turning to look at her again. "She is not regular at all."

"I do not care to be discussed as if I were not present," she said more sharply than was usually considered proper. Certainly, in the present circumstances, she would be excused by even the most ardent follower of proper form. Not that anyone fitting that description was present at the moment. A rare bit of luck for her and entirely overdue. "In fact, I don't care to be discussed at all, and certainly not evaluated."

"Can't be helped," Mr. Grey said in that odd, clipped way he had of speaking. It was most jarring. "You're unforgettable. People are going to remember you and talk about you. Smart thing would be to learn to like it."

That rendered her speechless for a full five seconds.

Unfortunately, before she could gather her composure, Lord Penrith added, "It is true, Lady Louisa. Certainly you must know that about yourself? You are unique, and that is always worth comment."

There was simply no answer to that. Was she to admit that no one had ever complimented her before, on any small particular?

Obviously not.

"I wasn't aware that Lady Louisa was the object of speculation and she certainly is not a topic for gossip," Blakesley said.

She could have kissed him.

Odd, to think such a thing of Blakesley. She didn't quite know where the thought had come from. It was the company, certainly. She had never been in such strange company engaging in such peculiar conversation before this instant.

It was very difficult not to lay the blame at Sophia's feet and, in fact, she saw no reason not to do so.

"Of course not," Penrith said quickly. "I hardly meant that."

"Then you must have meant," Blakesley said in a low and quite serious tone, "that she is, as any beautiful lady would be, mentioned when beauty and wit are discussed, as they always are, because they are so rarely combined in one woman. Of course you meant that Louisa Kirkland is that rare woman."

The men stared at each other in that particular way that men had of threatening each other without words. She had no idea why they did so when words were such effective weapons, but that was neither here nor there at the moment. Louisa could not help herself. She truly wanted to throw her arms around Blakesley's neck and kiss his cynical cheek.

Apparently even cynical, sarcastic men could rise to the occasion with the proper motivation. Penrith and George Grey must have provided the proper motivation.

Was it possible that she should lay *that* at Sophia Dalby's feet?

It did not seem at all likely.

"Exactly," Mr. George Grey said, his expression as inscrutable as ever, if one discounted the glint of lust in his eyes, which she was hardly disposed to discount. Really, the man, even for a savage, had no manners whatsoever.

It was not at all to her credit, but certainly convenient, that she was becoming almost inured to his expression as it related to her. He liked to look at her. He clearly found her desirable. Was that so horrible?

Certainly there were worse things.

Louisa felt a small smile of purely feminine satisfaction turn up the corners of her mouth. She really ought not to have smiled, but she did. He might take it as encouragement, and she certainly did not want that.

"I've looked," Mr. Grey said, his dark eyes almost captivating, almost because she was still so very aware of Blakesley at her elbow, vibrating like a harp in simmering anger. "I like what I see. I want you, Louisa Kirkland, and I mean to have you."

Louisa stopped smiling.

"I beg your pardon?" Louisa said, her voice a mere whisper.

"No, Louisa, he must beg yours," Blakesley said, facing Mr. Grey fully, his body a shield from Mr. Grey's gaze.

It was an effective shield. Unfortunately, Mr. Grey was rather tall and rather dark in his black coat with his black hair and his single shining silver earring dangling from his left ear . . . well, let it be said that he was difficult to ignore, no matter who stood in front of him.

"I will not," Grey said, his expression calm, one might even have said he was amused.

Amused?

"I have seen what I want. What can I do but go after it? She is not spoken for. I have asked Sophia. This woman is free to choose the man she will mate with. I would be that man."

"That is not quite the way things are done here," Penrith said, also looking slightly amused.

She was getting more than a little tired of everyone finding this amusing. It might be many things, but not a one of them was amusing. However, even though she was as sure of this as that she was wearing white, she distinctly heard a snicker from somewhere behind her. As it was directly behind her she could not help but think that someone was amused at her expense.

She, however, had too much dignity to turn around and look to see who was laughing at her predicament.

"Maybe they should be," Grey answered, looking at both Penrith and Blakesley with equal parts amusement and challenge. "You have known this woman for how long? Yet you have not made her yours. You must not want her. I do."

She could feel Blakesley's body go rigid with anger and she could not have been more delighted. Here, at last, was someone who was not amused by Mr. George Grey's aberrant behavior. She wasn't at all familiar with the customs and habits of Americans, but she did not quite believe that George Grey was at all typical. Certainly, even Americans must have some rules of deportment and rites of courtship. Certainly this grab and run technique would find no supporters even in America.

Though he had not actually grabbed for her and run. Not yet. But to judge by the look in his dark eyes, she suspected he was capable of it.

She never should have smiled at him. This is what came of smiling at strange men. Certainly Blakesley had never acted even remotely like this with her and she had smiled at him for years. There was obviously no point in mentioning how often she'd smiled at Dutton and what that had wrought.

"You can't have her," Blakesley said.

She chanced a quick look at him and was surprised to see an expression on his face she had never seen before; Blakesley, charming, impenetrable Blakesley, looked positively lethal.

Well, good heavens.

It was enough to make a girl want to smile again.

"Why not?" Grey asked.

"She is not a woman free for the taking," Blakesley said, taking her elbow in his hand.

"Well said, Blakesley," Penrith said.

For all that Penrith was supposed to be so devastating to women, he certainly was shy off the mark when it came to defending a woman from a savage. It did not speak well of him, not at all. He was hardly much of a rake if he couldn't best a single Indian in verbal warfare.

Blakesley gripped her elbow so tightly that it hurt, but she did not think it was wise to say anything about that now. Another look at his face was enough to advise her of that.

"We'll see," Grey said with a suspicious twinkle in his eye.

"No, we shall not see," Blakesley said.

He looked as if he were about to say more, but they were called to dinner at that instant, the duchess casting a very disapproving eye upon her as she and the duke marched into the red reception room.

Well, really, what had *she* done?

Nothing but smile at an Indian, and that done in a crowded room in the Hydes' own house. Really, if the Hydes didn't have better control of their guest list, why should she be held responsible because a minor incident had occurred while waiting to go into dinner, a dinner which should have started a quarter of an hour ago?

Being a duchess gave one the right of being completely unreasonable. It was likely the main reason why Amelia was so determined to become one.

Louisa, on the other hand, all thoughts of Dutton scattered to the sky, was simply determined to make it through dinner without being carried off into Hyde Park.

She didn't think her chances looked that good, not with the way Grey was staring at her as they proceeded into dinner.

IT was as they were pairing up to enter the red reception room, a long table laid out and gleaming with porcelain, crystal, and silver down the exact center, that Sophia made her way to Louisa's side and whispered, "You do seem to draw them in, darling. Like flies to manure. I had no idea that you attracted men so easily, and each one of them so earnest. You are to be congratulated. At this rate, you shall have your pearls back in hours. Or someone's pearls. Really, as long as you can cajole a strand from one of your many admirers, does it matter if they are the Melverley pearls or not? One fine strand of pearls will do as well as any other, is that not so?"

Of course, there were many phrases in Sophia's whispered speech which stuck out to Louisa. *Flies to manure*, certainly. *Attracted men so easily*, definitely. Was it true? And if it was, when had it happened? Certainly she had no recollection of men being inordinately taken with her. But there was that last bit, that bit about any strand of pearls being adequate to the cause.

Was that true?

No, absolutely not, because if it were true then she would be no better than a common . . . well, she knew very well what and she was not that. Not at all. Nor had she a wish to be.

But, to have pearls strewn about her, as Caroline Trevelyan had

had done just last week in this very house . . . that would have a certain satisfaction, wouldn't it? Especially if one of the strands were the Melverley pearls, *her* pearls. Wouldn't that be simple justice?

And retribution. So difficult to achieve true justice without retribution.

"I'm only interested in getting *my* pearls back," Louisa whispered to Sophia, because there was certainly no reason to tell Sophia every thought in her head. "And as to that," she said in a rush for they were entering rather more rapidly than she would have thought possible, though they were dining late and hunger could rush people so, "according to Lord Henry, the Marquis of Dutton is no longer in possession of the Melverley pearls. Henry himself has them."

Sophia eyed her like a rather plump lamb. It was not at all flattering.

"How very interesting. What does that mean, I wonder?"

"It means that some wager is afoot and—"

"And you mean to win it, obviously," Sophia interrupted. "How very clever of you, darling. Of course you must do all within your skill to win any wager even remotely connected to you."

It was the emphasis she put on the word *skill* which was so very insulting. Louisa felt herself bristling and was not at all concerned with hiding the fact.

"Naturally," Louisa said, though until that moment she had not given it any more thought than it took to be insulted and slightly confused. Something about talking to Sophia Dalby brushed silly responses like confusion to the floor. "I just wanted to make clear to you that Lord Henry has a plan to acquire the Melverley pearls for me, which means that our . . . discussion . . . of this afternoon—"

"Of course, darling," Sophia interrupted, again. "You have no need of me and my little plans for you. I'm quite certain that between you, you and Lord Henry shall manage it beautifully. I am so pleased for you, of course, but do be certain that all shall be concluded quickly as Molly is quite firm in her plans for Lord Henry's imminent marriage. But Blakes knows his mother's wishes. I'm sure all will be managed tonight and you shall have your pearls back before the wedding."

And with those words, she smiled, turned, and drifted into the general move to the red reception room and the table laid for them.

Louisa felt her heart drop into her hips, which was a terrible sensation to have just before going in to dinner. Blast Penelope Prestwick and her endless array of diamonds.

❧

"YOUR most irritating trait," Sophia said as she nearly bumped into the Marquis of Ruan, "is your habit of following me about. I sense you intend it as a compliment. It is actually more of an annoyance."

Lord Ruan smiled and said, "I've interrupted something. I hope it was a sordid appointment you had planned for later tonight."

"I do not engage in sordid appointments, Lord Ruan. You have mistaken me completely."

She brushed against his coat as she walked past him and managed to snag one of the small openings on her glove with a button on his waistcoat. It was a handy bit of work, and one she had used countless times before.

"We are ensnared, Lady Dalby," he said as they stood, her wrist to his belly. It was most provocative, which was precisely the point. "It feels entirely natural, does it not?"

"Release me," she said softly, looking up at him and giving him a grand view of her décolleté.

"Is that my cue to say 'never'? I'm dreadful at these comic operas. You must teach me my lines so that I don't disappoint."

"Too late, Lord Ruan," she said, giving him a brief, genuine smile. "I am freed."

She twitched her wrist and cast him off, walking as swiftly as the crowd would allow, getting as quickly away from him as she could.

He was offered a fine view of her back as she left him, which was all he was going to see tonight. It was so important to keep a man, especially a sophisticated man like Ruan, on his toes. One couldn't allow a man to become complaisant.

Particularly a man like Ruan. Ruan, she suspected, was rather more accustomed to having his way with women than would be tolerable for her. And, really, wasn't it always about what was tolerable for her?

Sophia smiled and made her way to the Duke of Edenham, her escort into dinner.

"You came," she said to him. "I promise you that you shall not be disappointed."

"You are on my arm," Edenham replied. "I am hardly disposed to being disappointed."

"Your grace, you are first among gentlemen."

"You're flattering me obscenely. What am I to expect tonight? To be drawn and quartered by dawn?"

"Is that what they're calling it now?" Sophia said with a sly smile. "Darling Edenham, would you rather be drawn or quartered first? I am entirely at your disposal."

Edenham laughed and patted her hand lightly. "Who is it you are punishing, Sophia? You are never so charming as when you are tormenting someone and you are being excessively charming, even accommodating. It is very unlike you."

"I'm so delighted that you're here that I'm not even going to bother to be insulted. For you, darling Edenham, only insult those who intrigue you. Now it is I who am flattered."

"I came because you asked me to honor the invitation and you know how I hate going about in Society," he said. "For that alone you should be flattered."

"And I am," she said as they entered the red reception room.

It was magnificently displayed under hundreds of white candles and the gleam of fine French chandeliers dripping with crystals.

The room was filling rapidly with the finest of London Society, the ladies in their pale gowns and glittering with the sparkle of jewels, the gentlemen in fine coats and waistcoats, their legs brilliantly displayed in white breeches. The current fashion was so favorable if a woman happened to enjoy the look of a shapely male leg. Which she did.

"But, darling, you were earnestly invited tonight, your company sought after by the Hydes and by everyone in this room, certainly. Certainly, by me."

Edenham looked down at her from his very elegant height, his dark brown hair falling forward over his brow. A most attractive man, and so eligible, why, the mind spun with possibilities.

"By you? I shall flatter myself this time and choose to believe it. But by them? No, I know better."

"If you are going to believe gossip, Edenham, then believe the gossip as I tell it. You are, as you well know it, a very desirable man. Why not act like one?"

"Meaning?"

"You know very well what I mean. You were not married from birth, darling, or can you not remember that far back?"

"Witch," he said, grinning reluctantly. He ought to do that more often, poor man. Humor was what was needed in Edenham's life, not the solitude he had shrouded himself in. "I am not that many years older than you, dear Sophia. Kindly remember that."

"Then act your age, as I do."

"You hardly act your age."

"You'd have to know my age to judge that, and I, for one, do not go about singing my age and other particulars to every shopkeeper in town."

"And I do?"

"You are a widower, Edenham. I am a widow. There. It is said. It is known. There is no more to it than that."

"You are simplifying."

"And you are complicating," she said. "See that lovely girl? The one with the curling ginger hair? That's Lady Louisa Kirkland, Melverley's older girl. Talk to her, your grace. Amuse yourself."

"What are you up to, Sophia? She wants a husband, certainly. All these young things want husbands, and I shall never be a husband again."

"Don't bore me with your pronouncements, darling. Certainly you shall marry again, when you meet the woman who can properly manage you, but Louisa is not that woman. She does not want you, so you are perfectly safe with her."

"She does not want me? Just like that? Does she even know me and yet she does not want me?"

Sophia laughed and said, "And you say you will not marry again? You are a perfect liar, darling. But you are safe from Louisa. She will not threaten you, at least not in any particularly harmful way. I'm fairly certain you will emerge relatively unscathed."

"It is when you qualify your facts that you frighten me, Sophia," he said, grinning down at her, for they both knew perfectly well that he would never be tempted by Louisa Kirkland. Ginger-haired virgins were not at all to his tastes. Not anymore.

"Enjoy your meal, darling," Sophia said with a smile. "And don't be afraid of these young things. Even you cannot kill them by conversation."

Edenham looked momentarily stricken by her comment and then he grinned ruefully. He needed teasing, poor dear, and she was just the woman to do it.

The table was set, the footmen at their places, and the company seated. All the pieces in their places. The game was begun.

Sophia could not possibly have been more delighted. It was going to prove to be a most delicious evening and she smiled in pure anticipation.

Thirteen

THE seating for sixty-four people for dinner was all prearranged, obviously. It was naturally presumed that Molly, the Duchess of Hyde, had done the arranging. If she had, she was a devious, vindictive woman.

Louisa found herself seated at one of the far ends of the table, the center being reserved for those of higher precedence as well as personal favorites of the Duke and Duchess of Hyde, who sat opposite each other in the dead center of the long table. Sophia Dalby was near the center, across from the intimidating Duke of Edenham, whom everyone gossiped could kill a woman practically by touching her hand through a glove, which was flatly ridiculous as it was perfectly obvious that the Duke of Edenham had to do much more than that to kill a woman, namely, marry her and get her with child. That, however, did the trick.

Edenham had buried three wives and had two smallish children to show for it. Even Amelia had not grown quite so desperate as to look at Edenham. Yet.

Lord Iveston was seated across and down a few seats from his father, the Duke of Hyde, who looked anything but happy to be in such a large room with so many people, even if it was his own house and those people his particular guests. Hyde, by all reports and certainly from her own observation, was rather peculiar for a duke in that he preferred his own company to that of any other. Unless it be the company of his wife, Molly, for whom, it was gossiped, he was completely faithful.

Again, most odd behavior for a duke or any man.

But as to Molly's character, it was perfectly obvious to Louisa that Molly must hate her completely, for she had placed her as far away from anyone who mattered to Louisa and who must matter to Molly. Namely, the sons of Hyde. Blakesley was at least ten people away from her, as were Blakesley's brothers, who numbered four if one included Iveston, which she did.

That was not the worst of it, of course. She could have enjoyed a dinner without Blakesley at her side, and had done so more than once at affairs of this sort, but what was the worst of it was that George Grey was seated immediately on her right and Lord Penrith on her left.

It was perfectly obvious to her that the Duchess of Hyde intended her to be ruined by the fourth course.

Across the table and far too distant to be of any service at all was Amelia, who, to judge by the slightly frantic look in her eyes, was feeling some of the same panic. Amelia, who could not possibly have earned either Molly's favor or enmity, was seated between the Marquis of Ruan and the Marquis of Dutton.

Yes, Dutton.

It was intentional, clearly. There was no mistaking Molly's intention. She wanted Louisa to see Dutton, to watch his every nuanced gesture toward her cousin and yet be able to do nothing about it. It was cruelty at its finest.

That Lord Ruan was added in was just honey on the porridge. Lord Ruan was, while not as lovely as Dutton, *dangerous* in a particular sort of fashion. While mamas throughout the ton warned their daughters about Dutton, knowing that their daughters would ignore every word, no word of warning was ever required of Ruan. Ruan was so dangerous, so worldly, that he was not even attempted.

And they were Amelia's dinner companions, if one discounted Aunt Mary, which one was regularly disposed to do as Mary was more frequently than not practically snoring into her plate by the second course. Mary, in this instance, was seated to the left of Ruan, where she would do no harm at all.

It was for perhaps the first time since she and Amelia had made their come out that Louisa wished for a sober chaperone.

From where she was sitting, Louisa could just make out Sophia sitting far down and across the table from her, sitting next to Blakesley, as it happened. Blakesley looked none too pleased at his placement, which was absurd as it was a family celebration of a dinner party and he could most likely have sat wherever he pleased. On second thought, if Molly, Duchess of Hyde, were her mother, Louisa had little doubt that she wouldn't be much pleased at all, even in such a small matter as to where she was seated to dine. Molly Hyde, who, now that Louisa thought about it, was from the American colonies back when they *had* been American colonies and for that reason alone was more than casual friends with Sophia Dalby.

It was all too very convenient and she was more certain than ever that going to speak with Sophia had been very near to consorting with the enemy. She was no closer to getting back her pearls, Dutton was miles away as the distance was measured across the dining table, and she had an American Indian breathing, quite literally, down her neck.

If she hadn't been so well brought up, Louisa would have hit someone.

"You don't look happy," George Grey said. "I could fix that for you."

"You are misinformed," she said stiffly, staring with what she suspected was longing in the precise direction of Dutton, who was saying something to Amelia at the moment, which resulted in Amelia smiling politely.

Good girl, Amelia.

Polite, but not enthusiastic. As Dutton was twelfth in line for some obscure dukedom in Northumbria, which was inhospitable at best, Dutton could not fail to be of no interest to Amelia.

"Don't listen to him, Lady Louisa," Penrith said softly, his voice as seductive as a siren's call. Though the sirens were supposed to have been women and almost certainly Greek, she thought the description more apt than not. "You look as you should and as you always do: completely lovely."

It was at that point that Dutton whispered something in the general direction of Amelia's ear. Amelia blushed and laughed rather more enthusiastically than was proper. Ruan cocked his head and studied Ameila in what looked to be surprise.

Amelia was looking less *good* by the minute.

Someone down table dropped a fork on his plate, creating a very disharmonious sound which perfectly coincided with her current mood. Louisa looked to the source and found herself staring at Blakesley. His blue eyes blazed down the table at her. Given her present situation, she could only respond in one fashion: she blazed her eyes back at him.

Did he think she was enjoying her current predicament?

Really, Blakesley could be so difficult. In fact, he seemed to relish being difficult.

Before she could look away, and she needed to look away for, if she was not mistaken, George Grey had put his fingertips on her seat and was a scant inch away from touching her thigh, Blakesley shifted his gaze, clearly indicating that she should excuse herself and meet him somewhere outside of the room. As the first course had just been served, she couldn't possibly leave now.

She was clearly communicating that with her eyes when Mr.

George Grey chose that exact moment to slide his fingertips under her leg just above the knee.

Louisa, without a moment's thought, signaled a footman to pull back her chair, stood, mouthed an excuse to his grace, the Duke of Hyde, who was likely a more sympathetic audience than his wife, Molly, and left the red reception room by the door that led into the yellow drawing room.

It was only then, in that large room that was deserted and barely lit by a pair of candlebra of five branches each, that she took a breath. It was a shaky breath, but she deserved it. Had she not escaped a savage Indian? Had he not actually *touched* her?

It was on her third, trembling breath that Blakesley entered the room from another, more secluded, doorway. He looked raging mad. Whatever was wrong with him? He had good placement at the table and she was quite certain that no Indian had mauled him.

"Do you want your pearls or not, Louisa? For if you continue on as you are, you will find yourself married to either an Iroquois warrior and living at lake's edge in North America or saddled with Penrith, who will use you abominably."

That stopped her for a full second, but she was a strong girl and recovered quickly.

"Are you saying that Penrith would use me worse than Grey? You must be daft. At least Penrith keeps his hands to himself."

Blakesley's expression grew quite hard at that, which was preposterous. *She* hadn't done a thing.

"Has he *touched* you?"

Even though she had seen Blakeley toss off a hard look in her direction every now and again, and therefore she could say quite assuredly that he did not frighten her in the least, there was something about *this* expression that gave her pause. Which was quite an unusual reaction for her.

Quite.

Blakesley took a step nearer to her, which brought him closer than was usual and which, in the dim light, made his eyes look almost menacing.

Louisa was in no mood to be menaced. Hadn't an Indian just touched her? Hadn't she endured quite enough from men this horrid evening? Hadn't Dutton made Amelia laugh?

"Louisa," Blakesley said, "answer me."

She wanted to tell him to leave her alone, to go rot along with every man in London and a few in Sussex whom she had little use for, to forget that she'd ever had pearls to lose or a heart to break.

She wanted to tell him that he could have Miss Prestwick and her shining black hair and her flawlessly set diamonds and that he had no right to ask about Mr. Grey or any other man.

She wanted to tell him that he had no right to mention her at White's.

She wanted to tell him that she didn't like at all where she was sitting at dinner.

She wanted to tell him that the evening was a dismal affair without his company and his comments.

She wanted to tell him that he was the most sarcastic man she had ever met and that he made her laugh as no other could, and that she quite possibly hated him for that.

Because Dutton never made her laugh. Dutton . . . she couldn't quite remember the exact color of Dutton's eyes, and that was because Blakesley's blue eyes were slicing into her heart. He had ruined Dutton for her and that was unforgiveable.

Couldn't he see that it was unforgiveable?

All those things and more were on the tip of her tongue to tell him, but she made the mistake, the simple mistake, of looking up into his eyes and seeing the warm flame of candlelight there and the feel of his hand on her arm and his breath on her skin . . . and then it happened.

She kissed him.

Oh, he didn't make it easy for her. He was Blakesley, after all, and a man doesn't change simply because he's kissed. He stiffened and then he froze, forcing her to do all the work, and it must be admitted that, as it was her first kiss, she didn't know what she was doing, not really, but she was earnest and eager and that must have showed because, just then, just when she thought she'd ruined the very last friendship she felt she had, Blakesley kissed her back.

Of course, that changed everything.

He touched her. With his tongue and his hands, and even his leg slid its way between hers, pressing against the fabric, pushing softly, urgently to nestle against her.

He was hot, his hands and mouth and leg.

He strained, his tongue pressing, dancing, pushing.

He pushed, pressing her against his length, forcing her to feel the hard, hot jut of his arousal.

He moaned briefly, a hot rush of air into her mouth and she shocked herself by moaning back, echoing him in this strange new language of beating hearts and grasping hands.

He wrapped one arm around her back so that she could not move except to move toward him, against him.

His other arm, his hand, touched her thigh, encased it and lifted, pressed, controlled her.

And his mouth devoured her.

And she devoured him in return.

Measure for measure.

Like for like.

She wrapped her arms around his shoulders, pulling the weight of his chest against her bosom, twined her tongue against his, held his bicep in her hand and would not let him move away from her, or take his hands off of her.

She hardly remembered it was Blakesley because the kiss consumed her and carried her along on a river of embers.

But it was Blakesley and couldn't possibly have been anyone

else because she could never have let herself run wild like this with anyone else.

Thinking, just now, gave her a headache.

Best just to kiss and kiss again.

She liked kissing.

Who would have thought it?

She opened her mouth a bit farther, to match him, just to match him, because he was Blakesley and she could trust him to teach her how to kiss, to make sure she was doing it right, and that she wasn't bungling it completely, and the kiss instantly became hotter and wetter and more . . . intimate.

Intimacy.

With Blakesley.

It seemed right somehow.

Safe.

Yes, safe, and because it was, she snuggled in deeper, running her hands under his coat and around his back, encompassing his waist nicely, firmly, and he had a nice waist, trim and taut, and of course she had known that about Blakesley because he could eat absolutely anything and never gain an inch, whereas she could not eat more than one sweet a day, which was horridly unfair because too often she had to watch Blakesley eat five desserts at once.

Desserts . . . kissing Blakesley was like eating a delicious dessert.

Delicious?

Louisa tilted her head and angled her kiss a bit deeper, pressing her breasts against Blakesley's chest, which was also nice and firm . . . and hot . . . and moaned in regret when Blakesley, for no reason at all that she could see, grabbed her by the upper arms and pushed her away from him. And rather roughly at that.

His eyes were blue coals, his mouth a thin line of repression, and he said, "God, enough. Enough. I'm blind with it."

Ridiculous nonsense. Blind? She had never seen more clearly. Blakesley's mouth and Blakesley's eyes and Blakesley's hands. She needed those hands, that mouth. She needed them to touch her, now.

So, what else was she to do?

She ignored him, which was only logical, and lunged toward him so forcefully that he took two or three steps backward and bumped against the door and somehow, because he was a man and had longer arms, she was sure of it, somehow he held her off.

But not before she had touched his chest with her hands, and run her hands fleetingly along his arms.

She'd got some satisfaction off him, anyway.

The flare of passion and surprise in his eyes just before he'd hit the door had been rather nice, too.

"Louisa! Stop!" he barked.

Wonderful. First he kissed her and now he spoke to her like an unruly pup. It really was not at all as she'd hoped the evening would turn out.

"What are you doing?" he snapped, straightening his waistcoat, his fingers lingering at the hem and fussing suspiciously there. Hmm.

"I thought *we* were kissing," she said, watching his hands.

"Yes," he said gruffly, "and if anyone had seen us, you'd be ruined."

"I'm not going to allow you to ruin me, Blakes," she said, mostly because she suspected it would annoy him dreadfully.

"My mother calls me Blakes," he said stiffly, his face looking quite angular in the shadowy light. She liked it. She liked everything about this moment, she decided.

The feeling of his kiss on her mouth still tingled, as well as her breasts and, as long as she was taking an inventory, a warm puddle of feeling was swirling between her legs.

She rather suspected that some warm something was doing things to the place between Blakesley's legs because he kept his hand suspiciously near his groin.

It really was too funny, and she wasn't the sort of girl not to take advantage of a man when he was so clearly vulnerable.

Smiling, she took a step nearer to him. Blakes, as she had suspected he would, took a step backward.

Oh, it was too, too easy.

"You can't mean that you've mistaken me for your mother," she said, twirling her lovely curl, which she suspected was rather the worse for wear and, strangely, did not concern her in the least.

"Of course that's not—"

"Or that I reminded you of your mother when I kissed you," she interrupted, closing on him. His heel hit the wall and he sidestepped a small console table of delicate proportions and kept the distance between them.

"My point," he said harshly, which couldn't have delighted her more, "was that it is a name used between intimates, Louisa, and you don't qualify."

"Don't I?" she whispered, pulling on her curl, watching his gaze follow her hand. "Can't we change that?"

"I beg your pardon?" he said hoarsely, his gaze riveting again on her face.

She took a step nearer to him and was delighted to find that he remained rooted to the spot. He was weakening, how lovely. Well, but didn't they always? Men were so weak when it came to these sorts of encounters. Everyone knew that. Why, just look at her father. He was like soft pudding when it came to women.

"I mean," she said softly, playing with him like a cat with a mouse, and didn't that just explain why cats always looked so contented? "I thought that, after our kiss that, aren't we? Isn't that enough intimacy to classify as . . . intimacy? Or is there more, Blakes? You would tell me if there were more, wouldn't you?"

He didn't move after that. Perhaps he couldn't; she'd like to think so.

She didn't know why she'd kissed him, what had prompted the

thought, though it was likely something Sophia had said since Sophia was known to be a bad influence on nearly everyone and, as strong-minded as Louisa was, she supposed even the worst influence would rub off on her eventually.

That remark about flies to manure and using what skill she could to win the wager still sang somewhere dark in her thoughts, but she didn't have time to bother thinking about that at the moment. Or ever. She had Blakes before her and he was practically hers for the taking, though what she was supposed to do with him or how she was supposed to "take" him were matters of some mystery.

Even though Melverley was a complete rogue, she still was more innocent than not.

She was being driven by instinct, which had its own delights, but little more.

It seemed to be enough.

"This is no game, Louisa, and I am not some toy you have recently discovered," Blakes said, seeing things a little more clearly than was entirely comfortable. Blakes was in the habit of doing that and it was one of his many annoying traits.

If she slowed down at all she would think of all sorts of reasons why kissing Blakes was a bad idea.

Best not to slow down then, obviously.

"Didn't you tell me that I had to behave in a certain way to get my pearls back? Isn't this what you had in mind?"

"This is all about your pearls, then?" he said, brows dipped low in suspicion.

"What else could it be about?" she said with a snap of annoyance. "I thought I was supposed to be seen with you, or was there more to the wager?"

"No one can see us now, Louisa," he said softly.

His face was almost in full shadow, the few candles in the room hardly sufficient to light more than their forms. She preferred it that way; it was much easier to be brazen in the darkness, which was likely why unmarried girls were discouraged from being alone with gentlemen in the dark.

"Which is why," she said, "I thought it a good time to practice."

"Practice what, Louisa?"

"Practice kissing, obviously. The way I understand it, I am to be seen more in your company than anyone else's, you win the wager, I get my pearls back, and then I am free to engage in my preferred behavior. As long as we are to spend time together, I thought I might as well learn how to kiss. Before it really matters."

She wasn't at all certain why she'd thrown that last bit in. It was bold, possibly reckless, perhaps even dangerous. But she was so very tired of men discounting her, ignoring her, and worse, some of them likely even avoided her.

Wouldn't it be lovely, just for once, to be noticed? To be pursued? To be *desired*? Even if it was somehow tangled up in a wager, it might be her best chance for . . . something. She wasn't certain quite what, but she wanted something more than she currently had and, naturally, she wanted it with Blakesley.

That seemed entirely reasonable to her.

Unfortunately, she hadn't anticipated the depth and breadth of Blakeley's response.

"Oh, this matters," he said in a soft snarl. "I am not for practice. I am not a game piece you move about the board in your efforts to win Dutton."

He knew about Dutton? Of course, she'd suspected that *he* suspected, but to have it so boldly thrown in her face, it was unbearable. Just how many people knew she had a *tendre* for Dutton?

"I never said—"

He took a step nearer and put one hand hard over her mouth, and with the other, he pulled her up so that she stood toe-to-toe with him.

"When I'm with you, you'll think of me. When I'm not with

you, you'll think of me. You'll do this because I'll kiss you until the only thought left in your head is of me, my mouth, my hands, my name. But I'll not ruin you, Louisa, never that. You'll be safe from that, but not from *me*."

He was breathing into her face, his eyes glistening and hard in the soft light, the sounds of his brother's celebration coming to them from beyond the door, his weight a presence she could feel against the soft muslin of her dress. He didn't move. She didn't move. She'd never known such force, such energy was hidden behind Blakesley's cool and cynical exterior. She was entirely certain that she wasn't meant to know, that no one was meant to know.

She breathed softly and held his gaze, their eyes locked, their breath coming in tandem.

When he moved his hand from off her mouth, she didn't move. He didn't move. They stared and studied each other until she thought she'd die from the examination. Things simply could not stand as they were. She did not care to be examined, especially by Blakesley, whom, it was suddenly clear, saw too much.

With the most casual inflection imaginable, she said, "Of course you'll not ruin me, Blakes. Did you think I'd allow that? What will happen is that I will ruin you."

He gave a short bark of laughter before she pulled him down to her and her mouth captured his again. He responded instantly. It was a kiss of passion, or that was her nearest guess. Perfect.

IT was less than perfect, that was certain. Amelia was seated nowhere near any available dukes, which surely was no accident, yet seated directly in between the lords Ruan and Dutton, which also appeared maliciously intentional. Amelia didn't know what she could have done to offend the Duchess of Hyde, but Molly seemed to have taken particular pleasure in seating her next to the exact two men she could have no possible interest in.

Dutton, for all that she could see, was a pure waste of skin. Rakes, and he definitely was one, held no interest for her at all. Why, even if he'd managed to be a duke she would have been hard-pressed to talk herself into pursuing him. Thank goodness there was no need. Dutton was not a duke, but he was her dinner companion, which meant she could not politely ignore him, as was her usual practice.

Ruan, on the other hand, was one of the best uses of skin and bone and muscle that she had seen in many years, and because of that, he was most dangerous to her resolve. Ruan was not a duke, but what Ruan *was* created problems. He was worldly, experienced, and handsome in an unfashionably rugged fashion. Ruan, truth be told, was a little bit frightening. The fact that Ruan was merely being polite to her and showed no special interest in her at all helped matters some, but only some.

But the worst aspect of her place at table, between two of the ton's most famous men of unmarried status, was that Aunt Mary was seated on the other side of Ruan, which clearly put her too close to Amelia. Louisa, mysteriously absent now for more than a few minutes, could evade Mary to some degree to pursue her amorous interests, but as Louisa's amorous interests were rigidly defined within the person of the Marquis of Dutton and not Mr. George Grey or the Marquis of Penrith, she didn't suppose not having to deal with Mary meant a thing to Louisa.

It shouldn't have meant anything to Amelia. After all, she was after a duke, and the closest duke to her at this precise moment was the Duke of Edenham, seated approximately fifteen people down from her and *across*, so there was no possibility of making any headway with him, not that she was certain she wanted to. Edenham was just the tiniest bit frightening, given his personal history. If at all possible, she'd prefer Iveston, or even Calbourne.

Though, at this point, after two Seasons out, she didn't suppose she could be very choosy. It was something of a miracle that there were three dukes or almost dukes available at once and one shouldn't, and she never did, look a gift horse in the mouth.

Though where the gift horse was, she couldn't quite determine.

At the moment, her problem was Aunt Mary, for even though she did not want to encourage an alliance with either Ruan or Dutton, she also did not want Aunt Mary to embarrass her. Mary was very close, *very* close, to doing so.

Aunt Mary, for as often and as deeply as she drank, was foxed. Completely foxed, as opposed to nearly foxed or almost foxed or on her way to being foxed, all of which were her usual states. Completely foxed was something of a novelty, and Mary could not have chosen a more inconvenient time to toy with her degrees of drunkenness.

Amelia had worked and planned and schemed, in the most ladylike ways possible, naturally, to achieve this invitation for more than two years, ever since she'd been made aware that Iveston's birthday was celebrated in this fashion, and she couldn't, she simply *couldn't* allow Mary to ruin everything now.

Penrith, observing from across the table, seemed distantly amused. George Grey had noted Mary's slumped form and slurred words and then proceeded to ignore everything but the doorway through which Louisa had passed minutes ago.

Which, truly, did strike Amelia as more than peculiar. Of what interest could Louisa have for him? Had he just not met her only this very day? And was he not a stranger of sorts to London and all of London Society? What had Louisa *done* to the man to arouse his rather intense interest in just a few minutes of conversation?

Whatever it was, she'd like to copy it to the exact detail and use it in her next brush with Iveston. Or Calbourne. Or, if matters grew truly desperate, Edenham.

She did so hope that matters did not grow desperate.

She also, rather forlornly, it must be added, wondered if matters were not already desperate.

"Matters are not so desperate," Ruan said softly, causing her to jolt out of her thoughts and stare at him rather more closely than was proper. How had he known what she was thinking? "The wine is likely stronger than she expected and has caught her by the heels."

Oh. He was speaking of Mary. Well, that was better, although not really.

It was at that particular moment, one could almost say, poetically ironic moment, that Mary signaled the footman to pull back her chair and in raising her hand, knocked her cap askew.

"Shoddy service, at best," Mary grumbled none too softly, apparently drawing the conclusion that a footman had knocked her cap. It would have been preferable, that was certainly true. "I'm not," Mary continued, trying to stand before the chair had been fully removed and banging her knees against the wood, which caused her to topple forward, which naturally necessitated that she brace her hands on the table. As they were eating soup at the time, it sloshed over the rim of Mary's bowl, as well as Lord Penrith's. Mr. Grey saved his soup by simply lifting his bowl mere seconds before Mary made contact with the table.

It was an impressive bit of timing and speed, which she supposed the Indians of the Americas were rather known for.

"I'd say she is," Dutton said in dry humor, finishing Mary's unfinished pronouncement. "Definitely and completely."

Ruan merely smiled and watched Amelia, which was not at all helpful.

"I'm not," Mary said again, even more forcefully and this time fully on her feet so that she could scan the table and see everyone. And everyone could see her.

Small wonder that Amelia had such trouble in snaring a duke with help of this sort.

"At *all*," Mary said, her voice rising in tune with her temper, "tolerant of this, your grace." Upon which, naturally, every duke in the room, including and most specifically the Duke of Hyde, stopped eating to stare at Mary. "Lady Louisa is gone missing. Lord Henry is gone missing. I insist that she be found. This is not at all regular, not regular at all."

And, of course it wasn't, but did making public statements about it help anyone at all?

Being sober, Amelia thought the answer obvious. Unfortunately, Mary was not sober. It was at times like these, when everyone at the large table, a table that sat sixty-four comfortably, stared at Amelia, obviously seeking signs of the same disposition or deportment in the girl that was so prominently displayed in the girl's chaperone, when Amelia felt the need of a good, strong drink.

Naturally, she said nothing of the sort, but merely kept a pleasant, proper, polite, slightly perplexed look on her face.

It was a brilliant bit of execution on her part and it was only spoiled by the fact that the Marquis of Ruan, still smiling, slid her drink closer to her.

⟨∞⟩

SOPHIA, almost twenty-five seats down from Mary, Lady Jordan, took a sip of her drink and smiled behind the rim of her glass. Where would the world be without chaperones?

"I do think she has a point," Sophia said in the general direction of both Robert Blakesley and George Blakesley, the second and third sons of Hyde.

Sophia was seated, providentially, right next to Henry Blakesley, Hyde's fourth son, and as his seat was currently and unmistakably empty, it made such obvious sense for her to cast her eyes in that direction and look with concern at Lord Henry's brothers. That Edenham was sitting in the same general vicinity and grinned at her comment she promptly ignored. Edenham had no part in this evening's entertainment, not at present, anyway.

"Do you?" snarled the Earl of Westlin, who was one of Sophia's most entertaining enemies and, by spectacular good fortune, her daughter's new father-in-law. They were now related. It was wonderful, for now, as family, she could torment Westlin until the day he died. Such fun.

It was somewhat unfortunate that Westlin had been seated across from her at dinner, but that he was five seats down made it more than bearable. He could see her, hear her, but was dissuaded from speaking to her. Perfection itself.

"But of course I do," Sophia said sweetly, which caused Westlin to frown in what he surely hoped was dreadful intimidation. Sophia laughed. "We can't have young, vibrant, unmarried people wandering about, can we, Lord Westlin? Surely such behavior among Britain's finest would lead to ruination?"

"You hope," he snarled, again.

Really, he was so limited in his forms of disapproval. She would have to see if she could help him improve on that. Westlin was a never-ending source of fun, made all the more amusing as he could not see it at all. Well, then, so few people saw themselves with any clarity at all, which made them even more amusing as a rule.

"Of course I hope," she said. "I hope we find them and that they have not got themselves into any mischief, though in such a well-run house as this, I hardly need worry."

A house with five unmarried sons in it. Was any house of that sort well-run?

Upon which the two Blakesleys closest to her stood as one, to be followed only slightly less closely by the youngest of the Blakesley brood, one Josiah Blakesley, who happened to be a particular and not altogether well-intentioned friend of Markham's. It was Josiah and Markham's poor luck that they had been dragged back from a frolic in Paris just the week before by John and his three sons. It was hardly to be expected that Josiah would cherish a friendship with George Grey, who he naturally saw as something of a jailor, though

Sophia was certain that would pass in time, not that it mattered in any regard. Men must be managed, that was all there was to it, and if they pulled against the restraints, then it was merely a question of providing them with the proper training.

She had absolutely no qualms about delivering the proper training. It made them so much better in the end, and really, shouldn't they be pleased at being improved?

Molly, Duchess of Hyde, looked about her as her sons rose and left the room as discreetly as possible, which was hardly discreet at all, gave her husband a particularly quelling glance, tried to proceed as if Iveston's celebration had not been so oddly interrupted, but was then made to watch as Iveston got up and left, to be swiftly followed by George Grey and, then, an odd smile on his face, Penrith.

It was as close to pandemonium as these evenings ever got before midnight after that. Dutton rose, almost knocking over his chair and the footman behind it, leaving by the main doorway back into the blue reception room. One would almost think he didn't want to find Louisa as anyone who'd been paying attention knew that she'd left the red reception room by the doorway into the yellow drawing room. And, if Sophia was not mistaken, and she never was in these sorts of situations, she'd heard the rather distinctive sound of a body being knocked against a door.

And anyone with any experience knew what that particular sound meant.

And she was definitely a woman with experience of that particular sort.

So it was, as the party split roughly in half to look for Louisa and Henry, that Sophia grinned and casually followed the crowd.

It was turning into such an entertaining and memorable evening, quite exactly as she'd expected.

Fourteen

BLAKES was quite a superb kisser. Not that Louisa had anyone to compare him to, but he certainly seemed to know what he was doing.

She wasn't, however, at all certain anymore that she knew what *she* was doing.

Whatever reason she had had for kissing him in the first place, if she had even taken the time to think of a reason, was lost now in the pure sensation of kissing him and of being kissed by him.

He was very, very good at it.

One would think that he'd be more insistent upon displaying his talent, but, oddly, Blakes kept pulling away from her, lifting his head, pushing her hands away from his monstrously thick waistcoat, to say the most extraordinarily meaningless things.

"If we're found, you shall be ruined," he said, and not for the first time.

He was holding her hands clasped within his fists, rather like warm shackles. It wasn't at all annoying, though she did like it better when she could touch him, her hands very modestly on his shoulders or around his neck. Well, fairly modestly, anyway.

"We shall be required to marry," he said, just before he brushed a kiss over her cheek.

"I've told you and told you, Blakes," she said, turning her mouth toward his, wanting to be done with this silly cheek-kissing business and on to the full effect of his mouth firmly pressed upon hers, "we shan't be found. I shall not be ruined."

"Yes, 'tis I who is being ruined," he breathed against her skin, his mouth whispering down her face to her throat, pressing itself against the top of her shoulder. She was *so* delighted to have worn a gown that presented her shoulders so flagrantly. "I believe you, I think. You have ruined me, Louisa. What do you intend to do about it?"

She giggled softly against his skin, her mouth brushing against his ear, and he responded by pressing his body against hers lightly, teasing her with its weight. She wanted his weight against her, that was the odd bit; she wanted to feel him press her down, her hips to his. Most peculiar, but there it was.

When one succumbed to instinct, one was left where instinct led.

Not at all reassuring, that, but as to being ruined, Blakes would never allow it. He was a very stubborn sort, consider only that he wouldn't let her touch him and would only allow their kisses to be of the briefest variety.

She happened to know that kisses could be quite lengthy affairs as she had once seen her father, the annoying Melverley, kiss one of his mistresses in the Theatre Royal for upwards of three minutes running. It had been most illuminating and, obviously, most disgusting.

"I intend to continue on, ruining you as best I may," she said. "Now, kindly kiss me, Blakes, I need the practice."

"Hardly that," he said, pulling away from her completely, even to the releasing of her hands from his.

Stubborn *and* contrary. She should have said nothing and let him think of it on his own, because surely he would have. He did seem to enjoy kissing her, which was only to be expected. She had decided in the last few minutes that she was imminently kissable and that it was a stellar quality to possess.

"You must go back in. You cannot stay so long away. Your absence will be missed. Is being missed," he added, his head cocked abruptly, listening.

There did seem to be some sort of commotion going on behind the door. Likely some footman had spilled the soup. It didn't concern them, here, in the flickering light, his mouth so tantalizingly close to hers.

Blakes took another step away from her and then another.

"It's just dinner being served," she said, stalking him greedily. She had to admit that Blakes was imminently kissable, too. How very convenient for her that he was so very available.

The noise spread and grew louder until it became, even to Louisa, a certain fact that they were being very quickly surrounded from behind the still closed doors to the yellow drawing room. There was no telling how long those doors would remain closed, and there was no being caught alone in the yellow drawing room. For all her jests about being ruined, it was a very real concern and she was very determined not to allow it.

It was so very unfortunate that she could think of no way to avoid it.

"*Do* something!" she snapped, backing away from Blakesley like a cornered rat.

"What did you have in mind?" he said sharply, just before he grabbed her hand and dragged her very willing body across the length of the yellow drawing room and into the Hyde dressing room and firmly closed the door behind them. The very same door of the very same dressing room where, not a week past, Lady Caroline and the Marquis of Ashdon had been caught in what was rumored to be a severely compromising situation, and what was in fact compromising enough to require them to marry the very next morning.

It did not escape Louisa's notice that Blakes had played some small part in that escapade, pearls, girl, dressing room, and all.

She turned a withering eye upon Blakesley and snapped under her breath, "What is it with you and this room?"

"What is it with you and kissing men with pearl necklaces?" he snapped back.

Well. That was uncalled for, certainly.

Stubborn, contrary, and *rude.*

"You are the only man I've ever kissed, pearls or not. And, by the way, when do I get my pearls back?"

"Is that why you kissed me? To get your pearls?"

"Whyever else?" she hissed, as furious with him now as she had been doe-eyed just moments before. Men were so contrary, causing her to change her opinion of him in the blink of an eye. Inconstant creatures, sowing inconstancy wherever they went and upon whomever they touched. "You certainly can't think that I would kiss you for no reason. I do have morals, after all."

"Yes, the sort of morals that allow you to kiss a man ardently and quite insistently, I might add, just for the reward of a pearl necklace. Nice, Louisa, very nice."

"You certainly can't be implying that I'd kiss a man without the promise of something as extraordinary as a pearl necklace! I'm hardly cheap, Lord Henry. Besides, it was to win a wager and regain ownership of *my* pearls! Certainly that lends the whole escapade, foolish as it was, I see now so clearly, a certain nobility of purpose."

"Only in your twisted little mind, Louisa," Blakesley snarled.

Twisted, mind you! The man was a monster, as changeable as a weather vane. He certainly had had no higher cause to kiss *her.*

Unless . . . had that been part of his wager at White's? To compromise the skittish Lady Louisa? For she was skittish with all men, her heart being so firmly set on Lord Dutton.

Oh, yes, Lord Dutton. Was he out there with the rest of the

rabble, looking for her? And if he found her with Lord Henry, what might that lead to?

Whatever it was, she wasn't certain it would help her and so she couldn't risk it.

"Thank you for . . . practicing with me, Lord Henry," she said with as much dignity as she could muster, which was considerable, considering that they were hiding in an unlit room in the middle of a ducal dinner. "I'm certain I shall use all you taught me to good purpose when I marry."

She waited for him to snap at her, some tight response that would attempt, unsuccessfully, to put her in her place, which was exalted.

He remained silent, but it wasn't the comforting silence of a dark and cozy room. Hardly. It was the complete silence of motion just before the striking of a snake.

Horrid man to try and jangle her nerves even more than they already were. The noise of the party seemed to surround them, ready to burst in upon them.

Blakesley did nothing.

At first.

She really should have just slapped him when she had the chance.

"You know better how the world works, Louisa," he said, his voice barely a whisper, yet as sharp as March wind. "You've been alone with a man and you've been kissed by him. No one will marry you now, unless it is I."

"No one will know," she said stiffly. She *hated* it when Blakesley got like this, so sure of himself and so supremely sure of her.

"Everyone will know and not because I will tell them. You look like a woman who's been kissed and kissed hard. Did you think it would not show? Did you think I could touch you and not leave my mark on you?"

"That sounds almost medieval," she snapped, lifting her hands to straighten her gown and check her hair. All seemed to be perfectly in order, if one discounted the condition of her curls, which felt more than a little . . . fuzzy.

"Does it?" he said, and she could hear the smile in his voice. Monster. "I suppose it does, yet it is true."

"I hardly think I should take your word for it," she said, forcing her voice to a matching whisper. The voices all around them were quite close now and it was not at all amusing or pleasant to contemplate being found in such a compromising situation, even if it was with Blakesley.

Surely, no one would imagine that she had surrendered to a few innocent kisses from Blakesley?

Of course, she hadn't actually surrendered so much as she'd attacked and the kisses hadn't been exactly innocent. Not if she were any judge of innocence, which she might not actually be any longer. *Oh, dear.*

Whyever had she thrown herself in the way of Blakesley's arms?

He clearly wondered the same thing for he said, "Why did you kiss me, Louisa? Why me?"

She didn't know what to say, so she was left with having to say the truth, bitter thing that it was.

"I don't know exactly, Blakes," she said softly. "Perhaps because I felt . . . safe with you."

Blakesley laughed once, a harsh, short bark of laughter, and said, "Ever safe, ever constant Blakes," he said. "I am not safe, Louisa. I am a man, like any other."

It was at that precise moment, a moment of raw reflection and confession, that the door from the drawing room into the dressing room swung open and Lord Dutton, of all people, stood with a throng of elegantly clad people at his back, throwing candlelight all over Louisa and Blakes and leaving them not one particle of comforting darkness to hide within.

It might have been the first moment that Louisa actually found herself more than slightly annoyed with Dutton. Certainly, and this was for the first time, his arrival was unwelcome.

Dutton's magnificent eyes went from one of them to the other, his very elegant mouth opened in slack-jawed surprise. Blakesley's many brothers pushed in behind him, scowling, and Sophia Dalby and Molly Hyde pushed in behind *them*. It really was most crowded and most, most humiliating.

"What are you doing in here?" Dutton asked.

"Hiding," Blakesley answered cordially, standing next to Louisa and taking her arm in his as if they were walking in to tea.

"What were you doing before that?" Iveston asked pleasantly, though curiously. Though, to judge by the gleam in his pale blue eyes, his curiosity may have been put on to please his mother, who looked anything but amused.

"Kissing," Blakesley said, again, oh so reasonably.

Upon which Dutton's gaze swung like a dagger to Louisa, who, having faced Melverley more than once since leaving the nursery, was up to the challenge. Oh, his look hurt her, but she was not going to give him the satisfaction of knowing it. She raised her chin and faced them all, including Molly. Molly's gunmetal gaze returned fire without so much as blinking.

Louisa dropped her gaze to the floor, but not before letting her glance slide over Sophia, who was smiling sociably at her.

"Molly," Sophia said sweetly, "I do believe you have the most scandalous dressing room in London. I simply must learn your secret."

Fifteen

IT seemed that the Marquis of Dutton could not quite believe it. Well, they made a good pair in that, at least, for Louisa could not quite believe it herself.

One would think that the party would have broken up, that, suffering from embarrassment of the worst sort, people would have scattered to the streets or at the very least, back to the dinner table.

That is not at all what happened because, after all, this was the very cream of London Society and they, more than any other class, loved a good scandal. The proceedings, for that is exactly what it amounted to, some special ton brand of social justice, took place in the Duke of Hyde's music room, which, as it was adjacent to the blue reception room, meant that every person who had no cause to be in the music room had their ears, shoulders, and noses pressed against the closed door in blatant and hilarious curiosity.

Louisa knew this to be so because it had happened in exactly the same fashion when Caroline Trevelyan, not a week ago, had disgraced herself and been ruined first in the Hydes' yellow drawing room and then in the Hydes' dressing room. Louisa had, without qualm, been one of those many with her ear pressed to the door as negotiations were made.

That the setting for her ruination was the same as Caroline's, and that Sophia had been an active and present force in both, was beyond coincidence.

Louisa knew that Sophia had a hand in her being ruined, she just *knew* it; unfortunately, she could not prove it. Also unfortunately, it wouldn't help her now if she could prove it. She was ruined, and she would have to marry Blakes.

As to that, Blakes didn't look entirely pleased by the prospect, which was completely absurd as he had most definitely been pleased by the prospect of kissing her. She wasn't a complete dolt. She knew what that particular bulge in his breeches meant and it was a bulge that had been most definitely pointing in her direction.

In fact, it still was.

"His feelings for you are more than a little obvious, are they not?" Sophia said quietly into the general noise of the room. "It's rather adorable, isn't it, how men just can't seem to hide their attraction to a particular woman? Of course, the current state of men's fashion does help so much in that regard. How else is a woman to know if her gown is of the right cut or her hair of the desired style? Men are so helpful in judging things of that sort, aren't they?"

"Exactly why are you here, Lady Dalby?" Louisa answered, avoiding the subject entirely, though she could not help it if her gaze went immediately to the appropriate, or inappropriate, region of every man in the room's breeches.

Dutton's line was, as ever, unmoved. Now that she was ruined, she supposed she could admit to having studied that particular area whenever the opportunity arose, that is, whenever she was in the same room with him.

Dutton was depressingly consistent in his lack of response and the maintenance of the perfect line of his leg.

Now that she was ruined, she looked around the music room and saw that not only was Blakesley's tailoring being put to the test, but also that of Mr. Grey, who had not relinquished his habit of staring at her whenever possible. And it always seemed to be possible.

George Grey was in the room because Sophia had sweetly reminded Hyde that George was her escort for the evening, which made no sense at all, but which Hyde had accepted.

Sophia was in the room as the direct result of Molly insisting she needed feminine support in this hour of her trial, the trial being obviously the inclusion of Louisa into her family.

Amelia was in the room because Aunt Mary was in the room, and Aunt Mary said that, conditions at the house being what they clearly were, she was not going to leave her unchaperoned niece to the clearly careless structure of Hyde House. Aunt Mary was still deeply in her cups and, horrifyingly, was determined to make things even worse than they currently were.

If that were possible.

Of course, Blakes was present, as well as all his brothers.

Naturally, that provided some small measure of delight for Amelia as she could now appear virtuous and concerned in regards to and compared to her ruined cousin. Amelia, Louisa noted cynically, looked delightfully fresh and innocent and spectacularly virginal.

Louisa had chanced a quick look in a mirror on her way to the music room and had been shocked to discover that she did not look fresh, innocent, or especially virginal. Her hair was tumbled and tossed, her mouth swollen and red, and her dress rumpled. The only thing she could say on her behalf, not that anyone cared to listen to her, was that *she* had not been tumbled and *she* had not been tossed. It didn't appear to matter, details of that sort. She was still a virgin, but that apparently was far from sufficient.

Blakesley had been right, though due to the crowd surrounding them and separating them, he didn't have the chance to say so. He did, however, choose that exact moment to lift his eyebrows in a sort of superior smirk.

"Lord Henry seems quite delighted by this turn of events," Sophia said. "And so he should be."

Louisa could only stare at her in dumb disbelief.

"He has managed things so well," Sophia continued, "as it has been perfectly obvious to me that he has been quite completely enamored of you for at least a year and likely two, though as Caroline was at a particularly difficult stage two years past I am not at all confident of my powers of observation during that particular Season. Still, he is a most attractive man and has quite a nice estate in Wessex, I believe?"

"Essex," Louisa supplied, still in a droopy state of what she assumed was shock.

"Ah, Essex, but am I not correct in that he has twenty thousand a year?"

Louisa was not going to be so crass as to discuss Blakeley's worth with Sophia, or to admit that she knew to the pound how much Blakesley was worth. Surely, those were the habits of a courtesan that Sophia had been unable or unwilling to discard on her marriage to Dalby.

But it was twenty-three thousand a year, not twenty thousand.

"I'm afraid he has not discussed that with me," Louisa said, which was the entire truth and had the added benefit of being evasive. "He also never indicated to me any sort of . . . feeling."

Upon which, Sophia chuckled, which drew the express attention of all the Blakesley brothers, including Iveston, who showed . . . stirrings . . . below their waistcoats.

This being ruined did open the door upon all sorts of observations and conversations. Certainly, Sophia would not be talking to her as she was now if her situation in Society had not changed drastically.

She could only wonder how Melverley would take the news. She hoped it killed him. Slowly.

"But, darling, of course he did," Sophia said lightly, drawing Louisa off slightly behind the harp. "How else is a man of this town, this country, this century, to show you his regard if not to accompany you in your pursuit of another man of his acquaintance?"

Louisa could feel herself blushing. Of course, there was that. She had suspected something, but not perhaps exactly this. Perhaps because it would have been a most inconvenient deduction, and she was all about doing what was most convenient for her. Certainly it had been convenient to have Blakesley's help in determining Dutton's next appearance. And certainly, she had never wanted to puzzle out his reasons for doing so.

Because she was not a fool and because she would have seen the truth for what it was and then, because honor was not altogether absent in her, she would have been required to stop.

Since none of that was an option that particularly appealed, she had not bothered to think of it at all. Life was so often more comfortable under those particular terms. She ought to know as she made something of a habit of it, which Eleanor was so quick to point out at every possible opportunity. Imp.

"Naturally, it was different in my day," Sophia went on, apparently completely unconcerned that she had launched into a soliloquy for a very unreceptive audience. "And, as you know, in my country. We are more direct there and, in that earlier, earthier generation, more . . . oh, perhaps the best word is *forceful.* Yes, forceful and direct, with none of this soft stepping and 'by your leave' which is so common today. Why, if Blakesley wanted you, why not—"

"Simply grab me up and cart me off through the forest?" Louisa interrupted, angry on behalf of Blakes, her country, and her entire generation.

"Well," Sophia said, smiling, "yes. Why not?"

"Because he is a gentleman!"

"Darling, that gentleman ruined you."

"No, Lady Dalby, I ruined him! 'Twas I who kissed him! Soundly and often."

At which point, because Louisa was arguing rather more loudly than she had intended, in fact because she had not intended to argue at all, the entire room turned to look at her. Dutton included, though why Dutton was in the room she had not yet puzzled out.

Into the startled silence that followed, all eyes eventually and almost poetically turned to consider Blakesley, who shrugged slightly and said evenly, "It's true. She kissed me. Soundly and often."

Upon which, Dutton looked suspiciously close to fainting, which she couldn't understand at all.

"Well done, Louisa," Sophia said into the pall that had settled upon them all. "It's so nice to see that someone in this day and age has the fortitude to fight for what she wants."

By which she must have meant that Louisa had wanted Blakes, which was completely absurd as she had wanted Dutton completely, exclusively, and in the face of all opposition, though her only opposition had been Dutton's rather marked lack of interest in her.

"Who's going to tell Melverley?" Molly said, still staring with extreme dislike at Louisa. Louisa, happily, was becoming immune to it.

"Oh, let me," Sophia said, stepping forward.

"No, allow me," Blakesley said. "I think you've done enough this evening, Lady Dalby." And he had the oddest expression on his face, not exactly displeased, but entirely suspicious.

"Have I?" Sophia said lightly. "I hardly noticed having done a thing. I think you must take the credit for this, Lord Henry."

"I thought we had determined that Lady Louisa was entirely responsible for this particular state of affairs," Molly said grimly.

Louisa was not at all certain she was going to enjoy having Molly Hyde for a mother-in-law.

"I did help," Blakes said in wry humor, upon which his brothers all laughed in that particular way men had of laughing at something completely unseemly, if not to say improper. She'd heard Melverley laugh in that fashion all her life. She had yet to develop an appreciation for it.

"I'm quite certain you did," Sophia said softly. "In fact, I'm not at all sure you didn't manage this all quite beautifully, Lord Henry, to get exactly what you wanted."

"I beg your pardon?" Molly said stiffly, to be swiftly followed by the Duke of Hyde saying, "What's that?"

Sophia shrugged delicately. "I am surely not the only person in Town to have noticed that Lord Henry has exhibited a certain fascination for Lady Louisa."

"I certainly have," Dutton said. "It's surely been too obvious to miss, even to the casual observer and none here can claim to be casual."

Upon which everyone in the room turned to stare at Lord Dutton, the sons of Hyde with the most unfriendly expressions upon their various faces. Well, it was to be expected. It was surely a point of honor that their brother not be seen to be a fool for love, which is exactly how Dutton had made him appear.

Of course, Louisa had not seen it, she most expressly had not seen it. She was so very good at not seeing those particular, uncomfortable things that she did not care to see. But this observation, made so publicly, did not put Blakes in at all a good light, and she simply could not allow it to stand. She was to be married to him, after all, and no husband of hers was going to be the subject of ridicule. No, the thing to do was to rescue Blakesley's reputation as it was in the very act of being destroyed by Lord Dutton and to do it immediately.

Let no one say from this point on that she was not going to be a good wife to Blakes. This act of personal heroism ought to silence any possible remarks on that immediately.

Louisa looked at Molly.

Molly looked right back at her.

"I certainly noticed no such thing," Louisa said. "Lord Henry has been nothing but kind to me, above reproach in all his dealings and in every conversation. He has been, and continues to be, a perfect gentleman."

"*I* certainly have no doubt of it," Molly said the moment Louisa finished speaking, which, of course, once again implied that Louisa was entirely at fault for the entire kissing adventure.

Which, actually, might have been true, but she didn't care for it to be put forth so publicly. Things of this sort had a life of their own and she was not entirely certain that the echo of this night would not be ringing still when her own daughters made their entrance into Society, and then what was she to tell them? That she'd married their father because she'd cornered him in the yellow drawing room and kissed him senseless?

No, that would never do.

"Now, Molly," Sophia said soothingly, "mothers simply don't notice such things about their sons, nor should they, as a rule."

Because, of course, no one would ever believe that Sophia Dalby did not pay particular attention to the smallest detail regarding her own son, the Earl of Dalby. He was a man, wasn't he? Sophia Dalby, as everyone knew, was something of an expert on men, though she hadn't proved very helpful to Louisa in reacquiring her pearls. Blakes had done far more for her on that score.

Louisa would likely end up married to the wrong man, that man being anyone not Dutton, but she would at least get her pearls back. If Blakes was correct about the particulars of the intemperate wager at White's. She never had quite got the gist of that.

"It's neither here nor there," Hyde said. "The deed is done. Melverley must be told of events as they stand. There is only one solution to this situation, no matter how it was arrived at. The girl is ruined. They must marry."

"There is another way," Mr. Grey said from a shadowed corner of the room.

Everyone turned in blank surprise for, it must be admitted, they had completely forgotten that he was even there. What part, aside from being Sophia's nephew, could he possibly have to play?

"You have something to say, sir?" Hyde asked, not unreasonably, which was more than a little insulting as it could not help but be noticed that Blakesley's family was not at all excited by the prospect of his marriage to her.

Which was completely preposterous. She was a marquis's daughter, wasn't she? Even if that marquis happened to be Melverley, that was not her fault, was it?

"I do," Grey answered softly, his dark form almost melting into the shadows, his twinkling black eyes the only part of him that moved at all. It was most disconcerting. "I want her. I have reason to think she wants me. I'll take her. Happy to."

And, naturally, everyone in the room turned to stare at her in terms varying from shock to grim satisfaction, grim satisfaction being obviously authored by Molly.

"*What* reason?" Blakesley snarled, looking at her and not at Grey. Well, *really*. It was turning into one of the most insulting evenings she'd ever endured.

"I'm a gentleman, too," Grey merely said, his mouth not even breaking the smallest smile to show that he was jesting. The man was a savage, truly, to savage her reputation so and on no foundation whatsoever.

"Darling," Sophia said to her in a voice just loud enough to be heard by all, even if she gave the appearance of whispering, "you certainly are a woman of rare qualities. I'm almost ashamed to admit that I had no idea of your . . . scope."

If it wasn't the final nail, it was a near thing.

"Have you kissed him, as well?" Sophia asked, smiling cheerfully, which clearly was the cruelest thing she could have done.

"Of course not!" Louisa said sharply, looking about the room for an ally.

She had none.

"Has she?" Molly asked Grey.

Mr. Grey merely smiled and kept his silence.

It was too, too much. Even Amelia and Aunt Mary were silent at this, for how could Amelia risk offending her possible future mother-in-law by aligning herself with Louisa? And how could Aunt Mary defend her charge when she was sleeping in a drunken sprawl on the corner of a smallish settee?

"If she's been ruined before now, I don't see why Blakes should have to shoulder it," George Blakesley said, his almond-shaped blue eyes narrowed in arrogant suspicion at her. She'd always liked George Blakesley, from a careful distance. He was Hyde's third son, blond like all of them, arrogant, as sons of dukes were wont to be, but pleasant enough.

He no longer seemed entirely pleasant.

"Well, there is that," Sophia said in a musing tone, as if discussing the merits of a particular operatic soprano.

"Does *she* have to be here?" Louisa exploded, pointing at Sophia.

"I want her here," Molly said. "I believe this . . . situation, will eventually require witnesses outside of the family."

Which meant that she was considering possible legal consequences?

"I only have your best interests at heart, Lady Louisa," Sophia said pleasantly. "Please trust in that, if not in me."

Which made no sense whatsoever, but then, nothing had made sense since she'd knocked on Sophia's door earlier in the day. What a horrible impulse that had been, born in a desperate attempt to get Dutton once and for all, a determination born so long ago now that she wondered how it had happened at all. Certainly Dutton's behavior in this room had done nothing to endear him to her. That might have been impulse as well, her sudden and consuming passion for him born two years ago almost to the night. Of course, she had been following a blind impulse when she'd kissed Blakes just a few minutes ago and look where that had led.

Clearly, she was far too impulsive for her own good.

Although, just as clearly, she couldn't think how changing now would help her.

"I want her," Mr. Grey said again, entirely unnecessarily. He made her sound like a cut of beefsteak, and, from the looks she was getting from the entire Hyde family, the resemblance was entirely accurate. "I don't see why she should have to marry Lord Henry because of a kiss."

"It was more than a single kiss," Blakesley said, not helping matters at all, at least as far as her reputation was concerned.

"But if you didn't–" Grey said.

"I did," Blakes cut him off. "I did completely. It was mutual, take my word for it."

"I guess I'll have to," Grey said with the oddest trace of humor to his voice. Really, these Americans were so odd and had such strange notions of propriety and the correct forms of conversation. It really did explain so much about Sophia to know that she sprang from American, that is to say, Indian, roots.

"We have rules here," Blakesley said, "rules of deportment. We've kissed. We must marry or her reputation will be ruined."

"Seems like she can marry anyone now and save her reputation. I'd be glad to get her," Mr. Grey said. "And I wouldn't need to be forced to take her," he added, staring meaningfully at Blakes.

Beefsteak.

Blakesley looked ready to pounce upon Mr. Grey, which was most kind of him and most chivalrous. Really, Blakesley had always been more considerate of her than any man she had ever known.

Of course, that wasn't saying much.

"Actually, Blakes," Robert Blakesley said, "you should consider it. It's a fair offer. More than fair."

Robert Blakesley, Hyde's second son and better known as

Cranleigh, had always slightly alarmed Louisa. He was blond, but barely, and his eyes were a glacial shade of blue, which somehow conveyed the impression that he would as soon spit in the king's eye as bow to him. He had the rather pugnacious look of his mother, a thoroughly American look, now that she thought about it, and one which did nothing at all to charm her. Though that may have been more because of her increased exposure to Molly than to anything to do with Cranleigh. She was, understandably, disinclined to ferret it out. It was enough that the whole of Blakesley's brothers seemed more than willing to have done with her.

"No," Blakes said, staring at Louisa as if she were the cause of the disturbance.

Which she was, but not in the drift of the current conversation.

"Really, this is so surprising," Sophia said almost gaily, "and such a strange turn. But, of course, perhaps it should be considered. It is so terribly tiresome to find oneself trapped into marriage. In that, I couldn't possibly agree with George more. He is absolutely right; a woman must choose. It is, however strange a notion here, completely ordinary in America and particularly among the Iroquois, which, of course, is all that George cares about at the moment. And who can blame him? Lady Louisa is quite a remarkable woman and any man of any sense would be delighted to . . . please excuse my phrasing . . . be delighted to have her. Isn't that so, George?"

"Yes," George said, without any trace of embarrassment at all. It was passing peculiar.

Yet, strangely appealing.

Perhaps there were some particulars of the American Indian culture that warranted closer inspection.

"But if we are to consider that, and as it was only a kiss or two, and as Lord Henry and Lady Louisa certainly had no marked regard for each other before tonight, perhaps it would be wise to contemplate other . . . options. That is to say, men," Sophia said in the most reasonable manner imaginable. Of course, what she was positing was not reasonable in the least. Consider other men? Now? It was beyond propriety.

Then again, kissing Blakes in the yellow drawing room and being caught with him in the dressing room had been beyond propriety as well.

Did it matter now if propriety's walls were breached?

Louisa looked at Sophia more closely than she had yet done, her own manner more curious than annoyed. She was surprised to see that Sophia was returning her look with one that could only be described as encouraging.

Louisa, against all inclination and training, held her tongue.

"As I said," Blakes snarled, "it was more than a kiss or two and I was hardly a disinterested party."

"Yet not the instigator," Sophia said sweetly. "Surely some leeway must be given you, Lord Henry. It was not your fault, was it? Should you be required to pay the fee? Hardly fair, in any culture."

"Listen to her, Blakes," Josiah Blakesley said, younger than Blakes by a year or two. "There's something to be said for it. And, don't forget that you're half American. Could be a loophole for us, if managed well."

"Josiah," the Duke of Hyde said stiffly, "hold your tongue. That is hardly to the point." But he did not, it should be noted, tell Sophia to keep her ideas to herself. Oh, no, on the contrary, Hyde sat himself down in the best chair in the room, crossed his well-clad legs, and said, "I'm sorry you were interrupted, Lady Dalby. You were saying?"

Lovely. It was so nice to be wanted.

"Of course, no one in this room would dream of maligning your virility, Lord Henry," Sophia said.

Louisa thought she might have seen Lord Dutton twitch slightly, some strange motion having to do with his mouth perhaps, but she wasn't certain and she didn't care to be certain. For the first time in two years, Louisa was not particularly concerned with what Lord Dutton was or was not doing. It was, to be blunt, something of a relief.

"In the interest of fair play, I merely," Sophia said, "thought it prudent to point out that I'm almost certain that there are options, that is to say, *men*, who have not yet been considered."

Louisa looked over at Amelia, who was sitting stock-still on the other end of the same smallish settee that held the snoring Aunt Mary. Amelia was sitting bolt upright and almost quivering with suppressed animation. Louisa knew the feeling well. They exchanged a look of shocked anticipation and, like wise women who saw clearly which hand held the winning cards, kept still. Sophia Dalby was many things, but not a one of them was stupid.

"This is absurd," Blakesley said, starting to prowl the room like a tiger on a frayed leash. "I'm going to marry her. She's ruined and I'm responsible."

"How gallant of you," Sophia drawled, "and how beautifully typical of you, Lord Henry. I have never known you to behave otherwise. But, shall we not consider Lady Louisa?"

"That's what I'm doing!" Blakesley barked.

"What I mean is," Sophia said in soothing tones, smiling calmly at Blakesley, "shall we not consider what would best serve Lady Louisa? By which I mean that she marry a man who truly wants her and who has expressed, before this unfortunate event, an interest in marrying her?"

"Who would that be?" Lord Dutton said, inserting himself into a debate in which he had not the smallest part.

It was also a question rife with insult and Louisa, for perhaps the first time, understood it as such. Lord Dutton, it appeared, could be rather insultingly rude. How unbecoming in a man who was so spectacularly beguiling in all other ways.

"Besides me, you mean?" Mr. Grey said dangerously, which had quite an odd effect on Lord Dutton. It was something to see, certainly, and she could admit that she'd never thought it possible, but Lord Dutton looked almost . . . nervous. It was certainly true that he couldn't quite seem to face Mr. Grey directly.

Well, she did not suppose Dutton should be faulted for that. Mr. Grey, even dressed in fine English wool, looked completely savage and entirely unpredictable.

"Of course, besides you, darling," Sophia answered for him, which was required as it was not entirely certain whether Dutton would have been able to answer for himself. "We are all aware of your feelings and, indeed, your intentions regarding the lovely Lady Louisa, and certainly you are to be credited with having flaw-less taste."

And here Sophia smiled indulgently and somewhat proudly at her nephew. As far as being received into a family, it was a far sight better than what the Blakesleys of Hyde House had proffered. Louisa, quite aware she was doing so, made a note of it.

There might be worse things than being married to an Indian; he was related to an earl of the realm, after all. A girl could do worse.

Why her gaze shifted to Dutton, she had no idea, but shift it did.

"Go on," Molly said. "You think there are others who might of-fer for her? Saving her from public ruin?"

"Well, I do think that cat is out of the bag," Sophia said with a shrug, "but, in the right circumstances, a woman's name being on everyone's lips is to her credit. I think this case will prove it to be so, especially as the lady has multiple offers. You are still in, Lord Henry?"

"Of course," he snapped, "and it's not going to be a public auc-tion, Lady Dalby. I'm the one who ruined her. I'm the one who shall marry her."

"I do believe that is for Louisa to decide," Sophia said, "ruined or not. Is that not so, Lady Louisa?"

It was difficult to read the look that Sophia gave her in that moment of shattered protocol, but Louisa was aware of one thing and that one thing proved the only point of interest to her. She was being given power. She had never, not even in the smallest detail, had any power at all over her life. Certainly she had been powerless in snagging Dutton for two long years and, in just that instant, it seemed she'd had quite enough of that. They were ready to deliver her, practically bound and gagged, into Blakesley's not quite willing enough hands.

Well. Perhaps not.

Certainly, given her present state of ruination, there was very little that could hurt her more.

"Of course," she said, echoing Blakes. "I don't see why I shouldn't explore my options. Whom did you have in mind, Lady Dalby?" she asked politely.

"Blast it all, Louisa!" Blakes yelled.

The commotion outside the music room door dulled as the throng hushed itself to listen. Oh, well. She was already ruined. How much worse could it get?

"Blakes! Kindly remember yourself!" Molly said in clipped tones.

"Of course, we could discuss this privately, but I do think, in the spirit of fairness, that the gentlemen in the room who have expressed an interest in matrimony should like to be aware of their potential competition for your hand," Sophia said calmly, and one could plainly see, in that moment, how she had so successfully negotiated countless arrangements for herself with various protectors. The woman was coolheaded, straightforward, and unsentimental. Louisa was frankly delighted.

"Appreciate it," Mr. Grey said solemnly.

Blakes grunted some sort of rude remark under his breath and stalked to her side of the room to stand directly behind her chair. It was obviously meant to be intimidating. If Louisa felt any slight inclination to be intimidated, which she might have done, not that she was called upon to admit it, Sophia Dalby was clearly unimpressed. That gave Louisa courage. She stiffened her spine, secretly wondering if that would give Blakes a lovely view into the shadowy line of her cleavage, and waited. She was rewarded by hearing Blakes take a thin breath and move slightly back.

Louisa tried not to grin. She was not altogether successful.

"There is the Marquis of Penrith, obviously," Sophia said, adjusting an earring.

"Obviously?" Blakes snapped out. "She just met him!"

"Yes," Sophia agreed charmingly. "Isn't it lovely when a man knows exactly what he wants and acts with such firmness of purpose? Lord Penrith met Lady Louisa by merest chance today and already he has declared himself quite completely taken with her. I do think that he would have hoped for a longer period of acquaintance, but as he is a man fully in his majority, I don't think that this little hiccup will dissuade him from seeking her hand."

"And he confessed all this to you? Today?" Blakes insisted, clearly not believing that any man *could* find her so instantly and completely compelling, the sod.

"I *was* so bold as to ask him," Sophia admitted, "but, yes. He confessed it all most readily. One might even say *happily*. That surprises you, Lord Henry? How very . . . peculiar."

"Damned peculiar," Dutton muttered and slumped down in his chair. As it was a very delicate chair of feminine proportions, he didn't look at all comfortable. Louisa was flatly delighted.

"I beg your pardon, my lord?" Sophia said.

"Nothing," Dutton said in the merest undertone.

"You did something," Blakes said, staring hard at Sophia. Sophia didn't look alarmed in the least. "You arranged something with Penrith."

"I?" Sophia asked innocently, her sable brows raised in query. There was no hope for it; Sophia Dalby was capable of many things, but looking innocent was not one of them. "What an odd remark, Lord Henry. If you are looking for the cause of his interest, she sits right in front of you. Don't tell me that you've never noticed how lovely and how original Lady Louisa is. Penrith certainly had no trouble recognizing her particular charms."

Louisa felt herself flush with pleasure. She wasn't inclined to believe a word of it, but they were such very nice words. Being occasionally drowned in flattery just had to be beneficial. She felt better than she had in years.

"What exactly did you say to Penrith?" Blakesley said, leaving Louisa so that he could stand in front of Sophia, who was standing not too terribly far from Dutton.

"Such suspicions, Lord Henry," Sophia drawled, smirking at him almost flirtatiously. "One would think you'd had experience in conspiracies of all sorts, but that couldn't possibly be true, could it?"

Upon which, Blakes scowled politely at Sophia and cocked his head in a gesture of impatience. Louisa had seen that particular look on his face before. It was only slightly alarming, which meant that Sophia would likely find it amusing.

"I merely pointed out to him the obvious," Sophia said lightly, "which is that it would only help his reputation as a man of discerning taste and impeccable breeding to be on cordial terms with Lady Louisa. Which it certainly shall. Or do you disagree?"

"No," Blakes said sharply, turning from Sophia to stare for a moment at Dutton. Dutton returned his look briefly and then dipped his gaze downward. Louisa still could not fathom why Dutton was in the room. He certainly had no part in this . . . negotiation. Unless he wanted to . . . bid . . . on her as well?

The thought should have given her chills of rapture. Strangely, she was only mildly curious as to what, if anything, he would say. She watched him from her seat, studying him for signs of what could only be called a breakthrough.

He was, as ever, completely silent in regards to her.

Oh, well.

Perhaps there were others who found her of intense and, dare she say it, matrimonial interest?

"I'm so glad to hear it," Sophia said cheerfully, promptly ignoring Blakesley to turn her attention to the Duke and Duchess of Hyde. "But before we allow this discussion to proceed further, I feel I must mention the Duke of Edenham."

At that, Amelia gasped.

All eyes, almost in unison, turned to Amelia, who had the grace to pretend to cough lightly and make something of a pretense of trying to catch her breath. But her eyes told it all. Her eyes were aimed right at Louisa and they had the most profound look of betrayal in their soft blue depths.

Well, *really*, she had done nothing to cause any sort of . . . animation in the Duke of Edenham. She hadn't even spoken to him!

What would have happened if she *had*?

The idea was positively delicious.

"Yes?" Molly said, still casting Louisa dark looks over Sophia's shoulder. "What of Edenham? You can't mean that he's taken with the girl. I had no idea she got around so much," Molly said. It was not at all flattering, not the way she said it.

"Oh, he hasn't actually been introduced to her yet," Sophia said blithely. "Or has he? Have you been introduced to the Duke of Edenham, Lady Louisa?"

"No, not that I recall," Louisa said, trying to sound as casual as possible. She thought she did a good job of it.

"She meets dukes every day, does she?" Dutton muttered to no one in particular.

"Well, I've met her and I like her," Iveston said, which really, considering the situation, was a remarkable bit of good manners. She could have kissed him for that, a chaste and proper kiss, naturally. She had no intention of kissing anyone as she had kissed Blakes ever again. Even Dutton did not tempt her, which in any other circumstance she would have considered remarkable. In the present circumstance, he was, oddly, merely a distraction at best.

"You're not a duke," Dutton said, which really was entirely too rude of him.

"And happy to wait it out," Iveston said, giving his father a very affectionate bow of acknowledgement.

Wasn't Iveston the most lovely of men? Such a shame that Blakes was nothing at all like him.

Louisa heard Amelia sigh a trifle loudly, turned to see what that was about, and was gifted with the most irritated look on Amelia's face. She then followed it by a less than subtle jerk of her head.

Apparently, even though she had not yet met him either, Amelia considered Edenham, as dangerous as he was, *hers* to either reject or accept.

The marriage mart was such a tangled wood on the best of days.

Actually, this might go down as one of the best of days. Certainly, she'd never had even a sliver of this much interest before . . . before visiting Sophia this afternoon.

Perhaps Blakes was correct. Perhaps this was all to do with Sophia and nothing whatsoever to do with her.

The best of days just got a little bit dimmer.

"As I was saying," Sophia continued, "the Duke of Edenham and I had such a lovely chat just before dinner was announced and Lady Louisa's name came up. I was given the impression that he came not only to celebrate Lord Iveston's birth, but to finally have a chance to meet Lady Louisa. He is a very forward-thinking man and would so enjoy marrying again. In any regard, I do feel his name, however lightly, should merit consideration in these deliberations. Perhaps he should be present?"

Louisa could not help herself. She primped, just slightly, but she did primp. Edenham, for all of his dangerous reputation as a literal lady-killer, was an extremely handsome man. And his estate was supposed to be in the finest condition, requiring no major updates for at least a decade, which had to be considered, naturally, as having a good income that went fully back into the estate was almost like having no money at all.

Blakes, who kept moving about the room like a shark in a bowl, laid a hand, a very firm hand, on her shoulder and said, "There's no need. This has all been very interesting, Lady Dalby, even amusing, but as I've said from the start, I will marry Louisa. I, and no other."

"But surely, Blakes," Molly implored—she actually *implored*; it was something of a miracle that she did not get down on her *knees*—"if there is interest from other quarters, I know it is not done, not in the usual cases, but this is hardly usual. This woman"—and here she looked daggers at Louisa. Aunt Mary snored on—"this woman has certainly manipulated events, and she kissed you, not the other way round, and, oh, Blakes," she said, actually managing to squeeze out the odd tear or two, "I did so hope for you to marry well."

Which, really, was the cap to the entire evening.

Dutton chose that moment to snort in derision.

That was the cap to the entire evening.

Upon which Blakes lifted her chin with his hand, and as he was standing behind her, she was forced to look back and up at him. Muttering what she assumed was an apology, Blakes leaned down rather more swiftly than gently, and kissed her. Hard. On the mouth.

Full on the mouth.

She even felt the slightest sweep of his tongue against her startled lips.

And still, he kept kissing her. Rather more thoroughly than was required to make the point, still, after a moment or two, she almost forget where they were and found herself relaxing deliciously into his kiss.

It wasn't quite the same with all the candles lit, but it was quite wonderful in a different way altogether. His hand held her chin quite firmly and his other hand came round and caressed her cheek so that she was quite completely encompassed and he was quite clearly in charge of the whole affair of what she would likely call *the music room kiss*, so there was no possibility of anyone in the room thinking that she had maneuvered Blakes into anything.

It was quite, quite the most extraordinary kiss in the most extraordinary of circumstances.

When Blakes finally lifted his mouth from hers, he kept her face captured in his hands and stared down at her, his eyes more gentle than she would have thought possible. She found herself smiling up at him and really couldn't think why. He had just ruined her completely and publicly and in so doing, he had saved her reputation.

It was so completely like Blakes.

It was so completely like him and so completely lovely that she took his hand from her cheek and kissed his palm in what was certainly more tenderness than she'd ever shown anyone.

The room was silent, heavily silent, which seemed to suit the moment somehow.

Amelia sighed.

Aunt Mary snored.

Louisa grinned into Blakesley's sweetly sardonic face.

"There you are," Blakes said, straightening up to face the room. "I have kissed her without any provocation whatsoever, beyond the obvious provocation of Louisa's blatant allure. I trust it is now obvious that I am fully capable of ruining a girl without any help."

At which point, Blakes winked at her almost cheerfully.

"You'll have to marry her now," Molly said glumly.

"Yes, I shall," Blakes said, looking across the room to where Mr. Grey stood.

Mr. Grey nodded his head once and crossed his arms over his chest in what appeared to be gracious defeat.

And *that* was the cap to the entire evening.

It should have been, but Dutton, who really did not know when to let things alone, something she had somehow missed in her two years pursuing him through the salons of London and two country house parties, said, "This is all to get back the Melverley pearls, you understand. A wager was made today. It's on the book at White's. In order to get her pearls, it must be proved to the Duke of Calbourne that Lady Louisa prefers Blakesley to me. That's all this is."

"Absurd," Hyde said. He had been a general during the revolt in the American colonies so he had quite an efficient way with a phrase. Terse, yes, but very decisive and oddly authoritative, even for a duke. "No girl ruins herself on a wager, not even for pearls."

"Check the book!" Dutton said. "Ask your son if it's not so."

The sons of Hyde looked at their brother and at her, clearly not at all certain whom or what to believe. It was particularly galling as it was apparently no secret to Dutton that she had wanted to marry him for far longer than was flattering to her.

She couldn't help but look to Blakes, to see his reaction, to gauge whether he was amused, enraged, or ashamed. She would kill him if he were ashamed for it would reflect so badly on her and on their imminent marriage. And they were getting married, no matter what Dutton said. She was ruined. He had ruined her. And she liked kissing him.

That was all there was to it.

"But, darling," Sophia said to Dutton, clearly amused and at Dutton's expense. It did much to calm Louisa, which was a frightening thought in and of itself. "Calbourne isn't in this room, nor was he in the yellow drawing room. By your own definition of this wager, Calbourne must be present to make a determination. And he is not. Clearly, this delightful conflagration of two hearts finally meeting is the result of pure desire and nothing less. Certainly whatever wager has been struck regarding the Melverley pearls is an altogether different situation and has nothing to do with this."

"No," Dutton said, pushing his hair back with a single hand, a gesture Louisa had always found dashing until this moment. "No, it's all about those pearls. Ask Blakesley."

At which point, Mr. Grey left his quiet corner without anyone noticing him, crossed like a shadow to Lord Dutton, and, before anyone, most especially Lord Dutton, knew what was happening, Mr. Grey hit Lord Dutton square on the jaw and then again in the vicinity of his eye.

Lord Dutton went down with a gush of expelled air.

Mr. Grey turned to Louisa, who stood with Blakes at her side, his arm about her in the most gloriously possessive gesture, and said, "My wedding gift."

And *that* was the cap to the entire evening.

Truly.

Sixteen

THE only thing left to do, besides the actual marriage, was to tell Melverley. Everyone, it seemed, was very eager to do so. Everyone except Louisa.

She didn't like having anything to do with her father, for any reason, on any occasion. This occasion, the occasion of her ruination and hasty marriage, was not one to promote any eagerness on her part.

Sophia, naturally, took the complete opposite view. She almost insisted on being present, even though there was no logical reason for her to be there and, strangely, for that very reason, Louisa could think of no reason to exclude her. Sophia was a force on the subject and Louisa, who was responsible for excluding her, could find no energy to do so.

She was to marry Blakesley.

Looking at him now, his hair gleaming in the light of music room candles, his blues eyes looking at her with a very clever twinkle, she could not quite believe it. What was more, she couldn't quite believe that she wasn't more upset about it. In point of fact, she wasn't upset at all.

She should so like to get him alone again and return that kiss he'd taken off of her, in front of his mother, no less. She'd pay him back for that. Somehow. She wasn't at all certain how a woman used her body as revenge against a man, but she knew someone who did know.

Louisa's gaze went to Sophia, talking softly with Molly, likely talking Molly into accepting her into the family.

Small chance of that.

But looking at Blakes, who was talking to his father and brothers, a circle of men who, by their look, were not at all displeased by his sudden fall into matrimony, she could not spare a thought for Molly. Blakes, she was suddenly certain, would manage everything.

"You look content," Amelia said softly. They were sitting on a pair of small chairs behind the harp. Mary was fully asleep on the settee, almost sprawled across it; no one thought it necessary to wake her as the situation had been settled, and quite well, without her. "I confess to being somewhat surprised."

"Because of the scandal?"

"No," Amelia said on a breathy chuckle. "I'm well aware that you have no fear of scandal, but because of Dutton, of course. You don't seem at all brokenhearted, and should you not be? He is the one you said you loved and wanted above all others."

"Yes, I said that, felt that," Louisa said, her gaze still on Blakesley.

Dutton had left the room after being helped up off the floor by Mr. Grey, of all people, and then, pushing credulity to the limits, Mr. Grey and Lord Dutton had left the music room together. It was, perhaps, not at all impossible that Mr. Grey was acting as a sort of guard against future misconduct on the part of Lord Dutton. Lord Dutton seemed to warrant that sort of special attention.

She had been so certain of what she had felt for Dutton. So very certain. For two years, she had wanted no one else, thought of no one else . . . and yet, she had kissed Blakes, and with that kiss, that first touch of his mouth to hers, she had all but forgotten Dutton.

Was it possible? Could she be . . . lecherous?

She'd seen it all her life, naturally. With Melverley for a father, how could she not? A lovely face, a plump wrist, a ripe . . . well, there was little point in cataloging the various attributes that could and did and would again lure her father into someone else's bed. She'd thought him shallow and flighty and led by passion when reason should rule. Yet now, with Blakesley's kiss still tingling on her lips, she had forsaken Dutton without a qualm and jumped, quite literally, into Blakesley's bed.

It was just possible that she was a wanton.

Did Blakes know?

And if he did not, should she tell him?

"I, for one, am delighted that you have finally seen him for what he is," Amelia continued, forcing Louisa to momentarily abandon her thoughts about her own, possibly, flagrant lechery, which, as everyone knew, soon led into blatant debauchery. "He is a rake, Louisa, and was never worthy of you."

But perhaps that was why she had been attracted to him, one rake to another?

What did one call a female rake? A rakess? Rakeine?

"I suppose not," Louisa said, studying the various sons of Hyde. Did she find any of them compelling, any besides Blakes, that is? Was she destined to cuckold Blakes with his own brothers?

It did not escape her notice, particularly as she was concentrating so fully on herself, that before today, she would never have considered cuckolding anyone for the simple reason that she could not have imagined that any man would want to . . . well, would want her in that way. But today had been a revelation of the most unbiblical variety. Today, she thought that perhaps it was highly likely that any number of men would want her in the most carnal terms imaginable, and that, strangely, she might be entirely capable of choosing from among many.

Aside from thinking of herself as lecherous, it was the most original thought she had ever entertained about herself.

Might she be . . . beguiling?

The events of the day certainly encouraged that conclusion.

Being beguiling was completely acceptable. Being a wanton was not.

The real question was if it were possible to be one and not the other. She certainly had seen no sign of it in her months in Town. One need only look across the room at Sophia Dalby for proof of the obvious fact that women who beguiled men were, in fact, rather wanton as a result.

Was there any help for it?

Certainly Sophia would be unable to answer her as she was both beguiling and wanton. It was most unfortunate that she could think of no one else to ask. Louisa cast a speculative glance to Amelia, who was quietly chatting on about how undeserving Dutton had been and how surprising the evening had been, all the while staring with demure charm at Lord Iveston. Amelia, to her credit, never wasted a moment in seeking to attain her goal of marrying a duke. Louisa had nothing but respect for a woman so supremely focused on a well-defined goal. Although Amelia was as innocent as she, though perhaps it was better said that Amelia was as innocent as she had been an hour ago, Louisa could not but wonder if Amelia, because of her clearheadedness and stark good sense, might know or be able to speculate on whether wantonness was an avoidable trait.

Louisa had nothing to lose by asking, and certainly Amelia *had* to know more about abstaining from certain appetites than Sophia. Though, as a married woman, perhaps it was not so much abstaining and refraining. All she had to do, really, was to keep her passions within the confines of the marital bed.

How difficult could that be?

Never mind that the ton was simply awash with people who couldn't seem to manage it. She was quite certain, because she was quite desperate, that she could do it. No matter that Melverley was her father. Or rather, in spite of it.

Oh, dear. The more she thought about it, the more hopeless it all seemed.

What if, dear God, Blakes could not satisfy her? What if her lusts were insatiable, as Melverley's clearly were?

"Louisa?" Amelia asked her, touching her arm to gain her attention.

"Yes?" Louisa said, dragging her gaze away from Blakes, who, she suddenly realized, was staring back at her. Who knew what he was thinking? Perhaps he could read her increasingly wanton thoughts all over her face.

The sad bit was that she had been thinking wanton thoughts, and in the midst of her trying very hard to think of how to save herself from wantonness. She was clearly a hopeless case.

"It truly doesn't bother you? To have to give Dutton up, I mean. Your plans, all your hopes that the two of you would . . ." Amelia said, stopping awkwardly as a blush fought to life on her cheeks. "What was it like?" she said instead, leaving the topic of Dutton altogether, at least for the moment.

Of course Louisa knew exactly what Amelia was asking, the problem was that she didn't know how to tell her what *it* was like without sounding like the veritable wanton she clearly was.

Life, she was certain, was going to be so much more complicated from this point on.

"Did you mind it very much?" Amelia said.

To which Louisa jerked her gaze, which, yes, had strayed to Blakes again, back to Amelia. "Did it look as if I minded it very much?"

Perhaps there was some hope for her. Perhaps she wasn't as lecherous as she felt whenever she looked at Blakes, and, yes, she'd once again allowed her gaze to settle on Blakes, which clearly was becoming something of a disagreeable habit, which surely she could break. Perhaps after they were wed. Perhaps then, these stirrings would diminish.

Perhaps, perhaps, perhaps.

Life did not appear altogether hopeful when one was forced to rely upon a series of *perhaps*.

"No," Amelia said, her blue eyes appearing suspiciously soft and dewy, "you looked . . . you looked as if you were being quite . . . quite, almost transformed by it. In fact, you haven't looked the same since he kissed you. I had no idea such a thing could happen, did you? Do you *feel* different?"

Yes, as it happened, she did. She felt exactly like a wanton. And it appeared she now looked like one as well.

❧

"SHE doesn't appear any the worse for it," Iveston said softly.

"I'd say she looks better," Cranleigh said.

"Try not to say anything," Blakes said. "I don't care to have my future wife discussed by you."

"I'm your brother," Cranleigh said.

"Exactly," Blakes said. "Brothers are exactly the wrong sort to discuss women one intends to marry."

"But women of the other sort are perfectly acceptable," George said.

"Only by default," Blakes said. "It's far better not to discuss women at all."

"It's clearly better to leave off talking and simply kiss them into ruin and marriage," Cranleigh said. "Got it."

It was going to be nearly impossible to keep his brothers from talking about Louisa for the next month, at least. It was going to be truly impossible to keep his brothers from talking *to* Louisa for the next few decades. Blakes understood in that instant that having his brothers realize his affection for Louisa and his delight in finally bringing her to the altar was going to be fodder for every conversation they would have for perhaps the rest of their lives. He didn't particularly enjoy contemplating that as he preferred his private life to remain private and his brothers, on most subjects, to remain silent. On the subject of women, especially. On the subject of his woman, definitely.

Louisa was his.

He wasn't at all certain how it had happened, namely, what had prompted her to so readily meet him in the yellow drawing room, which could easily have been managed, and to then kiss him like the veriest wanton, which could not easily have been managed, before he had his guard up.

He liked to think that he would have, given the appropriate warning, got his guard up in time to keep her from being ruined. But he wouldn't have laid odds on it.

He wanted her, had wanted her for more months than he cared to count, and to find that she wanted him, even in a purely physical sense, was better luck than he was willing to abandon. Actually, that she so clearly had wanted him in a purely physical sense was better than any wanting he could imagine.

Louisa, not that he had ever had any doubts about it whatsoever, was going to prove a very passionate wife. As she was clearly a passionate woman in all her dealings, it only made perfect sense. It was one of her charms, certainly, that particular brand of violence to her emotions and her boldness in behavior. He'd always found that amusing as well as intriguing. So many women of his acquaintance, Louisa's cousin Amelia for one, were so guarded and so correct in all their various interactions. It became not only predictable, but boring.

Louisa was never boring.

He'd found upon reaching his majority that boredom was a rather too constant companion and, once established, very difficult to abandon. If there was one thing he knew about his marriage to Louisa, and certainly he knew far more than one thing, it was that she would never bore him.

In fact, he knew beyond a shadow of a doubt, that she would excite him.

In point of fact, she excited him at this very instant.

Josiah laughed, his gaze upon the very tight fabric currently stretched across Blakeley's *tree of life*, as the saying went.

"You'll need to plant that in something, soon," Josiah said.

"Go back to Paris, Jos," Blakes said. "You're too coarse for London."

"Come with me and we'll plant trees together. The ground is rich and dark in Paris," Jos said, still laughing.

Blakes turned his back on his brothers, who were all chuckling by this time, and said to his father, "I'm certain the gossips are running low on fodder. Shall we not return to dinner?"

And so they did.

Seventeen

DINNER was an abbreviated affair, the food mostly gone cold, which no one seemed to mind in the least, the gossip having been served piping hot. Food could be got at any hour, but an *on dit* of this sort happened once a Season at best. That twice in a single week two girls of good family had been ruined in the dressing room of Hyde House was something of a miraculous event along the order of the immaculate conception, although completely opposite in *type*, of course, not that anyone cared.

It was to be expected that people kept leaving the table to disappear in the general direction of the dressing room, a rather large room, as dressing rooms went, but still, only a dressing room.

Hyde found it necessary to post a rather beefy footman at the door into the dressing room from the yellow drawing room. When that proved unsatisfactory, he instructed the butler to assign another largish footman to be positioned at the other door to the dressing room, the door reached from the bedroom.

Yes, it had come to that.

If that proved less than satisfactory, there was always the possibility of charging a fee for admission, though Hyde would likely frown upon that sort of thing. Molly, on the other hand, would think that when the opportunity of making a profit presented itself it was a fool indeed who looked the other way.

Sophia so liked that about Molly. She couldn't help but wonder if it was their American upbringing, but discarded that thought as implausible as their upbringings could not have been more different.

Sophia surveyed the table with a very pleased expression, which she knew annoyed Westlin down to the bone, which prompted her to smile all the more. Really, things were going so beautifully well that even Westlin sitting in her line of sight was becoming a boon.

"If the girl's to be married as soon as the license is obtained, it would seem that she'll have no use for me," Edenham said.

"Don't be absurd, your grace," Sophia said, sipping her wine and considering Edenham across the wide table. He was a most appealing man, the more so because he had such a pleasantly jaded view of things. Idealism and youthful exuberance were lovely by degrees, but one could so easily find them intolerable as a constant diet. These young girls and their marriage hopes, while entertaining, could become slightly tiresome. "There is always a use for a duke."

Edenham laughed softly, considering her in the candlelight. She enjoyed the fact that he was taking his time as she knew that she looked particularly well in candlelight.

"Sometimes a man wants to be more than a duke," Edenham said.

"A king?" Sophia said, smiling at him.

"A man," Edenham rejoined.

"But you are always a man, your grace. Did you doubt it?"

"I was only afraid that you might doubt it, or at least forget it."

"Hardly," she said, toasting him discreetly. "I'm not in my dotage, losing my teeth in my soup, no matter what you might have heard."

"You'll be relieved to know that I've heard nothing about you losing your teeth. On the contrary, they seem to grow sharper as the years pass."

"From cutting them on so many bodies, I should suspect," she said, enjoying herself immensely. How long had it been since she'd crossed swords so amicably with a handsome man of means?

Oh, yes, earlier today, with Lord Ruan.

Well, a woman could manage more than one man, if the men were amenable and compliant. And weren't they all?

"Would you care to gnaw upon me, Lady Dalby? Your appetite is not yet sated?" he said, clearly enjoying himself as fully as she. Lovely man.

"Is it ever?" she asked him, scandalizing Westlin, such a nice bonus.

"You're corrupting me," Blakesley interrupted with a wry twist to his lips. "What *shall* my dreams be tonight?"

"Oh, will you sleep?" Sophia said to Blakesley. "I shall have to try harder."

"Harder is not a word I want to hear, Lady Dalby. I am being pressed to the utmost at the moment."

"You or your breeches?" she said, laughing.

"I yield," he said. "But only because my mother can read my lips and will scold me later. I wither upon scolding."

"You must require regular withering, Lord Henry. Whatever shall Lady Louisa do to manage you? Not by scolding, I'll wager. There must be other, more pleasant ways to wither."

"I'm certain we shall manage together very well," Blakesley said, ending their bawdy exchange, which surely was an act of love and devotion that recommended him fully. That such a man as Lord Henry Blakesley should be so fully and obviously in love with Louisa Kirkland, it was almost enough to inspire one to write a sonnet on the glories of romantic love.

Almost.

"I'm equally certain," she said. "You are content with the match?"

"I believe you had no need to ask, Lady Dalby," he said, his eyes narrowed in sarcastic wit. "But if I am to be quoted, I am most content."

"You will speak to Melverley?" she said softly.

"I will," he said. "I am eager for it."

"I don't suppose I could cajole you into allowing me to come and watch. I do so enjoy watching a man fall into spitting fits, and certainly no one could be more deserving of one."

Blakesley eyed her carefully. He was a most observant man; one had to be so very careful around observant men. Fortunately, observant men were rather more the exception than the rule, so she was almost never required to be particularly careful.

"You have a special attachment to Lord Melverley?" Blakesley asked.

"My lord, I either enjoyed or endured a special attachment to many men," she said with a smile. "Do you require specifics?"

There, that ought to close that particular door of inquiry.

"I should say 'no,' to give credit to my breeding, but it is so very tempting to say 'yes.' Tell me this and I'll ask no more. Was Melverley endured or enjoyed?" Blakes asked.

"It's such a struggle to remember," she began.

"Not a promising start," Blakes said with a half smile.

"But I believe," she continued, "that at first I endured and endured until finally I found my enjoyment. It was a rough bit of ground, but eventually I found my passage."

Westlin, who was avidly listening to every word, slammed his fork down upon his plate, which resulted in a most inappropriate clang, which drew not a few disapproving glances in his direction, which resulted in a most delicious sense of satisfaction in Sophia.

Really, if one could not torment one's most enduring enemy and first amorous conquest, what was life for?

"I'm delighted to hear it," Blakesley said.

"For my sake or for his?" she replied.

"Why, for the sake of all men," Edenham said, reentering the conversation, "for what man wants to believe that he cannot do his part, especially with so lovely a partner? If Lady Dalby failed to find her feet upon that bit of ground, what hope for the next man who traveled the same road?"

"The point being that a man likes a road well traveled?" she asked Edenham pleasantly.

"Only in that it promises an enjoyable journey. Surely, a point both women and men can agree upon," Edenham said, dipping his head to her in salute.

"I couldn't possibly imagine disagreeing, your grace," she said, dipping her head in reply. "To an enjoyable journey. And to Lord Henry and Lady Louisa, may they find their feet quickly."

Henry Blakesley, who had fallen silent during her exchange with the Duke of Edenham, nodded pleasantly, but his eyes, those sharp blue eyes of his, considered her far too closely and with unpleasant sobriety. Observant men were truly the bane of a woman's life. She thanked Providence almost daily that they were so few of them.

As to that, best to get Blakesley's gaze trained elsewhere.

"You might think of applying for a special license, Lord Henry, to hurry things along," she said, indicating with her glass down the table to where Louisa sat surrounded by Penrith and her nephew George. "George may have yielded Lady Louisa to you, but I would not be as certain of Lord Penrith. He looks more determined than is seemly, though you are perhaps the best judge of that."

With complete predictability, Blakesley looked away from Sophia to stare down and across the table to where Louisa sat. Penrith did, indeed, look quite intent upon Louisa, which required that Blakesley look intently at Louisa as well.

Things were going beautifully.

THINGS were going horribly.

One would think that something as scandalous as being ruined would, well, ruin a girl, but the opposite seemed to be the case. Louisa simply could not dissuade Lord Penrith from making the most flagrant and flirtatious remarks directly to her face, and Mr. Grey, who previously had been most solicitous, now sat in supreme repose and watched it all with a quite savage-looking smile on his face, his dimple winking at her outrageously.

And Lord Dutton! Louisa simply could not fathom Lord Dutton. Whereas for the past two years getting his attention would have required her to break her leg over his very pretty head, now that she was ruined Dutton could not seem to stop talking to her.

The Marquis of Ruan was hardly better, though not nearly as talkative. He only stared at her with an altogether too knowing smile upon his rugged face, when he wasn't staring in what amounted to derision at Dutton, that is.

It was too, too much. It really was almost enough to make a girl want to avoid being ruined. There was such a thing as too much male attention and, clearly, being ruined invited it.

Why hadn't anyone told her?

Amelia was no help whatsoever. Amelia sat in what could only be described as dazed silence whilst Penrith, Dutton, and occasionally Ruan talked about her impending marriage to Blakesley both as if it were a fact already achieved and, simultaneously, a thing which could be avoided by the merest effort on their parts. And they were encouraging her to avoid it, marriage to Blakesley, that is, and yet speaking to her as if she had, in fact, been literally and physically *ruined.*

It was most embarrassing. She did not know at all what was the proper form in the current situation, not that she was convinced that *they* were exhibiting the proper form, but she did like to set an example when at all possible.

It didn't look possible in this particular instance.

"I don't know why I think it should spoil your fun, for you are clearly enjoying this, Lord Dutton, but I am not interested in being your guest at the theater. If I were to attend the theater, you know full well that Melverley has a box for the Season and I should use his."

"I should think you'd not want to share a box with your father," Dutton said. "I was not at all aware that you and Melverley were on such intimate terms as to share a box in the Theatre Royal."

"I am his daughter," she said stiffly.

Really, it was terribly rude of Dutton to allude to the fact that she didn't care to spend any time with her father in his box as it was a certainty that, if her father were in his box, he would not be in it alone and he would not be watching the theatrics. No, her father did other things in his box.

"Ignore him, Lady Louisa," Penrith said, his famous voice washing over her bare shoulder. It was most strange, but ever since she'd kissed and been kissed by Blakes, Penrith and his voice had almost no effect upon her. She could not have imagined a kiss to have such power.

Perhaps it was only Blakesley's kiss which did so?

Pity that she would never be able to put the theory to the test as she would have no opportunity to kiss anyone but Blakesley for the rest of her life. She was determined for that to be the case, for to even speculate otherwise would be to wander into wantonness and she was *not* going to be like her father.

"He only wants to best Blakesley," Penrith continued, and she did find herself looking deeply into his startling green eyes. Some things just could not be ignored. "Don't let yourself become a mere tool to that end."

"And what do you want, Lord Penrith?" Mr. Grey said, leaning back in his chair to look at Penrith behind her back.

"Only what we all want," Penrith said. "To do right by the women of our acquaintance."

"Is that what we all want?" Ruan said sardonically. "I'd always wondered. So good to have that settled, then."

"I've known Lady Louisa for far longer than you, Lord Penrith," Dutton said. "Do not lay your own plans at my doorstep."

"You have known her for far longer," Penrith agreed, "yet have not managed to escort her to the theater before now? How tardy of you, Dutton."

"Perhaps nothing was playing that he wished to see?" Ruan said pleasantly enough, yet entirely sarcastically.

Ruan was older than both Penrith and Dutton by some years; in fact, Louisa thought it highly likely that Ruan was older than Sophia Dalby, which, in some lights, made him seem as old as Adam in a very fallen Eden. In terms of these highly undesirable verbal exchanges, he was more than a match for both Penrith and Dutton combined.

It was patently obvious that both Dutton and Penrith were aware of it. Penrith took it in stride. Dutton was stumbling.

In all her months watching Dutton's every gesture, reading every forkful of food for nuance, she'd never seen him behave so oddly and so awkwardly. She couldn't have been that far off in her estimation of him; something was definitely wrong with him and she couldn't understand what it was.

More strangely, she couldn't summon the interest to actually puzzle it out.

"I've heard that there's a new play starting at the King's Theatre," Amelia said softly, clearly trying to set the course of their conversation back on the proper track, as it were.

"This has nothing to do with plays," Dutton said, staring at her from across the table, "and everything to do with wagers."

Oh, bother. Did everything in Town have to do with wagers?

"You should watch what you say, Lord Dutton," Mr. Grey said ominously. Louisa cast a quick glance at Grey; he looked as ominous as his tone of voice, but then, given that he was an Indian, he had the unfortunate tendency to look ominous for no cause whatsoever. It was likely a helpful quality in the forests of New York, but it had far fewer uses here.

Dutton looked at Mr. Grey and swallowed, his mouth compressed into a firm line.

Well, perhaps looking ominous was not a bad trait to possess on any continent.

"I would speak with you, Lady Louisa," Dutton said in a quietly intense tone of voice. It was most appealing. She could honestly report that she had never before heard Dutton speak so intently and so, dare she say it, passionately to anyone before for any occasion. She was slightly titillated, but only slightly, an important distinction and one she would make to Blakes if she found herself required to do so. "Alone, if you will allow it."

If she would allow it? She'd been trying for two years to get Dutton to speak with her on any topic and in any surrounding. Now, he was desperate to speak with her and *alone*?

Could life ever surpass this moment?

Apparently, her thoughts were written all over her face, which was indeed unfortunate, for Amelia said, "I should think that very unwise, Louisa."

Of course, it was unwise and if she were not already *completely* ruined, she should not have even contemplated it. But she *was* ruined. And she was going to marry Blakes, unless her father refused, which he would not do, as her father was far from being a fool and any father would be more than pleased to marry off his daughter to the man who'd ruined her, so that was not even worth bothering about.

She could admit that she'd only given it a cursory examination as to wisdom or folly, but in that brief scan of facts Louisa decided that she had absolutely nothing to lose by meeting with Dutton in another part of the house and almost everything to gain . . . namely, a chance to be alone with Dutton and to hear him speak to her on whatever urgent matter he'd invented to be alone with her.

Yes, she had absolutely everything to gain.

So, for the second time during the course of a single dinner, Louisa Kirkland excused herself and left her dinner to get cold upon the table. She left the red reception room as discreetly as possible, which was hardly discreet at all as everyone in the room could see her, and see Dutton leave a few moments after her, and watch Lord Henry Blakesley watch with an unreadable, but very interesting expression on his face, and then watch Sophia Dalby, who was rather famous for her outrageous remarks, whisper something to Lord Henry when Louisa and Dutton had been gone for more than a few minutes, which clearly prompted Lord Henry to leave his seat at table, to the outward display of annoyance from Molly, Duchess of Hyde, which Henry blatantly ignored, as everyone considered right as Louisa was to be his bride and Molly was only his mother.

And the final thing that everyone noticed, before things went completely to the dogs and a loud scuffle was heard from behind at least two doors, was that Sophia Dalby was smiling like the cat who ate the cream.

Eighteen

NATURALLY, Louisa had not intended to find herself alone in the Hyde House dressing room with Dutton.

Of course not.

How she had got there was still something of a mystery to her. She suspected it had a great deal to do with the air of mystery and concern which Dutton had thrown all over her like a wet cloak from the very minute she met him alone in the blue reception room. Alone, except for a stream of footmen and maids hurrying back and forth with the next course for dinner, but they hardly counted when a woman's reputation was in the wind.

Facing Dutton, alone, in the semidarkness wrought by the application of three candles in a rather nice silver candlebra, was seeming less and less interesting an encounter and more and more a foolhardy one. It was not to be ignored that Dutton was a very seductive man with a habit of success at dalliance.

She had, in fact, ignored that to a slight degree when allowing Dutton to lead her into the dressing room, he claiming that they were too likely to be intruded upon in the blue reception room, in the yellow drawing room, or in the music room, which had all been far more likely meeting places. She wasn't quite certain how Dutton had managed to get her into the dressing room, but the fact that she now found herself there did explain in large part his success at dalliance.

"You cannot marry Blakesley," Dutton said, his blue eyes appearing to lovely advantage in the candlelight, his hair falling, as it was wont to do, seductively over his brow in an almost poetic arch. "Not because of a stupid wager I made when more than half drunk."

He took her hand in his. She allowed it. How long had she dreamed of the touch of Dutton's hand?

Oddly, it did not move her as much as she had expected.

Perhaps if she removed her gloves . . . but she could not think of a way to get them off without seeming forward. Not that women who met with men in dressing rooms should have to worry about seeming forward.

She knew she was being ridiculous, but that didn't seem to help. She was still firmly on a course toward being not only ridiculous, but a disgrace to the Melverley name, which likely explained why she did nothing to remove herself from the dressing room.

Melverley had done more than enough to rub the gloss of respectability off his title; could anything she did make it worse?

She couldn't think of a reason not to find out. Again, she *was* already ruined. There was simply no place further to fall.

Dutton clearly understood that, which would explain why he had insisted on meeting her in the dressing room. She'd already been in this very dressing room with Blakes . . . although, put that way, it was entirely possible that being cloistered in a dressing room during a dinner at Hyde House with two separate and distinct men would do more than considerable damage to her reputation, ruined or not. There was being ruined in the normal sense of the word and then there was being scandalously ruined. Being ruined was bad enough; she didn't suppose she should allow scandal to be attached to it.

"How kind of you," she said, determined in that instant to exit the dressing room. "I do know of the wager, of course. Blakes was most clear about it. But thank you for being so concerned, Lord Dutton. I do appreciate it."

"But he shouldn't have told you of the wager," Dutton said, laying his arm across the doorway into the yellow drawing room, blocking her. It was a very large dressing room, really a smallish room decorated very simply, but even so, it was extraordinary how a man, a large man at that, could, by casually rearranging himself, make a room seem very, very small, and the doorway completely inaccessible. "What honor in that?"

"What honor, Lord Dutton, in making a wager about a woman and her pearls?" she said stiffly.

"But they are my pearls, Louisa, and I was trying to find a way to give them back to you."

"I suppose just giving them to me would have been too simple."

"Simple, yes, but isn't that how Caroline got herself ruined in a single evening? I was trying to spare you that."

Yes, well, she had become ruined anyway, so it seemed a ridiculous argument now and entirely off the point. The point being that she still wanted her pearls. Besides, making a woman the subject of a bet on White's book did not seem at all a route destined to keep a woman from ruination. Men never did see these things as clearly as a woman did. They were obviously hampered by the inescapable fact of being men.

"And now what's to become of my pearls?" she said, taking a step backward.

There was another door out of the dressing room, one which led into the gold bedroom, a room gilded from top to bottom in a magnificent and tasteful display of endless wealth. At least she hoped the Blakesleys possessed endless wealth as she had no wish to marry a man destined to become a pauper or, worse, have to delve into trade.

"Is that truly all you care about?" Dutton purred, his blue eyes going quite dark and sensual. Yes, she understood sensual; after kissing Blakes, how could she not? "The wager concerned more than that, or didn't Blakesley tell you the whole of it?"

Which, naturally, made her wonder if he *had.*

Which clearly meant that Dutton was nearly smoldering with the desire to be the one to tell her.

Anytime a man smoldered with desire, particularly as it was Dutton, she did feel it was best to let him proceed. Men who smoldered should be given every opportunity and every latitude.

Of course, she'd just made that up, but it did seem apt.

"I am as certain he did and you are clearly certain he did not," she said, eyeing him closely. "Perhaps you should tell me and then, when we have decided what is to become of my pearls, we can leave this dressing room and return to dinner. I cannot think that Blakesley would approve of our meeting like this, in such surroundings. You are a man of some reputation, Lord Dutton, as I'm certain you are aware."

She was quite pleased with herself, both her delivery and her choice of words. Of course, she had borrowed a good deal of it from a play she'd seen last year, but she was more than convinced that she was a better actress than Sally Bates, who had played an innocent miss with, considering the size of Sally's bosom, an unsurprising lack of innocence.

"I want to apologize first, for making the wager. It was most ill-considered."

Given the smolder in his blue eyes and the way his hair was, again, falling in a cascade over his beautifully formed brow, she was inclined to forgive him.

"It certainly was," she said in rather a more breathy way than she had planned to do. Her performance, which it surely must be, was slipping. Just as Sally's bodice had in the second act.

"I never should have put you in such a precarious position," he said, taking her hand in his again, though he still managed to block the door. She wasn't at all certain how men *did* that, become so ominously large whenever they chose. "Though I could not have anticipated that they would end in your marriage to Blakesley."

Well, of course, who could have?

"Not when I suspected that you had some small measure of feeling for me," he finished.

She hoped he'd finished. This was becoming most dreadfully awkward. She didn't know quite what to say, and no play she'd seen seemed to cover it. She clearly needed a French play for this.

"You must know that I hold you in the highest esteem, Lord Dutton," she said. It seemed safe enough and had the advantage of being the truth. "But I fail to see what that has to do with this ill-conceived wager."

"Only that it encompasses the parameters under which the wager was set. You see," he said softly, kissing her hand, which moved her not at all. *Gloves, again.* She truly had to find a way to remove her gloves if this attempt at seduction on Dutton's part had any hope at all of moving her. Was she a wanton or not? It seemed rather more urgent than not that she find out. "I thought that, even in possession of the pearls, that you would prefer my company to his. But that is not so. Or is it?" he said, taking the problem from her completely by sliding his fingertips into the hem of her glove and stripping it softly down her arm until it bunched at her wrist. He leaned down, that shock of hair falling forward and tickling her, just before his mouth kissed the inside of her wrist at the point where her blood ran blue.

She gasped.

He tugged, and she stumbled a step nearly into his arms. He pulled her glove from her, finger by finger, starting at the thumb and ending at the little finger and kissing her wrist and arm on the delicate and sensitive underside until she was gloveless, breathless, and speechless.

Yes, the glove had been the problem all along.

Dutton's mouth most definitely knew its way around a woman's wrist.

"Lord Dutton," she managed to say. She probably should have kept silent; he'd seemed more than content with her wrist, until she'd reminded him that she had a mouth.

"Louisa," he said, his voice as soft and urgent as she'd imagined on so many nights. Of course, she hadn't imagined the dressing room. "Forgive me. I had no thought that this would lead to marriage with a man you cannot love and little respect."

His words entered her ears at about the same instant as his mouth touched her lips. It was an extraordinary combination and one she didn't like in the least. His mouth was pleasant enough, she supposed, certainly nothing in line with Blakesley's rather torrid approach. As Blakesley's future wife, she was almost proud to note that Blakesley's kiss was a cannon fire to Dutton's slingshot. In fact, after a moment or two of tolerating his attack upon her, she was astonished to realize that she was bored.

Bored.

If she didn't already know that kisses could be something else altogether, she might have been shattered by disappointment. But there was Blakes and his mouth and, now that she paused to consider it, his rather more intense blue gaze and sharply amusing wit and lovely form, for she had felt small parts of it while kissing him . . . and what exactly did Dutton mean by saying that she couldn't love or respect Blakes?

She started speaking before she'd fully managed to push him off of her, which was a huge help in dissuading him in continuing to assault her.

"I must insist that you refrain from speaking so of Lord Henry," she said, trying to pull her limp glove out of Dutton's hand and keep him off of her in the same motion. It was less than successful as a maneuver. She had so little practice at these sorts of things and, truly, in Blakesley's case, she'd been pushing toward Blakes and not away from him, an entirely different proposition. "He, of course, has my love. Do you imagine I am the sort of person to kiss a man I do not love and intend to marry?"

Dutton looked down at her glove and then up at her with one brow cocked.

"You cannot possibly compare the two!" she said rather more hotly than was seemly, though she was probably long past worrying about seemly now. "I kissed Blakes and you kissed me! Surely you can see the difference."

"Not precisely," Dutton said.

At which point he looked entirely like a man intent upon kissing her again; she'd had experience of two now and was becoming, not immodestly, something of an expert on that particular look.

It was a point of good fortune for her that, as Dutton was moving to back her up against the wall, literally, he left his "post" at the door, which swung open with a bang of violent noise that made Dutton turn and her jump. And who was standing there but Blakes, looking like the wrath of God in a sapphire blue damask waistcoat, who took a quick succession of slicing looks at Dutton and her and her bare arm and her glove in Dutton's hand, and said, "Swords at dawn?"

"Swords at dawn," Dutton agreed, bowing to Blakes and then returning her glove to her with a smile of what should have been regret but was not.

And then, before she could catch a full breath to explain to Blakes how she had wound up in a dressing room, *their* dressing room, with Dutton, Blakes said, "If you wanted to take off your clothes, Louisa, you should have told me. I'm more than happy to oblige you."

That was the point when she thought that it, perhaps, had not been good fortune at all for Blakes to show up when and where he did.

Nineteen

"YOU are not going to duel with him," Louisa said, because it seemed wiser to speak of something else, anything else, but the removal of her clothing.

"Not now, no," Blakes said. "Now I am going to remove some of your clothes and, in the process, remind you most forcefully, that you will be marrying *me*."

"Of course I am to marry you," she snapped. "No one thinks otherwise."

"Don't they?" he said. "I wish this room had a lock," he mused softly. "I do think Ashdon would have appreciated a locked door as much as I do now."

She swallowed heavily and slid on her crumpled glove. Everyone knew what had happened within this room less than a week ago to Sophia's daughter Caroline; she had been thoroughly ruined and forced to marry the Earl of Ashdon the very next day. Why, it was all anyone could speak of still, though, aside from being ruined, everyone did admit that Caroline had looked rather delighted to have been ruined by Lord Ashdon.

There was something to that, surely.

"I think we should go back to dinner," she said. "Now."

"Because I spoke of locked doors?" he asked softly. "Don't worry. I shan't let anyone in to see you, locks or not."

"Lord Henry," she said firmly. "This is most inappropriate. And you seem to have got the wrong idea entirely about what, that is, about how I . . . how Lord Dutton and I . . . that is to say," she said hurriedly against the rising anger in Blakesley's eyes, "we were speaking of you!"

"How reassuring," he said drolly. "And your glove?"

"It's only a glove!"

"Did you remove it or did he? Don't bother to lie about it, Louisa. You know it's the first thing he'll tell me on the dueling field tomorrow. Men, as you may have heard, do talk about things of this sort . . . and women of that sort."

Women of that sort?

"That's entirely uncalled for!"

"The glove?" he said, smiling like a . . . well, like a shark. Not at *all* reassuring.

"He took it off!" she said, feeling that it vindicated her somehow.

It didn't come out right at all, she realized, watching the expression on Blakesley's face shift into something most appalling.

"What can I do but follow the great Dutton's form?" he said on a soft snarl. "He is the master, is he not? He is all you have wanted these past two years, is he not? What better course for me, the man you *will* marry, than to follow where he has so generously led?"

Oh, dear. That sounded most unpromising as courtships went.

He looked terribly angry and frightfully outraged, frankly more purely masculine than she had ever seen him, in a purely predatory way, obviously.

It was rather appealing, truth be told, though she didn't suppose he would appreciate hearing that at the moment, not when he was doing his best to be intimidating. And he was intimidating, she just found it so compelling, which she was quite certain was not the

reaction he had intended. Oh, well. She would try to display discretion as the better part of valor, holding her tongue and her opinion while he backed her against the wall and . . . what, stripped her
bare?

Oh, dear.

Being ruined certainly did have its advantages.

"You don't look at all as frightened as you should be, Louisa," he
said, walking slowly toward her. He didn't have far to walk; it
wasn't *that* large a room. She backed up as he came on, her gaze
held by his, until her back hit the wall with a soft thump of finality
and dead ends.

"I shouldn't think you'd want your future wife to be frightened
of you," she said stoutly, lifting her chin and meeting his gaze.

"You clearly don't know a thing about how a proper marriage
works," he said, lifting her face with his hands, his fingers tangled in
her dangling curls, ruining her perfect curl completely and unre-
lentingly. It was past fixing now, certainly. "Of what use are you to
me if you are not cowed into behaving properly?"

"I'm not at all certain I can be cowed into any sort of behavior,
Blakesley," she said, "not proper and not even improper."

"You don't think so?" he said, grinning like an imp from Hell.
"Let's try, shall we? For myself, I prefer improper from you. For the
world, you shall have to learn how to behave so as not to bring derision upon me. A simple formula for success. Learn it, will you?"

"Blakesley, you have the most sublime sense of humor," she
said, grinning back at him, her eyes challenging him outrageously.
"Do you honestly believe you can force me to anything? Why, I
have defied Melverley for years and all he has to show for it is a
head of gray hair and four missing teeth. I think you should protect
your hair and your teeth, for I am quite certain I should not find
you at all attractive without them. And you are so very attractive
now. Let's proceed from there, shall we?"

"You find me attractive?" he said, lifting her chin with his thumbs, his fingers bracing her face tenderly, no matter what he said.

"I presume you have a mirror?" she said tartly. "You can see for yourself that you are devilishly handsome, if one cares for devils, that is. How fortunate for you that I do."

Upon which he grinned and pulled her face to his and kissed her as she so well deserved. It was such a relief to be kissed by Blakes after the mistreatment and mismanagement she had suffered under Dutton. She felt her heart trip, her head spin, and her pulse pound—in a word, all the things she expected should happen when a woman was properly kissed. She really didn't know how Dutton had managed it all these years. Clearly, he was living on legend, and she couldn't possibly imagine how the legend had first started. Perhaps with his father?

In any case, she had no time to think about Dutton, not when Blakes was doing his best to drive her wild.

Blakes was so very good at driving her wild.

His tongue teased hers, and his hands played in her hair, pulling at her curls, strand by strand, one by one, until her hair tumbled down around her shoulders in what she was certain were tangled coils and not one bit attractive. Blakes didn't seem to notice that her hair was not the thing. Blakes was too busy elsewhere. He pressed her back against the paneled door and kissed her hard, hard, until her breath came in gulps and gasps and she had her arms wrapped around his neck, breathing in the scent of him, the feel of him against her breasts, pressing, the weight of him a gift she was shocked to find she hungered for.

He did not pull away from her this time. No, she held him fast, a prisoner, caught in ruining her as she was in being ruined. A perfect pairing. It was only fair that they should share in it, tumble into it, falling as far and as deep as ruin could deliver them.

Her breasts ached and felt hot and full and she moaned into his mouth and demanded more, more ruin and more falling, more heat and more madness.

Blakes, that devil, untwisted her arms from around his neck and held her from him, his eyes like blue coals of passion and determination and what looked like anger. Let him be angry. Let him also be determined to follow passion and Louisa when they led him. Was that so difficult?

He smiled, a lopsided thing, and pulled a chair to him by its wooden back. It was a simple chair, well made, upholstered in pale blue silk on its seat and graced by careful carving on its open back. A pretty chair. Blakes sat in it when he should have offered it to her. The lout.

He sat, his legs splayed out, his smile still crooked, and, grabbing her by her hips, pulled her into the space between his legs. Her gown was thin, the finest muslin, fragile and nearly sheer in the candlelight, and she could feel the hard heat of his hands through the fabric.

It was horrifying, to be manhandled so, like a common actress in a side street.

She liked it. She liked the look in his eyes and the smile on his face and the ease with which he handled her.

She *was* a wanton.

Perhaps, if no one but Blakes were to know, it wouldn't be too scandalous. Certainly, he would tell no one. What man wanted his wife to be known as an unrepentant wanton? A secret wanton would have to suffice, however unrepentant.

"I am going to ruin you, Louisa," Blakes said in a voice just above a whisper, the sound so low and so intense that the hairs on the back of her neck rose in a chill of warning. "I am going to ruin you so completely that no man will have you, save I. I'm going to ruin you so that no man's touch will ever satisfy you, save mine."

"I suppose you're going to do it by talking," she said, taunting him, wanting to hurry him along, unable to bear the tension of pure waiting.

Blakes laughed, a mocking sound that filled the silent room like ripples of light.

"You can't bear it, can you?" he said, studying her, molding his hands to her hips, feeling the bones of her joints with his thumbs. "You don't know what I'm going to do and you'd rather be beaten to death by my hands than wait in fear."

"An overstatement of absurd proportions," she said, lifting her arms to try and rearrange her hair, a pointless exercise, but Sally Bates had done it in the second act of that abysmal play and it had done wonders for her bosom. And stretched her bodice ties to breaking, or nearly. "Have you always been given to exaggeration and melodrama, Blakes? I had no idea."

"There's much you have no idea about. But not for long." And with those words he grabbed her derriere with one hand and lifted the hem of her skirts with the other. A wash of cold air ran over her legs in a slow sweep of motion as he lifted and lifted . . . and lifted. "And I've seen your bust often enough to know it's quite fine. You can relax."

Relax? Impossible.

She did not try to argue with him for she knew that would only amuse him; besides, she was more than curious to see where these strange and slightly marvelous sensations would lead. And she was more than a little certain that Blakesley's hand would lead her there.

Wanton.

Well, there had to be worse things a woman could be. She would think of some later, when she wasn't so distracted.

"You are very quiet, Louisa. You're not going to faint, are you?" Blakes said as he methodically caressed her leg from the ankle to the knee, the fabric of her stocking increasing the sensation, magnifying it. Ripples again, ripples of sensation.

"No, though I may scream," she said, trying for sarcasm. She thought she'd likely missed it. She could barely stand, what with Blakesley's hand on her leg and his eyes studying her like she was an experiment he was conducting.

"My plans exactly," Blakes said, his smile deepening as his hand rose higher.

He was skimming over her thigh now, a tickle, a brush of skin against skin, a caress that teased.

"Did you bring me here to tickle me?" she said.

"I didn't bring you here at all," he answered, his smile lost. Oh, yes, she shouldn't have reminded him about Dutton. The fact was, *she'd* forgotten about Dutton. And hadn't Blakes promised he would accomplish exactly that?

Blakesley's touch, that gentle thing he'd been practicing on her was abandoned for something altogether more primal.

"Stand still," he commanded. "Don't move or make a sound, Louisa. I'm going to have my way with you and you're going to let me."

"Or what?" she said, daring him. Really, she didn't know what had gotten into her.

Of course she did. Blakesley. He'd ruined her by kissing her. He might as well ruin her by touching her where, frankly, she was desperate to be touched.

"Or I'll not give you back your pearls," he said, watching her face.

It hardly seemed the time to tell him that she hadn't thought about her pearls for simply hours and the entire matter of her pearls seemed, well, given the fact that she was ruined, completely irrelevant. If he thought threatening her with her pearls was an efficient whip, she wasn't going to be the one to disillusion him as to their inefficacy.

"Oh, no," she said flatly, forcing herself to face him when all she wanted to do was to close her eyes in abject shame.

His hands were under her skirts, both hands, and her skirts were at her hips. She knew that her legs were sticking out for him to see, a completely shameless posture, that her nether regions would soon be as completely bare to him, and she was determined, because she was clearly a fool, not to back down in fear and timidity.

She was afraid and she was timid, certainly about this, but it wouldn't do at all for Blakes to see it. They were to be married; every inch of skin revealed sealed their fate more firmly, and even now the stage was being set for their future dealings. She was not going to enter in with her head bowed and her hands shaking, hoping for the best and preparing for the worst.

She was not going into marriage as her mother had.

"You don't want your pearls back?" he said, his hands stilled as he studied her face.

"Did I say that?" she snapped. "Tell me, Blakes, do you even listen to me?"

"Not usually," he snapped back. "Especially not when you look as you do now."

Yes, like a wanton with her skirts around her waist. What man would care what a woman said at that point?

"How completely typical," she said, staring down at him, at his golden head and his cynical blue eyes, which did not look at all cynical at the moment. Blakes, dear Blakes, looked almost vulnerable. Angry and vulnerable. It was a combination she understood perfectly. "I suppose you even prefer it when I am as I am now, exposed, helpless . . . voiceless."

Blakes laughed, a short bark of laughter, and said, "Louisa, you are the worst liar I have ever known."

"I suppose you'd prefer it if your wife were an accomplished liar," she said, smiling in spite of herself and her exposed legs and his wandering hands.

"No," he said, his smile fading. "No, but we both know you shall never be voiceless. Not with me. Particularly as I plan to have you screaming in the next few minutes."

"If I scream now will you stop talking and kiss me?" she said.

"Kisses first," he said, standing, dragging her skirts with him in one fist, his other hand grabbing her neck and pulling her toward him, "screams later."

And then he kissed her. Finally. It was everything it should have been. Deep and hard and hot. Her breath caught in her chest and exploded there, sending heat spiraling upward and down, coiling in perfect curls of fire and longing. His hand pressed against her derriere, his fist releasing her dress to grab the woman beneath. She met his kiss and arched into his hand, moaning, but not screaming. Not yet. She would not give him that just yet.

His hand moved to the front, to the apex, to the quivering, slippery folds of her sex, and he cupped her.

She was hot. Wet. Trembling.

She wanted to buckle against him, sobbing out his name or some such trite nonsense. Blakes would lose all appreciation of her if she became, literally, weak-kneed. She locked her knees and held on, her hands gripping his coat, her mouth locked on his, breathing his breath, anchoring herself in his arms.

He fingered her folds, softly, testing her. She moaned and writhed against his hand. But she did not scream.

She would not scream until she could do nothing *but* scream, and she was a long way from that. She thought.

Blakes seemed to think differently.

He plunged a finger inside her, a violent action that matched her mood exactly. His mouth still possessed hers fully, his tongue filling her, commanding her to respond. She didn't need to be commanded. She was with him fully, eager to be ahead, to lead him on, to control his passion as he controlled hers.

"I'm in you, Louisa," he breathed against her skin. "Start screaming."

"Make me," she said, staring him down, but she couldn't see him, not really. She was passion blind, her eyes unable to focus, her thoughts chained to his hand and his mouth, assaulted and enjoying every second of it.

He scowled, a look that screamed sensual promise, and plunged his finger into her faster, harder, his thumb brushing against a tiny bud of explosive sensation she had no idea she possessed.

She bucked against his hand, fighting for more contact, fighting against the assault of his hand. She couldn't understand herself, not what she wanted, not what she should have wanted. It all disappeared when she looked into his eyes or plunged into his kiss. Or was plunged into by his hand.

"What are you doing to me?" she whispered against his neck, her mouth almost smothered in his cravat.

"Ruining you," he said, his voice hoarse and low. "Possessing you."

"You . . . you do it very well," she said, her voice breaking into a high-pitched gasp at some particular motion of his fingers. "The result of much practice, no doubt."

"Shut up, Louisa, and let me ravish you in peace, will you?"

"Lord and Master, I suppose, is what you had in mind," she said as he spread her thighs and plunged deeper, watching her, his blue eyes glittering.

"Oh, I think I've mastered this," he said, his fingers doing mysterious and wonderful things, things which . . . things which . . . *oh, dear.* "What say you?"

"Shut up, Blakes. I need to scream."

And she did.

Blakes grinned, which she supposed was allowable as he *had* earned it.

She collapsed against him, her legs truly now completely unable to support her, which pleased Blakes inordinately. He withdrew his hand and allowed her skirts to fall back to the floor, sat down in that very pretty chair, and pulled her onto his lap. She was, she was mortified to admit, clutching his shoulders as if he could keep her from falling off the edge of the world, which is exactly how it felt, and breathing so forcefully and so shakily that she was afraid she must sound to him as if she were on the point of death.

Blakes didn't seem to find any of this extraordinary in the least, which was just the tiniest bit irritating. In fact, Blakes couldn't seem to stop grinning. It was, she decided when he actually began to *whistle*, completely annoying.

Of course, it was at that precise moment that the door to the dressing room opened. She tried to jump to her feet, but Blakes, still in that same aggravating mood, held her fast and turned to face the open door, looking, she suspected, like a man about to enjoy an afternoon tart at his leisure. She, naturally, was the tart.

"Oh, *there* you are!" Molly said, eyeing first Blakes and then Louisa. Upon which, she added, "I should have known."

"We thought we heard a, well . . . a scream," Iveston said, looking over his mother's shoulder. He looked decidedly unconcerned for a man who had heard a woman scream.

"I'm certain you did," Blakes said before she could get a word out.

At which point, Molly's gaze went directly back to Louisa. She looked entirely displeased.

"I'll see about getting a special license," Hyde said, looking appropriately grim and ducal. "It might be best if we not wait the usual length of time for these things, special circumstances and all that."

"Special circumstances, to be sure," Molly said, turning on her heel and walking off. She had a bit of a time doing it as the way seemed to be clogged with bodies.

Louisa elbowed Blakes in the midsection, which proved to be the prompt he needed to release her. She stood, albeit on shaky legs, but she did stand and looked more closely at the opened door and beyond into the yellow drawing room. It *was* clogged with bodies, the bodies of the dinner guests, who, having become convinced that salmon was a shoddy affair when compared to the *affaire* going on in Hyde's dressing room, had left the table en masse. To see her. To see Blakes. To see what they were up to.

Which only required that they look at Blakesley's breeches at a particular point to see exactly what was up and what was pointing.

Melverley, when he heard of it, and of course he would, would not be pleased.

Louisa smiled.

Twenty

DUTTON was waiting for Blakesley when he arrived at Hyde Park for their dawn appointment. Of course, dueling was frowned upon and there would be hell to pay if they were caught, which hardly mattered as they had no intention of being caught. Besides which, as the whole of the cream of London Society had a fairly good idea of what was to happen this morning and had laid wagers on the outcome, it would have been very bad form for any of them to have reported it or made any attempt to stop it.

A wager was a wager, after all.

Speaking of wagers, Dutton and Blakesley had one which required settling, and Calbourne, there to officiate the duel, was not shy about setting that wager to rights.

"Before we begin," Calbourne said from his lofty height, "there is the matter of the pearl wager. By the terms, it is clear that Lady Louisa did, in fact, choose Lord Henry over Lord Dutton within the proscribed time and, therefore, Lord Henry has won the wager. In case of permanent injury, I do think it would be best if that wager be paid out now."

"You must think he's going to get the best of me," Dutton said, testing his foil. "I shan't be able to pay if I'm dead, shall I?"

"And that would be such a pity," Blakesley said, his voice tight. "Pay up, Dutton. Let's finish our business. I have another appointment in two hours and would not be seen in a lather."

"Going to beg her hand from Melverley, are you?" Dutton said softly.

"Try not to provoke him, will you?" Penrith said.

Penrith had come as Dutton's second. Iveston had come as Blakesley's. It was most convenient as all parties present knew the particulars of last night's events and no tedious explanations as to the source of the animus between Dutton and Blakesley were required. For all that men liked to pretend that they were above such concerns, they truly did love to know every *on dit*, and this duel was going to prove one of the finest of the Season.

"Will you pay your debt or not?" Iveston asked as Blakesley removed his coat.

"Of course I shall pay it," Dutton said, handing his coat to Penrith. "Am I not a man of honor?"

"I don't know," Blakesley snarled softly. "Are you?"

After that, it became very difficult for Calbourne to keep them from each other's throats, which clearly meant that it was the precise time for the duel to begin.

They were well matched in form and skill and temperament. Naturally, it made for an interesting and more than usually exciting duel.

The dawn was hazy and moist, the trees casting heavy black shadows over the trampled grass, the men grunting as the birds of the day sang their first notes.

Louisa, watching from behind a particularly large tree with her cousin the Marquis of Hawksworth at her side as her unofficial chaperone, grunted in concert with every grunt of Blakesley's.

"You don't think they shall do each other a serious injury, do you?" she asked Hawksworth.

"Not at all," Hawksworth answered, as if he had seen innumerable duels in his twenty years.

Ridiculous bit of male superiority, and so typical of males in general. Why, just look at Blakesley and Dutton, jabbing and slicing the air in an effort to skewer each other over . . . well, over her. It was not at all flattering. In fact, it was flatly irritating. What if Blakesley were killed, or worse, maimed? Who should marry her then and save her reputation? Not Dutton, that was certainly true.

"You are completely ruined, according to Amelia," Hawksworth said almost casually.

"Completely," she said. "Are you going to fight a duel for my honor, too?"

"Blakesley seems the right man for it," Hawksworth said, "especially as he's the one who ruined you."

Louisa cast a speculative glance at her cousin, just a glance as she didn't want to miss the duel, and these things were rumored to be over and done with very quickly. She didn't want to miss what was certain to be her only duel.

"I think you may be a coward, Hawksworth," she said. "Certainly that cannot be said of Blakesley, who fights Dutton for my honor."

"He fights Dutton for his own honor, Louisa," Hawksworth said, not even bothering to appear insulted. "No one has insulted me or even Amelia, why should I be desperate to fight?"

"You *are* a coward, aren't you?"

"Because I am not eager to get myself filleted? And over a woman?" Hawksworth laughed under his breath. "Fine. I am a coward."

It was at that moment, the moment when she was going to seriously chide Hawksworth for not displaying the proper manly traits, that Blakesley's foil sliced a neat line along Dutton's shirt, leaving a slim trace of blood behind. Louisa gasped and clapped her hand over her mouth. The last thing she wanted was to be found out and cast out. Actually, the last thing she wanted was to see Blakes bloodied.

Apparently, Dutton felt similarly for he spread wide his arms, tipped his foil down in a gesture of elegant defeat, and said, "Has honor been satisfied, Lord Henry?"

Blakes took a hard breath, staring at Dutton through the brightening day, and tipped his sword down. "Well fought, Lord Dutton," he said.

"Lord Henry," Dutton said, bowing just before he handed his sword to Penrith.

"You will not bother Lady Louisa again," Blakes said.

"That I will not," Dutton said.

The two parties swiftly departed the park after that, but not before Blakes looked over to where she stood with Hawksworth and smiled stiffly. Louisa gasped again softly and buried herself behind a very large and very dirty tree.

"Do you think he saw me?" she whispered to Hawksworth.

"Assuredly," he answered, adjusting his glove, looking at her in bored sophistication. Blasted Hawksworth, to behave so annoyingly; she thought of him more as a brother than a cousin and he knew just how to annoy her because of that closeness.

"How could he have?" she snapped, pulling her cloak closer about her. It was dark blue and should have blended her into the wooded background.

"Perhaps because you gasped and shrieked with every thrust of Dutton's blade?" Hawksworth said.

"I did no such thing!"

"You did exactly that, cousin," Hawksworth said. "It was most distracting to me; I can't think what perils you put the combatants in because of your womanish behavior."

"At least I am no coward!" she said as they turned to leave the scene.

"How could you possibly know that?" he asked, a smile hovering over his lips.

"Did I or did I not manage two men into ruining me on a single night? If you think it takes no courage to be publicly ruined, you are truly the callow youth I always believed you to be."

"Cousin, I apologize," he said, taking her elbow like the finest of men, which is what he was reputed to be, outside of the family, that is. "You are no coward. But can you brazen your way into marriage? That will be the true test of your mettle."

"Of course I can," she said with more confidence than she felt, even after watching Blakesley's heroic display on her behalf.

"I'm so relieved to hear it," Hawksworth said, "for if you cannot, then I don't see any way to avoid fighting a duel for your honor. That would be most inconvenient as I am an acknowledged coward."

❦

"DID he just say he was a coward?" Matthew Grey asked.

"A jest," his father, John Grey, answered him as they slipped back into the darker shadows of the wood.

They had watched the duel, of course. As warriors, they were interested in acts of valor and of aggression, and they had not been disappointed by the morning's entertainment. Sophia had told them of it, naturally, knowing they would find it instructive. John had seen enough of Englishmen, and French, to understand the nuances of their battle games, but his sons had not. Or, perhaps it was more accurate to say that his sons could always learn more.

They were, to a man, very well educated in how the different nations of the world conducted battle and built empires.

It was all very well to understand a man's weapons, but it was far better to understand his thoughts and the way his mind turned.

"She was here," Young said, looking at his brother George. "To watch him."

"He fought for her," George said. "She had a right to be here."

"But the English would not think so," John said.

"Yet he saw her and did not send her off," Young said.

"He knows her," George said softly. "He has an understanding of her."

"I am not as certain that she understands him," Young said.

They were walking almost silently through the wood, their bodies draped in shadow and worn leather, their voices hushed and soft, like the rustling of leaves. They moved quickly, effortlessly, without undue caution but not without care, back to Dalby House. Back to Sophia and her world.

"He will teach her," George said as Dalby House rose white and solid before them.

Twenty-one

WHILE the Duke of Hyde went about acquiring a special license, not a difficult task as he was so very well connected, Blakes was in Melverley House to meet with the Marquis of Melverley regarding his marriage to Louisa.

Blakes had brought Iveston with him, mostly because Iveston refused to be left behind at Hyde House. Iveston, however, waited in the small salon whilst Blakesley faced Melverley in the library, an impressive room that looked to receive a fair amount of use. Which, it must be admitted, struck Blakesley as very strange indeed as he knew Louisa was not interested in books and he strongly suspected that Melverley was of a similar disposition. Melverley was far too busy seeing to his many pleasures to bother about sitting quietly in a room alone to read. What Melverley enjoyed doing could not be done in solitude, unless a man were very, very desperate and, in London, no man was required to become that desperate.

Melverley, aged, dissolute, and struggling with gout, did not rise as Blakesley entered. He had hardly expected him to. Melverley, an old rake with a reputation for insolence and arrogance, rose for very few. Melverley had been close with the Duke of Cumberland, the Prince of Wales's dissolute uncle, and Cumberland was rumored to have learned all his dissolute ways from Melverley. They had been known to share their liquor and their women with equal freedom and with equal jocularity. Blakesley knew it to be true.

Melverley, red-haired and stout, his nose a web of broken blood vessels and his blue eyes pale and bloodshot, eyed him coldly as he made his way across the carpet. Blakesley, accustomed to dealing with his mother, who, while not bloodshot and stout, was formidable in the same fashion, was not intimidated or alarmed. In fact, he was slightly amused.

Melverley was about to be dealt a blow. Melverley, seducer of women, was about to face the seducer of his daughter. It had definite comic possibilities, not that he would see it.

Melverley, on top of everything else, had a rather underdeveloped sense of humor.

"My Lord Melverley," Blakesley said with a bow.

"Lord Henry," Melverley said, "what do you require of me so early in the day?"

It was eleven in the morning, but Blakesley understood very well that Melverley likely hadn't gone to bed, that is, to *sleep*, until after dawn.

"I shall be brief, Lord Melverley," Blakes said. "I have come to ask your permission to marry Lady Louisa."

Melverley eyed him from beneath bushy brows heavily mixed with silver. "Why should she marry you? The fourth son of a duke? She can do better, sir. She *ought* to do better."

Blakesley bristled only slightly and said, "I have ruined her, my lord. I must and will marry her. Hyde is seeing now to getting a special license, to put her under the protection of our name at the earliest convenience."

Melverley scowled into his teacup and breathed out heavily. "She allowed it, I suppose."

"I beg your pardon?"

Melverley looked up at him, and the animosity in the man's expression was potent. "She allowed it. She allowed you to ruin her. You didn't rape her, I take it."

"I did not rape her, no," Blakesley said, all thoughts of comic possibilities erased completely. "But as to allowing it, I'm not at all certain what you expected her to do to stop it. You are as aware as I that a man, intent upon his pleasure, will accept no boundaries to his desires."

And that was putting it delicately where Melverley was concerned. The rumors about him were legion and legendary.

"Nonsense," Melverley growled, staring up at Blakesley without a shred of embarrassment. " 'Tis the woman who calls the step; a woman of her rank and disposition calls the tune as well. You'll not convince me that Louisa did not do this for the express purpose of shaming me, which she has failed to do. And with the fourth son, no less. She could have at least shown some sense and aimed higher. Certainly some duke or earl could have been managed into ruining her. You, Lord Henry, have been made a fool. I will not join you. You will not marry her. Let her be ruined. She is like her mother before her, intemperate, unsubmissive. Let her learn, if she can, the price of rebellion."

Blakesley was at a complete loss for words.

Melverley, unfortunately, was not.

"Good day to you, sir. I hold that you are not responsible."

And with that, Blakes was escorted from the library.

ELEANOR watched as Lord Henry was escorted from the library, saw the expression on his face, watched him exchange a few soft words with Lord Iveston, watched Iveston's look of shock, watched them leave the house with rather more agitation than they had entered it, which she knew because she had watched that as well, and concluded, accurately, that Melverley had spoiled Louisa's chances for a good marriage with a man who clearly and devotedly loved her.

It was completely like Melverley, and she had suspected something very like this would happen since hearing of Louisa's ruination at Hyde House last night from Amelia. Amelia, as was to be expected, was not at all inclined to tell Eleanor anything, but Eleanor was not to be put off. She knew *something* had happened by the state of Louisa's hair. In the end, Amelia was convinced to tell everything she knew, which was quite a bit, actually, because Eleanor had told her that she'd be far more likely not to be ruined herself if she knew exactly how a girl could so easily become ruined in the first place.

Actually, it hadn't sounded very easy once she'd heard. It sounded very complicated with lots of comings and goings and witnesses. Eleanor wasn't entirely certain how Louisa had managed to pull it off, but her respect for Louisa was infinitely higher as a result.

Not an easy thing, to become ruined by exactly the right man.

And Louisa didn't have the benefit of all those plays and novels to give her any ideas on the matter. Really, it was quite an impressive bit of work.

Eleanor waited until the front door closed, the butler was out of sight, and then ran upstairs to Louisa's room. Amelia and Louisa were waiting for her, Amelia's expression hopeful, as was her disposition, and Louisa's skeptical, as was her disposition. Eleanor hoped her expression was one of intelligence, as she was fairly confident it was her most dominant trait.

"What did he say?" Louisa asked, putting aside her cup of tea.

"I didn't actually hear what was said, Louisa," Eleanor said. "You know how Anderson lingers whenever Melverley is about. I couldn't get near without being noticed, but I *did* see Lord Henry as he left, he came with Iveston, by the way. What a handsome pair they make." Amelia blushed. She would. Iveston was in line for a dukedom. "They did not look at all happy, Louisa. In fact, Lord Henry looked quite displeased and . . ."

She couldn't quite bring herself to say it. Louisa was not so hesitant.

"Displeased and?" Louisa prompted.

"Shocked, I should say," Eleanor said.

Louisa said nothing for a moment. She merely looked at the carpet under her bare feet. Louisa liked to go about barefoot whenever possible, a habit that Melverley abhorred, which merely cemented the habit into Louisa's repertoire of abhorrent habits.

"He's refused him," Louisa said finally, tucking one foot underneath her, her free foot toeing the carpet. "He's refused to allow me to marry Blakesley. I should have anticipated this."

"He'll never hold to it," Amelia said. "He wouldn't. It will make all of you scraps for scandal."

"Why should he care about that now? He's been the subject of scandal for forty years. He's used to it," Louisa said.

"But you're his daughter," Amelia said.

Upon which, Louisa looked up at Amelia, her gaze encompassing Eleanor, her eyes so blue they blazed, and said, "Not according to him, I'm not."

Which explained everything, naturally.

❧

"AND he gave you no explanation? No cause for such an action?" Iveston said.

"No. He blamed *her*, if you can believe it," Blakes answered.

"Knowing what I do of him, I suppose I can believe it," Iveston answered.

They had walked to Melverley House as it was not far and the weather was pleasant for April. Blakesley was now glad they had; he needed to walk, to move, to think. He had not anticipated this, though he could not but wonder if Louisa had. She knew her father. It was not unlikely that she would have guessed his response.

Yet what woman gently bred could have anticipated this from a father?

Louisa, as he knew her, could have.

And that remark about her seeking someone of higher rank to ruin her, had she been hoping Dutton would do the deed for these two long years? Is that why she'd followed him, trying to catch his eye and his interest, so that he might be tempted into ruining her?

To what end? Melverley would not marry her off, even ruined.

Blakesley could not reason it out.

"You still want her," Iveston said. It was not a question.

"And mean to have her," Blakes said.

"Then I think we need wise counsel, and I can think of only one who can give it, giving you what you want in the person of Louisa Kirkland."

Blakesley knew exactly whom Iveston meant. He had come to the same conclusion, for there was only one person in London who was devious enough to outwit and outmaneuver Melverley.

Sophia Dalby.

SOPHIA Dalby watched the skies roll back in a bank of solid gray cloud. The rain came down gently, gusting softly against the windows. She sat by the fire in the white salon, sipping a cup of coffee, listening with increasing interest to the very unusual, but not at all unexpected events as they had transpired at Melverley House just an hour past.

It certainly was the perfect distraction for a rainy afternoon, and it was so reassuring that London, as ever, could be counted upon to produce one *on dit* after another. One truly could not ask more of a town than that.

"But I'm not at all certain I see the problem, Lord Henry," she said, smiling pleasantly at them. "You have behaved honorably from the start. If Lord Melverley wishes to punish his daughter in this peculiar fashion, why, it can be no concern of yours. Your reputation will hardly be tarnished by his actions. In some circles, it might even be enhanced."

Blakesley looked ready to kill. It was such a good look for him, for any man, really. Men did so enjoy running about and killing things. It was just good manners to give them the opportunity to do so.

"And what about Louisa?" Blakesley snapped.

"I think Melverley made the point very well, Lord Henry," she said calmly. "Louisa Kirkland is none of your concern."

"I made her my concern when I kissed her," Blakesley said. "She will remain my concern until the day I die."

"But only if you are married to her . . . and have written up your estate to see to her welfare after you are gone," she said.

"Naturally," he bit out. "The point in my coming here is to find a way to marry her."

"To force Melverley to allow him to marry her," Iveston said for clarification.

Such a lovely man, Iveston, so unlike Blakes on the surface; one so cool and quiet, one so cold and sharp. It was difficult not to give in to the speculation that they were rather more alike than they appeared on the surface. Siblings were so often that way. Why, just look at she and John. So different. So alike. In all the ways that mattered, that is.

"And you came to me," she said sweetly. Men absolutely abhorred women who spoke sweetly when they were in a high state of agitation. Which is, of course, exactly why she did it. "I'm deeply flattered, but not a little confused. How, exactly was I supposed to help you? I have no connection to Melverley and I certainly cannot think of any cause which would allow me to intrude upon what are clearly family matters of the most intimate sort. Or did you have an idea?"

Of course he did not. If he had, if the two of them together had managed a single thought, they would be running about even now, attempting it.

"You must know Melverley," Blakesley snapped, giving into his rather sharp temper by fast degrees. It suited him completely.

"Of course, I *know* Melverley, but we are hardly on intimate terms," she said politely, and then added, "or did you mean to imply otherwise?"

"No, of course not," Blakes said stiffly, running a hand through his hair in distraction. Really, she had never seen Blakesley look more delicious. Louisa was such a lucky girl, to have acquired a man as delightful as this.

"Try to relax, Lord Henry," she said. "Surely, this problem you face has an obvious solution. One which I am surprised you did not stumble to on your own."

"And that is?" he said, giving her his most cruel and dangerous look, she was quite certain. It was most charming on him. What a delightful time Louisa was going to have with this man and what interesting children they would produce.

"I see I am required to lay it out for you," she said, considering them both over the rim of her cup. "For two men of the world such as yourselves, I'll admit to some surprise that it didn't occur to you earlier. But never fear, I shall not breathe a word."

"What *is* it?" Blakesley snapped.

Sophia smiled, delighted at his anger and impatience, for how else did a man of Blakesley's temperament express love? He was too guarded to fall to one knee and burst into tears, something which, delightfully, could not be said of the Prince of Wales. Prinny was so deliciously unguarded.

"Only that Lady Louisa has been ruined and once ruined, forever ruined. By you, as it so conveniently falls. You have ruined her, Lord Henry, and she, by all appearances, enjoyed it immensely. If Melverley refuses to allow her to wed, denying you the opportunity to make all right, then what is left but for you to continue on as you have done?"

"I beg your pardon?" Iveston said, his fair cheeks flushed, his quite remarkable blue eyes burning.

"I have not been sufficiently clear," she said smoothly, putting aside her cup. "I will amend. The girl is ruined. There is no future for her other than that of every ruined girl of every badly produced farce in Drury Lane. She is not to marry. Well then, she must find a protector. Why should it not be you, Lord Henry? You clearly have an affinity for each other, or am I mistaken? Was she merely a diversion for you?"

Blakesley looked at a loss for words. It did not last long.

"You would have me take her on? You would have her turn lightskirt? *That* is your solution?"

"Darling," she said with a soft snarl of warning, "I am not the one who lifted her skirts. What she is, what she is faced with, is your doing, not mine."

"I intended to marry her!" he barked, his face enraged.

"Yet made no provision for doing so," she said coldly. "As a plan, it was dismally ill-considered. But," she said, smiling again, "not unsalvageable."

"This is not a plan," Iveston said, "unless it be a plan for ruin."

"Darling," she said softly, looking at them both. Really, men were, by and large, such children when it came to love. They saw no nuance at all. It was charming, in a pathetic sort of way. "Louisa *is* ruined. There is no going back from that, is there? What we must consider is how to achieve what we all want from this particular point onward."

"What plan is required for making her mine?" Blakesley said, staring at her with almost hatred. Of course, he would turn his feelings for himself outward, at her. What else was a man to do when he hated the very thought of what he had done? "She is mine already."

"How very romantic you are, Lord Henry," she said. "But, allow me to instruct you. She is not yours because you have kissed or," she said, watching him closely, "put your hands where they had no right to be." He looked up at her with a scowl of warning. Perfect. It was as she had suspected. There was only one way to achieve wrinkles on muslin of the precise pattern as Louisa had displayed after coming out of that dressing room for the second time. "A woman about to enter the world of the demimonde must, from the very start, have a sound financial agreement on paper before any other intimacies are allowed."

"She is not—" Blakesley stormed, cutting her off. Really, he could get most aggressive on the topic of Louisa. How delicious.

"Allow me to continue," she said, interrupting what was certain to be a very long and very heated torrent of completely powerless commands. "You want to marry Louisa, yes?"

At his nod, she said, "Melverley denies you, yes?"

This time he didn't bother to nod, he kept his response to a scowl. Very predictable of him, but he was in a state of high agitation. He couldn't be expected to be his normal, engaging self at such a crisis of the heart.

"You, clearly, must force Melverley's hand, yes? How else to do so, darling Blakesley, but by following the only avenue *he* has left open to you both?"

A light of understanding slowly lit his eyes. Finally.

"Start the legal arrangements to pay for her, and make certain your clerk is not at all discreet. She will require a house, servants, an allowance, but I trust you know how to proceed on the particulars." Blakesley nodded, looking askance at Iveston.

"I don't know if she will agree to it," Blakesley said.

"I think you underestimate her, Lord Henry," she said, "but I will certainly speak to her, if you think it necessary."

"I'm not at all certain she will want to speak to either of us," Blakesley said.

To which, there was no response that could be made politely as it was almost ridiculously clear that Blakesley did not understand the situation as it stood between Louisa and Melverley at all.

&

MELVERLEY did not understand the depth of her rage at all, to think she would abide by his pronouncements regarding Blakesley and her marriage to him. Because Louisa was going to marry Blakes and her father was not going to stop her. He was acting out of pure spite, an emotion Louisa understood far too well. Yet, it must be admitted, it did give her an advantage for she was so very accustomed to thinking up ways to thwart Melverley's cruelty and indifference, and so, Louisa was able to devise the perfect hammer with which to bludgeon Melverley with.

It was as she was devising a way to get past Anderson so that she could hie off to Dalby House, that Sophia was announced.

They met in the drawing room, a lovely room of pleasing proportions and good light done in shades of fawn and blue, over a pot of tea that grew rapidly cold. Neither woman was in the frame of mind to dawdle over refreshments of any sort, even on a day that had gone quite cool and rain-soaked.

"Shall we pretend and speak of polite things or shall we speak as women?" Sophia said, watching Louisa.

Louisa was wearing a lovely gown of a quite unusual shade of pale wheat with black embroidery dancing about the bodice. It was quite a bold pattern and it suited her completely, which she had known when she had it made, but which was confirmed in Sophia's appreciative gaze.

"I'm going to marry Blakes," Louisa said in answer.

"Do you know how you're going to manage that?" Sophia said.

"I'm going to force Melverley to agree to it."

"And how shall you force him?"

"I'm not completely certain of that," Louisa said, hating to admit defeat on even the smallest point, but, truthfully, if she were going to outwit her father, she needed the help of the one woman in London who was known for her ability to not only seduce any man she wished to seduce, but to outwit any man who had the misfortune to cross wits with her. "I'm only certain that it can and must be done."

"Of course it can be done, darling," Sophia said with a smile, "and I know just how to do it. If you will follow my counsel on this, you shall have the joy of not only having Blakesley for your very own, but of thwarting Melverley in the bargain. Will you trust me? Will you do as I instruct?"

Familiar words, and she had no pearls and no Dutton to show for trusting Sophia and following her counsel. Why did that not seem to matter to her now? Now, it was all of Blakes and Melverley.

Now was all that mattered.

"I shall obey your every word, Lady Dalby," Sophia said.

It was certainly ironic as she had never spoken any such sentiment to Melverley.

Twenty-two

MELVERLEY was in the habit of attending the Theatre Royal on most Thursdays during the Season. He did this not because he particularly enjoyed the theater, but because he did particularly enjoy letting Society see his latest toss. Emily Bates, sister to Sally Bates, who was rumored to be pregnant and shuffled off to a town outside of Newcastle until delivered of the child, rumored to be Melverley's in fact, was his latest toss. She was a nice bit of baggage, pink-cheeked and dimpled, who giggled in bed.

Sophia knew this because she'd been told so by a man who'd been in bed with Emily and witnessed it for himself. Naturally, as she was as discreet as the next person, she was as happy to name the gentleman as, well, the next person.

"Richborough told me everything, naturally," Sophia said. "He also told me that she giggled during his most ardent moments, which I am not at all certain speaks more to her or to him. Certainly, there are many things a man may do at that particular moment which would make any woman giggle. Particularly with Richborough."

"You are not speaking from experience?" Anne Warren asked, looking at Sophia with some amusement.

"Don't be coy with me, Anne. You know full well that not only is Richborough the most indiscreet gossip of any man in Town, but that I am, unfortunately, in a very good position to know what dear Emily was giggling about."

"I believe I am supposed to be too innocent to discuss these matters with you, Sophia," Anne said. "Or at least I can pretend to be."

"And certainly you should pretend to be with Stavey, for he does love to protect you, but as women, we must be honest about these things. For our own protection, you understand."

"From what are you protecting her?" Dutton asked, having come up behind them in their box.

"From whom, would be a better question and would be my answer," Sophia said without pause. "From men such as yourself, Lord Dutton. You are remarkably quick to soil a woman's good name."

"But not a good woman's name," Dutton said. "A fine distinction."

"Certainly, we cannot be speaking of Lady Louisa," Anne said, taking up the argument briskly, "for she is as good as her name."

"Until events at Hyde House ruined both her goodness and her good name," Dutton said, staring hard at Anne. Anne was not moved. Sophia smiled and worked her fan, watching Anne manage Dutton. She did it very well for a girl not yet twenty-one. "Events which I had no part in. At least, not at first."

"I believe that discussing Lady Louisa is hardly discreet or in her best interests," Anne said.

"And why should you care about her best interests, Mrs. Warren? I was not aware that you were on good terms with Lady Louisa," Dutton said.

"I am on good terms with any woman who must defend her good name, Lord Dutton, from gentlemen who find vast amusement in ruining the same. I have been about in the world, Lord

Dutton, a fact which I think amuses you, but which has given me a taste for that which I do not and never will want," Anne said.

Sophia was truly impressed. This was a fine display of moral superiority and nothing would annoy Dutton more. It was an excellent piece of work for Anne and she was managing it brilliantly.

"And that is?" Dutton said, his blue eyes cold with anger.

"Oh, don't press her, Lord Dutton," Sophia said. "You are certainly no fool and therefore know very well what Mrs. Warren does want and that is Lord Staverton, and he wants her, darling man, and they will marry next month and be very content and positively boring in their respectability, which must predict that you and I will have very little cause to visit them. But speaking of visits, how did your dawn visit with Lord Henry go? I have heard so little of it, yet it promised to be so vastly entertaining."

"We had good exercise, Lady Dalby," he said, shifting his gaze away from Anne with such cool disdain that it could only be taken as a compliment of the highest degree. "What's more, we came to an end of our disagreement."

"And was there not a wager between you?" Sophia asked.

"There was," Dutton answered, "and he won it, I'm sorry to report."

"How very sad for you," she said. "Perhaps you will have more luck in your next venture."

Whereupon Dutton's gaze drifted back to Anne's with almost magnetic precision. How completely delicious.

"Perhaps I shall," Dutton said.

"Oh, hello, Markham," Sophia said, turning in her chair to offer her son her hand. Markham, the Earl of Dalby, kissed it lightly and then greeted Mrs. Warren with the same courtesy. Markham greeted Dutton with a nod and a half bow, which Dutton returned, his gaze most determinedly not on Anne. It was completely charming. "Are you sitting with us this evening or have you made other arrangements?"

"I thought I'd stay for the first act," Markham said, "if there's room."

"I was just on my way out, Lord Dalby," Dutton said, bowing to the women. Anne all but ignored him. Sophia smiled prettily and watched him go. Markham followed him out and said something in a subdued voice before returning to them.

"What did you say to him?" Sophia asked as Markham sat down and crossed his legs.

"I simply reminded him that Mrs. Warren was very dear to you, and therefore to all the Trevelyans, and as he had made something of a name for himself with Lady Louisa Kirkland, he should avoid doing anything similar with Mrs. Warren," he said. "I hope I have not embarrassed you, Mrs. Warren, but I do see it as my duty to protect you from rakes of that particular variety."

"And how many varieties of rake are there, Markham?" Sophia asked. "And what sort of rake are you?"

Markham smiled at Sophia and said, "Mother, there are certain things, indeed, many things, which a man does not discuss with the ladies of his family."

"All the truly interesting things, no doubt," Sophia said. "Never mind. I shall find out all by myself. Now, where are you off to after the first act?"

"Uncle John has something planned for us, I am not at all sure what."

"For all you boys?" Sophia said.

"Yes, we *boys*," he said wryly.

"Now, darling, I am quite aware that you are a man and that it is of the utmost importance for a man to think of himself as a man," Sophia said. "It is only for what cause he thinks of himself as a man that interests me. Now, certainly it must be admitted that Lord Henry Blakesley is most assuredly a man. His very acts prove it to be so."

"Because he ruined a woman?" Markham asked.

"Don't be absurd, darling," Sophia said. "It takes no ability at all to ruin a woman. It is what he does after that which proves or disproves his manhood. And I am not speaking of this morning's duel."

Which had been exactly what he had been on the point of saying.

"What then?" Markham asked, his sable brows quirked quizzically.

"Why, what he's doing now, Markham."

Upon which Markham and Anne Warren looked across the theater at the bank of boxes on the other side. It was, as ever, a sea of people lit up like individual gems in a jeweler's case, glittering and gesturing, talking and pointing, and behaving in any manner they found entertaining. The play on the stage had started, but the play within the confines of the walls of the Theatre Royal was already in full swing, each player watching for his particular moment of notice.

As it happened, all eyes were on the Duke of Hyde's box, for there, in full view of at least two hundred people, most especially the Marquis of Melverley and his woman of the hour, were Lord Henry Blakesley and, without chaperone and wearing a completely inappropriate but most becoming gown, Lady Louisa Kirkland.

They were alone.

They were plainly observed.

They were, to everyone's delight, behaving most, *most* indecorously.

Sophia smiled fully and, gesturing with her hand toward the Hyde box, said, "That's what a man does, Markham. Not only does he ruin a girl, but he does it in full view of her father."

"ARE you certain he can see us?" Louisa said.

"Everyone can see us, Louisa," Blakes answered.

"Then you best get on with it, Blakes. Seduce me, will you?"

Blakes looked over at her and said sarcastically, at least she assumed it was sarcastically, surely he couldn't have *meant* it, "It's better if you help."

"What am I supposed to do? Lift up my skirts and plant my feet on the rail?" she hissed, trying to look unconcerned and sophisticated and all the qualities courtesans were supposed to drip off of them like rainwater. She wasn't sophisticated, not in this. And she was very, very concerned.

It wasn't the easiest thing in the world to do, ruin oneself publicly and revenge oneself on one's father, but Melverley was just the sort of father that required such effort and sacrifice and plain strength of purpose from a daughter. Thank heavens she was accustomed to it, the effort and strength, that is. She was not at all tolerant of sacrifice and saw no need to make a habit of it. Just this once should be more than enough.

It had to be.

She just couldn't imagine doing anything of this sort again.

"It sounds promising," Blakes said in a rumble of what she could only hope was desire. "But I don't think you have it in you. And before you object and prove to me that you do, I don't have it in me to allow it. So keep your skirts about your ankles, Louisa. I almost think being here with me, alone, is enough to make the point."

"You obviously have no idea who Melverley is," she said, using her fan to obscure her face so that she could study her father.

He hadn't noticed her yet. Or if he had, he hadn't reacted to her yet.

But others had.

She could see Sophia in her box, Mrs. Warren at her side, looking ethereally beautiful. She truly did dislike that woman. Between them sat the Earl of Dalby, a most impressive-looking man, tall, lean, with enormous dark eyes, which, at the moment, were staring directly at her.

As was Lord Dutton, sitting in his box down one and over two from the Dalby box, a fact she knew almost as well as she knew the location of the Melverley box as she had learnt everything possible about Dutton in the past two years. His gaze, so direct and so smoldering . . . it sent a shiver down her spine. He'd fought a duel because of her, because he'd kissed her and Blakes had taken great exception to it. As he should have done. Blakes had kissed her first . . .

Oh, very well, *she* had kissed *him* first and that had, in effect, settled everything. She had, for reasons she had yet to bother to figure out, chosen Blakesley. She also was, for reasons she had not yet bothered with, not upset in the least to be stuck with Blakesley.

She had wondered, however, if Blakesley was the tiniest bit upset that he was now stuck with her. Because of her, and Dutton, for she did feel that the blame ought to be properly shared, Blakesley had fought a duel this very morning, not that she had mentioned the fact to him because women, stupidly, were not supposed to notice things such as duels and debauchery and gambling debts that destroyed family estates. It wasn't her fault if she weren't stupid enough not to notice things of that sort. Particularly debauchery, as it lived, one might well say, in her very own house.

Her gaze went again to Melverley and his latest woman, a woman who looked rather a lot like that actress, Sally Bates of the straining bodice. Melverley was looking down this woman's bodice, and she appeared to enjoy having him look.

Perhaps Blakes would enjoy a peep down *her* bodice? It was clearly, to judge by Melverley, a known expert in debauchery, the thing to do when with a woman of uncertain reputation. One could only imagine that, with enough men staring down a single bodice enough times, a woman's reputation would become very certain indeed.

"Look down my bodice," she whispered to Blakes from behind her fan.

"I beg your pardon?"

"I suppose you never once thought about looking down my bodice?" she said, shooting him a dark look of exasperation.

"I suppose you expect me to admit to lecherous thoughts about you and your bodice?"

"It would help if you could be at least a little enthusiastic about debauching me," she said sharply, snapping her fan shut. "I thought we agreed that this was the way to get what we want from Melverley."

"At the moment," he said tightly, "the only thing I want has to do with your bodice and how it gapes just enough to make me very irritable."

"I suppose that you will find fault with either me or my bodice and that, henceforth, all your irritable moods will be laid at that particular door?" she said, dipping her shoulders forward so that her bodice gaped a little more, only in an effort to achieve their goals, of course.

"That sounds reasonable," he said, leaning forward and, she assumed, looking down her bodice to the very creamy swells of her breasts.

She had quite nice breasts with not a single freckle to be seen. She only hoped he noticed the good care she had taken of her breasts all these years, years in which no one seemed *ever* to notice her or her breasts. High time that ended.

"Blakes," she said stiffly, eyeing him coldly, "no one in this theater will ever believe I am being compromised, let alone debauched, if you don't do something which gives the appearance of being, well, debauched."

"What would you suggest, Louisa?" he said politely, still looking down her bodice with rather more discretion than the situation required. Really, this was hardly the time to be discreet. "Shall I lift your skirts, spread your legs, and dive in?"

"Blakesley!" she said, opening her fan and truly using it to cool herself. She could feel a hot blush rising from the absolute base of her breasts all the way up to her hairline. Hot sweeps of embarrassment and, yes, the smallest bit of rising passion, roared up her throat and face. She was completely certain that the actors on the stage could see her quite clearly and, worse, could read her thoughts. "That's entirely too . . . blunt."

"You want blunt, Louisa?" he said softly on a snarl of passion. "Look down and see how blunt I am."

Yes, well, she did look down, and there he was. Blunt and bold and pointing directly at her.

She couldn't help it. She smiled.

"Amuses you, does it?" he said.

"A little," she admitted, mostly because she sensed it would annoy him. She did not know what it was about Blakes, but she got such a thrill out of annoying him mercilessly. "I suppose it's allowed for a ruined girl to find amusement in the man who ruined her, especially in this particular fashion, on this particular point."

"Point?" he said. "Clever, aren't you, and so very safe here, in the Theatre Royal. What will you do, dear Louisa, when I've got you alone and no one can hear you scream?"

"Why, Blakesley," she said, leaning very far forward so that she was quite, quite certain he could see most, if not all, of her flawless breasts, "if no one can hear me scream, then most certainly no one will hear you."

Blakesley smiled. A little smile, a half smile that he quickly swallowed so that he could scowl at her. "And how will you make me scream, Louisa? I can't wait to hear your plans for me."

"I," she said, thinking fast and coming up with very little, "I shall kiss you."

"I've been kissed by you. I did not scream."

She didn't know what made her do it. She didn't know where the thought came from. But, for whatever reason, her gaze fell again to his very erect manhood, and she said, "It is where I shall kiss you that shall make you scream, Blakes."

It was then that Blakesley hauled her up by her waist, swearing something unintelligible, or at least a properly brought up girl would have found it unintelligible, then backed her against the back wall of their box and kissed her deeply.

It was a most satisfying conclusion to her maiden efforts to get herself debauched.

One could not but wonder precisely how long she would remain a maiden if things continued on as well as they had begun.

Twenty-three

IT didn't take Aunt Mary very long at all to realize that Louisa was gone and that there had been a falling out of sorts concerning Louisa, Blakesley, and Melverley. Mary couldn't get any details from Eleanor, which was a point of some pride for Eleanor, but she was confident she could bludgeon them out of Amelia, a point upon which Eleanor was far less confident. Amelia could be rather soft when pushed, which only proved she was not any daughter at all of Melverley. In the Melverley household, one learned early on how to push back.

Things being as they were, namely, that Eleanor was not going to be forced into divulging any information about Louisa's whereabouts, and Mary having quite a bit of experience in how easy it was to lose track of Eleanor's whereabouts, resulted in Amelia being sent for. As it was evening and Hawksworth was on his way out anyway, he accompanied Amelia to Melverley House. Hawksworth, it was obvious, was more than a little curious.

Hawksworth, knowing very well both Louisa and Melverley, should have been able to puzzle it all out on his own. But then, Hawksworth was notoriously lazy, so he likely couldn't be bothered and would much prefer having everything spelled out for him, rather like Aunt Mary in that, actually. Aunt Mary was suspicious and experienced in dealing with Amelia, Louisa, and Eleanor, but she had yet to find a satisfactory method for preventing any of them from doing whatever it was they particularly wanted.

It made for a most convenient and congenial relationship, at least from Eleanor's perspective. She was quite certain that Aunt Mary, somewhat haggard and usually hungover, would likely disagree.

Those were the perils of being the only woman alive in two families who could function as a chaperone for two, almost three, marriageable daughters. Eleanor had determined from an early age that such a future was not to be hers. She could see no benefit at all to being an elderly woman without a husband; certainly in fiction they did not fare well at all.

Hawksworth, lounging in fashionable boredom on a long sofa in the library, eyed the women casually and with almost insulting lack of interest, his longish blond hair splayed out on the pillow beneath his head. Eleanor had never had more than a passing interest in Hawksworth, even if he were her cousin. He was the heir apparent to her uncle, the Duke of Aldreth; he was handsome; he was rich; he was, as a result, very tired of life at the profound age of twenty. She found *him* altogether tiresome.

"Hawksworth," Aunt Mary said, "how lovely to see you. You're not in Paris with the rest of them?"

Paris because the Treaty of Amiens had just been signed, which meant that Paris was free of war and therefore open and available to the wastrels of the world. Eleanor knew this because she did, after all, read Fielding. *The rest of them* being the other youngbloods of London, who were all, presumably, in Paris behaving as perfect wastrels.

"I'm back," Hawksworth drawled. "I shall go over again, as the mood strikes or does not strike, Aunt Mary. Is that why you asked us over? To discuss my travel plans?"

"No," Aunt Mary said, pretending to be cowed by his rebuke, but she was not. Aunt Mary had so much experience in dealing with overbearing and underchivalrous men, namely, the men her sisters had married, that she was very well accustomed to behaving in whatever ways pleased the men while simultaneously behaving in whatever ways best suited herself. Eleanor had long ago come to the conclusion that she liked that about Aunt Mary and that, even though often drunk, Aunt Mary was not often stupid.

"I asked you to come because, well . . ." Aunt Mary hedged.

Eleanor moved as quietly as possible to the farthest corner of the room, a corner almost completely drenched in shadow, and stood stock-still. Unseen was as near as she was going to get to being unnoticed. She, of course, knew what Aunt Mary was about to say and she had strong suspicions about where the discussion would lead. If she were correct, and she knew she was, then she would be sent from the room as it would be decided that she was inappropriately young and far too innocent to hear the particulars of the conversation as it pertained to Louisa.

She was not too young at sixteen to hear the particulars, but she would certainly remain far too innocent if she were ushered from the room.

"Yes?" Hawksworth prompted. Eleanor noticed that Amelia was looking around the room, likely trying to find her own shadowed corner.

"I seem to have misplaced Lady Louisa," Aunt Mary said.

"I beg your pardon?" Hawksworth said, sitting up slightly.

"Louisa is not at home," Mary said. "I don't know where's she gone. You don't think she could have eloped, do you? With Henry Blakesley?"

"She might have done," Hawksworth said, sitting up fully now.

"Certainly, it would serve. She would thwart Melverley and acquire Blakesley. A double gain, that."

"Don't be absurd, Hawks," Amelia snapped, standing up to walk over to her brother, her *younger* brother, and scowl down at him. "If you'd been in Town as often as you ought to have been, you would know that Louisa is and has been interested in only one man since her coming out, and that man is not Henry Blakesley, but the Marquis of Dutton. She would hardly gain what she wants by marrying Lord Henry."

"She's ruined now, Amelia," Hawksworth said stiffly, standing to face his sister, "she'll take whatever man she can and be thankful for him. If Blakesley is willing to have her, she'll be wise to snatch him up. She was silly enough to let him ruin her in the first place, it's only to be expected—"

"But Dutton ruined her as well," Amelia interrupted. "He could still be managed to the altar. If a male member of this family had the brass to do so."

Eleanor almost giggled at that, which would have seen her tossed from the room like so much garbage. She swallowed all sound, stilled all movement, though she did so want to clap for joy over Hawksworth's set down. He so deserved it, lazy sot.

"The point is"—Aunt Mary interrupted what was certain to become an argument between Amelia and Hawksworth that would entertain the servants of Melverely House for the following week as they repeated every word amongst them—"that Louisa is not here and that, given events as they have so recently transpired, I do think that she must be found, if only to be saved from herself."

"She is ruined, Aunt," Hawksworth said. "Saving her, even from herself, is certainly beyond our doing."

"Of course, *you* would say that," Amelia said sharply, "for it might require you to get up off the sofa."

Hawksworth, lazy to the last, saved his most energetic of looks for his sister. Amelia, it appeared, appreciated the effort made on her behalf. Certainly, they should all be glad when or if Hawksworth ever showed any sign of effort on any point.

"You have no idea where she could have gone?" Hawksworth asked Aunt Mary, turning from Amelia with flagrant irritation.

"She has gone to the Theatre Royal," a male voice, which was not Hawksworth's, said.

They all turned to the sound of that voice. He was tall, lean, dark, that was what registered first. Then, his clothing: leather leggings, some scrap of fabric hanging down over his manly bits, a coarse linen shirt. A knife.

A very large knife, almost a short sword. It glinted in the candlelight, a mesmerizing glow of deadly metal.

Then, his face. Deep-set eyes under a slash of ebony brows. Prominent cheekbones. A bold and hawkish nose. An angular face that was in want of shaving.

He stood in the room, his back to the open window behind him. Open because the rain had stopped and the evening breeze had been fresh and cool.

Eleanor looked around the room. In front of each open window stood another just like the first, younger, but just as savage. Just as foreign.

"You will not intrude," he said. "You will stay here."

"I think not," Hawksworth said.

"Think again," one of them said, the oldest of the younger set. *Indians.*

This time, Eleanor could not help herself. She clapped her hands for joy.

IF Sophia had been any less sophisticated than she was, she would have clapped for joy the very instant when Blakesley trapped Louisa against the dark back wall of their box and, to judge from his position, kissed her into oblivion.

Things were proceeding so nicely and without needless interruption, too. That was so important in events such as these, to keep things moving forward, as it were. Sophia rose to her feet, smiling meaningfully at Anne and Markham, though she had grave doubts as to whether Markham would understand what she meant, though she was certain that Anne would explain everything as needed, and walked out of her box and down a short flight of stairs and, knocking lightly, entered Melverley's box.

He was engaged in sweaty activity with Emily Bates, his breeches loosened sufficiently to get the job done, Emily's skirts lifted, her cheeks pink, her gaze wandering about the theater. Sophia smiled and winked at her and held her finger to her lips, watching Melverley at his toils, rather like Hercules, though certainly not as well formed as Hercules must have been.

When Melverley, who had a revoltingly white arse sprinkled with curling red hair, grunted and lurched for perhaps the twentieth time, though it could have been merely the third, she was simply too revolted to be relied upon for an accurate count, she decided she simply could not wait any longer and must speak out.

She was completely certain that Emily, young and struggling as she was to maintain even the display of ardor, would thank her.

"Lord Melverley," she said lightly, grinning when he jerked to a halt and swore a curse into Emily's bodice. "How delightful it is, bumping into you this way. Though, I suppose that is not quite accurate. 'Tis Miss Bates whom you are bumping into, so to speak."

Melverley, thankfully, covered his most unappealing arse, and stood, clumsily, to face her. Emily, by the look of it, was struggling not to grin and to appear properly embarrassed by the interruption. Dear Emily would simply starve if she ever had to rely upon her acting skills alone.

"Are you lost, Lady Dalby?" he said gruffly, still adjusting his breeches as he faced her.

"No, but I am so very afraid that you are, Lord Melverley. You seem to have quite completely lost your way with your elder daughter," Sophia said, looking at Emily, who read her nicely enough, smart girl, and who, mumbling, left the box to them. Melverley did not look pleased, but then, when did he ever?

"Louisa is none of your concern," he said, still gruffly because the poor man simply had no other way of communicating. It would have been distressing if it were not so amusing.

"She certainly is proving to be none of *your* concern, though Lord Henry Blakesley does not seem to mind giving her the attention she deserves and, perhaps, requires. How like you she is. How gratifying it must be for you, to observe at least one of your daughters following in your deliciously debauched footsteps."

"What the devil are you talking about, Sophia?" he said. Gruffly. "Lord Henry ruined her and she can stay ruined. 'Twould teach her well."

"I'm not precisely certain what you think it will teach her, unless it be how to live a life debauched, which, while it has a certain appeal, is not the route most men choose for their daughters."

"You know as well I, as well as all of London, that she is none of mine," he said. Yes, *gruffly*.

"Darling Melly, they do say that the father is always the last to know, but I do think you are pushing it. Louisa is all yours, from her ginger hair to her stubborn will and, I hesitate to say it to your face, her sharp tongue. How could you think otherwise?"

"Westlin told me as much," he said. "Margaret warmed his bed. She even admitted it once."

"Darling, Westlin thinks he has fathered every person of ginger hair between the ages of twenty-five and two who live within fifty miles of Town. It is a rare conceit, and I am quite certain he expects everyone in Society to indulge him, but I see no reason why I should, nor why you should. Can you?"

His poor battered face, for he did suffer from an extremity of color about the nose and chin that was most alarming, grew thoughtful and still. Poor dear, thinking was proving something of an effort after decades of fleshly indulgence. Well, he required managing, a tender leading string to prompt him to the correct conclusion.

"Her mother confessed," he said, belligerently, which did prove some improvement over gruffly.

"Darling, of course she confessed," she said in a gay tone. "Let me guess as to how the stage was set for that particular performance. You were then, as you are now, prone to dalliance. Westlin had started his rumors, all to benefit himself, which even you must admit. You accused her, the scent of another woman likely still fresh upon your skin, and she . . . ? She was supposed to play the long-suffering wife, true to the end, as you played Othello and smote her down?" Sophia laughed to see the look on his face. "Melly, you simply must stop living your life by some play or other you've seen. What did you expect her to say? She'd been accused, you were neither faithful nor discreet, and you presented her with the perfect revenge. I applaud her for taking it. What woman would not?"

"She could have denied it," he said.

"In the face of your disbelief?" she said. "Admit it, Melly, remember Margaret as she truly was, not as you've rewritten her in your memory. Could she have been faithless to you? Did she not love you? Was she not a good wife, a credit to your name?"

Melverley looked very thoughtful, melancholy, almost on the point of tears. How very well-deserved they were. He had behaved abominably, and he should repent of every foul deed from the day he first tupped a dairymaid to this.

"I should kill Westlin," he finally said, having composed himself to the best of his ability, which was not great, poor man.

"Westlin is not your problem, Lord Melverley," she said. "Louisa is. She has been ruined and will continue to be so and more so if you do not step in and make all right."

"You mean, to marry Henry Blakesley."

"Precisely."

"She could do better."

"My dear Lord Melverley," Sophia said, gesturing across the theater, the shouts and catcalls rising, "she is being done better even now. By Lord Henry. What you will not give, will be taken."

It was then that Melverley, who really must get his head out of a lady's skirts more often and look about him, saw what everyone else in the Theatre Royal was seeing, and commenting upon, loudly. Namely, that Lady Louisa Kirkland, eldest girl of the Marquis of Melverley, was almost certainly being tupped by Lord Henry Blakesley in a box at the Theatre Royal. She seemed to be enjoying herself far more than Emily Bates had done, but Sophia did not think that Lord Melverley would appreciate that distinction being pointed out to him.

"And you doubted she was your daughter, Melverley," Sophia said brightly. "You must be blind."

Twenty-four

"I'M not going to take you here, Louisa, pressed against a wall at the Theatre Royal," Blakes said, holding her at arm's length and breathing hard, rather like a man who was fighting for his very life.

Poor man. He was having such a difficult time resisting her. What was she to conclude but that she was irresistible to him?

"I think, Blakes," she said, smiling at him and licking her lower lip. He nearly moaned. It was extraordinary. She was enjoying herself completely. "I think that I shall have you anywhere I want you. I think, darling man, that you are powerless to resist me."

"And you want me powerless, do you?" he said, his blue eyes glinting like rubbed pewter.

"I'm a woman, aren't I? Naturally I want you powerless, at least where I am concerned."

"Darling Louisa," he said, mimicking her, "if you think that you have all the power here, now, you are very, very stupid. I don't mind, you understand, for a man does not require intelligence in a woman, particularly if she has a firm bosom and a solid arse, but I had thought, once, that you possessed some small bit of intelligence. Oh, well," he said with a rather nasty grin, "we shall have to make do without, shan't we?"

"Whatever do you mean?" she said.

She was very well aware that he was baiting her, but she could not fathom his reason. She was ruined. He had ruined her. Her father had to be punished for it somehow. And they had stumbled upon this happy solution. Why did Blakes have to muddle it all by thinking so much?

He did have the unfortunate tendency to complicate things. She would have to work on that.

"Only that, as ruined as you are, I'm not at all certain that Hyde will allow *me* to marry *you*, no matter what Melverley decides. I have done my part, certainly."

"I presume you mean the part where you ruined me?" she snapped.

"I thought your supposition was that you had ruined me?"

"Blakes, you know perfectly well that only a woman can be truly ruined, and I am most sincerely ruined!"

"You most certainly are," he said. "Which would mean, I presume, that I can take you or leave you, as the mood strikes me."

"Something certainly will soon be striking you, Blakesley," she snarled, grabbing him by the arms and trying to shake him. He was, most annoyingly, unshakeable. He stood like a rather stupid rock embedded in the soil, and with all the capability of a rock, too. "You have ruined me, in your father's very house, and you shall do all within your power to make it right."

"Ah, my power. I have so little, you see," he said, smirking at her as if this were a jest of immense proportions. "Your father denies me. My father, after this night's exhibition, will certainly deny me. We are, it seems, left without options. Except, naturally the option of me setting you up somewhere, somewhere not quite as respectable as you are accustomed to, but nice enough for all that. I shall set you up, give you a generous allowance, and see you at my pleasure. In fact, I have begun the arrangements today, as Lady Dalby so helpfully instructed."

"Lady Dalby! I should have known," Louisa spat.

"The only thing left, of course," he continued, all but ignoring her, "is for me to decide just when and where I will take you and, having sampled the goods, decide how much I will settle on you."

"Blakes, you have the most appalling sense of humor!" she said, crossing her arms over her breasts. It was all well and good to *play* at being a girl on the town, but it was altogether another to actually have to *perform* as one. "You know very well that you love me and want to marry me."

"Do I?" he said softly, pressing her back into the darkness, away from the catcalls of the crowd and the leers from the peers all around them. Was this to be her life now? "When did I tell you that?"

"You told me that," she said, lifting her chin and her hopes, "when you sat by my side at every event in Town for the past two years."

"The two years that you were chasing Dutton?" he said. "Is that when I declared myself and you heard my vows?"

Oh, he would make everything so difficult. Leave it to Blakes to want to poke and prod every little thing, even ancient things like her ill-founded fascination with Dutton. How was she to have known that Dutton couldn't kiss and couldn't make her blood roar? It was even worse that he couldn't make her laugh and, as Blakes well knew, only *he* could make her truly laugh.

"Blakes, you know very well that I *allowed* you to ruin me. That speaks volumes, if you would only admit to hearing the tune. Do you think I would have kissed you if I didn't know that you cared for me? *Deeply* cared for me? Really, I can't think why you are being so argumentative all of a sudden. You know perfectly well that you want me desperately."

"And you, Louisa?" he said on a soft growl. "Do you want me desperately?"

"Isn't it obvious?"

"Not quite," he murmured against her mouth, almost kissing her, but not quite. He truly did have the most malicious sense of humor.

His hands were doing wonderful, scandalous things to her breasts, teasing them, taunting her, and his mouth, that wicked mouth, breathing, tickling, tantalizing her without truly satisfying her.

She could hardly think for wanting his mouth on hers and his hands on her, and yet he was mumbling something against her skin, which was irritating in the extreme. The man needed serious instruction in debauchery; she was quite certain that there was no need for this endless *talking*. Certainly, there were far better things he could be doing with his mouth.

"Melverley pearls," he whispered just before he kissed her. It was not nearly enough of a kiss to satisfy her, as he almost immediately moved from her mouth to her throat to her chest to her . . . right breast. Finally, he seemed to have the idea of the whole thing.

And then he stopped and lifted his head and said, in an almost conversational tone of voice, which he was obviously putting on just to annoy her, "What about them, Louisa?"

"What?" she gasped, thrusting her breasts at his mouth with a moan of longing. "What about what?"

"Your pearls. This all started because of the Melverley pearls. What shall we do about them?" he said.

It was with some relief that she noticed he was struggling for composure and to keep his hands still, though they were snuggled just beneath the shadow of her breasts and he seemed to be having a bit of a time not moving them about. Blakesley was far less immune to her particular charms than he cared to let on. She had the most peculiar urge to giggle for joy.

She squelched it, naturally.

"I don't care," she said, making a grab for his head, to pull it down to her mouth, which he rudely avoided by pinning her arms to her sides. She did have the satisfaction of having her bodice gaping open in his general direction, but her skirts were firmly planted around her ankles and he didn't seem particularly eager to repeat his performance of the Hyde House dressing room. Really, she had never known Blakesley to be so ill-tempered and stubborn. One would almost think that he didn't *want* to seduce her.

"I thought you cared very much. I thought you wanted them back at any cost."

"Almost any cost," she said, deciding that trying to fight her way toward Blakesley's mouth was indecorous and, possibly, indecent. She relaxed against the wall and took a deep breath, hoping that the jut of her breasts would distract him.

He did, in truth, seem mildly distracted, at least for a moment.

It was not a pleasant moment; she was becoming seriously in doubt as to her powers of appeal. Could it be possible? Might he actually be able to resist her?

"I tried to get them for you, at almost any cost," he said, staring at her bodice, his gaze moving slowly down to her skirts. She tried to think of some way to encourage the direction of his gaze, but couldn't, other than trying to tackle him by wrapping her legs around his waist. She was completely certain that such an attack would be both indecorous and indecent. And she would likely miss.

"Yes, that was very nice of you," she said softly, staring at his mouth. He seemed to respond well when she stared at his mouth; it helped a great deal that she enjoyed his mouth immensely. "Did you get them? The pearls?"

His gaze left her skirts and went back to her eyes. Oh, well, she supposed she could entice him with her eyes as well as her skirts.

"Do you care so much, Louisa?"

Something in his voice, some small sound of pain and longing, made her forget all about his mouth and his hands and even her skirts to let her gaze linger on his face.

He was not a beautiful man, her Blakes, not beautiful and seductive as Dutton was, but startlingly male and strong and intelligent.

And she found that far more beautiful and seductive than any lovely face could be. When she looked at Blakes, she could barely remember what Dutton looked like, and she couldn't remember anything that Dutton had ever said. Blakesley's words hung about her like jewels, every sentence golden, every word a pearl of humor and insight.

It was all so clear. She could see it all so clearly, now that he had forced her to stop and think. It was not a comfortable habit, and she was entirely certain that she would not adopt it. This one moment of introspection would just have to be enough for him.

"No," she said, staring into his eyes, letting down the gates into her heart that had been put in place so long ago, a defense against Melverley. "I *don't* care."

"I have the necklace, you know," he said, watching her, waiting.

"But whatever will you wear it with, Blakes?" she said, smiling softly.

"I could give the pearls to my mistress," he said, leaning closer, which was very stupid of him, really. She could attack him at any time now. Poor Blakes, getting so careless of his virtue.

"You should only give them to the one you love," she said, pulling his face close to hers and kissing him on the edge of his mouth. "Give them to your mother."

Blakes started laughing then and pulled her into his laughter as he pulled her into his arms.

"A strand of pearls will likely warm things enough for Hyde to give his permission for me to marry you. He likes you, you realize," Blakes said, wrapping one arm around her waist and with the other hand, lifting her skirts slowly. Finally. "Hyde likes redheads."

"As does his son," Louisa said.

"As does his son," Blakes repeated just before he kissed her. About time, too.

Twenty-five

IT was perfectly clear to Melverley, indeed to everyone in the Theatre Royal, that Louisa was being thoroughly seduced and irretrievably ruined by Henry Blakesley. What was less certain was how far the seduction was actually progressing and if, once fully engaged, Blakesley would marry her.

"I must admit to a bolt of nostalgia," Sophia said, hovering near Melverley's elbow, though his linen truly was past due for washing, "for it was in this very theater that I lost my virtue to . . . well, I suppose it would be very indiscreet of me to name names, even at this late date." And she laughed to punctuate the moment. Melverley, as was to be expected, did not take it in stride.

"You don't mean to say you lost . . . but that's not possible, for I know you were taken up by Westlin before your arrangement with Dutton."

"Oh, darling, of course I didn't mean my actual virtue, but my virtue specifically as far as Dutton was concerned. And I do think it dreadful of you to name names. Dutton is certainly dead, but his son lives on, and you know how it distresses these children when the past is paraded out for them to see. And now Louisa and I shall have that in common. How lovely for her, to lose her . . . oh, but I suppose it may already have been lost in that wonderful dressing room at Hyde House. I simply must have a carpenter in to see to my dressing room. It is most definitely not performing as it clearly could."

Which produced the precise result she had planned for.

Melverley, who did so love to bluster and storm and speak gruffly whenever he possibly could, shouted out across the theater, which was such a huge success that all the players on the stage stopped their performance to watch and listen, for surely this moment was the most entertaining play of all, to Blakesley in his box,

"You can and shall marry the girl, Blakesley!"

Upon which, Blakesley appeared at the rail, looking deliciously disheveled, his waistcoat all but stripped from him, his hair a perfect halo of wantonness, and, smiling, held his hand out behind him to catch Louisa to his side. She looked just as wanton and disheveled and, plainly, fully debauched. As a pair, they grinned at each other and then at Melverley. And it was in complete perfection of purpose and with ringing clarity that *Louisa* called out across the theater, "Of course he shall, for I shall have no other!"

At which point, most delightfully, the entire theater rang out in applause and calls of good cheer. It was one of those rare moments when London, all of London, seemed in the same state of high good humor.

RUAN watched Sophia in Melverley's box and could not help smiling, not that he tried. She had done it. He didn't know precisely what or why, but he knew that look of hers by now, that smiling, satisfied look, that *I've done what I set out to do* look. She'd had it when her daughter had been ruined by Ashdon and she had it now, watching Louisa Kirkland being ruined by Henry Blakesley. Apparently, Louisa had been encouraged to forget all about her passion for the Marquis of Dutton. Just like that.

Nothing happened just like that, not without a considerable bit of help.

It did seem strange to him that Sophia Dalby appeared to enjoy helping girls of good family, starting with her own daughter, get ruined. But the evidence was blinding.

As was the woman.

She was fascinating.

He wanted her.

The problem, as he saw it, was that getting her might be more of a challenge than he'd thought. She was not a woman easily won nor easily managed, though, again, watching Henry Blakesley and Louisa Kirkland leave their box, Louisa's hair a complete ruin, it was clear that Sophia found it very easy to manage others.

He was not too proud a man to learn from his betters and in this, Sophia just might classify as his better.

He wanted her.

He meant to have her.

The thing to do was to watch and learn how best to acquire her.

With that thought foremost, Lord Ruan left the Theatre Royal. He'd come alone and he left alone, though he was beginning to wonder if being seen with a woman was the surest way to get Sophia's attention.

What sort of woman would annoy her most?

He grinned, in a better humor than he'd enjoyed for the past week.

ELEANOR watched the Indians in her house and felt such absolute joy that she could barely breathe. She had her very own Indians, in her own house, and she could study them at will. Every rumor of them was being proved true.

They were a handsome race. So very true.

They were savage in their dress and deportment. Also true.

They were stealthy and ruthless. Obviously true, for they had successfully entered her home and kept them successfully sequestered without the servants knowing a thing.

It was a brilliant bit of work. She was immensely impressed. Eleanor had not a thought of being distressed or anxious because, after all, these men, savage as they were, were relatives of Sophia Dalby and Sophia was a countess and, really, who needed to be afraid of a countess's relatives?

"Hawksworth," Amelia said softly, as if no one would hear her, but of course, they all could, "*do* something."

"What do you propose?" Hawksworth said in a completely normal tone of voice, which irritated Amelia obviously and instantly.

Amelia and her brother had one of the most peculiar sibling relationships Eleanor had ever seen; Amelia was one of the calmest, most soft-spoken of women in every situation with every sort of person. Certainly, she was all that was kindness and tact with Louisa, and who knew better than Eleanor how impossible that was to accomplish? Yet with Hawksworth and only with Hawksworth, Amelia lost her gifts of patience and kindness completely. Of course, Hawksworth *was* irritating, Eleanor was not arguing that point at all, but it was that Amelia lost all capacity for patience and good humor when in his company and only in his company.

Actually, it was rather like her relationship with Louisa. Eleanor, naturally enough, felt far more provoked and was equally certain that she managed her emotions better than Amelia seemed capable of doing. Of course, she fully expected her relationship with Louisa to improve by leaps once Louisa got married because then, obviously, they would so rarely see each other.

Of course, she would write her weekly, but it was so much easier to be pleasant in a letter than face-to-face, especially as she was almost certain that Louisa would not be writing her. In point of fact, Eleanor was not entirely certain that Louisa was literate.

But that would be her husband's problem. One did wonder,

however, who could be found to take on the job of husbanding Louisa.

"You are her sister," one of the Indians said to her. He was the youngest of the three sons, and he had the most remarkable blue eyes. He was standing, his legs scandalously displayed, his dark chest clearly visible through the opened edges of his shirt; why, he was almost nearly naked. Eleanor could not stop staring at him and, thankfully, had been raised in a household that did little to discourage her from exploring her interests. She was very interested in Indians in general and these Indians in particular. And this Indian in very particular.

He was very, very handsome in a perfectly marvelously *savage* way.

Why, she could feel a shiver down to her very toes.

"Whose sister?" she said softly, because, while she could and did explore various topics, she did not make a habit of displaying her varied interests to Aunt Mary.

"The other redhead," he said. "Louisa. Your hair is the same."

In point of fact, her hair was not truly the same; hers was darker than Louisa's brilliant orangey red, and hers was almost straight while Louisa's was quite vividly curly. But, yes, they both had red hair. She did find herself wondering if all redheads with white skin looked alike to Indians.

"What is your name?" he asked. He was not holding a knife, not the way John Grey was, but he had one in plain sight, in a scabbard attached around his waist. It looked appropriately savage and slightly irresistible on him.

"Lady Eleanor Kirkland," she said. "What is yours?"

"Mr. Matthew Grey," he said.

"But that is not your Indian name," she prompted, because, truly, wouldn't it be lovely if he had some marvelous name like Running Wolf or Tall Fire or something equally poetical?

"It's not?" he said, and while his voice and his expression were completely solemn, she just knew that he was laughing at her.

Strange, but in all her thoughts about American Indians, she had never imagined them as having a sense of humor and she certainly, in her secret dreams, had never imagined that an American Indian would find it necessary to make fun of *her*.

Sometimes reality could be distinctly disappointing.

"Surely not," she said with great dignity. She had read all about Indians, after all. He couldn't fool her on a subject as basic as the common practices of the average Indian on the naming of children. Why, she'd read an entire chapter on it, though, admittedly, it had been a short chapter in a very old book. Still. "It's a well-known fact that Indians on both the North and South American continents name their offspring names of significance, of personal significance," she clarified.

"Matthew Grey's not significant?" he said.

Again, it was becoming horridly obvious that he was mocking her. She didn't find anything remotely amusing about it, and it was becoming more and more clear to her exactly why Louisa hadn't wanted to discuss Sophia's American relatives.

They were, it was proving, highly unpredictable.

"Not significant in the proper way," she said. Really, did he require instruction upon the customs and habits of his own people? How very odd. "For instance, what is your father's name?"

"Mr. John Grey," Matthew, for what else was she to call him, answered solemnly.

"I mean to say, what do *you* call him?"

"I don't call him much. He calls me," Matthew said pleasantly. It was very irritating.

"Very well, what about your brothers? They *are* your brothers?"

"Yup," he said. "George is the older and Young's the younger. I'm the youngest."

"Oh, yes, Young," she said in some excitement for this was more directly to the point, "now from where does that name spring?"

Matthew looked at her in open bemusement and said, "Because he's John the Younger. Younger than John, his father. Young."

It was *very* irritating.

"Matthew," John the Elder called from across the room. "Come here."

Upon which, Matthew turned and left her without a polite word to ease his parting and stood at his father's side. Young and George were already in attendance upon their father, Mr. John Grey, as if any proper Indian would have such an ordinary name, and they were all staring at Aunt Mary. It was most peculiar. Even Hawksworth sat up from his slouch on the sofa, something he had not done in at least ten years.

"This is Lady Jordan," John Grey said.

Whereupon the boys bowed and kissed Aunt Mary's hand, which was completely ridiculous as she was almost positive that Indians did not kiss hands in the French style, and, most peculiarly of all, Aunt Mary stood straighter and with more pride than she had in Eleanor's memory and smiled with rather more warmth than was necessary at John Grey. It was the most peculiar event of an entirely peculiar evening.

Aunt Mary looked as Eleanor had rarely seen her, and the shade of the beauty she had been, she and her two sisters, shone out with a pale glow. Her hair, still pale, but mostly gray and silver strands from Eleanor's earliest memory, seemed almost to sparkle in the candlelight and her blue eyes shone. She looked almost lovely, standing there, smiling up at Mr. John Grey, almost as if she knew him. In fact, now that Eleanor thought about it, Aunt Mary had not seemed very much alarmed at the sudden appearance of four Indians in their midst, and she certainly did not seem alarmed now.

She seemed, beyond all reasonable expectation, to be pleased.

Eleanor did know a fair bit about people and events and things; she did read quite a lot and it was nearly impossible not to learn a good deal about a great many things from books. For some peculiar reason, which she could not puzzle out, the events of the past quarter hour did not fit in with anything she knew.

It was most distressing.

"You have lovely sons, John," Aunt Mary said, which, it must be admitted, was entirely too familiar, even if he were an Indian. "I am so glad for the chance to get to know them."

"We've met," George said with a lopsided grin, "but I was busy seducing your niece. Sorry."

"Yes, well," Aunt Mary said, "you clearly take after your father in that. Though I do remember him as being rather more successful at it."

To which John seemed to grin, though it was rather difficult to tell as his features bore a remarkable resemblance to chiseled granite.

"Now, don't count me out," George said. "It was hardly a fair fight. Her heart was set, and there was no turning it."

He was referring to Louisa, obviously, as her heart was clearly and relentlessly set on Lord Dutton. Everybody knew that, even Indians new to Town. Poor Louisa, to have made such a cake of herself.

Hawksworth was standing at this point, something of an exertion for him, and walking over to where Aunt Mary stood with what could only be termed her admirers. It was quite extraordinary. She didn't even, and this was the truly extraordinary bit, appear drunk.

"You know my aunt, sir?" Hawksworth asked of Mr. Grey, which truly, given Hawksworth's temperament, was a gigantic effort. "I would ask how."

"I have been in England before this," John Grey answered. "I know not only Lady Jordan, but knew each of the Whaley women. Before they were married. And after."

"You knew my mother?" Hawksworth said.

He clearly was not pleased by the thought. Eleanor understood the feeling entirely. *Her* mother had known an Indian, and told her nothing of it?

"Yes," John Grey answered, his dark eyes revealing nothing, but nevertheless showing the gleam of amusement.

These Indians certainly did enjoy their inexplicable jests. It did not seem at all a very Indian sort of thing to indulge in. Though, perhaps because they were part English, that would explain what Eleanor could only think of as a discrepancy. Certainly Indians should never be jolly. That would be absurd.

"In what capacity?" Hawksworth asked Mr. Grey, which surely was most inappropriate of him, and in mixed company, too. "I mean to say, how did you meet?"

Well, that was slightly better. It might have been the rather frigid look in Mr. Grey's eyes when he'd asked the first bit that had resulted in asking the second. Hawksworth was not known for his bravery, not that she blamed him in this instance.

One thing was very true about Indians: they did appear most formidable.

"I don't believe that's any of your concern, Hawksworth," Mary said, showing more steel than she had in ten years. "Both of my sisters are deceased; clearly their memories are buried with them. My memories are my own. I don't care to share them with you."

Well.

Eleanor looked at Aunt Mary with more interest than she had ever done.

"It's enough that you know," Aunt Mary continued, "that I have an old acquaintance with Mr. Grey and that I am pleased, *very* pleased, to renew it."

It was the way she said *very pleased* that was astounding. It did appear that Aunt Mary might be something of a lightskirt, at least where Mr. Grey was concerned.

As far as that, seeing Mr. Grey and his sons up close, Eleanor was entirely sympathetic. They were, as a group, compelling. Individually, they might actually be irresistible.

"But if it is a question of honor," Hawksworth said, speaking to Mary and, in effect, ignoring the Greys, which Eleanor did not think quite wise of him, "I must insist upon—"

"What would you do?" Matthew asked, which really was remarkable, to interrupt a marquis that way. It simply wasn't done and certainly never by a commoner. It was becoming increasingly clear that the Greys did not think of themselves as commoners. "You have no heart for battle, even when the honor of one of your women is at stake."

"I beg your pardon?" Amelia said, staring at her brother. "What is he talking about, Hawks?"

Hawksworth looked uncomfortable; it was a look which suited him completely.

"Dutton and Blakesley dueled this morning. I took Louisa to watch," Hawksworth said, looking slightly sheepish.

"That was highly improper, Hawksworth," Aunt Mary said, which was truly remarkable as everything about Aunt Mary spanning the past twenty years was beginning to look improper. "A duel is no place for a woman."

"Or a man unwilling to fight," George said.

Upon which Hawksworth cleared his throat and said, "It wasn't my fight."

"It should have been," John Grey said, which appeared to be the final word as every man in the room fell silent after that.

"I am concerned, Mr. Grey," Aunt Mary said, "about my niece Louisa. She is not here and she should be."

"She is at the Theatre Royal, Lady Jordan," Mr. Grey answered conversationally, "being ruined by Henry Blakesley. Again."

Amelia sighed and sat down again, her hand to her brow. Hawksworth didn't seem to know what to do with himself, so he sat. He liked to sit and did so at every opportunity.

Aunt Mary, on the other hand, looked at Mr. Grey in a state of excited agitation.

"Melverley is at the Theatre Royal, I believe," she said.

"Exactly," John Grey said. "It was necessary. To move things in the right direction."

"He'll have to insist," Aunt Mary said.

"He will," Mr. Grey agreed.

Upon which, Aunt Mary sat down with what could only have been a sigh of relief.

"Oh, thank goodness for that," she said, which was something of a surprise, as most chaperones and aunts did not wish for their nieces' ruination.

"Thank Sophia," John said.

Aunt Mary looked up at John Grey, her blue eyes thoughtful and perhaps resigned.

"I suppose I must," Mary said.

Twenty-six

BEING a duke carried with it many advantages, one of which was the ability to make things happen upon a moment's notice. That the elder daughter of Melverley had been repeatedly ruined and that one of the sons of Hyde was willing to marry the girl was the subject for not a little gossip and the speedy acquisition of a special license to marry.

Lord Henry and Lady Louisa were married, appropriately, in the yellow drawing room of Hyde House.

"I met you here, in this room, you know," Blakes whispered to Louisa just minutes after the ceremony.

"You remember where you met me?" she said. "You're just trying to convince me you're a romantic, and I'll believe many things of you, Blakes, but not that."

"It was in the yellow drawing room," he said, "two years ago at the assemblie."

"Everyone attends the Hyde House assemblie," she said, walking the short distance to the fireplace.

"You were talking to Amelia."

"I'm always talking to Amelia."

"You were wearing white."

"Who doesn't?"

"You were wearing white silk with a pale green sash and the Melverley pearls."

She looked up at him, completely ignoring everyone in the room, her eyes wide with disbelief and profound appreciation.

"You *are* a romantic," she said.

"Only since meeting you," he said, taking her by the arm and leading her to the door to the dressing room.

"That's a very romantic thing to say, Blakes. Are you going to make a habit of saying pretty things to me"—Louisa stopped and looked around her at the dressing room—"and are you going to make a habit of saying them in this dressing room?"

"I've developed a fondness for this room," he said.

"I can see that."

"I've developed a fondness for doing certain things in this room."

"Only in this room?" she said, starting to laugh. "That could be a problem, don't you think?"

"Only if my parents object. And they're hardly likely to do that."

"Oh, come now, Blakes. They certainly must dislike me . . ." Her voice trailed off and she looked at the floor between Blakesley's feet. The mood was broken, and they knew each other too well not to know who and what had broken it.

"My father," Blakes said, lifting her chin with his hand, "is fascinated by you, as am I."

"Oh, really, Blakesley," she said, taking a firm breath.

"You know my mother," Blakes said. "It surely must be obvious the type of woman he prefers."

"Yes, well, I suppose that's possible, but your mother—"

"Is old friends with Sophia Dalby," he interrupted. "You can't think that any of this"—and he made an impatient motion with his hand—"was by chance? I'd love to know how they managed it between them. I can't see *how* it was done, but I know it *was* done. We, dear girl, have been managed, and expertly. I wish I could resent them for it. But I can't. Can you?" he asked in a soft whisper, his romantic heart laid bare.

"Not at all," she said softly in answer.

But she did not look certain of anything, least of all his declaration; Blakesley knew all of Louisa's looks and looking uncertain was surely new for her. Blakesley closed the distance between them, wanting to hold her, not wanting to see the empty ache flickering in her eyes.

"What is it?" he said softly, his arms wrapping around her narrow waist in a solid coil of love and possession. "Don't bother to lie."

"I never lie!" she snapped. "You ought to know that."

"Which I do, which is why you will tell me. What is it?"

She sighed, her ribs expanding to strain against his arms. His arms would not release her.

"My father was most exquisitely brought to heel, insisting upon our marriage," she said, her voice small and tight, almost childlike. It was most alarming. "But what brought your father to heel, Blakes? And your mother? They have been opposed to me from the start, and no matter what history ties Molly to Sophia, your mother cannot be pleased to have me in her family. She has made that more than clear more than once."

"They were in this together, I tell you—"

"Don't be absurd, Blakes," she interrupted, her voice snapping and breaking into threads of hurt. "No woman would arrange for her beloved son to marry me."

His arms tightened around her in concert with his heart. Darling, incandescent, violent Louisa, broken into bits by her father as a girl, she had refashioned herself into a woman who could withstand him. Yet she bore the scars, a tracery of brokenness, and they were what made her beautiful, like glazed and fired porcelain, gleaming in fragile strength.

"She did," he said simply. "She has."

"She hates me."

"How very fortunate that you did not marry her, but me." Louisa squirmed in his arms, but he did not loosen his hold on her. He never would. "I love you."

"I don't believe it."

"Give me time," he said, kissing the top of her flaming red head. "You will."

That silenced her. He would not have thought it possible. Clearly, declaring oneself as a hopeless romantic with the soul of a poet was the way to subdue Louisa's will to fight. How he wished he had known that two years ago.

"What do you love about me?" she said, her face buried in his shirt, hiding from his gaze.

"You are entirely lovable," he whispered into her flaming hair. "But I am not such a fool as to categorize your assets. You would run me to ruin if you knew how foolishly and completely I love you. No, a man must have boundaries."

"How arrogant you sound, Blakes," she said softly, and he could feel her smile against his shirt, her back relaxing to arch into his. "I don't think I shall tolerate arrogance from you."

"I'm quite as certain that you shall," he said, smiling at the wall of the dressing room, of all things. "I know exactly how you shall be managed, Louisa. You shall enjoy it completely."

"You sound very certain," she whispered back, pressing her hips against his.

"I am certain of many things. For one, my parents are most pleased by you. For another, Melverley is an ass."

"Very certainly," she said, leaning into him, wrapping her arms tightly around his waist.

The silence encircled them, not an uncomfortable thing, and

they clung to each other, which was entirely right. Still, one thought hovered. . . .

"What of Dutton?" he asked, bracing his chin on the top of her head.

Louisa jerked out of his embrace, her eyes flashing in annoyance. He was as charmed by her annoyance as he ever was. "Dutton? What has he to do with anything? Do you think me a fool, to have tasted you and somehow still hungered for Dutton?"

"You did hunger for him."

"You will allow that most of the women of the ton find him fascinating," she said hotly. Before he could answer her, she said, "You will admit that he is handsome and eligible and a rake."

"All the things a woman finds irresistible," Blakes said flatly, not quite as amused as he had been.

"Precisely," Louisa said sharply. "Of course, he is very obvious about it, is he not? How could I have known that you were far more rakish than he could ever dream of being? I ask you," she said, smiling crookedly up at him, "has Dutton ever ruined a girl at the Theatre Royal?"

"Well," he said slowly, starting to smile.

"I mean, of course, a girl not already ruined in some other fashion by some other man."

"Then, no," Blakes said solemnly, "I should say not."

"He certainly is jealous of you, Blakes," she said. "I'm not a little afraid that you have set the bar entirely too high in the ways and means of ruining fine young girls, and what happens after that but that it becomes the fashion to debauch girls in dressing rooms and theaters? I daresay, you could well become legendary."

"I suppose I could live with that," he said, pulling her into his arms and leaning down to kiss her as she ought to have been kissed five minutes ago. Silly man, he required so much *prodding;* she would have to work on that with him.

He kissed her deeply, as was her preference, and her skirts were up around her waist without any prompting on her part, surely an improvement. He found her wet and hot and ready, and he did exactly as he ought to have done upon finding conditions so favorable.

He debauched her beautifully.

This time, she was able to wrap her legs around his waist, and not miss, and to kiss him and hold him to her without being restrained. Although, being restrained had its own pleasures, which she was certain she could induce Blakes to explore later. As things stood now, they were quietly debauching each other while their wedding guests waited beyond the door.

Louisa was not unaware, for she did listen to interesting rumors as avidly as the next person, that Caroline Trevelyan had been deflowered in precisely the same manner less than an hour after her marriage to Lord Ashdon. Up against a door, a dining room door, as the story went, and witnessed to a strange degree by the Duke of Calbourne. Louisa, who could admit to a healthy competition with Caroline, had *three* dukes at her wedding and was being deflowered less than *half* an hour from the last words spoken at the marriage ceremony.

By any measure, she had won. She had Blakesley, did she not?

"IT does the heart good to see a man so well matched in his passions, does it not?" Sophia said to Molly.

"There were times, I do confess, when I doubted that they'd manage it," Molly said. "I should have known you would see it done."

Sophia and Molly smiled at each other in true feminine understanding. Hyde shook his head, and said, "It was very much of a mess. I think the whole thing could have been handled without so much mud and blood all round."

"One must consider the combatants, your grace," Sophia said. "I do think that it would have been highly unlikely for Louisa to walk straight into Henry's arms. They both needed the proper motivation. How fortunate that Dutton was available and exactly the thing, not that he knows it, poor dear. I do think he has suffered a frightful blow to his confidence. And so well deserved, too."

"I can't but think this has something to do with his father, Sophia," Molly said softly, leading them gently away from Hyde, who, as a former general in the king's army was not at all equipped to understand the brutality of warfare as women waged it. "Dutton had rather a bad name going for him, and Melverley"—she shuddered—"did and does do himself no good turn by being so often out in Society. The world would think better of him if they saw him less often."

"You are of such a suspicious frame of mind, Molly," Sophia said sweetly, casting a glance over the room.

The ceremony had taken place in the yellow drawing room, so touchingly symbolic, and, the sounds of passion being blissfully achieved coming to them from beyond the dressing room door notwithstanding, the party remained happily chatting until breakfast could be served.

All were there, all who mattered at that precise moment in time. Her brother John, his sons, Lady Jordan and the children of her sisters, Melverley and the Duke of Aldreth, Amelia's father, all the sons of Hyde, Markham. Lives entwined, the skeins twisting back twenty years and more, all seemingly content to let the past lie in shadow, quiet and still.

But not Sophia.

Sophia forgot nothing.

It was such an advantage that they did forget. It made everything so much easier.

"You had no thought of Melverley and Cumberland, no thought of Westlin and Dutton when you arranged for Louisa to be ruined by Hyde's son?" Molly asked, her bright eyes alive with interest and no condemnation.

Molly was an old friend and had been witness to much of it. But not all.

No one needed to know it all.

"They are well matched, are they not? She is ideal for him. Whether Melverley made her that way or God, I do not know and it does not pertain. She came to me, Molly, not I to her." Sophia shrugged good-naturedly.

"She *is* good for him," Molly said. "What is more, he knows it. It takes little more for a marriage to thrive than that."

"And yet they have so much more," Sophia said just as the faint sounds of muffled screaming could be heard from the direction of the dressing room.

They sounded distinctly masculine.

Well done, Louisa.

It was not long after that, that Louisa and Blakesley reentered the yellow drawing room from the red reception room door. It would have been flagrant in the extreme for them to have entered from the dressing room door and, even though their courtship had been excessively public and extremely improper, some lines just had to be drawn. The line in their particular circumstance was at the dressing room door.

It was completely charming.

Melverley, upon seeing Louisa and understanding what had just occurred, nodded approvingly, which, of course, he would, and even went so far in his exuberance as to kiss Louisa on the cheek.

Louisa looked extremely shocked.

Eleanor, her fetching younger sister, looked appalled.

Yes, well, that was understandable, surely.

"You told him Westlin's not her father," John said, having come up behind her as silently as usual. As usual, she had heard him coming.

"Of course. It made everything so much easier for Melverley."

"Melverley *is* her father," John said.

"Of course he is, in every way that matters," she said, looking up at her brother in perfect accord. "The English have odd customs about bloodlines. He mistreated her, and her sister, because of Westlin and his constant boasting."

"How do you know that Melverley's seed did not make her?" John said softly. They were speaking in near whispers in the far corner of the room, her nephews making a ring about them, a ring of defense to give them privacy in this far from private place.

"Melverley's seed makes nothing," she said, watching Melverley, watching Eleanor. "Every rumor of his begetting a bastard, I have started."

"To protect them."

"It was little enough," Sophia said. " 'Twas mostly for Margaret, and she is gone. What is left but to see to her daughters?"

"Westlin fathered Louisa," John said. "Did she use him again to create Eleanor?"

"No," Sophia said. "Westlin was done with her."

"Then who?"

Sophia looked at John and smiled. "Ask Mary."

Epilogue

IT might have been because of the weather, which turned unsea-
sonably cold and windy for April, but directly after the Kirkland–Blakesley wedding things quieted down considerably for that
specific element of London's population that did not enjoy quiet
even when in the country, so how could they possibly be content in
Town?

Markham, John, and the boys had taken themselves off to
Marshfield Park, the Dalby estate in Dalbyshire. It had been
Young's idea as he was the least interested in Town life and had required a respite of sorts in the woods and fields of Dalbyshire. She
was completely certain that they were having a wonderful time and
were likely stalking things right and left.

Caroline and Ashdon were still at Chaldon Hall, likely giving
no thought at all to the many things that needed to be done on the
Curzon Street house in Town that Westlin had given them as a wedding gift.

Sophia spent the time productively. She was still reinventing the
white salon, and because the weather was so unpleasant, she was
having the tradesmen come to her with their bolts and sample

cases. The walls were to be covered in blush white damask wallpaper, which would look particularly well at night in the candle's glow, and the furniture, which was to remain the same, would be recovered in moss green velvet. She was almost certain. Certainly there was no rush, and she was still considering when Freddy entered the white salon.

"You have a caller, Countess," he said, grinning from ear to ear.

"At this time of day?" she said. It was not yet noon. Far too early for callers. "I'm too busy at the moment, Freddy. I would like to decide about the fabric today or I shall never get it all done before the party I intend to give for Caro and Ashdon when they return to Town."

"When's that to be?" he asked.

"Before the end of the Season, surely. Caro will want to show Ashdon off and she simply can't do that from Chaldon Hall. She will also want to say her good-byes to Markham and John and the boys before they leave for New York."

"And when's *that* to be?" he asked, walking over to the bolts of fabric leaning against the window and looking them over.

"I'm not quite certain," she said. "I'm not at all sure that they've done everything they possibly could to make things interesting while in England."

"Things did get interesting," Freddy said with a wry smile. "About that, one of those interesting things is standing in the foyer, waiting to see you. Lady Jordan."

Sophia immediately lost all interest in the various fabrics tossed about the salon and said, "How very interesting. I will see her immediately, naturally. Please show her to the yellow salon, would you? I shall be in directly."

Before Sophia had finished checking the order of her hair in the mirror, Freddy entered the white salon again. She turned from the mirror to face him in some surprise, when he said, "You have another caller, Countess. Lord Henry Blakesley. With a parcel under his arm like it's made of solid gold. He made it clear that it's for you."

"A gift?" Sophia said. "How lovely. Such a thoughtful man. I'll see him immediately. Show him in here, will you, Freddy? I think the disarray will charm him. And do see about providing Lady Jordan with some refreshment. A pot of chocolate, perhaps. I do seem to recall that she was very fond of chocolate."

Blakesley was shown in a few moments later, looking quite handsome in a pair of well-cut pantaloons and perfectly tailored coat of blue superfine. Marriage seemed to quite agree with him.

And he had brought a gift. Could a man be more accommodating than that?

She greeted him warmly, as she did routinely when a man brought gifts, but in this case, she was truly happy to see him. He looked spectacular and more content than she had ever seen him. It was so nice when things of this sort worked out so very well.

"Lord Henry," she said, eyeing him appreciatively, "how marvelous you look. Is that a new coat? It fits you to perfection. Are you seeing a new tailor?"

"Yes, actually," Blakes said. "Louisa insisted."

"She would," Sophia said with a discreet smile. "Men are invariably better turned out once they have a woman to please. Married men, of any situation, are always better dressed than bachelors."

" 'Tis a wonder any of us ever get married, then, as slovenly as our natural habits are."

"Oh, a woman can see beyond a stained cuff, Lord Henry," Sophia said as she sat on the sofa near the fire. "She sees what can be, with the proper effort and skill."

"How true that is," Blakes said, eyeing her in his usual cynical way. She so enjoyed Blakesley; he never failed to grasp the point. "And hence my visit. You are a woman, Lady Dalby, with very much sophistication in exerting the proper effort and skill required for any situation I've ever heard of. I know that somehow, some way, you are directly responsible for . . . well, for Louisa."

The dear man looked most distressed, the emotion of the moment clearly more than he was willing to disclose. She quite understood. One did not romp about Town dribbling emotion here and there like a leaky pipe. It promised to lead to the most disastrous and unpredictable results, which clearly should be avoided at all costs.

"Lord Henry," she said, leaning forward, "you do yourself an injustice in trying to do me honor. I did nothing, I promise you."

"You did *something*," he said, having quite got hold of himself again. "Louisa won't tell me, naturally, but I know she came to you for counsel in reacquiring the Melverley pearls, but that's all she'll say."

"And what did become of those pearls, Lord Henry? I did hear a rumor that you had won some sort of wager with Lord Dutton and that he had paid you in pearls. Is Louisa now wearing her delightful pearls again?"

"I think, Lady Dalby," Blakes said, looking at her in blatant amusement, "that you are far better informed that you like to let on. But, to answer you, Louisa has lost all interest in that particular item and has chosen to give them to her sister, Eleanor."

"How very generous of her," Sophia said. "It is not many women, in fact, I can't think of one offhand, who would give up such a precious item. She clearly found something she values far more than mere pearls."

Upon which, Lord Henry Blakesley smiled the most delicious smile and ducked his head. It was completely charming. She could not possibly have been more delighted.

"Which brings me to the reason for my visit," he said. "I wanted to thank you, for whatever you did or did not do, and, knowing that the blanc de Chine cup is no longer in your possession, and hearing a rumor"—and here he smiled most sarcastically—"that you were re-doing this room around a new theme altogether, I have brought you this."

And he unwrapped the coarse wool bundle which he had been balancing on his knee, to reveal a smaller bundle wrapped in fresh linen strips, which upon being unwrapped revealed the most exquisite vase of celadon porcelain. He handed it to her and she took it as gently as if it were an infant child. It was hexagonal in shape with floral lacework cut into the sides and it was the most brilliant, clear, leaf green in color.

"You are fond of Chinese porcelain, I trust?" he said.

"Very," she said softly.

"This is from the royal household of the emperor Qianlong. I hoped you would find a suitable spot for it."

And for the first time in her life as it had begun in London all those years ago, she said words she had never thought to say again. "It is too fine. I have done nothing to warrant such a gift, Lord Henry."

"I have Louisa," he said. "Without you, I would not have her, no matter what you would say to deny it. Take the vase, Sophia," he said softly. "I have to thank someone or I shall go mad."

"And Louisa knows of this gift?" she said, looking at him and starting to grin.

"She wanted to give you the Melverley pearls. I convinced her that, by her grandmother's wish, they should stay in the family. Yes, she knows of the gift," he said, starting to smile. "She wouldn't mind a bit if you renamed the white salon the Blakesley Room."

"I shall consider it," Sophia said on a laugh of pure pleasure.

IT was on that buoyant note that Sophia bid Lord Henry good day and went in to the yellow salon to greet Lady Jordan.

What a surprising day it was turning into. When life slowed

down in London, the citizens revolted, forced to find their own amusements. How lovely for her that they seemed to be drawn to Dalby House.

Lady Jordan was sitting not at all serenely on one of the yellow silk sofas. She looked uncomfortable. She also looked sober. It was quite startling.

"How good to see you, Lady Jordan," Sophia said, signaling Freddy to bring in more chocolate. "You are looking very well and on such a blustery day, too. How do you manage it? I have been closeted within, scarce brave enough to venture out."

It was a pleasant enough lie, and entirely harmless.

"Thank you for seeing me, Lady Dalby," Mary said somewhat stiffly. "I have enjoyed seeing Mr. Grey again, though I think he is out of Town now?"

"Yes, he went to Dalby House with the boys, though I should stop calling them *boys* as they are very much men, but they required some time in the country, as you may imagine. Coming to visit, which I always so enjoy, is something of an effort for them. I do hope that Caro can spend more time with them before they must leave."

"Yes, I should say so," Lady Jordan said blandly, clearly not at all sure how to move from small talk to the real purpose of her visit.

"And how is Lady Eleanor, now that her sister is wed? Is she eager for her own nuptials?" Sophia said, smiling politely.

Mary jerked and frowned. "Hardly. She is but sixteen, Lady Dalby. Too young for thoughts of that sort."

"I would say that is a matter of personal inclination, Lady Jordan, wouldn't you?"

"Lady Eleanor's inclinations are entirely appropriate for her tender years."

"I agree with you completely," Sophia said pleasantly. "Lady Louisa is a contented bride?" she asked, changing the subject.

"So it would seem," Mary said, not at all cheerfully.

"I'm delighted to hear it. I have not seen Lord Melverley out lately, though, as I said, I have been rarely out myself, but he is well? The exertions of the wedding did not tire him?"

Lord Melverley had never found an event yet that tired him, unless it be the task of parenting his daughters.

"Not at all," Mary said. "And I must thank you, Lady Dalby. Mr. Grey made it clear to me that without your help, the situation with Louisa might have turned out differently than it has done."

It was said with some discomfort, with a great deal of hesitation and even a slight hint of distaste. But it was said. Sophia could not help being a little impressed with Lady Jordan's fortitude.

"Nonsense," Sophia said. "I'm sure you put too much upon me, Lady Jordan. Does not love always find a way?"

According to the poets, it did, but both Sophia and Mary were too old and too experienced to listen to poets.

Upon which Mary looked at her, and Sophia calmly returned the look.

"I thought you had arranged the Earl of Westlin for her," Mary said quietly. "Arranged with Westlin for her, for Margaret. A tawdry jest, a wager, something."

"The only thing I would arrange for Westlin is a hanging," Sophia said just as quietly.

"I did not understand about Melverley then," Mary said. "Living in Town, one understands things so much better."

"Very true, I'm afraid."

"You tried to help Margaret, did you not? She needed to give Melverley a child."

"And he has two," Sophia said. "He should have been most content, but some men do not have the facility for contentment. Why blame ourselves when that proves to be true?"

Mary jerked again, her gaze going down to the floor and then to the windows and then to the hem of Sophia's dress.

"You believe that?" Mary said, her voice just above a whisper.

"Of course I do, and so should every reasonable woman,"

Sophia answered. "Some men refuse to be pleased. It is very sad for them, naturally, but that is all."

"Did John tell you? About us?" Mary breathed.

"Of course not," Sophia said. "It is only that I see things, perhaps those things that others would prefer not to see. John has always been and ever will be the soul of discretion."

"You don't mind?" Mary said, lifting her eyes to look deeply into Sophia's. Mary's eyes were very pretty still, a clear and light blue, and so beautifully tilted at the corners. She had been a rare beauty in her day, as had her sisters.

"I never mind when people find their happiness, even if it only lasts an hour. Certainly, I have found mine often enough not to begrudge you my brother for a season."

After that, they said nothing, but sipped their chocolate and let the rainy afternoon slide by, closing old wounds, erasing old scars. It was, truly, a lovely way to spend an April day.

IT was some time later, when Lady Jordan had left Dalby House and Sophia had almost decided upon a lovely pale green silk damask for the sofas and dark green damask of the same pattern for the chairs, all perfect compliments to her remarkable celadon vase, that Freddy announced yet another visitor.

For such a dreary day, it was proving highly productive.

The white salon had been cleared and reordered, still famously white, but with the addition of a single stroke of celadon, which was truly a spectacular piece, when Lady Amelia Caversham was announced and gracefully entered the room.

Amelia was dressed in white muslin sprigged with a delicate green design, by happy chance, and looked quite at home in the white salon. All except for her tense expression, that is. The girl looked positively intense, which was such an unusual choice for her. Amelia was ever and always pleasing and pleasant, truth be told, almost to the point of plainness, which was such a pity as she was such a good-looking girl: fine white skin, shining blond hair, which was so popular at present, and eyes of a delicate and unusual shade of blue. Truly, she was the exact type that poets made famous.

"How lovely of you to come and see me today, Lady Amelia. You have brightened my day considerably. But, where is your chaperone, Lady Jordan?"

"I," she said slowly, "I am not quite certain, Lady Dalby. She was out, and I suppose, in my eagerness, I left before she returned."

"Eagerness? How flattering," Sophia said. "I was the source of your eagerness?"

"Lady Dalby," Amelia said, "please excuse me for being forward, but I . . . I was most impressed, that is to say, actually I found myself astonished by the chain of events surrounding Louisa's marriage to Lord Henry Blakesley. She is, even more astonishing, quite completely content in the marriage, and I . . . I, well, you may not know it, but we had our come out together and attended most functions together, with Lady Jordan, of course."

"Of course," Sophia said politely.

Sweet girl, a bit scattered, but being on the marriage mart for too long could do that to a woman of a sensitive nature. It only remained to be discovered if Amelia Caversham was of a sensitive nature. She did hope not. Sensitive natures were such a nuisance.

"And now, now," Amelia continued, holding her neck very still and straight, showing it to best advantage, which was certainly wise of her, but her eyes were darting all over the room. It was not in the least attractive. "I suppose that I don't know what's to become of me now. I am at a loss, Lady Dalby, and I could not but wonder if you, you would be so kind as to . . . help me."

"Help you do what, Lady Amelia?" Sophia asked with a smile of complete understanding. Of course, everyone in Town knew exactly what Amelia needed and what she clearly needed help in achieving. "I am afraid I do not quite comprehend you."

Amelia looked appropriately uncomfortable. She squirmed a bit and her eyes did more jumping about and, truthfully, she came very near to knocking over a rather expensive Directoire table that John had brought with him from Paris. It was the latest thing in French design and, of course, she was the first to have one. If one could not be the first, there was hardly any point to French design, was there?

"Lady Dalby," Amelia finally got out, her cheeks flushed most becomingly. "Lady Dalby, I would very much like to marry . . . to marry . . ."

"Yes, darling, you would very much like to marry. Of course you would. Perfectly natural," Sophia said, for how could she resist the smallest and most innocuous of torments?

"I mean to say," Amelia continued, which showed such pluck, it surely did and spoke so eloquently of the girl's character. Sophia was delighted to see it, she truly was. "What I mean, Lady Dalby, is that I would very much like to marry a duke, and I would very much like your help in acquiring one."

"Why, darling," Sophia said, leaning forward and taking Amelia by the hand, "that sounds positively riveting. I'm quite sure that, between the two of us, we can manage to snare one duke, don't you agree?"

Claudia Dain is an award-winning author and two-time RITA finalist. She lives in the Southeast and is at work on Sophia's next attempt at match-making.